OF PRINCES AND DRAGONS

BOOK 2

THE LORDS AND COMMONERS SERIES

LYNNE HILL

Second Edition 2019

Created with Vellum

OTHER BOOKS BY LYNNE HILL

The Lords and Commoners Series

Of Lords and Commoners Book 1

Of Princes and Dragons Book 2

Of Gods and Goddesses Book 3

A Gods and Goddesses Novelette

A Woman's World Series

A Woman's World Book 1

Lost Powers Book 2

A Collision of Worlds Book 3

This book is dedicated to Tony and Kalin.
Thank you for putting up with me while I wrote these stories!

DRAGON

He is known the world over
Yet what is a dragon?
Is he a hero or a villain?
That is a matter of where one is from
In some parts, the dragon is a symbol of good luck
One who drives away evil spirits
He is wise and strong
Still others view him as a symbol of greed and power
A violent and destructive creature
A truly evil being
Can he be both — a wicked hero?

PROLOGUE

Vallachia strolled in a high mountain meadow. The lush green forest around her felt familiar. The evergreens were similar to the ones near her childhood home. A small mountain lake was nestled in the bottom of the basin. It looked pristine and refreshing. Her thoughts strayed to how wonderful a good swim would be when she saw him. On the opposite side of the lake stood the figure of a burly man. He wore a long black chlamys, the bottom of which brushed the grass beneath his feet as he moved toward her. His clothes were not simply black; they were the type of black that stole all the light. This was in deep contrast to her flowing white gown alight in the bright summer sun.

With a closer look, her lips parted in amazement. She knew him. In fact, she had been waiting centuries for him. After hundreds of years she had finally found ... Teller. Her initial trepidation about the intimidating figure was replaced with joy.

He is alive! she thought. Regardless of his deadpan stare, her heart leapt into her throat. She smiled but the gesture was not returned; his face remained emotionless.

"Teller, it is me, Vallachia."

His silence caused a shiver to pass through her. His dark eyes studied her with an eerie hunger. She forced her feet to cautiously move toward him.

Teller's body doubled in size ... then tripled. His skin turned blood red and his clothes melted away. His body continued to grow and morph. Scales formed across his skin.

Vallachia instinctively backed away. She found herself staring at a dragon, whose head towered above the tallest trees. Her heart drummed in her ears. The beast's shiny golden eyes focused on her. His massive head swung through the air as it lunged for her. His sword-like teeth were about to rip into her when she awoke with a sharp inhale.

CHAPTER 1 COPENHAGEN 1354 AD

It had been a year since they ended the plagues in Europe, in which rogue vampires decimated half the human population in some regions. The High Court of Elders, led by Lord Chastellain, in turn eliminated more than half of the vampire population, thus restoring the fragile balance between humans and vampires. This allowed the Court to move into a time of peace, which called for a celebration.

Even the hundreds of vampire skulls had been removed from the main entrance to Lord Chastellain's castle. This was a great improvement as far as Vallachia was concerned. Gardeners were brought in and the palace looked majestic once again, like something out of a children's fairy story.

Mari, Sonia, Mary and Elizabeth were with Vallachia in her chambers getting ready for the festivities. Vallachia rejoiced in the feminine energy. It was a welcome change. They were able to put their swords to rest and at least pretend to be normal women. Even wearing a poofy silk brocade was tolerable for Vallachia. It was nice to feel and look womanly — especially since it was only for the evening.

This gala would be different, which concerned Vallachia. In the past she had always danced with Prince Elijah, Lord Chastellain's only son, but this time he had a different partner. Vallachia was not looking forward to having to dance with anyone else or possibly *everyone* else.

Elijah often had mistresses in the past, probably more than Vallachia knew about. However, this new woman was different. She was the first one Elijah was candid about being with. Over the past year their affair had developed and was no longer a secret.

She called herself Patricia. She and her father were refugees — of sorts — from Southern Europe. They came to the Court to learn how to feed without killing and they now lived here in the castle. Undoubtedly she and Elijah would be together at the dance. He seemed happy and this in turn pleased Vallachia. The problem was that Elijah had always kept unwanted suitors away; now Vallachia would have to deal with them herself. She was planning to escape shortly after the formalities were over and her dutiful appearance as a high-ranking member of the Court was fulfilled.

At the long table set aside for the leaders, Vallachia sat to the left of Lord Chastellain with Riddick by her side as was customary. Riddick was their commander in chief. Behind the lord stood John, waiting in the shadows, always at the lord's behest. John was the lord's top advisor. To the right of the lord sat his son and Patricia.

After the lord's brief speech and celebratory toast, Elijah and Patricia moved to the dance floor. A man approached Vallachia but Riddick stood and glared at the poor fellow. The stranger quickly did an about-face, retreating swiftly. This was a common reaction to Riddick's massive form, for which Vallachia was grateful.

"Come, let's dance," Riddick grabbed Vallachia under the arm, pulling her to her feet — not giving her a choice in the matter.

He still does not know how to ask a woman to dance, as a true gentleman should. At least he has not completely changed, Vallachia smiled to herself.

They moved gracefully around the dance floor.

"You look beautiful, Val," Riddick said. "It is nice to see you out of your battle garb and dressed as a proper lady."

"Now you are going to be a gentleman?" Val gave him a playful smile.

"No, not entirely."

"It is good to know that you are still you. Though, I have to admit it is nice to be out of my armor."

Riddick chuckled, then his expression turned serious. "How are you faring?"

"I am well. Why do you ask?"

He rolled his eyes and glanced toward Elijah and Patricia, thus pointing out the perceived problem, "You are no longer his favorite mistress."

Val laughed; that was what this must look like. "Elijah appears content and that is all that matters."

Riddick studied her face. "You are sincere. You are not upset in the least?"

"No and I have no reason to be upset."

Riddick shook his head. "You are the most peculiar woman I have ever met. I have watched you and Elijah for the better part of one hundred years, you are obviously in love with him."

Vallachia was thoughtful for a moment. *Is it that obvious?* She decided that it probably was.

"I swear," Riddick continued. "Even after so many years I have not figured you out. I suppose I never will."

"That is because you don't know the whole story. I was never Elijah's mistress. The truth is I love someone else." Riddick looked at her with a glint of hope so she quickly added, "I'm still in love with a boy from my childhood."

"Your childhood? Wouldn't he be at least fifty years dead by now?"

"No, I turned him into a vampire." She said this last word quietly, as if it were a secret — a terrible secret. "Surely he is not dead. He is out there somewhere."

"Why haven't you gone to him?"

"I'm always looking for any sign of him but I don't know where he is."

"And he has not bothered to find you?"

Val shook her head no and fought the tears that were threatening to form in her large crystal-blue eyes.

"Everyone knows who you are in our world. He could have easily found you. So he is either dead or he does not want you."

Vallachia refused to believe either one of those options. She would not believe it. Yet his words were still painful and she fought the urge to rub the aching sensation out of her heart, even though she knew it would not help.

"Don't you think it is high time you let him go?" Riddick said this in the softest voice she had ever heard him use. He knew his words had hurt her. "You know ... you remind me of ... her."

Vallachia's eyes widened in surprise at this odd comment. She barely noticed when he leaned in close, as if to kiss her. "Who do I remind you of?" For ninety-two years she had wondered about his past — his human life. *Will he finally tell me?* He had always shut down when anyone asked him about it. Curiosity consumed her.

As his lips were about to reach hers, someone tapped Riddick's shoulder and he turned to see who it was.

"May I?" Lord Chastellain said, as he gave Riddick an icy stare that said he was getting too close and needed to back off.

Vallachia frowned. Wonderful, the lord is playing the part of a jealous lover.

Riddick gracefully swung her around and held her hand out to Chastellain. "Of course, My Lord," he bowed slightly and gave Val a sarcastic smile that said, *Enjoy*, before he strode off.

Val watched after him for a moment, not wanting him to leave. *What did he mean by that? Who do I remind him of?* But Riddick was gone and she was left to dance with Elijah's father — the ruler of all vampires.

"Riddick is correct, my dear," he said.

"About what, My Lord?"

"It is long past due that you move on and forget about that boy from your childhood."

"You were listening to us?" Her voice was full of disgust.

The lord was not flustered or deterred by her tone. "You are going to lose him," he glanced toward his son.

Vallachia followed his gaze. She did not fancy the thought of Elijah marrying. She would lose his friendship, for his bride would not approve of their relationship. Not to mention, his bride would occupy much of his time.

"You are very well aware that a man can only wait so long?" Chastellain said.

Vallachia wished she knew where Teller was, because then she could decide. She would gladly choose Elijah if she knew there was no hope for her to be with Teller. However, as long as there was a chance — no matter how small — she would hang on. She had always had a strong sense that she was meant to be with Teller. The way it felt when they touched was unique. Surely she would never feel that way with anyone else. He was the only one for her. This was one thing she was certain of. They must be together, someday, somehow.

These thoughts were uncomfortable and dancing with Lord Chastellain was even more discomfiting. With a slight bow Val said, "If that is all, My Lord, then I am going to retire. I am rather tired." This was a lie — her mind was racing and she did not want to dance anymore unless it was with Elijah. And he was otherwise occupied.

CHAPTER 2 COPENHAGEN 1354 AD

Vallachia headed straight for her balcony and gazed out over the enchanted city of Copenhagen. She wished that her girlfriends would join her, as they would distract her and lift her spirits. She had always been good at staying busy, never an idle moment. She took no time to dwell on Teller or her love life in general — or rather the lack of a love life. Her friends were enjoying themselves, as they very well should. They had earned it. She should have been with them and normally would have.

However, tonight was different. Teller was all she could think about. How is it that after all these years he still has so much power over me? Is that what true love is? I suppose not. If he still loved me, he would have found me by now.

Vallachia tried to make herself think of something, anything besides Teller. *Focus on work — politics,* she told herself. This was what normally consumed her life. Her thoughts strayed to the previous year, one she usually tried not to think about. It had been grueling. However tonight she did not know which was worse; thinking about fighting the vampire plagues of 1353 or thinking of Teller. While the Court had managed to stop Ramdasha's new vampires from destroying Europe, they still had not found him — the leader of the resistance to the Court. Ramdasha wanted to rule a world where vampires lived free and humans were subjugated to the superior vampire race. Undoubtedly, he was regrouping somewhere. But where, the Court did not know.

A swirl of air softly surrounded her, interrupting her musings. The swooshing of large wings filled her ears. She could tell who had landed behind her by the lovely musky scent. She did not turn to look at him. "You should not be here. You belong with Patricia."

"No, I belong with you," Elijah whispered in her ear. The way he said it meant that he should be with her forever, not only at this precise moment. "Father informed me that you were upset. Is that true?"

Val did not answer as they continued to gaze out across the ever-growing city in the distance.

"He also said that if I was not careful, I would lose you," Elijah added.

"I received that lecture as well. Why has your father always been so determined to see us together? Why does he even care?"

"He loves you."

She chuckled. Love had never been a part of her relationship with the lord.

"He does. And he knows how much you mean to me." Elijah looked thoughtful for a moment. "In the beginning he thought you would make a prized bride for me."

Val rolled her eyes — something she had learned from Riddick. The last thing she wanted was to be someone's prize. "I'm glad to meet his standard."

"Of course, you have become much more than that over the years. You have been indispensable to the Court. You are our secret weapon. Your ability to win allies and fight when needed has proven that you are a better leader than either of us could have predicted. The Court needs you. We would not have been able to reclaim the North and maintain control without you."

"I have not done anything special — no more than you or Riddick or Samuel," Val countered.

"You are too modest. That is one of the many things I love about you. We would be lost without you — I would be lost without you." Elijah put his arms around her.

Val gave into the embrace and buried her head in his chest. It felt wonderful. They had not been this close in quite some time, perhaps since they had been trapped in Ramdasha's old cavern in Constantinople. That had been when she finally admitted to herself that she loved Elijah.

"I never wanted to be a leader," Val said. "I don't want power. I simply want to protect humans and the vampires I care about."

"That is precisely what makes you a good leader," he whispered. "You should be by my side as my queen. Father knows this. In fact, everyone knows this except for you." Elijah sighed. "Do you know how hard it is to be this close to you and yet you are still not mine?"

Val pulled away from him. "You should get back to Patricia or you will lose her."

"That is inevitable. She is growing impatient because I will not ask her to marry me."

"You should marry her. She pleases you."

"No, she doesn't. If you truly want me to be happy, then you will marry me."

Vallachia's stomach began to ache. The night had been trying. She was tired of thinking. "Surely I alone am not responsible for your happiness, My Lord." She gently pushed him away. "You should go to her."

Elijah smiled his handsome crooked smile. "I suppose I can leave now that it is clear you are alone."

Val finished pushing him away with a hard shove that would have thrown a human across the room.

Elijah gave her a wink — which he'd learned from Riddick. "I'll call on your lady friends for you. They know how to make you feel better." He always knew what she needed. Then he was gone.

Val smiled. *Riddick is a terrible influence on us*. He was teaching them impudent behavior — eye rolling, winking. Then her face fell. *Elijah is going to break Patricia's heart.* Vallachia's heart ached for Patricia.

Vallachia sat on the large overstuffed settee in her chambers and rubbed the faint scar on her right palm. The scar that she received the day she had saved a small boy in her village. Teller had asked her to marry him that night. *He loved me once, why has he not come for me?*

It was not long before she heard Mari in the hallway. "Give me a moment to speak with her." Mari was talking to their other girlfriends. Then there came a soft knock at Vallachia's door.

Oh, no, Val thought, *here we go.* "Come in."

In a flash Mari was at Val's side on the settee. "What is going on?" Her voice was that of a concerned mother trying to comfort a small child.

"I have been thinking about Teller."

"I know you loved him dearly. You were meant to be with him at one time ... but no one has heard any word of him since ... he was turned." Surely she was going to say, "Since your father's death," or even worse, "Since Teller killed your father." She had carefully chosen better words. "Perhaps it is time to move on?"

Val let out a frustrated moan. "You are the third person to say that to me tonight."

"Well then, perhaps you should listen." Mari kept her voice soft.

An angry heat caused Val's cheeks to redden. "I can't! I won't! Don't you understand?"

"Very well." Mari nodded. After hesitating she added, "However, I would hate to see you lose Elijah because you are waiting for someone who will never come."

It was silent for a long moment while Vallachia let the tears fall. They needed to fall; she needed to get this out. Mari put her arm around Val, who then laid her head on Mari's shoulder.

"Do you want me to help you search for him?" Mari whispered.

She is a good friend, Val thought.

The door flew open as Mary, Elizabeth and Sonia barged in.

"That is enough sulking. No more talk of men. They are all arses — that is why I prefer women," Mary declared with a broad smile.

They most likely thought Vallachia was upset because Elijah was with Patricia. That was fine with Val. She did not want to talk or think about Teller anymore — or Elijah for that matter. Soon they were drinking fine wine while playing cards. Their laugher raised Val's spirits.

CHAPTER 3 COPENHAGEN 1354 AD

After leaving Vallachia and retrieving her friends for her, Elijah retired to his chambers in hopes of being alone. Unfortunately, being alone was not possible. Patricia sat with her arms and legs crossed while reclining on his bed. Her down-turned mouth spoke volumes. Elijah was in no mood to readdress her needs, which he could not fulfill.

Elijah's thoughts had been of Vallachia. *She loves me. I know she does. There must be some way to get through to her.* Although he had not been able to figure her out thus far, so why would tonight be any different?

"Might I ask where you disappeared to?" Patricia's voice was full of accusation.

Elijah let out a heavy sigh. *Not again.* "That is no concern of yours."

"That answer is proof of your guilt. You were with *her* weren't you?" An angry light flickered in her eyes.

"I am guilty of nothing. I will do as I please."

"You think that because you are *the prince* that you can have as many women as you please? Well, I won't stand for it!"

"No one is asking you to. I have told you before, you should go. You deserve better — someone who loves you and will be faithful to you."

"You are a fool for loving her!" she yelled.

"And you are a fool for loving me." Elijah's voice remained calm and flat.

Patricia's anger gave way. A tear rolled down her cheek. "What do I have to do to make you love me?"

"There is nothing anyone can do to make someone fall in love. Believe me, this is one lesson I have learned over the past few hundred years."

"Vallachia does not love you. I do! I'm here — she is not. Don't you see? It has been the better part of one hundred years and you still have not won her heart. You only want her because she is the only thing you have not been able to have. The entire world is at your command, everything ... except for her. If you were able to finally have her then you would no longer want her."

That is enough. Elijah clenched his fists. Surely Patricia was wrong. He had loved Vallachia for a long time and he always would. That much he knew was true. "You had better watch your tongue! You know nothing of Lady Vallachia and our relationship."

"I know she turned you away ... again, as you came here alone."

No more fighting. I have to end this. "Get out." Elijah's voice was low and emotionless.

Patricia appeared in front of him with desperation in her large brown eyes. Her lovely face was wet with tears. She pressed her lips to Elijah's. In between kisses she breathed, "Don't push me away. ... Give me more time to make you see that I am the one for you. ... I can please you, if you give me the chance."

Elijah wanted to laugh. Patricia could never take Val's place in his heart. Elijah was convinced that Patricia was like all the others — selfish, petty and only interested in the status that marrying the prince of vampires would give her. If Vallachia were to marry me it would be because she truly loved me and nothing more. Val is not concerned with power or wealth. She is selfless. Val is the only woman I can fully trust as a companion. Other women are out for little more than personal gain. If I could have Vallachia I would never let her go. She will be mine ... someday, he thought.

Patricia loosened the ties to the top of her gown and one side of her brocade slipped over her shoulder, leaving it bare. As she pressed her body to Elijah's she pulled his chlamys off.

He pushed her away but she placed her lips to his in a hard and feverish kiss. It did not take long before he gave in. Her sensual curves were too tempting. Soon he found himself returning her kiss. With ease and half by accident he ripped the top of her delicate silk gown off.

She pulled him down onto the bed with a triumphant smile.

There was a weak voice urging Elijah to stop but the dreaded guilt would not fully come until he woke. In the meantime he would allow himself to enjoy her and deal with the contrition later.

UPON AWAKENING, Elijah slid his uncomfortable arm out from under Patricia. She rolled away from him, exposing her naked back. She was still asleep. Her tangled brown hair fell onto the pillow. Her hair reminded him of one of his first lovers who had taught him a valuable lesson. After her, he tended to keep women at arm's length. He could not recall her name at first. She had been named after one of the great empresses who had ruled Rome on her own, with no husband at her side. *Irene — yes that was it — or was it Zoe? No, that was not right either. Dora, after the beautiful Empress Theodora — that was it.* Elijah's thoughts drifted to his youth. ...

CHAPTER 4 CONSTANTINOPLE
600 AD

"Once we are married and I am crowned a ruler of the vampires, I will change everything. Vampires will rule this world," Dora proclaimed as she lay next to Elijah. Her brown eyes sparkled with ambition.

Elijah had no doubt that Dora was serious. Being young and a relatively new vampire he was petrified by her words. Father and his allies had recently formed the High Court of the Elders and decreed that vampires would not rule over humans. Dora's words were treason. Lord Chastellain would have her killed if he discovered her plans. While Elijah could not help but admire her determination, it was becoming clear that she did not care about him. She was only with Elijah because she wanted to be in power.

Elijah ran his hand gently through Dora's hair. *Father will surely have her head if he learns of her plans.* "Do you love me?" his voice was soft.

"Of course." Dora did not meet his gaze.

She's lying. This realization was sudden and painful, as if a stone had been heaved at Elijah's head. What she truly meant was, "Whatever you want to believe, you insignificant child." Which Elijah largely was at the time but he was a fast learner. Dora was older and wiser than he, with a greed that ran deep. He studied her lovely face. Only her eyes provided a glimpse of her true age. He gave her a weak smile as he stood to dress.

Looking back on it now, it was clear to Elijah that she did not deserve the name Theodora, after the grandest and most generous empress to rule the new Roman Empire. Her name should have been Irene, after the cruelest of empresses. He finally could see Dora for who she was. He wished that she loved him but this was not the case. She might even have despised him. Elijah was her way to the top and she would not stop at vampire domination; she would make humans her slaves. For all he knew, she might have been planning to kill his father and then him once she was crowned ruler of the night. Elijah's jaw tightened, yet he managed to keep his expression impartial so she would not be able to deduce that he was on to her.

Elijah knew what he had to do. He had to be quick, as Dora was strong and fast. Surprise was his best chance of defeating her. Moving as quickly as possible to the sword stand not far from the bed, he seized the nearest weapon and without pause pivoted into a powerful swing. His sword easily severed her pretty head from her lovely body.

It was his first vampire kill but far from his last. Killing traitors of the Court was to become customary in his life and falling for the wrong woman was a mistake that he would never make again.

That was why he would always want Vallachia. She was the only woman he had ever met who cared nothing for power or wealth.

CHAPTER 5 COPENHAGEN 1354 AD

Upon awakening, Vallachia's first thought was of Riddick's odd comment at the celebration the previous evening. Filled with curiosity, she dressed in her trusty and comfortable tunic and breeches and headed out to find him. Hopefully he was truly ready to talk about his past. At the very least, she had to try to get it out of him.

Some of the lord's guards informed her that Riddick was in the armory working on a new sword. This was not a surprise. Fighting and weapons were his life; when he was not training with weapons he was making them. That was where she found him, hammering away on red-hot metal. She quietly watched him for a time. He was incredibly focused on his work and she did not want to disturb him.

From the back he resembled Teller. With his broad shoulders, olive skin and dark hair, he very well could have been Teller working in his father's smithy shop. This thought was unsettling so she shook her head to get the image out and turned to leave.

Riddick must have caught her movement out of the corner of his eye, or perhaps he had caught her scent, as he suddenly looked up from his work.

"Sorry to bother you," Val said. "I will come back when you are not so busy."

"No, it is fine. I figured you would be looking for me after my comment last night." He dropped his hammer on the table with a deafening clank and eased the new sword into a large vat of water, which sizzled in protest. Steam filled the air. "I'm done anyway. Though I wish I had not mentioned her."

"Why?" Val asked.

"Because now you will not leave it be until I tell you about my past. I have no choice now but to relive it. Anytime I start to think about the past I busy myself. This helps to push it from my mind."

"I know it must be difficult for you to talk about because you have not told any of us anything about your human life. It may be helpful for you to talk about it. It might even make you feel better ... somehow."

Riddick sat on the high workbench. "I don't know about that." He shook his head as he lowered his chin to his chest.

Vallachia moved to sit beside him. "I'm not sure why but I always feel better after I talk about things that are bothering me." This was true, she felt better after talking to Mari last night. "Please tell me, who was she?"

"My wife, Natalia."

"You were married!" Luckily Val was sitting or she might have fallen over in shock. It was impossible to imagine Riddick as a married man.

"She looked a lot like you. She was tall and had long golden hair ... like yours. When I first saw you in Ramdasha's cavern I could not take my eyes off you. I was hoping beyond hope that you were her; that somehow, she was not dead and had been turned instead. Of course, it did not take me long to realize that you were not her." He fell silent for a moment, as memories came flooding back. He did not want to continue.

"Please, tell me about her."

"Natalia was much like you in other ways as well. She was stoic and thoughtful most of the time and only bold when it was needed. She tirelessly cared for an elderly woman who had lost her family. She was a bright light in the darkness. The only light in my life and when that light went out ... " Riddick's eyes were full of affection when he looked at Vallachia, as if he were seeing the wonderful wife he was describing. Perhaps at times they were one and the same — in his mind at least.

"Natalia and I had grown up together in a small town outside of Venice. After a couple of years of marriage we were beginning to think that we were not going to be able to have children. That was when we found out that she was with child. It was one of the best days of my life." Riddick smiled weakly before a shadow fell over his face. "In one horrible night I lost my beloved and the child she carried." His voice was deep and his face contorted with pain.

Vallachia put her hand on his shoulder. "I'm so sorry, Riddick."

Riddick shook his head and took a deep breath. This seemed to help him recover. "Of course, at the time I had no idea what or who had killed her. I could not fathom that one of the townspeople would have been capable of killing her. I convinced myself that it must have been an animal attack."

This sounded familiar. Humans often had no idea what to make of the senseless murders vampires left behind. "She was killed by a vampire?"

Riddick nodded. "After their death I buried myself in work, as I still do, I suppose. As a carpenter, life was simple. Building was the only thing that made sense. Only a couple of days after coming home to find my wife's bloodstained body, I was approached by a wealthy merchant named Leopoldo. He wanted me to build his new home. I was grateful for the vast amount of work it would take to build the manor he was requesting. He befriended me and I eventually came to trust Leo. It was not long before we became virtually inseparable. He helped to fill the large void in my life. Of course, looking back on it now it all makes perfect sense. After a year or so of gaining my trust, he finally revealed his true nature to me. He expected me to be scared, yet I was not. I was intrigued with the power he had. He spoke about being a vampire as if it was the best life possible. He essentially thought he was a god. He made it sound wonderful and I begged him to turn me. I wanted to be like him — a god. A human life no longer appealed to me. My hopes and dreams died with my wife. The strength and power that Leo had were appealing. In fact, it was beyond temptation. I thought a vampire life was the answer to all my problems. I believed that somehow I could exchange a pain filled human life for a carefree immortal one."

"So he turned you?" Val asked.

"Aye, Leo gladly granted me my wish. Yet, he had not bothered to inform me about the need for human blood. This made the first couple of months as a vampire very difficult. I became even more depressed after my first kill. I felt like a fool, I had been seduced by the devil himself and did not see Leo for what he truly was until it was too late. After my first feeding, I also realized that it was a vampire who had killed Natalia. As I held a dead human in my arms with the same wounds on the neck that I had found on her body, I knew it had been the work of a vampire."

"Had Leopoldo killed her?" Val was sitting at the edge of her seat, anxious to hear more.

"He convinced me that he had no idea who had killed her. I believed him — I wanted to believe him. In order to deal with this new life I found a way to not feel. I quickly became cruel and numb. This was a welcome reprieve from the pain of my human life. I was able to stop mourning for Natalia and our unborn child. Leo and I remained friends. He offered me a room in the workers' quarters, which were many times nicer than my tiny home. After a year or so, I eventually moved into a large room in the manor itself. As more of the villagers came up missing or dead at our hands, the townspeople grew suspicious of us. We knew we had to be moving on soon." Riddick gave Vallachia a weak smile. He found it endearing how completely enthralled she was in his story.

"Please go on."

"Becoming a vampire increased my desire for power. I reveled in the strength and speed, it made me want more. My ambitions grew and I wanted to work my way to the top. I had an insatiable need to be the best. A small-town life made me restless. I was bored. Leo, on the other hand, was content. He wanted to find another remote area to settle in. I wanted to find a leader of our kind. I had heard rumors of a vampire lord in Constantinople. This led to an argument between Leo and me one night. ... "

CHAPTER 6 OUTSKIRTS OF VENICE 1223 AD

"We shall head for Rome," Leopoldo said. "I know this charming little town outside the city. We can easily travel to Rome to feed, which will give us more prey to choose from. We will be able to go unnoticed."

"I plan to head for Constantinople," Riddick said. "This thriving capital has the most to offer. It is full of riches and a powerful Vampire Lord; come with me if you wish."

Leo's eyes flashed with anger. "You will not leave me! I made you. You *will* come to Rome with me."

Leo's fury at the mention of going their separate ways took Riddick aback. "I will do as I please and it pleases me to see what awaits in Constantinople."

Riddick turned to leave but Leo appeared in front of him, his expression was full of worry. "There is no need to be greedy. I have plenty of wealth, enough for the both of us. What is important is that we stay together. Can't you see?"

Riddick was confused by Leo's desperation. Leo was acting as if they were ... lovers!

"Please don't leave me!" Leo took Riddick's hands.

Leo's strange behavior was concerning to say the least. They had become good friends but clearly Riddick meant more to him than that. Leo wanted to control Riddick – to own him. Riddick's blood began to boil as his confusion gave way to anger. He pushed Leo away. "What has gotten into you?"

"You can't leave me. I have been alone for far too long. It took me ages to find you."

"What are you saying, Leo?"

"I can't believe you don't see it. I'm in love with you. That is why I did what I had to do." Leo's voice was little more than a whisper.

Riddick's vision blurred. The world faded away. There was only an intense focus on the man standing in front of him. Riddick's hand found Leopoldo's throat. "*What* did you do, Leo!"

Leopoldo shook his head and struggled in Riddick's grip. Riddick slammed Leo against the wall, which cracked behind him. "Tell me!" Riddick's face was only inches from Leo's.

"I killed your wife so we could be together," Leo choked.

Riddick's vision completely burred. The world went dark, as if someone blew out the only lamp. "You killed them! I trusted you. I thought you were my friend!" Riddick sank his teeth into Leo's neck tearing out a large piece of flesh. This made it easier to rip Leo's head from his body.

CHAPTER 7 COPENHAGEN 1354 AD

"I set Leopoldo's manor ablaze and walked away, never looking back," Riddick said. "That kind of betrayal is hard to comprehend. Someone I trusted – who claimed to care about me – only to learn he had killed my family. I became even more cruel and heartless after that. I did not trust anyone and would not let others get close. I feared they would only betray me. This attitude made it easy to quickly climb the ranks in Ramdasha's coven. It suited my ambitions well. That was ... until you came along and changed everything."

Vallachia was speechless as Riddick finished his gruesome tale. She laid her head on his shoulder and in return he laid his head on hers. They said nothing for quite some time.

"Thank you for telling me," she whispered.

Riddick looked into Val's sparkly blue eyes. "Do you want to know why I'm so protective of you?"

Val nodded.

"Because the hardest part about losing Natalia was that I hated myself for not being there to save her. It was my job to protect her and I failed. I have vowed never to fail again. I will not let anything happen to you."

"Oh, my dear Riddick, I am not her. I'm not your wife and it is not your responsibility to protect me."

"I am well aware of that, though this protectiveness for you was why I could not let Ramdasha kill you and why I chose to kill my own men and leave Ramdasha for the Court." Riddick paused as he struggled for the words. "It was as if by saving you I could somehow make up for my past failure."

"Riddick, my wonderful friend, there was nothing you could have done to save your wife. You were a human and the killer was a vampire. Her death was not your fault."

Riddick nodded in agreement but Val could tell he was not fully convinced. Perhaps his head knew that he was not to blame for Natalia's death, yet his heart told him different.

"Aye but I am a vampire now. Therefore, failure is not an option this time." After a pause he added. "In the beginning it was hell, having to watch you with the prince. It was like watching another man with my wife, it was almost more than I could bear. There was even a time or two when I thought about killing him."

"I cannot imagine. I wish you had told me sooner."

"Why? Would it have changed the way you feel about me?"

"In a way, perhaps. I have trusted you for a long time. You have more than proven your allegiance to the Court. Yet, now I understand you better. You are like a brother to me." Val put her arms around him.

Riddick sighed. "That is all I will ever get from you, is it not?"

"I am afraid so." Val frowned.

He pushed her away. "That is what I thought." After a long pause, he added, "You know being here with you in the North has allowed me to become more like my old self, my human self."

Val smiled. "I'm glad for you. I like you much better this way. It has been a long time since you had to kill humans to survive. Perhaps this allowed you to regain your humanity."

Riddick had slowly recovered his compassion and morals over the past years, and he was no longer the ruthless vampire Val met over ninety years ago.

Vampires must learn to let go of their conscience if they are to survive as killers. Once they become virtually emotionless, the killing no longer bothers them and they can be content with themselves. The problem is that this makes them callous, thirsty for power, greedy and vengeful. The image of Ramdasha came into Val's mind, as this description fit him perfectly.

"What is going on here?" came a voice from behind them.

This brought Vallachia out of the ponderous state she had fallen into. She turned to find Elijah and gave him a smile. "Riddick was telling me ... a story."

"What kind of story?" Elijah asked with apprehension. He was not entirely sure he wanted to know what they had been discussing.

"Do not make me tell that wretched story twice over, My Lady." Riddick stood in order to put some distance between himself and Val.

"The story is yours and yours alone. Tell it only when you wish and only to those whom you wish to hear it," Val said.

Riddick looked relieved. "Well then, I hope to never have to tell it again. You can be my storyteller."

"If that is your wish, I would be honored. Elijah really should know. It explains much about you."

Riddick nodded. "I don't care whom you tell. All that matters is that *you* know."

Val gave him another hug. "Thank you."

Riddick was uncomfortable under Elijah's concerned stare so he quickly retreated claiming he had work to attend to.

Elijah crossed his arms. "What is going on?"

"Riddick finally told me the story of his past. It is terrible and now I see why he tried so hard to bury it." Then it dawned on Val. "How did you know I was here?" The armory was not a place she frequented.

"John thought it was interesting how you went stalking about looking for Riddick early this morning. As you had never done this before, he thought it would be of interest to me."

Val narrowed her eyes at Elijah. "Then you came looking for me. Is John your spy?" This was concerning on a number of levels. *Has John always been watching my movement in the castle? If so, why?*

"In a way, I suppose. He is a nosy little fellow. He knows everything that happens within these stone walls."

Val did not even try to hide her irritation. She had come to think of John as Lord Chastellain's number-one minion. He virtually worshiped the lord. Now she saw him as a viper in the shadows — always lurking. The lord's eyes and ears — ever present. It was infuriating that Elijah could have as many mistresses as he wanted and yet Val could not even talk with a friend without being followed — suspected even.

"Am I not allowed to converse with an old friend in private? Riddick has become like a brother to me. He cares about me and I him," Val said.

"Of course you can. Don't blame John, he is simply doing father's bidding. He has been instructed that you and Riddick are not to be alone. Never mind the fact that that order was given almost one hundred years ago."

"And yet here you are — checking up on me."

Elijah nodded. "Yes, that is correct. I don't want you to be with anyone else. I still want you for myself."

This lowered Val's defenses. She gave him a weak smile and put her arm in his as they walked. "You should trust me."

"You are right, I should." Elijah was not fully agreeing with her.

"You also must hear Riddick's story!"

CHAPTER 8 LONDON 1457 AD

For many years, Vallachia had secretly hoped that Teller would come for her. He could have easily found her, as everyone in the vampire world appeared to know who Vallachia was. As time passed it was no longer a secret, she admittedly dreamt of the day he would turn up looking for her. Yet time continued to slip away, day following day like each gentle wave slowly reshaping the shoreline. There was no news of Teller.

After almost two hundred years — well, one hundred and ninety-six years to be exact but who was counting? — Val was beginning to think that it was a real possibility that Teller was dead. Surely by now he would have turned up in a vampire coven somewhere and they would have heard of him. Many times over the years she'd had the strong desire to search for him.

On several occasions Val stumbled across false leads. She had searched for him, to no avail. At this point she did not know where to start to look for him. Perhaps he had wandered to the farthest reaches of the East. She had only heard tales of these strange and distant lands. Her home was now Copenhagen and at times still London. With the ongoing search for Ramdasha, she had too much work to do here to travel very far east. Continually working to gain and maintain alliances for the Court had become her life.

The year was 1457 when she finally found Teller. She ran toward him. He turned slowly and gazed at her with a deadpan stare. Before she reached him, he transformed into a massive red dragon. His long teeth were about to engulf her. She woke with a sharp inhale. *That horrid dream again!*

This was odd because Vallachia had not dreamt of Teller in a long time. It was incredibly real. For a moment she truly believed she had found him. Looking around to get her bearings, she remembered she was in Mary and Elizabeth's room. She was visiting them in London. She stayed with them in their chambers in Lord Alexandru's new castle, which was over a hundred years old. This was slightly awkward, as Mary and Elizabeth had become lovers.

Vallachia had only been there a couple of days when Hector came to the door to inform her that her presence was needed back in Copenhagen.

"Is everything well?" Val asked.

"Yes, My Lady, it is simply an important diplomatic errand. Lord Chastellain says it requires your expertise."

"I will leave straightaway. Thank you, Hector."

"You've only just arrived," Elizabeth complained.

"Please do not look at me like that. You make me feel even worse," Val said.

"That is precisely the point." Elizabeth gave Val a devious smile, one a child might make after getting away with stealing a forbidden sweet.

"Surely you could get away with murder when you look at people in such a manner," Val said.

"Of course she can get away with murder. She is a vampire," Mary scoffed.

Val laughed. "Sorry I must be leaving already. This has been increasingly the case with the growing threat from Ramdasha. It seems I haven't been able to spend as much time as I would like with you."

"Surely it is the young lord's fault. Elijah can't stand being away from you for too long," Mary said.

Val gave Mary a hard shove, tossing her onto the bed.

Mary laughed heartily at Val's irritation.

"Since we are not to travel alone, perhaps you two can be my escorts back to Denmark?"

In no time the three women were speeding through the air, quickly making their way eastward. Within the hour they landed on Vallachia's balcony in Copenhagen. Mary and Elizabeth settled into Val's quarters where they would be staying while they visited.

Val headed straight for the Great Hall, only to find the lord and Elijah waiting. She greeted Elijah with a hug and a smile.

Then to Chastellain she gave a slight bow and said, "What is it, My Lord?"

"Have you heard of Prince Vlad of Wallachia?" The lord always went straight to business.

"Yes, My Lord. He is said to be a merciless ruler who has recently risen to power. He has earned the nickname 'the Impaler,' as this is his most favored intimidation tactic." Val paused. "Is he a vampire?"

"Yes. We have been watching him for quite some time. He follows our laws, as it appears that no humans suspect that he is a vampire. His fortress is not far from our hometown. He married into the Draculesti family roughly one year ago and has used that name to take control of Wallachia. It is crucial that we gain his support. He has amassed large armies under his command, both human and vampire. He could be our most important ally and we must ensure that Prince Vlad does not side with Ramdasha. That is why I am sending my best. This is possibly your most vital mission to date. It may be dangerous so I want you to take extra men as well."

The usual entourage — Samuel, Riddick, Mary, Elijah and Val — as well as five of their top warriors set out for Wallachia at once. Mary often accompanied them on important or potentially dangerous missions. She had become the commander in chief of Lord Alexandru's branch of the Court in London. She, quite literally, fought her way to the top with her superior combat skills.

It was not long before they landed on a large terrace leading to an immense castle high in the Carpathian Alps. From here Vlad could keep watch over his kingdom to the south. To the north, the mountain ridges intertwined like the backs of a school of fish in shallow water. The closest mountains were a lush green and the distant mountain-tops appeared to be a deep-sea blue. The sun shone through the clouds making the colors stand out and fade in multiple hues of greens and blues, creating a sense of motion.

They paused to admire the view. Vallachia missed these mountains. Her original home had been nestled safely in their heart. It would have been heavenly to simply remain here. She would have been content to stare at the beauty before her for all time.

Elijah lifted the large knocker on the huge castle door and let it fall. A loud banging sound echoed through the mountains behind them. This pulled a reluctant Val from the view and brought her back to the important mission at hand. A servant slowly opened the door. Val noted that he was human.

CHAPTER 9 WALLACHIA 1457 AD

"We are here to speak with Prince Vlad of the Draculesti Family. We are from the High Court of the Elders," Elijah announced.

"Yes, of course. The master is expecting you. Right this way, Sire." The servant led them to a large room to await Prince Vlad. "I will inform the master of your arrival."

Vallachia thought the Chastellains were ostentatious but this place put their castle to shame. It was decorated with large wall hangings and chandeliers. There were many coats-of-arms on display representing the Draculesti family. They contained red serpent-like dragons twisting and curving their bodies to form odd shapes. Flames spewed from their mouths. For some reason this reminded Val of her recent nightmare about a dragon.

The largest of the paintings was titled *Voivode Vlad*. "Prince Vlad." Vallachia translated out loud. She looked up to find herself staring into the face of Teller. "Good God!" Val grabbed Elijah's arm in an iron grip.

Elijah followed her gaze to the large painting. "Oh shit," was his only reply.

Vallachia's blood turned to ice and her hands trembled. Her

protective instincts for Elijah took over. "You have to get out of here. He will not be happy to see you. You being here won't help to get him on our side." She pushed Elijah out the door from whence they had come.

"Do not leave her side," Elijah commanded Riddick.

Samuel and one of the guards left with Elijah.

"What is going on?" Riddick asked.

Val decided that he needed to know what they were getting into. "You remember that boy from my childhood — the one I told you about?"

"Aye." Riddick furrowed his brow.

"That is him," Val pointed with her thumb to the grand painting behind her.

Riddick studied the massive man whose face was spread across the wall, "Shhhit."

"That appears to say it all." Val's breath was uneven. She rubbed the scar on her right hand in a vain attempt to make the trembling stop. This moment had been a long time coming. *Have I truly found him?* For some reason she was filled with trepidation. *I should be happy. Why am I ... scared?*

"So this was your childhood love? Well, he is handsome and built like Riddick. He's modest too." Mary's smile was full of sarcasm.

"Yes, I know. This is not right." Vallachia looked around at the over-furnished room. Everything was new and extravagant. "Something is wrong. This is nothing like the young man I knew back in Ludus." Prince Vlad's moniker rang through her head, *The Impaler*. He was most likely incredibly dangerous. She had always thought of Teller as kind and simple. Yet nothing about this place was kind *or* simple.

Riddick took Val's hands. "You are shivering." He put his arm around her and rubbed her shoulder, as if to warm her but that was not the problem. "All will be well. Take a deep breath."

Vallachia did just that as the far door on the opposite end of the large room swung open. She jumped which placed her against

Riddick. This was not a good place to be, so she quickly stepped to the side.

Teller's eyes focused on her for a moment, then moved to Riddick for an even longer moment. He slowly approached. His face was emotionless — the same deadpan expression from Val's dream. She half expected him to transform into a dragon. Teller was more handsome than she remembered but he was different, cold, maybe even cruel. His eyes were dark, almost black — not the forest green she remembered.

"Well, Well. What have we here? I wondered when *the Court* would pay me a visit," Teller exclaimed.

Teller had been waiting for "the Court" to show up but not Vallachia. He was not waiting for her. Of course he wasn't, how stupid she had been. She took a step forward. She wanted to go to him — to throw her arms around him — but something in his hard stare held her back. *He is ... not right. There is something ... evil about him.*

"This is not who I expected to find you with, Vallachia." Teller gestured to Riddick. "Where is your *prince?"* He said the word "prince" with disdain — exactly as Riddick once had so many years ago.

This sent a chill down Val's spine. "His name is Elijah. He is not here and he is not 'my prince.'" Val was glad her voice came out steady because that was not how she was feeling.

"So you have gotten rid of your prince and moved on ... to him?" Teller gestured to Riddick again. Teller's gaze had hardly left Riddick.

Vallachia could feel Riddick's anger before he spoke.

"You arrogant arse! You know nothing about her and you do not speak to the Lady Vallachia in such a disrespectful manner." Riddick's voice boomed as he moved forward. In a flash they were within feet of each other.

Mary and Val jumped in between them. Val could feel their overwhelming male essence. These two men wanted to kill each other and they did not even know each other.

Val glanced around. The Court's guards had formed a half circle around Riddick. Teller's guards had his back. She had to do something. "Both of you stop!" She turned her attention to Riddick. "Please,

Riddick." She struggled to keep her voice calm as she placed her hand on his chest and slowly pushed him away from Teller.

Riddick's breathing was heavy. When it slowed, Val turned her attention to Teller. "We only want to talk."

Teller seemed to have regained some control as well. "Fine. I will speak with you — alone." Teller was shrewd, as he kept his gaze on the threat, which was Riddick.

Val turned her crystal-blue eyes to Riddick.

"No. I will not leave you. I can't!" Riddick said.

She gently took his chin with her thumb and index finger and gazed at him intently. "I'll be fine. I need to speak with him." Val knew that this was the only way they would get anywhere. She had to try to find the old Teller. He was in there somewhere — she could feel it.

"No!" Riddick said.

"All of you get out!" Val commanded. Without Elijah in the room Val was the ranking officer. They had to obey.

"Don't do this, please," Riddick whispered.

"I have to. It is our only chance of negotiating with him. No harm will come to me."

"You will answer to Elijah then?" Riddick was not supposed to leave her side for *any* reason. Elijah would be furious with Riddick.

"Of course." Val gave him a reassuring smile.

Riddick nodded yet was clearly not thrilled about having to leave. He grabbed Mary by the upper arm to lead her out. He gestured for the rest of their men to follow.

Val took a deep breath and tried to calm herself. She slowly turned around to face Teller — or was it Vlad?

CHAPTER 10 WALLACHIA 1457 AD

Once Teller was sure Vallachia's guards were retreating, he gave a hand gesture and his men exited the Great Hall out the opposite door.

Vallachia watched him for a moment trying to get a feel for him. He wore a thick dark mustache, in the style of this region. It hung down around his mouth. She did not care for the mustache, yet it succeeded in making him look older — which was surely why he wore it. She was searching for any sign of Teller and saw none.

Vlad swung his forearm out with his palm up. "You wanted to talk, so talk." His voice was full of irritation.

Val wanted to ask what had happened to him. Instead she said, "You have done well for yourself." As soon as the words left her mouth, she remembered Chastellain saying Vlad had married into the powerful Draculesti family. *That is how he managed all this.* It was as if someone slid a dagger into her stomach. She actually flinched in pain. *He is married! That is why he never came for me. I am such a fool!*

"You have done well for yourself as well. It is wondrous how marrying the right people has made us into more than we could ever have hoped."

"I never married."

"Ah, then the rumors are true; you are simply the young lord's mistress."

"No. I'm not that either." The anger welling up inside her was welcome because it eased the suffocating pain in her stomach.

"Then how did you get to the top?"

"I am a skilled emissary and a well-trained fighter. I am a servant of the High Court of Elders."

Teller issued a derisive chuckle. He clearly did not believe her. His iridescent black silk chlamys flowed elegantly behind him as he paced. "I can't believe you would serve that malevolent king, after all the horrible things he has done."

"I don't do it for him —"

"Then you do it for your beloved prince," he interrupted.

"No. I fight for the Court because I want to help protect humans. I know which side is the right one."

"Yes, of course. That is the reason, to save precious humans." His mocking tone was meant to infuriate her.

It was working.

They were not getting anywhere, so Val decided to change the subject. "Where is your ... wife?" She almost choked on the last word.

He smiled with malice. "She ... became *indisposed* not long after our wedding."

Val's stomach turned. "You killed her?"

"She was human and would only have gotten in my way. She had to be *dealt* with." Teller showed no sign of remorse — no emotion at all.

He has gone completely mad. She could no longer refrain, "It appears that your father would be proud of you. What happened to you?"

Teller's deadpan expression turned to an angry scowl.

The face of Vlad. At least it is an emotion, Val thought.

He slammed his fists into the oak table in front of him.

The tabletop cracked and Val jumped. He is not stable. He's on the edge and could explode at any moment.

Teller pointed a condemning finger at Vallachia. "You know very well what happened to me. You were there. You did this to me ... or have you forgotten?" He put his chin to his chest and rested his fists on what was left of the table. He took a couple deep breaths to regain control.

Val said nothing for a long moment, giving him time to calm down. Her mind raced for some way to get through to Teller, her love. She thought of how it had felt when they touched after she had been turned. She wanted to know if that feeling was still there. *Perhaps he can feel it too, now that he is a vampire. It might help me to get through to Teller. He must still be in there ... somewhere. He has to be!*

Val slowly moved to his side and put her hand over his fist on the table. She felt the shocking sensation in the palm of her hand. It moved up her arm.

Teller looked at her with wide eyes. This was in stark contrast to the previous intense narrow-eyed stare he had worn. He pulled his hand away. "What was that?"

Val was relieved to see that his eyes only held curiosity. The anger was gone. She took his hand, wrapping her fingers in his. "I don't know. Perhaps it is an indication of the way we feel about each other." She allowed herself to enjoy the sensation for a moment before removing her hand but he tightened his fingers around hers.

Once again Teller's expression changed. His eyes went from being full of curiosity to being full of hunger. As she stepped away, he grabbed her waist pulling her to him. Before she knew it, his lips were on hers. His mouth moved down her neck, kissing every inch along the way. Her entire body was on fire. She could not think or even breathe. Finding his lips she kissed him back. It was not until she heard the rip of fabric that she began to be able to think.

"Stop." Val could barely whisper in her breathless state. She gasped for air so she could force out a louder, "Stop!" She tried to pull away but it was useless.

Teller pushed her and she tumbled to the ground. She tried to escape but he was too quick. He was on top of her before she could get away.

"No!" Val tried to push him off.

Suddenly Teller went flying back. He landed gracefully on his feet. The momentum caused him to slide backwards.

"She said stop!" Elijah exclaimed. He had apparently thrown Teller off.

Now Teller's expression was murderous. "You!" he roared. "I have been waiting a long time to see you again." He marched toward Elijah.

Val jumped in front of Elijah and backed up against him with her arms out protectively. "No! Teller, please don't."

He looked between Elijah and Val for a moment. "I don't know what makes me angrier, that he had the nerve to interfere or that you are defending him."

Teller was clearly not used to restraining himself. He was used to getting what he wanted whenever he wanted it. His voice was dark and deep, not the voice Val remembered. *Is Teller truly gone, leaving only this monster behind?* Her chest ached. *How many times is he going to break my heart?*

Teller seemed to regain control. As if reading Val's thoughts he said, "Teller is dead. He died with your father many years ago. My name is Vlad. Actually," he corrected, "it is Prince Vlad to you. Now get out of here, before I change my mind."

Elijah had moved to her side, ready to fight if needed. Neither of them wanted to turn their back on Vlad. After an intense moment, Vlad spun on his heel and walked out. His regal chlamys billowed out behind him.

Before Vlad exited the room, he turned to Elijah. "I know why you came. Tell your father I will never join him. I will not follow anyone. I am in this for myself. I will reclaim Constantinople and become Emperor. I will single-handedly restore the Eastern Roman Empire to its former glory. I do not have time for your petty vampire struggles." Then he was gone.

Vallachia felt as if her body was falling in on itself. Somehow, she remained standing on her shaky legs. She had never been more confused. Part of her wanted to run after him and — equally — the other part wanted to run away and never look back. She doubled over in an attempt to simply breathe.

Elijah unfastened the gold broach from his chlamys and swung the fabric over her shoulders to cover her torn tunic. “Let’s get out of here,” he whispered.

CHAPTER 11 THE BEGINNING 1262 AD

Teller sat up in bed and put his head in the palms of his hands. He rubbed his eyes trying to clear the cloudiness from his thoughts. *Where am I?* He surveyed his surroundings. The bloodstained body of a woman lay beside him. She was mostly naked.

Another mess to clean up, he thought with irritation. The room around him was sparsely furnished and rundown. He moved to the window of the unfamiliar room and peered out. *Targoviste — that is where I am.*

Vague memories slowly came back to him. There were many women — most of them naked — and lots of blood. The last clear memory he had was of fleeing from ... somewhere. He remembered the pain in his eyes when the sun came up. He had stumbled into a village tavern, yet could not recall the name of the place. The people around him smelled like his mother's cooking after he had been out chopping wood all day — no, they smelled even better than that. Even though he had been salivating with hunger, he managed to control himself until that night when the inn grew crowded.

A local woman had approached him at the bar. She sat on his lap. "Hello, handsome. Do you want me to show you a good time?"

Teller could not recall what she looked like. All he remembered was her sweet scent. It was as if she were waving a slab of beef in front of a starved lion. He sank his teeth into her neck. a brief scream escaped from her before all that remained was her limp body. Other women screamed and men hollered. One man charged after Teller. "He killed Camilla, after him!"

Teller disappeared in a flash.

That was it — I had to flee Ludus. Yet why did I leave home? Teller sat down hard on a wooden chair, which had a broken arm. The memories came back faster now. Adam! I killed Adam that is why I had to leave. Vallachia! Where is she? I must find her. No, that's absurd! I killed her father. She would not want to see the likes of me. In fact, if she never saw me again it would most likely be too soon.

He moved to look out the window for the second time. The trees had leaves and the grass was green. *Summer,* he thought. *Have I been here a matter of days or an entire year or more?* He could not recall *which* summer it was.

Teller took the broken chair and wedged it against the door so no one would easily come in and find the woman on the bed. That would have to do until he could get rid of her. He quickly dressed and did his best to clean himself in the washbasin. With his cloak over his head, he checked the street to see if anyone was around. He saw no one and leapt out the window down three stories. He entered the tavern through the front door.

The man behind the long and well-worn counter declared loudly, "Well, there he is. Sleep late again, eh? You had better get yourself a job, boy, so you can pay your tab."

Teller pointed his finger at the innkeeper and scanned his fuzzy brain for the man's name. "Petru, right?"

"Well, at least you remembered my name this morning. You know, son, you had better lay off the drink."

No doubt Petru was referring to ale but that was not the problem, it was blood that Teller needed to refrain from. "Thanks for the advice. I really need a mead, make it the sweetest you've got." Teller was hoping the sweetness would help clear his head. He needed to think.

"Oh no, sonny, not until you pay up."

"I will get you money today."

"Aye, that is what you said yesterday and the day before that, as a matter of fact. You will get nothing more from me until I have money right here." Petru jabbed at his palm with his index finger.

A man sitting in a dark corner of the room spoke, "I will pay for the boy's mead, Petru. Make it two." The stranger motioned for Teller to join him.

Teller cautiously approached. He surveyed his surroundings for any signs of danger. There was only a handful of old-timers sitting around sipping meads and ales. He reluctantly took a seat across from the stranger.

"My name is Sergiu." He held out his hand in greeting.

Teller took his hand, only to find that it was as cold as his. Teller looked at him with surprise and the stranger gave Teller a knowing nod.

"And what do you call yourself?" The stranger had to ask as Teller had not offered his name.

"Vlad," Teller replied. It was the first name that came to mind. He was not entirely sure why he chose it. He supposed it was because it reminded him of the male version of Vallachia or Val.

"Oh, Teller," Petru yelled across the room. "Before I forget, a man came in here yesterday lookin' for ya, while you were out. Said he was trying to find his son. Called himself Ivan; that mean anything to you?"

"No. Just get us some mead, Petru." *At least Father cared enough to look for me,* Teller thought.

"Teller, eh?" Sergiu questioned.

"Not anymore."

The stranger nodded in understanding. "Well, Vlad is a better name."

"What do you want?"

"I only want to help you." Sergiu issued a friendly smile.

The stranger had a kind face, yet Teller was not entirely sure he could trust the man. He narrowed his eyes. "Help me? What makes you think I need help?"

"It is time you wake up. Look around you, boy. You cannot live like this forever. Listen to what people are saying about you," Sergiu glanced toward two old men seated by a window.

One of them was saying, "What a waste — a handsome boy like that already a no good drunkard."

"He should be out working, raising a family, doing what normal young men do," the other old man added.

"What is your point? I'm not a normal man anymore," Teller said.

"I'm well aware of that. I have been watching you for some time. We are vampires and there are no limits for us. You could be anything — become anyone. I don't like to watch others waste their lives."

"Then stop watching me."

"The locals are also beginning to suspect your involvement in the disappearance of the ladies of the night. You should be warned that if you keep this up you will gain the attention of the High Court of Elders."

"Who in hell are they and what do they have to do with me?"

CHAPTER 12 WALLACHIA 1262 AD

"The High Court of Elders will have everything to do with you if you don't pull yourself together. They will kill you in an instant," Sergiu informed Teller.

"Good. Then this miserable life would be over." Teller's voice was monotone. He had not a care in the world. He was incapable of feeling anything but hopelessness. "I don't even know what year it is and I do not care."

Petru brought them two mugs of mead and retreated. "Thank you," Sergiu said loudly to Petru, then to Teller he spoke softly, "You are worse off than I originally thought. The year is 1262."

Teller could not believe it. He had been in Targoviste an entire year and did not remember most of it.

"Believe me I know it is difficult in the beginning," Sergiu continued, "but you will get better at controlling your thirst. You will start to see this life for what it truly is — a gift. I implore you not to waste it. You can be so much more than you are now. You can be anything you aspire to be. You must have something to live for?"

Vallachia's perfect face with her large crystal-blue eyes appeared in his mind and he shook his head. "Not anymore."

"Then forget your past, make a new future. Find a new reason to live."

There will never be another Vallachia, he thought. "Why do you care so much? I mean, why bother with me? It would be easier to let me waste away until this Court or whatever it is, finds me and kills me."

"I see potential in you. You could be great. Besides, what makes this life worthwhile for me is helping my fellow vampires. What brings me pleasure is saving my kind from being killed by Lord Chastellain's Court."

At the mention of the name Chastellain, Teller sat up straight in his chair, finally interested in the conversation. "What did you say?"

"Lord Chastellain and his son. They swiftly and mercilessly kill vampires who reveal their true nature to humans."

"You are telling me that Lord Chastellain is the leader of our kind!"

"The undisputed leader, yes. It appears you have heard of him."

"This day could not possibly get any worse. Why am I not surprised?" Teller simply had to ask, "There is a lady, her name is Vallachia, have you heard of her?"

"Aye, yes. I have only heard rumors of her beauty. She is to marry the young lord, so it is said. Though there has not been any formal engagement announcement, which leaves some to speculate that the lovely young Lady of the Court is the prince's current mistress. What is his name?" Sergiu looked thoughtful.

Hot blood rushed to Teller's face. "Elijah," he said through gritted teeth.

"That is right." Sergiu looked pleased but grew concerned when he saw Teller's face.

"Are you sure — Vallachia is with Elijah?"

"Of course, everyone in our world knows this."

Teller could no longer contain himself. He let out a yell of frustration. The chair legs scraped noisily against the floor as he stood. He threw the terra-cotta mug across the room and headed for the door. This was all in one swift motion. The mug shattered across the adjacent wall. He had to get out of there before he tore this godforsaken place down with his bare hands.

"I will add the mug to your tab. Hopefully you are headed out to find work in order to be able to pay me," Petru said.

Teller ignored the innkeeper. Pulling his hood over his head he stepped out into the sun and was gone. He ran for a long time until he reached the top of a nearby mountain. The edge of a cliff finally stopped him. He sat down hard and became lost in his thoughts.

How could she possibly be with Elijah, after everything they did to me, to her, to us? It has been a year since we were together. No doubt Vallachia has accepted Elijah's proposal by now. They may already be married. She is not the type to be someone's mistress. Not to mention Elijah would marry her in a heartbeat — who wouldn't? Teller's chest was tight, as if he were bound by chains that were tied to horses. The horses were pulling in opposite directions causing the chains to crush his torso. He could not escape. "She is mine!" he yelled. "Or was — she should be mine." Teller spoke the last part quietly. He wanted to sink his teeth into someone.

Sergiu appeared at his side. "You know you could have flown up here. It is even faster than running."

Teller gave him an incredulous glare. "You are mad. What on earth are you talking about?"

"How long have you been a vampire and you have never flown? No wonder you're melancholy. Flying is the best part about being one of us. It is past time you learned." With that he gave Teller a firm kick to the back. This was the last thing he expected Sergiu to do and he went tumbling off the cliff.

As Teller sped toward the ground far below, his only thought was, *Thank God, this will surely kill me*. But he was not that lucky. Massive black wings spread out on either side of him. They seemed to suspend him in the air. He found himself gliding gracefully through the sky. The stinging in his eyes demanded his attention. He had to pull his hood back over his head. Laughter came from beside him as a large winged creature appeared there. Sergiu spiraled and moved through the air with ease. The sun did not seem to bother him.

"Come on," Sergiu said. "Don't simply glide, try to fly."

"How?"

"Move your wings."

How on earth do I intentionally move something that I did not even know I had? Teller concentrated on the muscles in his back and to his surprise the wings moved.

The two vampires slowly ascended higher. Teller looked around in amazement at the tiny world far below.

"Now you can't tell me this is not worth living for?" Sergiu said.

Teller gave Sergiu the slightest of smiles. *It is incredible!*

They flew all day and well into the night. Sergiu landed with ease on the side of a steep hill covered by prickly evergreens. Teller tried to slow himself with little success and ended up crashing into a tree. The branches broke with loud cracking sounds as he fell through the tree, eventually landing on his arse at Sergiu's feet. He was covered in tiny cuts and scratches.

Sergiu roared with laughter, as Teller stood and brushed off the pine needles and twigs. "Come, you can stay with me, if you like." His voice was full of light and life.

Was he always this happy? Teller thought with irritation, as he plucked a pine needle out of his hand.

"Flying today was the first time you have smiled since I spotted you over a month ago," Sergiu continued.

No doubt that was true. Teller had had no reason to smile, not since he killed Vallachia's father — losing her forever.

Sergiu walked a short way up the hill, crouched down and disappeared into a small dark opening in the side of the mountain. Teller reluctantly followed. For about ten or fifteen paces they had to walk almost doubled over. Then the cave abruptly opened into a large round stone room. Sergiu must have brought in some provisions because chairs, blankets and pillows were scattered about haphazardly.

"This is where you live?"

"Yes. Granted it is modest. Yet it has more than I need and the best part is that it is free. Not to mention noisy obnoxious humans with their sweet scent don't bother me here."

That does sound pleasant — for a change, Teller thought.

Sergiu laid out a blanket on the hard, cold floor of the cave. "Get some rest. We have work to do tomorrow."

Teller realized how tired he was. He stretched out on the blanket and vaguely wondered what *work* Sergiu was referring to, as he drifted off.

CHAPTER 13 COPENHAGEN 1386 AD

Elijah did indeed break Patricia's heart. She waited another year for a proposal that never came. Shortly after, she married another from Norway and moved to be with him. Elijah did not seem to care that she was gone. In fact, he seemed relieved.

Vallachia felt bad for Patricia but she seemed to be in high spirits at her wedding. And Vallachia had to admit that she was glad to once again have her dance partner. Things returned to normal between the two old friends.

"I had the horses saddled. Will you come for a ride with me?" Elijah asked.

This was one of their favorite pastimes. Vallachia slammed her book shut. "I would love to." How her life had changed. She was no longer a servant to her family — not that caring for her family had been terrible, by any means. Now she was like Elijah, an aristocrat, a noble. Not only did she have plenty of time to go on leisurely horseback rides, she didn't even have to saddle her own horse.

How has this happened? she wondered. "Don't you think we could at least prepare our own horses for riding?"

"Why?" Elijah honestly did not see her point. He had been born into the aristocracy and had no idea what it was like to be a commoner.

Vallachia hoped that that was something she would never forget — what it was like to have to work hard every day simply to survive. "Never mind," she said.

In no time they were galloping southwest leaving the manicured castle grounds behind. Many lengths ahead was a secluded lookout which they often enjoyed flying to. It was a rock cliff that overlooked a wider part of the Oresund. Vallachia and her friends had spent much time there and loved to dive off the sheer cliff into the freezing water. On this day, she and Elijah decided to try to ride there.

Vallachia gently kicked her horse's flanks and headed south.

"We have to go around the gorge. The horses will not be able to make it," Elijah said.

"It is only a small gorge, surely they can cross it. It will be faster to head directly south, rather than travel all the way around the ravine," she replied.

"We should not risk it. Traveling southwest is the best route. Then we will cut back to the Oresund staying on the main road."

"Fine, you go your way and I will go mine."

"We should not split up."

"It is broad daylight. Our enemy will not be out at this time. Nor would he dare to venture so close to our home. He is not that brave ... or stupid."

"Remember, Ramdasha is older than you. He too will be used to the sun by now."

"Yes but not many of his men will be old enough to venture out in the daylight. He would need all his forces to attack us on our land. There is no danger today. Come on, I dare you — my path is better. I will race you there."

Elijah smiled his devious crooked smiled — the playful one she had grown to love. Without another word he kicked his horse and was swiftly heading southwest.

"Hey!" Val protested. *That is not fair. He has a head start.* She kicked her horse and turned the reins toward the south. Once she reached the gorge her horse, whom she called Baby, balked and would go no farther. It was the dead of winter and only a small frozen stream was visible in the bottom of the wash. In the spring, it would become a raging river. It was however deeper than she had remembered. They usually flew to the lookout at night. From the sky it did not appear as steep and treacherous.

"Come on, Baby, you can do it." She coaxed her young mare forward.

The horse jerked her head back in protest.

"I will help you, Baby. You can do this." Val softly patted the horse's long silky neck. She pictured Elijah speeding down the road. He could stay at a full run and he would be at the lookout soon. She thought about flying the horse over the gorge. *No that would be cheating,* she thought.

With more gentle prodding, Baby took a step down the embankment. Her hooves slid and her shoulders moved exaggeratedly from side to side as she tried to slow her steep descent. When they reached the bottom, Val kicked Baby's flanks to get her to run up the far wall out of the gorge. Baby pushed off with her powerful hind legs, which propelled them up the other side. Baby was a good horse, well trained, did as she was told. Yet, she could not make it on her own.

Not far from the top she lost her momentum and slid back. Val had already positioned her feet on the saddle and leapt into the air. Her hands briefly touched Baby's croup as she did a back flip off her. Val landed gracefully behind the horse. With one powerful shove Baby was able to make it up out of the gorge.

Once safely on the other side, Val rubbed her muzzle and neck to calm her. "You see? I told you we would make it, Baby."

The horse snorted at Val. No doubt she was cross about having to maneuver the gorge. Val leapt into the saddle. Now they could beat Elijah, if they ran as fast as the wind.

They had not been racing through the forest for long when Baby came to a sudden stop rearing up on her hind legs at the edge of a clearing. Val had to lower her chest to Baby's neck so that she did not slide off the horse onto the ground. Val did not try to force Baby forward as she could hear and smell the danger as well.

In the clearing before them, a pack of wolves closed in on their prey. She leapt from Baby who neighed a warning as Val headed toward the danger. Val could see a horse's large brown back laying on the ground — unmoving. Beside it lay a shivering foal. Unlike its mother the foal was alive. The wolves had formed a circle around their precious winter meal.

Val stepped forward with Baby's reins in her hand but the horse was reluctant to follow. Baby's back legs trembled. Val released the reins and gave her a firm slap on the rear. Baby sped away faster than Val had ever seen her run. She would head straight for home. She was a smart horse, who knew where to find safety, food and shelter. The pack would not follow Baby when they had a free meal laid out in front of them. The choice between wasting energy chasing a healthy horse when a fresh motionless one lay at their feet was of no consideration.

Val had set her sights on the foal. In a flash she stood over the baby horse surrounded by ten wolves. The largest of the pack bared his long yellow teeth and let out a low deep growl.

"Mine are bigger," Val said out loud. With that she hissed and opened her mouth wide revealing her two-inch fangs.

The Alpha wolf paused. He growled and the Beta and Kappa wolves to the right and left of him lunged for Val.

She would not use her sword — that would be too easy. She grabbed the large toothy mouth closest to her by the lower jaw and the scruff of the neck. With an easy twist followed by a brief whimper the dog fell limp to the ground. She had snapped its neck like a twig. As the next attacker was about to sink his hungry teeth into her shoulder she threw her arm up with such force it broke his neck as well.

She stepped forward as the Alpha howled for the rest of his pack to attack. The Alpha leapt toward her. She caught him by the neck and held him up. It would have been difficult to find a neck vein through all that thick winter fur. She bit into the shoulder joint between his chest and front leg. Vampires knew where the nearest and largest veins would be. They could hear the blood pulsing and the smell was strong. It was as if they could "see" the veins. She drank heartily. The blood was bitter — not sweet and nourishing like human blood. When the wolf's heartbeat slowed, she dropped him to the frozen ground with a thud. He was still alive; he would recover. She looked around at the stunned pack. *They are only trying to survive the long winter*. Val's heart sank at the thought.

"I only want the foal. You can have the mother." *Perhaps this is what happens when you live too long — you start talking to wild animals,* she thought. The poor half-frozen foal was trying to gain protection and warmth from his mother who would never wake. Val took her coat — which had cost more than any horse was worth — and wrapped the colt in it. She swept him up into her arms and took flight. A couple of wolves had cautiously moved in and snapped at her heels as she ascended into the sky.

Back at the stables, Val laid the foal down on fresh dry straw in an empty stall. As she did, a twig fell out of her coat, which still warmed the baby horse. She picked up the twig and studied it. It had the deepest dark-green leaves with sharp points and a few bright red berries clung to the stem. "Holly, the winter berry," she whispered. *Of course!* She had not thought about it before but the clearing had been full of holly shrubs. She turned her gaze to the foal, "I knew it! I was meant to save you." After making sure the foal was warm and safe she flew to Elijah. He would be worried.

In no time Val landed by Elijah's side at the overlook.

Relief filled his iron-grey eyes. "Where were you? I was ... " Her mischievous smile caused him to pause.

"I have a gift for you. Come!" She took his hand to lead him away.

He smiled triumphantly. "I told you the road was faster." He glanced around and added, "Where is Baby?"

"Almost back to the stables, most likely. Come. We must hurry."

"What is going on? You've only just arrived."

But she had already jumped onto the back of his charger. "It is a surprise."

Elijah sighed and quickly positioned himself in the saddle behind her. They rode swiftly home, giving his fat yet powerful steed some much-needed exercise.

CHAPTER 14 COPENHAGEN 1386 AD

Once back in the stable, Vallachia said, "Now, close your eyes."

"What are you up to, Val?" Elijah reluctantly closed his eyes and let her lead him into the foal's new stall.

"You may open them."

Elijah smiled when he saw the foal wrapped in her coat.

"I saved him from a pack of wolves. He was lying next to his dead mother."

"I thought I smelled wolf blood on you."

"I had to save him and I knew that he was meant to be your horse."

Elijah gave Val a questioning look, so she continued, "Because I found him in a grove of this." She held out the twig with the dark green leaves and bright red berries.

"Hollis," Elijah whispered as he took the twig from her.

"You remember."

"How could I forget? Your first horseback ride was on Hollis — whom I had found in a holly grove. He was an excellent horse."

"I hope this foal will serve you as well as Hollis."

Elijah bent down and rubbed the colt's neck. "I will name him Hollis as well." He spoke softly as not to further scare the already frightened youngling. "He needs warm milk." Elijah disappeared through the stall door and called down the long corridor for the stable boy.

The servant quickly appeared.

"Bring me the large red mare who recently had a foal. We must see if she will take to this new foal. She has plenty of milk for two."

Vallachia was not sure why Elijah could not have fetched the new mother himself, as it would have been faster. It was a very old and ingrained habit, she supposed. People became accustomed to having others do everything for them.

In no time, the stable boy led the large red mare into Hollis's stall. They watched as the mare sniffed the foal and moved away. She knew it was not hers. She sidestepped and slightly kicked her rear leg, pushing the foal away when he tried to nurse on long wobbly legs.

This big red mare had been Val's but as soon as her horses had babies she gave up riding them. Young fillies were more fiery and energetic. Giving birth seemed to calm them. Val preferred spunky horses, perhaps because they resembled her. Yet soon Baby would go into estrus and Elijah would breed her to his charger. It happened every time. Then Val would have to find a new spirited young filly to ride.

"Do you think she will allow him to feed?" Val asked.

Elijah frowned. "Sometimes it works but more often mares reject foals that aren't their own. Let us leave them alone and give them time to get used to each other."

"Come on, Mama. Don't be stingy with your milk," Val said as she turned to leave the mismatched pair.

They checked back on the horses after a good half hour. The mother was still reluctant.

"Soon Hollis will grow too weak to stand and feed." Elijah furrowed his brow. He gathered a rope hanging on a nearby nail and tossed Val an apple. "Here, distract the mare with this."

The Court had fall apples stockpiled in the cellar solely for the horses — as they did not eat them. If their own orchards failed to produce enough, Elijah would have apples imported from the south. Their horses were indeed spoiled.

As Val fed the mare the apple, Elijah deftly tied her front legs together and then her back legs. Now the mare could not easily move away from the hungry foal. Hollis began to nurse eagerly. Elijah picked Val up and swung her around.

"It worked! You are a genius," Val declared.

Eventually Elijah had the mare's foal brought to her. "She will need extra rations of apples and more hay but she is healthy and will easily be able to feed them both."

Hollis thrived and grew into a magnificent steed. Once fully grown he stood over sixteen hands high. This was much taller than any of the other horses they owned. He had a shiny honey-colored coat with a long blond mane and tail. His tail would sweep the ground when he walked. Hollis was quite a sight to behold. Elijah would spend time with him every day. He trained him and hand fed him apples. This he did himself because he wanted Hollis for himself. The horse grew to know and trust Elijah above anyone else.

CHAPTER 15 WALLACHIA 1262 AD

When Teller woke his thoughts were hazy. He looked around the dark cave but this time reality returned to him more quickly. *Sergiu! I'm in Sergiu's cave. The year is 1262. I can fly! Vallachia is with Elijah.* He let out a moan and rolled over pulling a pillow over his head. He wanted to find someone to sink his aching fangs into. This would help him to forget about her.

"Come on, lazybones, it is time to get up," Sergiu beamed.

"Are you always this genial? Because it is grating on me." Teller tossed the stale pillow off his head.

Sergiu threw a chalice of water in Teller's face, causing Teller to sit upright.

"What was that for?"

"Here," Sergiu said as he handed Teller a steaming cup of strong smelling brew.

This lessened Teller's anger, as the substance smelled delectable. "What is it?" Teller wiped the water off his face with the sleeve of his tunic.

"My favorite drink. I call it 'Sergiu's secret brew.' It is simply mint and sage leaves that I have gathered from these mountains. I dry them to perfection and steep them in boiling water."

Sofia, the healer in Teller's village, used to create medicines in this manner but Teller had never heard of drinking such a brew for enjoyment. He took a sip of the hot liquid and moaned, "This is wonderful." It was nothing like Sofia's horrible tasting concoctions. Teller's head cleared, so he eagerly took another sip. He looked around to find that Sergiu had bundles of dried plants hanging about the cave.

Sergiu wore a look of satisfaction. He was pleased that Teller was enjoying his special brew.

Teller followed him out to a small fire burning in front of the cave entrance. Apparently this was where he heated the water for his drink. They sat around the fire and watched the sunrise. Nothing but lush green mountains surrounded them. This place was peaceful and isolated. Without the bothersome scent of humans, Teller's head was already clearer than it had been in a long time, possibly since he had become a creature of the night. The brew seemed to help as well. The problem was that a clear head let in the pain — all that he had lost; a perfect human life, all the lives he had taken. *How can I possibly live with myself?*

"That is quite enough brooding, my dear boy. Tell me, what skills do you have?" Sergiu said.

It was a relief to Teller that Sergiu did not appear to want to know about Teller's past, because he did not want to talk about it. Sergiu was only concerned with the future.

"Well, I am fairly good with metal," Teller answered.

"Excellent, a fine skill. One that can make you money."

"Why do I need money?"

"You are going to need something to do besides sit here all forlorn staring at the mountains for an eternity. For starters you need money to be able to pay back that poor innkeeper. Not to mention, you will not get very far dressed as a peasant. You need money to buy better clothes —

"I don't want fancy clothes. I don't need anything ... except blood."

"How else will you ever make something of yourself?"

"Who says I want to make anything of myself? And besides I can steal clothes when needed."

"Simply because we have to kill to survive does not mean we have to abandon all morals. You will feel better about yourself if you can make your own way. Living an honest life, as honest a life as possible anyway, will empower you. Just because we need human blood does not mean that we have to become thieves as well. You can start by refraining from all the blood — it makes you dim. I only feed every four to six weeks, I suggest you do the same."

"Four to six —

Sergiu narrowed his eyes at Teller.

"Fine, I will try."

"Then you can start by getting a job to pay Petru back."

"Oh, shit."

"What is it?"

"I left a woman's body in the room back at the inn."

Sergiu slapped Teller upside the head with the back of his hand. "You see? Too much blood makes you dim!"

"Ouch." It hadn't been a hard slap, only enough to sting a bit and to get Teller's attention. He deserved that, he supposed, so he let it go. He was not convinced that an honest life was the one for him. Yet working with metal again did sound appealing. "So, you are in opposition to Lord Chastellain and this Court of his?" Teller asked.

"Absolutely not. The Court is in the right. Vampires should remain hidden from humans, as this is what is best for everyone. There would be chaos if humans knew we existed. I am grateful they are in power and I'm not saying this simply to save my own head."

"Yet you told me you enjoy saving vampires from their clutches."

"I believe some vampires are worth saving and capable of change. I've seen it. With a little guidance they can learn to control themselves. Lord Chastellain prefers to sever heads first and ask questions later — if you know what I mean." Even this Sergiu said with a smile.

How can anyone be so jubilant all the time? Teller wondered. Sergiu's words were confusing; either the lord was the enemy or he was not. There is no in between ... or is there? Irrespective, Lord Chastellain is my enemy — he tried to kill me. Not to mention his son is no friend, if for no other reason than stealing Vallachia from me. Teller narrowed his eyes and his frown deepened.

"I already told you, that is enough of your self-pity and loathing. First things first, today we will find you a job in a smithy shop. We will head to the southeast region of town. That way we will hopefully avoid anyone who may be looking for you in the northwestern part of Targoviste, where they know you by the name of Teller and now the killer of the woman in Petru's tavern. It will be best for you to go by Vlad from now on." Sergiu appeared to have everything already planned out for Teller's new life.

They sat in silence for a moment staring out over the seemingly endless array of the Carpathian Mountains. "This could all be yours someday — if you pull yourself together."

Teller looked at him with curiosity. *What does he mean by that?*

CHAPTER 16 WALLACHIA 1262 AD

Sergiu and Teller took flight for town. It did not take long for them to locate the local smithy for the southern region of Targoviste. A man in his late forties was hard at work in a small one-room smithy shop.

Sergiu boldly approached the man. "Pardon me, kind sir, it looks as if you could use an extra hand around here?"

The smithy eyed Sergiu with suspicion. "I can't afford any help, mister. You best be on your way."

"Ah but you *will* be able to afford help and much more after you see what this young gentleman can do. He will make you triple the money you make now, if not more."

The man studied Teller. "You look strong enough, but I'm barely making ends meet, I could not pay you."

"How will you be able to get ahead if you do not have help? There is no way you can do it all yourself; get the metalwork done, tend to customers, not to mention, keeping the fires stoked."

Teller could almost see a new line form on the smithy's face. The weight of Sergiu's words caused him to slump.

"That is why you had best stop wasting my time and let me get back to work," the smithy said.

"Just one day. Give the boy one chance to prove how much help he can be to you. You do not have to pay him for the day's labor if you still think he is not worth it."

"What?" Teller demanded. He did not know which was worse, the insult to his skill or the fact that he had to work for nothing. "I am not a slave."

Teller turned to leave but Sergiu stopped him. He spoke quickly and quietly so only Teller could hear. "Don't worry about the money. It will come once he sees what you are able to do with a vampire's strength and stamina."

Teller studied Sergiu for a moment. Teller could see that he was genuine. His only motive was to help Teller. Teller was already growing quite fond of the man. Teller gave him a nod and turned back to the smithy. "My name is Tel-Vladislav and this is Sergiu." He held his arm out to the smithy, which was received. This was a common gesture when making an acquaintance but more commonly used when making a deal. In this case it was both.

"My name is Darius."

"Pleased to meet you." Teller was anxious to show this man what he was capable of. "Let's get started, I'm sure there is plenty to do."

"You've got that right, young man," Darius said. "I'm at least a month out on orders. That is what I tell my customers but truthfully I will be lucky to have their merchandise to them in that short amount of time."

The front of the shop was a simple open-air counter where people placed orders or picked up their new metal goods. The shop itself was a small dirt-floored room behind the counter. He pointed to a stack of small pieces of papyrus with orders on them.

"I was working on an order of knives for a tavern. You can start on a small job." Darius thumbed through the orders. "Here you go. A friend of mine needs a new axe head. That should be easy enough for you."

Teller had a hard time hiding his scowl. *Easy enough indeed.*

"I will help out in the front," Sergiu offered. "I can take orders and give folks their merchandise. Besides I need to keep an eye on this one." He pointed to Teller. "To make sure he stays out of trouble."

Teller glared at Sergiu and Darius looked concerned.

"Don't fret, you don't have to pay me," Sergiu said.

"Well then, what are we waiting for?" Teller said. In no time he had a perfectly formed axe head, as smooth as a silk scarf. With his supernatural strength he could easily pound the molten metal to the desired shape. Darius was still hammering away on the first knife for the tavern when Teller placed the hot axe head into a cooling trough. The protesting water hissed and sizzled, filling the air with steam.

"What are you doing, boy? That axe cannot possibly be ready for cooling?"

"See for yourself." Teller lifted it out of the water with the tongs and placed it on the table.

Darius inspected the axe with awe. "It is perfect, how —"

Sergiu had been thumbing through the orders. "This looks like an important one. A lord is requesting fifty swords. No doubt they are for his guards."

Teller looked at Sergiu with wide eyes — he could read. Only a handful of people in Ludus could read, Teller was not one of them. Not that he had much interest in sitting around reading, even if there had been someone to teach him.

"An educated man," Darius said. "I have learned enough to write down orders, otherwise I would never remember them all."

"Aye, scarcely enough. You did not spell 'sword' correctly," Sergiu stated.

Teller threw the axe head to Sergiu who swiftly caught it. "You can make yourself useful and sharpen that."

Sergiu frowned at Teller; yet moved to the sharpening stone.

"I will have the swords ready by morning for the lord's order," Teller declared. "They will be the finest he has ever seen."

"No one can make that many swords in one day," Darius said.

But Teller was already busy at work. Darius headed home late that evening and Sergiu and Teller stayed up all night. Sergiu sharpened the swords once they had cooled. When Darius came into work early the next morning, he found sixty beautifully-crafted razor-sharp swords leaning against the wall and Teller had already moved on to the next round of orders.

Darius studied the swords. "I have never seen such craftsmanship. The lord will be pleased. Why did you make more than ordered?"

"Once the lord sees these swords he will want more," Sergiu said with confidence. "It will then be easy to sell the extra ones to him and, if we are lucky, he will place another order. In fact, I have been known to sell fish to fishermen. Why don't you let me deliver the swords?"

Sergiu's ready smile made him hard to deny and easy to like.

"Very well. The lord will be delighted to have them so soon and that will allow me to get to work here," Darius said.

"Actually, I will be out of materials by the day's end," Teller said. "It would be more productive if you keep me supplied with raw metal, wood and the like."

Darius moved to survey his sorely diminished stockpiles. "My metal supplier will not be coming through town for another couple of weeks."

"Then go to him," Teller suggested.

"I suppose I could take the cart to his mine outside of town. I've never had to do that before. With three of us working it does change things." Darius already appeared lighter. His back was less bent under his burden and fewer creases lined his face.

By the time Darius returned with a cartload of iron ore it was dusk.

They were out of raw metal and Sergiu and Teller had dozed off in a couple of wooden chairs.

Sergiu woke Teller with a swift kick. Then to Darius he said, "The lord was pleased beyond measure. He bought all sixty swords and placed an order for one hundred more. It appears he is more than confident in our work." Sergiu tossed a large bag of gold coins to Darius.

Darius opened the leather bag and blinked at the shining coins inside. "This is ... wonderful. I did not expect to get this money for months. I will be able to pay my debts. The miner did not want to let me leave with the ore today. I will be able to pay him tomorrow. He will be relieved. I am grateful to you both."

"You will be able to pay me, as well," Teller added. It was not a question.

"Yes, indeed. It appears that you are well worth it. I have never seen anyone work with metal the way you can. It is ... uncanny."

Teller melted down the next round of iron. Over the next three days he finished the last of the back orders and started on the lord's new order of swords. Customers were thrilled to get their metalworks so quickly. As word spread about what they could do, the orders poured in. With Darius keeping Teller supplied with materials and Sergiu taking and delivering orders, Teller could usually keep up with the work during the daylight hours and nights were spent flying. Being so busy did not allow him time to think about Vallachia; not to mention his unquenchable thirst for blood.

At the end of the first week Darius handed his two new helpers a sack of coins, much more than he had agreed to pay Teller in the beginning. Sergiu hadn't expected any pay, of course.

"You both deserve this and more," Darius said. "For the first time I am not simply scraping by. My debts are paid and my family is well taken care of. I will be able to pay you more next week, if you keep working at this pace."

That night in Sergiu's cave, Teller stretched out on a bedroll. He gazed at the cave ceiling with contentment.

"Did I not say that the money would come?" Sergiu said.

Teller rolled over onto one elbow and handed Sergiu his bag of coins. "Do me a favor and take this to Petru. It will more than pay for my debt. I would do it myself but I should not be seen around there."

Sergiu smiled and took the bag. "See there, it feels much better to do good when we can. We greatly helped Darius this week and to pay Petru is the proper thing to do."

For the first time in a long time Teller felt satisfied with himself and his life. He was also tired after a long week of hard work. He drifted off into a deep sleep.

CHAPTER 17 WALLACHIA 1262 AD

The next month went along much the same. The money was rolling in for all of them. Teller was relieved to wake with a clear head. He almost believed that he was normal again. Then came the reminder that he was not — the need to feed stirred inside. It came abruptly when Darius brought his family to meet his new help.

Darius had four daughters — no sons — hence not having any help in the shop. Two of his daughters were married and two remained at home. The two younger daughters and Darius's wife filed into the tiny shop. Their delicious scent was too much for Teller.

"This is Vladislav and Sergiu," Darius said. "They are the ones I have been telling you about. Their help is ..."

But Teller ran out of the shop covering his mouth and nose to try to hide the dangerously long eyeteeth that formed in his aching jaw. This also helped him to not breathe in their sweet scent.

In a flash, he was across town. He had not paused to grab his cloak so he had to stay in the shadows. He spotted a man walking down the street ... alone.

"Pardon me," Teller said, from the shade of a large cathedral. "Would you be so kind as to come over here? I'm in need of assistance." He tried to sound desperate, which was easy — he *was* desperate, mad with the pain of hunger.

"Of course, how may I help?" The stranger approached.

Teller doubled over and waited.

"Are you alright?" the man asked.

As soon as he stepped into the shade, Teller grabbed him by the shoulders and sank his teeth into the stranger's neck. It was like slowly waking up, coming back to consciousness, as the man's blood calmed the raging monster inside. Teller laid the man down on the street and ran, careful to remain in the shadows. Once far out of town under the shade of a large tree, he paced, trying to gather his thoughts.

Who was I fooling? I am nothing more than a killer — a taker of innocent lives. This is all I will ever be — a cannibal.

His thoughts strayed to home. His mother used to say, "This is our life and we must learn to make the best of it." She would often say this after a particularly-bad night with his father. Sometimes she could not come out of the house until the bruises healed. As a child, Teller thought she was only making excuses for Ivan and his cruelty. She was simply justifying her helplessness in a terrible situation. Teller had resented her for it. As a simple-minded child, he had wished she would leave her husband and get them out of that terrible home.

Of course, where would she have gone and how would she have fed us? I can see that now, she did not have any good choices. Yet she still found happiness even with my father. In actuality, her attitude was remarkable.

Now her words had a new meaning for Teller. "Things are the way they are, so make the best of it. If I must be a killer, I could at least make the deaths count. I can eliminate anyone who stands in my way." He said this out loud, even though he was utterly alone. He could feel his ambitions growing deep within. This was the start of a new Teller. In fact, Teller was all but gone. He was now Vlad.

CHAPTER 18 FRANCE 1431 AD

The High Court of Elders had many years of peace after suppressing Tarantism and the plagues across Europe. Balance had been restored to the world since vampire numbers had been greatly reduced. Humans repopulated and thrived once again. The Court continued to maintain their current allies and search for new comrades. Once again Vallachia's job became more diplomatic in nature, which was greatly rewarding for her.

It was not long — well, for vampires, as it had been about twenty years — before the Court heard rumors of Ramdasha regrouping. They often traveled south on missions searching for him or someone who could tell them where he was. However, he remained well hidden.

By the fifteenth century they were sure that Ramdasha was trying a different tactic. Instead of creating numerous new untrained vampires who randomly caused trouble, he was building a large well-trained army in order to fight the Court in a battle for domination of the vampire world.

The Court had eyes and ears throughout Europe and beyond. They were continually looking for Ramdasha. Lord Chastellain had to pay his scouts well, as it was a dangerous job. Not to mention, the money helped to ensure that they remained loyal to the Court. Sometimes the scouts would not return. The lord assumed they had found Ramdasha and been killed or had defected. Either way they were dead to the lord.

Late one night the Court's top emissaries, Riddick, Mary, Elijah and Vallachia, traveled to visit a new coven of vampires in France. Their mission was to gain the coven's support before Lord Belleaire could. Belleaire remained loyal to Ramdasha and was very influential over the vampires of France.

As they flew over a large human army camp, Elijah beckoned for his entourage to land. Once outside the camp he whispered, "Do you smell that?"

They walked through the camp, following their noses. A man appeared in the distance. He was clearly not human. He moved too gracefully and smelled as only a vampire does. As they approached the figure, it became apparent that it was not a "he" but rather a "she", dressed as a man, as Mary and Vallachia were. The woman had a pleasant face and appeared to be quite young.

She clasped Elijah's forearm and gave it a firm shake, "I'm Joan of Arc," the vampire said. "And you are?"

They had heard of her. She was the woman who was leading the French army against the British.

"My name is Lord Chastellain."

"My Lord." She gave a bow. "Of course, I know of you. It is an honor." She gazed at him for a moment, "I thought you would ... appear older."

"That would be my father you are thinking of. Please, call me Elijah."

"I see. It is an honor to finally meet you." Joan turned to Vallachia, "And you must be the fair and gracious lady of the Court."

"I don't know about all that. My name is Vallachia." Val reached for her hand. "It is nice to meet you."

"No. The pleasure is all mine." Joan held onto Val's hand. "I have idolized you my entire life. Even as a child I was told stories of the beautiful Queen in the North who never ages. She who rules with love and compassion."

Val looked at Elijah for clarification. He chuckled and shrugged to indicate that he had no idea what Joan was talking about.

"I am no queen," Val said.

"Of course you are. Once I was turned and I learned of Lord Chastellain and his Court, it all made sense — the stories were indeed true. I knew then that you were an immortal vampire. You are our queen, whether you know it or not."

Val opened her mouth to protest but Joan continued, "We follow you. You are our leader."

Val shook her head. This was madness. Was this truly how she was viewed by their kind? Could it be that humans told tales of her as well? This simply could not be. "Well, I sincerely doubt all that nonsense," Val said.

"I also heard you were incredibly modest. This I can see is true as well."

Val proceeded to introduce Mary and Riddick. This helped her to change the subject.

"Please join me in my tent." It was only at this point that Joan released Val's hand as she beckoned them to follow.

Once inside a large tent, Joan went to a thick book on her nightstand and held it up. It was the Bible. "You, as well as this, are my motivation and inspiration. My father was a very spiritual man. Thankfully, he taught me to read."

"My father was a deacon. I too am immensely grateful for how he raised me." The two women smiled at each other for a moment. They seemed to have a connection and an understanding between them that Val could not fully explain.

The fact that Joan managed to keep her faith after being turned into a vampire caused guilt to wash over Vallachia. She had all but given up on God after being turned. She wished she could be like Joan — still devoted. In fact, a feeling of inferiority settled in Val's stomach.

"How wonderful it must be to still have such faith. How do you manage it after being turned?" Val asked.

"Some things you know here." Joan tapped the center of her chest to indicate her heart. "Not up here." She tapped her forehead.

"So you don't think we come from the darkest depths of Hell?" Val said.

"It is impossible to say where our kind comes from but one thing I do know is that my purpose in life is a worthy one. The work you do with the Court is also honorable. I would argue that we are all doing God's work. That is enough for me."

Val nodded. Even if vampires were the demonic spawn of the Devil, then at least she worked tirelessly to stop the worst of them.

"Well, I am sure you did not fly all this way to talk about religion," Joan said.

"We are on a diplomatic mission and happened to stumble upon your camp," Elijah explained.

"Ah, so you did not come here seeking me out." Joan looked relieved.

"Not exactly, though I am glad we found you. Tell me, do you support Lord Belleaire?" Elijah asked.

"Certainly not. He is a tyrant. I am loyal only to France," Joan declared.

"I do have one more question for you, Joan. Do any of your men suspect that you are a vampire?"

"No. They see me as being rather strong for a woman, that is all."

This answer seemed to pacify Elijah as he relaxed, leaning back into his chair. His "interrogation" was over. Joan was free to carry on about her business as long as she did not let humans discover her true nature and she did not support the enemies of the Court.

"When you are done here, perhaps you will consider joining us in the north?" Val asked.

"I would like that very much, as soon as I get the bloody British out of my country." Joan smiled with confidence.

Vallachia half considered herself to be British. London was one of her homes but she did not like what King Henry was doing to France. They spoke about politics and religion for quite some time. Riddick was about to fall asleep when Elijah decided it was time for them to go.

"I hope we will meet again soon. Take care of yourself," Vallachia gave Joan a hug and Joan appeared not to want to let go.

Once back in the air Elijah said, "She reminds me of you, in some ways."

"You know, for just having met Joan of Arc, I am quite fond of her," Mary said.

"I bet you are," Riddick added with a jesting smirk and a playful elbow to Mary's ribs.

"Not like that, you pervert." Mary tackled Riddick. They tumbled end over end, falling through the night's sky. With a hardy shove Mary pushed him away. They gracefully spread their wings to stop from plummeting to the earth.

Their meeting with the young vampires of France was a wash. They were reluctant to cross the cruel Belleaire but Vallachia convinced a couple of them to come to Denmark. These were two new vampires who desperately wanted to learn to feed without killing; thus the mission was not a complete loss. Plus, they had met Joan.

CHAPTER 19 COPENHAGEN 1431 AD

Six months after they first met Joan of Arc, Mary landed on Val's balcony in Copenhagen. Mary did not knock. She barged into Val's chambers, pulling her from the settee where she had been reading. "We must go! Joan is in trouble. She needs our help."

Val had never seen Mary so full of panic. Val turned to Mari, who had been reading on the other end of the settee. "Tell Elijah I am on my way to London." Val grabbed her favorite sword from its stand by her bed and she and Mary were off.

In just under an hour the two women landed on the outskirts of London. They could smell the putrid stench of burning flesh. Val and Mary looked at each other with wide eyes. They ran.

"No! Surely they have not killed her!" Mary said.

They followed the smoke plumes through the city. In no time they arrived in a public square. Three human-like figures tied to stakes were the central attraction. The blackened bodies still smoldered.

Val appeared behind an old woman — one of the last remaining onlookers. "Pardon me."

The woman jumped at Val's sudden appearance.

"Who were these people?" Val asked.

"A witch. Called herself Joan of Arc, and two of her guards." She gestured to the figures with a crooked finger.

Val shook her head. "No." She put her arm around Mary who had tears streaming down her cheeks.

"It can't be. We are too late," Mary moaned.

"Now young ladies don't go cryin' for the likes of that woman. She was a witch and a traitor to England, no less."

Vallachia slowly lifted her head to glare at the woman. In one swift step Val was towering over her. "You are a fool for an old woman. Joan of Arc was no witch, she was a saint!"

Val felt a twinge of guilt because the woman was now trembling. She backed away from Val and lumbered off as quickly as her old legs would carry her. Val felt a swoosh of air and turned to find Elijah and Riddick. Mary was on her knees, her face still wet with tears.

"What happened?" Elijah eyed the charred figures with dread.

"It is Joan — they killed her," Val managed, as the tears finally came. She bent down and hugged Mary.

"Oh no," Elijah breathed. He knelt down, wrapping his arms around both of the grieving women. They stayed like that for some time.

"We have to take her ashes to France," Val murmured. "It is undoubtedly what she would want."

Mary nodded in agreement.

"I'll fetch something to carry the ashes," Riddick said. He was relieved to have something to do. The emotional scene was not his greatest strength.

It was not long before he returned with three relatively small barrels. They had most of the charred remains in the barrels when men rode up on horseback. They wore the royal armor of King Henry's guards.

"Halt there! What do you think you are you doing?" one of them demanded. He was obviously in charge.

"We are to dispose of the ashes at King Henry's behest," Elijah lied. He spoke with an almost flawless English accent.

The men looked at one another with confusion.

"That was to be our job," the leader declared.

"That is odd. You had better take it up with the king." Elijah went back to work.

"That I will. What is your name, boy?"

"John of Dale." Elijah was quick with his lies.

The leader of the guards appeared skeptical but slowly turned his horse back toward the king's castle.

"Hurry," Val whispered. "They won't be gone for long."

"It would be a shame to have to kill them," Mari spat. "Ignorant murderers that they are."

They quickly sealed the barrels and disappeared even quicker.

They stopped briefly at Alexandru's to send word to Elijah's father that they were heading to France on a brief order of business.

AT LEAST JOAN OF ARC was given a proper burial in France. The uncrowned King Charles was in attendance at her service to honor her sacrifice for the country that was rightfully his.

"I don't understand. How were they able to capture her?" Mary asked.

"I don't know," Val said.

"She was a lone vampire, with only a human army around her. If she were injured they could easily have captured her," Elijah offered.

"They put her to death so quickly," Mary said. "I heard of her capture and two hours later she was dead."

"They may have noticed her uncanny healing ability. This would explain the witch accusation. It most likely scared them so they executed her straightaway, before she could be fully healed," Elijah said.

"I should have stayed and tried to save her. I was sure we had plenty of time to rescue her. There should have been a long-drawn-out trial, giving us plenty of time to free her."

"Please, Mary, stop berating yourself. It is not your fault," Val said.

Elijah put an arm over Mary's shoulder. "Besides you may have been burned with her if you had not come for us first. We have done everything we could."

Val placed an arm around Mary's waist. "Let's go home."

CHAPTER 20 WALLACHIA 1262 AD

Teller, or rather Vlad, did not return to the smithy shop until early the next morning. Having to kill the man in the street the previous day had set him back. But he would not allow himself to be addled again.

When Darius came into the shop, Vlad had been working for hours.

"Glad to see you are feeling better," Darius said.

"I often find it difficult to be in confined spaces with lots of people."

"I have never heard of such a thing. Bit of a loner, are you?"

"Aye, something to that effect. You know, we desperately need more space. I could use a larger work area and we need room to stockpile supplies. We should invest in the vacant building next door."

"I don't know. That would be quite an expense. I must think of my family and their needs. Perhaps in a year or so all of my daughters will finally be married, then I could expand."

Vlad narrowed his eyes at Darius. *A little man thinking small.* Vlad forced a smile. "Of course, all in due time." Inside Vlad was fuming. *No one will hold me back.*

A few days later Vlad noticed a girl watching him out of the corner of his eye. Begrudgingly he stopped pounding on the metal before him. "Yes?" His voice was full of irritation. *Where was Sergiu?* He always dealt with the public and Darius was out cutting wood for the furnace, which now rarely cooled.

"Hi. My name is Sabina. I'm Darius's youngest daughter." The girl peered up at Teller with a shy smile.

"Aye, I remember. What do you want?"

Sabina seemed flustered by his short tone. She had a tiny girlish face and mousey brown hair; yet she was attractive enough. "I wanted to introduce myself since we did not properly meet the other day. You know, you are greatly helping us. Mother thanks God every day for you and Sergiu coming into our lives. Father is no longer exhausted when he comes home from work. He takes walks with us in the evenings and —"

"Tell your mother that it is nothing. Now I must get back to work."

"Don't you ever take a break?" Sabina smiled playfully and took a step closer.

Oh no, Vlad thought. "No, not usually." He turned to stoke the fire.

"Are you hungry? I can get you something to eat." She moved to stand even closer.

Sabina's words reminded him of Vallachia and now he was doubly irritated. He stood to his full height and towered over her. "You seem like a nice girl. You need to stay away from me. I really don't want to hurt you." With that he walked out of the shop in order to get away from her mouthwatering scent.

"What do you mean — hurt me?" Sabina said to Vlad's back.

Once outside the shop he spotted Sergiu and headed straight for him.

"Where are you going?" Sergiu asked.

"I'm trying to get away from Darius's daughter. Keep her away from me, will you?"

"Ah, I see. Sure thing, my friend. Wouldn't want you to kill that nice young lady now, would we? That would mess everything up. After all, we have a good thing going here."

With that Sergiu headed for Sabina who was now standing at the front of the shop. He put his arm around her shoulder and led her away. She looked back at Vlad; clearly not wanting to leave.

Vlad could hear Sergiu telling her, "You really should not waste your affections on Vlad, my dear. You see, he is infatuated with a princess, a foreign one, no less. I'm constantly telling him that he needs to forget about her but he is vastly stubborn. He simply will not listen to me."

~

FOR THE NEXT month Vlad easily kept up with orders. Flying was an enjoyable way to pass the nights. Vlad continued to avoid Sabina. Sergiu would intervene most of the time. She invited them to dinner and Sergiu politely refused. A time or two she managed to catch Vlad alone — which truly said something of her determination. Vlad would quickly exit the shop when she refused to leave.

Surely, she will get the hint, he thought.

The next time the monster stirred from within, Vlad was ready. He had been patiently biding his time. It came late one evening while Vlad was in the shop with Darius and Sergiu.

"When will you two young gentlemen marry and start families of your own?" Darius asked.

"That life is not for me," Sergiu said in his usual cordial manner.

"You know, Sabina has grown quite fond of you, Vlad? You two would make a lovely pair."

Vlad appeared behind Darius. "You don't want me for a son-in-law," he whispered in Darius's ear.

Darius started at Vlad's sudden closeness.

Vlad bit deeply into his neck before he could turn around.

Sergiu jumped to his feet. "Have you gone mad?"

Vlad let Darius's body fall to the dirt floor. "He was holding me back. This is my shop now. We have a lot of work to do."

For the first time since they met, Sergiu's smile was gone. "I was actually starting to like the old man. What about his family? Who will care for them?"

"They are my responsibility. They will be well cared for."

Sergiu nodded. "Very well — but it is your job to get rid of the body."

Vlad left Darius in the street not far from the shop. That way everyone would know he was dead. His family could mourn and Vlad could carry on with the business.

Vlad and Sergiu attended the service three days later. Afterwards Vlad informed the family that he would continue to run the shop and gladly provide for them. Darius's wife and Sabina proclaimed that they were indebted to Vlad. The oldest of the daughters was named Martina. With two young children in tow she simply glared at Vlad.

The very next day, Vlad took most of the money they had and bought the building next to the tiny shop. He hired two young boys — whom he could pay next to nothing — to sharpen finished products, keep wood stocked for the furnaces and take the cart to get supplies. Sergiu was in charge of money, orders, sales and the like. With his ready smile and uncanny way with people, he was the face of the new shop.

As Vlad spoke with the carpenter who was to build the addition to the back of the shop, Martina marched up to Vlad and jabbed her finger in his chest. "This was my father's. It was his life's work. You can't simply show up, from God knows where, four days after Father's death and change everything. He always wanted to keep his business small and after only two months of working for him you think you can simply take over!" she was yelling at this point.

The carpenter shrank away. Vlad gave Martina a devilish smile and closed the space between them. "And who is going to stop me?"

Martina backed away. "I tell my sister all the time that she is a fool for falling in love with you. You very well may be the devil himself!"

Vlad smiled with pleasure as he completely agreed. "Your father lacked vision. I will make you and your family wealthier than you could have ever imagined."

Sergiu stepped in between the quarreling pair and addressed Darius's daughter, "Honestly, love, I would not antagonize him. He has quite the temper, not to mention we are all upset over your father's death."

Martina glared at him. "I am *not* your love and Vlad does not appear to be upset in the least. He is only gaining from Father's death. In fact, he is probably the one who killed him."

"Now, now, dear, those are strong accusations. You are simply upset. We can discuss this matter when you are not so distraught."

"Don't patronize me! I am not a child!" Martina said.

As she stormed off, her fiery red hair swayed in time with her hips. She was spirited and intelligent although not overly pretty — Vlad liked her.

Sergiu's heart sank when he saw the look on Vlad's face. "Oh no. Don't get any ideas. Leave her alone. You have done enough damage as it is."

CHAPTER 21 WALLACHIA 1262 AD

The business flourished. Soon every noble far and wide came to Vlad for their metalworks. He had the best products and a remarkable delivery rate. He received orders from as far as Constantinople and Venice. Two more smithies were hired, yet Vlad was still the main smithy, as he was by far the best and the fastest. He ran a high-production outfit that turned out high quality work quickly. He had more money than he knew what to do with. Ironically, they did not need much living in a cave.

By the year's end he started construction on a manor not far from the shop, as well as three slightly smaller homes for Darius's family. One was for his wife and unwed daughters and the other two were for his married daughters. He also gave the widow a hearty stipend every week. This was more than enough for food, clothes and the like.

Sergiu tried to teach Vlad to read. Vlad despised it. Reading was as boring as sitting around doing nothing during the long nights. Irrespective, due to Sergiu's persistence and possibly a high functioning vampire intellect, Vlad was reading quite well by the year's end.

Once Sergiu was confident in Vlad's reading ability, he turned his attention to teaching Vlad different languages. Sergiu was ancient. He could speak most any language. His favorites were ancient Greek and Latin. These languages were close to the dialects Vlad had grown up with, so they were relatively easy to acquire. It was similar to speaking with an accent in some ways. Soon they moved on to some of his other cherished languages, which were Turkish and Arabic. Sergiu had spent much time in the near east. These were completely foreign to Vlad and much more difficult to understand, let alone speak. Still, having Sergiu endlessly repeat odd sounding words and phrases to Vlad was better than reading Homer's massive works for the hundredth time. Overall, it was not a bad way to pass the long nights.

Sabina held on to her infatuation with Vlad. Late one night while he was going through supplies next door she managed to catch him alone. She simply smiled with affection and moved in close.

"What are you doing here?" Vlad asked. He noticed that he was more in control. Sabina smelled tempting but he thought he could refrain.

"You know why I am here. Stop pretending that you don't."

"I have never been kind to you, so why do you keep coming around?"

"You provide very generously for us. What could be kinder than that?"

"That is simply out of duty, nothing more. I feel contrite for what happened to your father."

"And why is that? It is not as if his death was your fault." She was close enough that she rolled up on her toes and kissed him.

Vlad let her. *Will I lose control?* When he did not, he placed his hands on her shoulders and gently pushed her away. "I cannot do this to you. You are so young and innocent."

Sabina's eyes filled with tears. "I'm not that much younger than you. It is because you don't love me, isn't it?"

Vlad nodded. "It would not be fair to you."

"Because you have some childish dream of a foreign princess!" Her heartache gave way to anger.

He glared at her and she stepped back a pace.

"That princess will be mine someday and you will do well to never speak of her again." Though Vlad had no idea how, he knew this was true. Someday, perhaps when he was wealthy enough or powerful enough, he could win Vallachia back. He took a deep breath to calm himself. It dawned on him; as Sabina's caregiver he had responsibilities other than simply paying for that fancy dress she wore. "In fact, as your provider, it is high time I found you and your remaining unwed sister suitable husbands."

Sabina blinked, causing a tear to roll down her cheek. "No, please. I only want you."

Vlad spun on his heel and was off on a new mission — to be a matchmaker. Also, feeling more in control of his lust for blood gave him the urge to want to test it. He knew Martina's husband would be out all day in the fields, as it was harvesting season. It was the opportune time to pay her a visit.

Martina was surprised to see Vlad, as he had never come to the home since it had been built. "To what do we owe the pleasure?"

"It is a small matter I wanted to discuss with you," Vlad said.

"Well, my husband is out, so why don't you come back when he is here?"

"My business is with you." He swiftly moved past her into the home.

"I see. ... Can I ... get you something to drink?"

"Can you make up a brew?"

Martina's brows came together in confusion, so Vlad continued. "Say some mint leaves or the like, steeped in hot water."

"I have never heard of such a thing. I can offer you ale, wine or mead."

Of course, the only things humans ever drink, Vlad thought. He had grown quite fond of Sergiu's brew. Perhaps it was because it was served hot, reminding him of blood. "An ale will do."

Martina poured ale into a stein and placed it on the table. She gestured for Vlad to sit.

He did not sit or take the ale.

"So what is it that brought you here?"

"I have been thinking," Vlad said, "it is about time your two youngest sisters wed. I wanted to know if you had any ideas regarding who might make good husbands for them?"

"You should speak with Mother about such matters. She will know better than I. Although, I suppose it is time they married." She fidgeted nervously with the front of her dress.

This made Vlad smile. "Where are your little ones," he inquired.

"They are lying down for their mid-day rest."

Perfect, he thought. This was just as he had hoped.

"If that is all, then I must get back to the cleaning. I must make the most of my time while my children are asleep." Martina turned, as if to leave the room. "I am sure you can find your way out."

Vlad appeared behind her. Martina jumped as he whispered in her ear. "There is another reason I came here." He gently brushed his lips across her neck and ran his fingers down the length of her arms. The large vein in her neck pulsed — enticing him. He had to resist, as there was something else he needed.

Martina turned to face him with wide eyes.

He wrapped his arm around her waist and pulled her against him. She tried to push him away but could not escape his unyielding grip.

"What are you doing?" she demanded.

Reminding himself to be as gentle as possible he placed his lips on hers. His mouth moved to her cheek and down her neck.

Her body relaxed and she kissed him back. She gave a shiver. "Why are you so cold? It is the middle of summer."

"It is simply the way I am." Vlad pressed his lips to hers, harder this time and ran a hand over her breast.

Martian let out a soft moan.

This time, when she pulled away, he let her. Vlad knew he had her. She would not refuse him.

She took him by the hand and led him upstairs.

When it was over, Martina shivered beneath Vlad. He quickly rose and placed a blanket over her naked form. "I had better be getting back to the shop. If you have any ideas about suitable matches for your sisters, do let me know." He pulled his tunic over his head.

She glared at him. "You truly are the devil."

He smiled. "You have no idea." Then he was gone.

CHAPTER 22 WALLACHIA 1262 AD

The following day, Martina barged into the shop demanding to speak with Vlad in private. Once alone in the warehouse she whispered, "What was that about ... yesterday?"

With his arrogant smile, Vlad crossed his arms over his chest. "I am afraid I do not understand."

"Was it to prove something — to put me in my place?"

What is she talking about? Vlad shook his head to indicate his confusion.

"I challenged you after Father's death and you wanted to prove that you are in control — that you can seduce me whenever you want. Is this some sort of manly game to you?"

Vlad chuckled and placed his hands on her shoulders. "You are overthinking this entirely, my dear. I am an unwed man and men have needs. There is nothing more to it than that. Is it not better than breaking a young girl's heart?"

"Perhaps it is *you* whom we should find a bride for. But not my baby sister, you stay away from her ... and me!"

Vlad's smile broadened, as he had the feeling that she did not truly want him to stay away.

Martina growled in frustration. "You and that boasting smirk. You are infuriating. I hate you!" With a flash of bright red hair she stormed away.

Sergiu appeared at Vlad's side. "You seduced Martina?"

"It wasn't too difficult."

"You cannot do that to a married woman!"

"Don't be ridiculous, Serg. With my long list of sins that one is nowhere near the top. As a matter of fact, I thought you would be pleased."

"And why is that?"

"She is still alive."

Both men stared at the door where Martina had exited.

"Do women truly ponder everything in such a strange manner?" Vlad asked.

"Aye, especially when it comes to matters of the heart. They are baffling and mysterious creatures. I have found that life is much easier if I leave them alone." Sergiu looked at Vlad as if he were a proud father. "You are in control of your thirst. I am afraid my work here is done. You are doing well for yourself. My faith in you was not misplaced."

Vlad frowned. "You are leaving?"

"Surely I am needed elsewhere."

Sergiu left that afternoon. He took only a small bag and very little money, though Vlad offered him much more. Sergiu promised he would stay in touch and that he would visit whenever he passed through.

Vlad searched for a reason for him to stay but came up short. If it had not been for Sergiu, Vlad would most likely be dead. He was much more than a friend; he was a mentor and the face of his business.

Sergiu was certain that Vlad would easily find his replacement for the shop.

That night, Vlad stared at the fire where he was heating water for a brew. The silence was unbearable. Sergiu was not there pestering him into reading the latest book he had come across or offering a history lesson.

The cup in Vlad's hand was in pieces before he fully realized he had crushed it. He kicked the water pot off the grate in the fireplace. A couple of blows from his fists left large holes in the wooden wall.

Vlad's chest heaved with every breath as he finished destroying his living room. In a flash he took to the sky.

By morning he was back in his shop. The best thing to do was to stay busy. Vlad had plenty of obligations between the shop and finding husbands for Darius's daughters, Sabina and Corina.

The following evening Vlad paid a visit to Darius's widow. Over wine he asked, "Don't you think it is time your two youngest daughters married?"

The widow's lined mouth turned downward. "Yes, I suppose so. Yet I will miss their company. They are all I have left."

"We can find them husbands nearby, so they will not go far. You can help with the grandchildren. Who knows, someday you may find a man — a widower perhaps?"

She issued a weak smile. "Vlad, my dear boy, you are too kind."

"Well, that is a matter of opinion. The men who work for me would tell you otherwise."

A glimmer of hope flashed in her eyes. "Are you here to ask for Sabina's hand in marriage."

"I am afraid not. I have no intention of marrying."

Her forehead wrinkled with concern, revealing her age. "This will be difficult news for my little girl. She does fancy you."

"Once she is married to a fine young gentleman and has a couple of children she will forget about me. Let us start with Corina, as that may be easier. Any prospects for her?"

"I think she may have an interest in a boy down the way. His name is Ciprian."

"Splendid. I have heard of him — good family. I will speak with the boy's father tomorrow about the matter."

"That will make matters easier. Without Darius we must wait for proposals, as it would have been up to him to find husbands for our daughters. Women should never approach a man about such matters."

And yet women often do, now don't they? Vlad was thinking of Sabina's forwardness. "Of course, I am glad to help." He stood to leave.

"Vlad, please remember that such matters are not simply business ventures."

"Matters of the heart never are."

These words — which he had stolen from Sergiu — seemed to ease her mind. She appeared relieved as she rose to show Vlad to the door.

IT TOOK some negotiating over the dowry but once Vlad offered to build Corina and Ciprian a home next to her mother, the deal was quickly sealed and a wedding date was set. Corina was excited when Vlad told her the news. *One down, one to go,* he thought. *Although, surely Sabina will be more difficult.*

CHAPTER 23 WALLACHIA 1262 AD

Vlad left Martina alone as she had requested — for a time. One day when he knew her husband would be out, he decided to pay her a visit. He waited for the home to fall silent, indicating that her children were napping. This time he entered the back door and did not bother to knock. She was busy sweeping the kitchen. He appeared behind her and wrapped his arms gently around her waist.

Martina jumped. A scream escaped her lips.

Vlad laughed. It had always been amusing to scare people — *my mother, Vallachia...* he quickly pushed the thought of Vallachia out of his head. As a vampire it was all the easier to startle people.

Martina turned to face him and slapped his chest. "You cruel man!"

He leaned in to kiss her.

"Stop." She pushed the palms of her hands against his hard chest to no avail.

This caused him to pause and look at her, yet he did not let go of her waist.

"You cannot come here uninvited and ... " Martina's eyes filled with sorrow. "You don't know what it was like — having to face my husband when he came home the evening after your first visit. He was exhausted from a day of hard work in the fields and I had to pretend as if nothing had happened. Then finding myself hoping you would come back. I am a terrible wife to have such sinful thoughts."

"Do you want me to leave?" Vlad was prepared to go if she demanded it.

Martina banged her fists on his chest. With a helpless sigh, she breathed, "No."

He lifted her chin to look into her eyes. "Then let us enjoy each other while we can."

Martina pressed her lips to his. He picked her up and she wrapped her long legs around him. That was how he carried her to bed.

Afterwards he rose to leave. Her children could wake at any moment.

"Your heart is as cold as your skin."

Vlad gave her a genuine smile rather than the usual sarcastic one. "And your heart is as warm as you are. You are a good woman and a good wife. Don't be so hard on yourself."

For the first time, she returned the smile.

It was indeed more difficult to find Sabina a husband. Vlad first approached a young smithy he had hired. He refused the offer, stating that he had plans to ask another to marry him when he had saved enough money for the dowry. There were not many other unmarried men nearby so Vlad approached the son of a farmer who lived near Martina. He thought this would be acceptable, as Sabina would be close to her oldest sister.

"I will not live outside of town!" Sabina yelled as she ran out of the common room.

Vlad's heart raced and blood rushed to his face. "You are an insolent child! Surely you would never speak to your father in such a manner?"

"You are *not* my father!" Sabina yelled down from her room upstairs.

He moved up the stairs. To do what he was not sure, as one strike from him would kill the poor girl.

Sabina's mother placed her hand gently on Vlad's forearm. "Please, I beg you, don't make her move to the country. Give her some time ... to ... get over you."

Her soft voice calmed Vlad enough to gather his wits about him. She reminded him of his own mother when she had tried to reason with his enraged father. Vlad took a deep breath. "Very well. One year at the most. I will find someone who lives in town and who is from a decent family. Sabina *will* marry that boy. It is your job to reason with her. She will die an old maid if she continues to wait for me. Do you understand?"

The widow nodded solemnly. "I will speak with her, in due time. She will marry next summer, to whomever you choose."

"Good woman." Vlad left swiftly before he killed the widow out of frustration.

CHAPTER 24 WALLACHIA 1263 AD

Sabina was indeed married that next summer. The miserable girl was utterly downtrodden at her wedding. She never smiled and did not so much as acknowledge the groom. However, the groom was elated. No doubt this had something to do with the nominal dowry he had to pay — which was essentially a gold ring for Sabina — and the new home he would be moving into, at Vlad's expense. It was a great relief for Vlad to have the last of the girls married.

Darius's widow died within the next ten years. Vlad's obligation to the family was officially over with her passing and all four of Darius's daughters having husbands to provide for them. Still, if they needed anything they could find him at the smithy shop. When Corina's youngest boy fell ill, Vlad paid for the doctor. He rather enjoyed having the responsibility. It made him feel useful and in control.

Vlad carried on his affair with Martina for that ten-year period as well; until one day she said, "You do not look a day over twenty, how can that be, my love?"

He gently ran his cold hand across her warm face tracing the now present lines around her eyes. "We can't do this anymore."

"I feared this day was coming." A tear ran down her cheek. "I will miss this. I look forward to your ... visits."

"You are intelligent and brazen. That is why I chose you."

Martina smiled. "Is this really goodbye?"

Vlad nodded and stood to dress. Her sobs were muffled by her pillow. He had to get out of there. He could not stand the tears. *Next time don't carry on the affair for so long,* he advised himself. *Don't allow them to become so attached.* Or was it he who risked becoming attached?

Vlad also had to fire his help and rehired new young men. This was a pain and slowed business down as the new help did not know what they were doing. On the plus side, these new men would work for less. This change was necessary in order to avoid the questions about how Vlad had not aged a single day over the past decade.

The years continued to fly by. The business flourished and Vlad eventually became one of the largest landowners in Targoviste, aside from a handful of nobles who had been given their lands by birthright.

By the year 1285, Vlad had begun to avoid people from his past as best he could. He scarcely left the back of the shop during daylight hours. Sergiu's human replacement, in the front, was instructed to relay messages from the public. Remaining in the back helped him to circumvent the customer who would ask about his youthful appearance. He had to tell a number of people that he was Vlad's son, Vlad the II. If only he had a bani for every time someone said, "That is remarkable! You resemble your father perfectly."

It was around this time when Sabina managed to find him in the warehouse. It had probably been over ten years since he had seen her. He heard her approach but figured it was one of his workers. He had let his guard down, as there had not been any word from Darius's daughters in many years. Normally he would have disappeared if one of them came looking for him, thus forcing them to leave a message with the man in the front.

Sabina stared at him with an open mouth. "How... ?" she was at a loss for words. "How is it that you look entirely the same?"

She must have been about forty years old and looked it. In fact, he had heard she was a grandmother now. "What can I do for you, miss?" he asked with his usual short tone.

She was momentarily baffled. "Vlad, it is me, Sabina."

"Vlad was my father. What do you want?"

Her eyes filled with tears. "Vlad never married! How could he have a son?"

Vlad was in no mood to make up a false family history. "I'm busy." He turned back to his work. Is it possible that after all these years I am still breaking this poor girl's heart? Surely not.

Sabina narrowed her eyes. "Then where is your father?"

"He died a few years back." He headed for the main shop.

"It is Martina. She is asking for you — er your father."

Vlad abruptly stopped and turned toward her. "Why?"

"She is ill, very ill. She is adamantly asking for you — for Vlad. Do you have any idea why she would want to see him so badly?"

"No." He left Sabina in the warehouse.

The front manager stood when he saw Vlad. "There you are, sir. I need to know what you want me to do about —"

Vlad simply grabbed his ever-present cloak by the back door and was gone. He sped to Martina's home. A handful of her grown children were in the kitchen. With the slightest jump he landed in the second story window to her bedroom. He knew she would be alone — her husband had died several years ago.

Martina slowly turned her head toward him as he approached her bed. She looked dreadful. There was no doubt she was dying.

She greeted him with a smile. "Sabina found you. I'm so glad." Her voice was little more than a whisper.

"Aye, I'm here." He knelt down beside her bed gently taking her fragile hand in his strong youthful one.

"I wanted to know something."

"What is it?" His voice was soft. He figured it was about his agelessness or his coldness or how he managed to get to her house from town so quickly without so much as a horse or how he could simply appear in her window — any number of the numerous oddities about him.

"I have a confession."

Vlad's brows raised with curiosity.

"I always hoped I would have a green-eyed baby. All those times you visited, yet I never did. Why did I never have your child?"

That was not what he expected. He was thoughtful for a moment, as he had never thought about it. "We — well I — must not be able to have children."

"Oh, you poor dear! Is that why you never married?"

Here she was, on her deathbed, pitying him. "Enough about me. I'm here to see you and to see if there is anything I can do to help."

"You were always so kind to me," she tried to sit up but this caused a bout of coughing.

"No, don't do that. You need to rest." Vlad helped her lay back down.

Martina placed her hand on his cheek. "Still so beautiful, my mysterious Kamadeva."

His puzzled expression led her to continue, "When my sisters and I were children a trader from the Far East came into father's shop looking to have his axe repaired. The four of us girls would often go with Mother to take Father food while he worked. As the man waited for his axe, he sat us down and told us tales of his gods. The one who stood out the most was Kamadeva. The man called him the god of love and desire. This god's favorite pastime was luring young maidens into the forest in order to seduce them," she gave a shy chuckle that ended with a cough. "That was when Mother thought we had heard quite enough and she gathered us up for home. Of course, we remembered this part of the stranger's story the best and my sisters and I often joked and even dreamt of meeting such a god as we grew into women. You were my Kamadeva."

Vlad ran his hand down her long grey hair. It saddened him to remember how vibrant and red it once was. Most likely he did not deserve such a comparison to a foreign god but he replied, "I'm pleased that that is how you remember me."

Martina closed her eyes and leaned her head into his hand. Soon her labored breathing stopped.

No, he thought. He stood and a frustrated yell escaped from him. He was out the window in an eyeblink.

I should be dead, as well. Why aren't I dead? I am stuck with this cursed life forever!

CHAPTER 25 VENICE 1354 AD

It was an unusually cool spring night when Riddick, Elijah and Vallachia left their manor in Venice to feed. They had been in town for quite some time on Court business — as always. They had been cleaning up loose ends from the long battle with the black death. It was important that the Court had a presence in the south. They had to work doubly hard to maintain their few allies in the region. Not to mention they had the best chance of finding Ramdasha from this outpost. Venice marked their southernmost "border" — as loosely defined as it was.

As the members of the Court made their way through a dark street, a large group of men approached. Judging by their slurred speech they had been drinking all night. Not to mention they could smell the spirits oozing from the men well before they could see them.

Elijah and Riddick smiled to each other. The three vampires slowed and let the men come to them.

The ringleader spoke as soon as he spotted the handsome trio. "Well, well boys. Look what we have here; two incredibly rich men, by the looks of them. And a pretty young lady the likes of whom should not be out at this unfavorable hour."

"I bet they've got at least a handful of gold coins on 'em. Perhaps some silver as well," another of the men declared. Some of the men brandished their knives and a few had swords.

Elijah took a step forward and tossed his bag of coins up in the air and then caught it. The coins noisily jostled about — taunting the men. "I suppose this is what you are after," Elijah said.

The men's eyes were full of greed as they watched the bag of coins. "Think of all the drink and women we could buy with that," one of the ruffians said.

"Forget the whores. I want to have some fun with *this* beauty."

Elijah had had enough. He moved to throw the bag of coins but Val gently placed her hand on his forearm to stop him. With the sweetest smile she could muster, she turned her attention to the group of men. "I'm afraid none of you boys could handle the likes of me."

This brought a round of whistles and rude heckles.

"But I could," Riddick said.

Elijah and Val both shot him a glare.

"What? I'm simply stating a fact." Riddick defended himself.

Elijah's arm was barely a blur, as he threw the bag of coins directly at the ringleader's head, knocking him unconscious. The man fell to the ground and gold coins flew in every direction. Blood dripped from the man's forehead. This sent the remaining men scrambling for the gold. They showed no concern for their wounded leader. Some even stepped on him in their frenzy. The vampires moved in.

"Try not to kill them," Elijah said.

Slowly and as humanely as possible they rendered most of the men unconscious and fed from the last three as they tried to flee. Once all the men lay peacefully in the street, they gathered Elijah's coins.

"These men will have severe headaches tomorrow and it won't only be from too much drink," Riddick said. Something caught Riddick's eye. One of the men had a finely crafted sword. Riddick swiftly kicked the sword into his hand with the toe of his boot. "The craftsmanship of this sword is superb. It could almost be one of mine. But I did not make it."

"How can you be certain? It looks similar in quality to your weapons," Elijah said.

"No. It is not mine. See the smithy's signature mark here?" Riddick pointed to an engraving.

Val and Elijah looked closer. The letter 'V' was elegantly inscribed where the sharp edge met the handle.

"You would think a vampire crafted this," Elijah said. "It is far too nice a sword for this bunch. They must have stolen it."

A vampire smithy — Teller! Val thought. "Where did this sword come from?" She could not hide the eagerness in her voice.

Riddick spun the handle of the sword around in his hand and examined it further with his expert and critical eye. "There are no other markings. I can't tell where it came from."

As soon as the local smithy opened for business the next morning, Vallachia entered the small steamy shop.

"Please, sir, can you tell me anything about this sword?" She handed him the weapon.

The man inspected it briefly and frowned. "Aye, it is made in Targoviste. As are many of the swords in these parts."

Vallachia's heart jumped into her throat. *It very well could be Teller!* "Would you be so kind as to tell me how to find the smithy who made this?"

The man sighed. "He owns the largest smithy shop in all of Targoviste. You can't miss him."

"Thank you very much!" She almost hugged the man but refrained. Could it be? Could Teller have made this very sword? Could he be in Targoviste now?

As she turned to leave, she overheard the man muttering to himself, "Damn that smithy. He has stolen yet another customer from me."

It took some convincing but Elijah and Riddick eventually agreed to accompany Val to Targoviste. They were not about to let her go alone and they knew she would go with or without them for protection.

"We have been through this before, My Lady," Riddick said. "You need to forget about this fellow."

Elijah was also less than thrilled with the idea of looking for Teller.

"I am terribly sorry, Elijah but I must know if it is Teller who made this sword. This is the first clue I have gotten in a very long time. I need to know if he is well."

VALLACHIA ENJOYED SEEING TARGOVISTE AGAIN. It truly had not changed much since she was young. The first people they encountered gladly pointed in the direction of the largest — and the only — smithy shop in Targoviste. Apparently, all smithies had to work in this shop, as it was the only place in the city that produced metalworks. Vallachia wandered off the main street and up to the front counter. She struggled to suppress her excitement. *What if Teller works here?* She frowned. *What if he does not?* She tried not to panic at this last thought.

"Pardon me," Val said to the two men behind the counter. "Does a smithy by the name of Teller work here?"

"Teller? No ma'am. I have never heard of anyone by that name."

Val deflated, like someone draining a water-skin. "Who do you work for?"

"That would be Vlad, Madam."

That explains the 'V' on the extraordinary sword Riddick found. "May I have a word with him?"

"Afraid not. He is out at the moment."

The two men behind the counter looked identical. They had to be twins or at least brothers who were very close in age. It was the other one who spoke, "He is most likely with one of his mistresses. He sneaks out around mid-day 'cause he knows their husbands will most likely be away."

The other man gave his brother a disapproving glare. "Shut that flapping mouth of yours, Costel. Do not speak of the master like that in front of customers."

This confirmed it for Vallachia — the man they were speaking of was not Teller. *He would not seduce married women.*

"We can give him a message for you."

"That won't be necessary. I must have the wrong man and I must be leaving town. Thank you for your time." *I may never find Teller,* she thought. She struggled against the darkness that threatened to consume her, as she headed back to Riddick and Elijah who were keeping a watchful eye on her from down the street. Elijah looked relieved when Val shook her head no, indicating that she did not find Teller. Val could not help but rub at the pain in her constricted chest.

The three old companions weaved their way through the streets as they left town.

VLAD ROUNDED a corner and caught an unusual scent. It differed from the scent of humans. For some reason Sergiu came to mind. Yet, it was not Sergiu's scent. *It must be other vampires,* he thought. He followed the scent, rounding corner after corner but there was no one in sight. *I must be hallucinating. What am I doing wasting time? I must be getting back to the shop. I'll be working late as it is to fill that order from Constantinople.*

Meanwhile, Vallachia took flight from the woods not far from her lost love.

CHAPTER 26 WALLACHIA 1354 AD

Over the decades leading up to 1354, Vlad grew bored and restless. With no other vampires around he was often alone. Sergiu visited at least once every couple of years, yet never stayed more than a month's time. Once he had deemed that Vlad was doing well, he would disappear again. After his random visits Vlad would feel even worse — more alone and trapped than ever. Sergiu would invite him to accompany him on his travels but Vlad had to man the shop. After all, it must be run properly. Targoviste was his home — or was it his prison?

Vlad could not have human companions for any length of time as their questions about his agelessness were difficult to answer. He was forced to keep people at arm's length. It was increasingly difficult to pretend to be human in this ageless body. There were no more responsibilities for Darius's family. There was nothing he wanted to spend his ever-accumulating wealth on. And the worst part was that he was no closer to getting Vallachia back. He felt like a hollow vessel endlessly pounding away on red hot metal. It no longer brought him pleasure, neither did his latest mistress.

Vlad was bound to the smithy shop. By the summer of 1354 this downward spiral had led to sloppy feeding habits. Instead of going across town to feed, he often killed closer to the shop, leaving the bodies in the street instead of burying them.

Teller also became less choosy about whom he killed. Initially he had only fed on the occasional drunkard, who often went unmissed in the city. Now he would feed on anyone. Upon awakening he would be dazed. He did not care. *Maybe the Court will come for me and end this miserable life? Maybe Vallachia will finally find me?* He often dreamt of her walking into the shop. Her face was radiant and beamed even brighter when she would see him. He dreaded waking from those dreams.

It was an unusually warm fall night in 1354 when Vlad woke to the sound of an angry mob making its way to his manor. He shook his head to clear it. By the time the men arrived, Vlad stood on his front porch leaning against a column. *This is going to be fun. Perhaps in number they will have the strength to kill me — I hope.*

A group of a hundred men surrounded the front of Vlad's home in a half circle. They were chanting "Killer, Killer." Many were armed with swords or spears. Vlad had no weapons about his person and wanted none.

"There he is — Vlad! He has not aged a single day," one elderly man yelled.

Then a man Vlad had fired from the shop for being indolent, yelled, "He has the strength of ten men. I have seen it myself, the way he can sculpt metal — it's not natural."

Vlad slowly moved down the front steps with the usual confident and sarcastic grin on his face. It was the expression of a man who had nothing to lose.

"He is responsible for the deaths. I know it!" another man yelled.

As Vlad approached the mob, the men nervously stepped back.

One daring man stepped forward and said, "Vlad, come with us peacefully. You are to be held accountable to the people for the recent murders around town."

Vlad's smile broadened. "Come and get me then."

"That might as well be an admission of his guilt," one man declared and yet another man yelled, "Get him!"

Two men charged toward Vlad with swords drawn. He easily dodged their slow and wild swings. He moved too quickly for the human eye to follow. His fist found one man's jaw; the bones cracked loudly as he flew fifteen paces back. He landed in a heap at the foot of the mob. In an instant Vlad turned and threw a punch into the other swordsman's chest, caving it in and sending him flying back as well. Neither man moved. They were both dead before they hit the ground.

Someone yelled, "Tie him up!" Two lassos went over Vlad's head and shoulders, tightening around his torso and pulling from both his right and left side. He pulled the two thick ropes apart as if breaking a twig.

"Is that all you've got?" Vlad roared. He moved a couple of paces toward the crowd. They retreated a couple of steps back. A handful of men in the rear of the mob made a run for it.

"He is the devil," one of them declared.

"Aye," Vlad conceded. "I'm the devil who has seduced half of your wives. The other half were not worth my time." This was not entirely true — the point was to provoke them. He wanted them to kill him or at least try. Perhaps he simply wanted the fight.

The insult worked, as numerous men charged him and a handful of spears spiraled toward him. He easily evaded them and caught one spear as it flew through the air. He spun it around jabbing the sharp end into the chest of the first man to reach him. He lifted him up with the spear and swiftly forced the dull end of the weapon deep into the ground. This left the dying man suspended in the air on the end of the spear. Vlad quickly dodged other blows.

Shoving his foot under a spear on the ground, he kicked it into his hand. Swiftly spinning it around he impaled another attacker and staked him up in the same fashion as the first. The man's blood ran down the spear onto Vlad's hands. The sight and smell of blood overwhelmed him. He could feel the familiar aching sensation in his jaw. Two more men were impaled before the rest backed away. Many more men had retreated at this point.

Who could blame them? They had no idea what they were up against when they came for me.

The remaining brave — or stupid — men stared at the monster before them with wide eyes and mouths agape. Long fangs protruded from Vlad's lips. He was covered in the blood of his victims. A low growl came from deep within and eventually emerged as a furious yell. Some men stumbled and fell as they tried to flee. Vlad grabbed the nearest man by the back of the neck and sank his teeth into him. After the lifeless body fell to the ground, Vlad leapt into the air while spreading his jet-black, ten-foot wings to their full extent. As the powerful wings lifted him, they sent dirt swirling up into the faces of the few who remained. He ascended high into the sky.

CHAPTER 27 WALLACHIA 1354 AD

Vlad could hardly think. He moaned and rolled over, pulling a blanket over his head to block out the faint light coming from the small cave opening. He was accosted by a musty smell so he threw off the old blanket and surveyed his surroundings. *That's right, I'm in Sergiu's cave,* he thought. Last night's slaughter slowly came back to him. He let out another moan and rolled over, hoping to force himself back to sleep. *If only I could not wake for an eternity.*

An old and familiar scent registered with Vlad. He sat up quickly to find Sergiu by a small fire outside the cave. Undoubtedly, he was heating water for a wondrous brew — something worth getting up for.

Vlad pulled his hood up to cover his burning eyes as he stepped out into the bright morning sun. Usually the sun was only a slight nuisance, but not on mornings when he had had too much blood the night before — such as this morning. His head throbbed and his eyes stung even with the hood to shade them. He plopped down next to Sergiu.

"There you are, lazybones," Sergiu said, by way of greeting. "I was not sure when or if you would ever wake."

Vlad slapped his shoulder. "You are a sight for sore eyes, old friend."

"That was one hell of a way to get my attention. You knew I was in Trebizond. You could have simply sent for me. You did not need to slaughter half of Targoviste."

"How did you know I was having trouble ... again?"

"I'd heard rumors of the unrest in this region. I figured you had something to do with it, so I headed this way. Unfortunately, I stopped to visit some companions along the way. Little did I know how bad you were or I would have arrived sooner." Sergiu handed Vlad a cup of brew. "I may have been able to prevent your little escapade last night. I am glad I found you before the Court did. Thankfully they have other concerns; they are keeping their eyes and ears peeled for any sign of Ramdasha's next move."

"Who is Ramdasha?" Vlad asked, only half interested. He preferred to focus on the cup of warm water, which smelled mostly of mint with a hint of jasmine. He held the cup greedily with both hands, simply inhaling the hot steam. It helped to clear his head.

"I swear, my dear boy, you ought to get out more often. You have never heard of Ramdasha?"

"You are the only vampire I know. I only get news of our world from your scarce and brief visits."

Sergiu's eyes widened. "In all these years you never encountered any other vampires wandering through Targoviste?"

"Not that I'm aware of."

"Well then, it is high time you mingled with your own kind." Sergiu studied the vast mountainous expanse before him.

Vlad followed his gaze. The thought of meeting others like him was not appealing. He quite enjoyed being the strongest and fastest around. Yet, he did wonder what they would be like.

"I spent some time with the Court in Denmark the first part of this year," Sergiu said. "I mainly went out of curiosity and to attend Lord Chastellain's celebration of one year of peace after ending the vampire plagues. Thankfully, Targoviste managed to go untouched by the plague. Though parts of Hungary were badly affected by the young rogue vampires."

Vlad shot his gaze to Sergiu. "Did you see her?"

"Aye and now I understand what all the fuss is about. The Lady Vallachia is quite lovely. She rules to the left of Lord Chastellain. Prince Elijah hardly leaves her side. He is very protective — perhaps even possessive of her. Who could blame him?"

This was not exactly news, yet rage boiled inside Vlad. If Sergiu is trying to make me feel better, it is not working. Her position to the left of the Lord bequeaths her with the status of third in command. That is remarkable. How did she manage to gain such a high rank in the Court? "So they are married?" He managed to choke the words out through gritted teeth.

"Not as far as I can tell. The gossip around the castle is that the lovely pair are engaged. Yet with no wedding date set and the years continuing to pass, many assume they are clandestine lovers. Though everyone knows this, so I don't know what the secret is. Honestly, they appeared to be... friends. At this particular gala the Prince danced with another. This came as a shock to those around me, it was all anyone talked about, as Elijah usually dances solely with the Lady Vallachia."

This was difficult to hear. Yet, hope swelled in Vlad's chest. *Maybe Val is not married and Elijah is with another.*

"It is very difficult to get near the lady," Sergiu continued. "She is well protected and rarely alone. I tried to speak with her during the dance. I wanted to ask her about her relationship with the Prince and to see her reaction when I told her of you. Yet as I approached, a very large man," Sergiu paused and eyed Vlad for a moment. "Much like you in some respects — anyway this guard, Riddick, I believe he is called, gave me a look which made it clear that I was not to take another step toward her or he would rip my heart out of my chest — with his bare hands, I'm sure."

"So she has no news of me?"

"I'm afraid not. I did not think it appropriate to sneak into her chambers, which are directly across from Prince Chastellain's. With my luck she would yell for her prince and the Court would have my head. Unlike you, I do not have a death wish. She is unreachable to someone such as me. Sorry my old friend, I did try."

She may not be married. For the first time in a long time Vlad had a purpose. He stood to leave but Sergiu rose and clasped his forearm.

"And where do you think you are going?"

"I have to see her."

"Slow down there, son. You cannot simply show up at the High Court's Castle expecting to take their most prized possession. She is highly coveted by all who follow the Elders. It would be suicide."

"Just as well. I cannot carry on like this any longer." This life is worth nothing without her. She loved me once, maybe she still does and if not the Court will kill me. It is the perfect plan. I will get what I want no matter the outcome; as I will either get Vallachia back or I will be dead.

Vlad took another step forward but was stopped by Sergiu's secure grip.

"Very well, I understand. You want to win the affections of the Lady of the Court. Then I implore you, let us be smart about this, Teller. Let me help you," Sergiu pleaded.

The use of his human name got Vlad's attention, as well as the concern in Sergiu's eyes. This was enough to stop Vlad from flying north. Sergiu truly cared for Teller and did not want him to head off on a mission that would most likely end in his death. Sergiu was the only one who was truly fond of Vlad. This made Sergiu the only one he would listen to. Vlad slowly nodded and sat back down.

"Good man." Relief swept over Sergiu. They sat in silence for a time before he added, "Are you certain it must be *that* particular woman, as there are many beautiful vampire maidens."

Vlad narrowed his eyes and the muscles in his jaw flexed.

"Very well, I had to be sure. It makes sense, I suppose. You always did like an unviable challenge."

Vlad's mind raced. *A challenge, that is what I needed and Vallachia was the perfect prize*. He pictured her standing by his side on the high balcony of a large palace overlooking these mountains — their home. "That's it! I have riches but no power. I need a castle to win her back. I must become royalty, as this is what she has become accustomed to."

Vlad's brow furrowed, as he had no idea how to become a noble. There is a thick impenetrable line between nobles and the working class. You had to be born into the highest of social ranks. One could not get there otherwise. Yet Vallachia had — because of Elijah. Come to think of it there were many tales of commoners becoming royalty. Some of these stories were even true; such as Emperor Justinian changing Roman law so that he could marry the beautiful Theodora. She was even rumored to have been a lady of the night before they wed, though no one would have said so to the emperor. But how did a man become royalty?

Sergiu was thinking along the same lines. He had been silent and thoughtful before his face lit up with excitement. "That might work! We can strategically maneuver our way into a noble's court. You have plenty of money so you can dress as a noble. Perhaps a minor one at first, as no one will have heard of you. With your speed and strength you can quickly prove your worth and climb the ranks of a human army. Then perhaps once you have enough status you can eventually wed a princess. Then, with the family name behind you, you will be unstoppable."

CHAPTER 28 WALLACHIA 1354 AD

"Once I have the name and an army behind me, I will be powerful and the Court will finally hear of me. Perhaps *she* will come to me." This sounded promising to Vlad — an excellent strategy and next to impossible. *That is why I will succeed. I will become royalty, one way or another!* With a new goal, life flooded back into Vlad. He had a purpose and a plan. *It is time to get to work.*

Sergiu was content as well and ready for the task ahead. "Now you are using your head, my dear friend. You will have to wait a couple of decades before you return to Targoviste. You will have to stay away until the mess you made last night passes into myth and legend. When I arrived at dawn, I found your mansion ablaze. The townspeople torched it as they removed the impaled bodies from the courtyard. I figured you would come to our cave and that is, of course, where I found you. Why don't you travel with me? You should meet some of our kind and refine your fighting skills. Then we will execute our plan."

That night, well after dark the two old friends entered Vlad's smithy shop. Buried in the back of the storage room was most of his gold. It was quite a substantial pile of treasure and took them several trips to get it all to the cave. They buried most of it in the back of the cave. The following day Vlad signed all his properties over to Sergiu who would put them up for sale the following day.

While they were waiting for the estates to sell Vlad decided to pay two of his workers a visit. They were brothers — twins actually — who went by the names of Cosmin and Costel. He could not tell them apart. They constantly had to correct Vlad when he got their names confused, which was most of the time. They were, however, fiercely loyal to Vlad. They had not been part of the angry mob the night the local men came for him. The brothers were obedient, completing any task without question or complaint. Clearly these two were the best and hardest workers Vlad had ever had. He had dreaded the day he would have to fire them due to his lack of aging. Now the idea of leaving them behind was bothersome. He had a notion that as vampires they would be equally as loyal and useful. He decided to see if he was right.

Late one night Sergiu and Vlad sneaked into the twins' modest home. They shared a small room with bunk beds. They were young and unwed; this would make them perfect companions — Vlad hoped. Vlad went to the one sleeping soundly on the bottom bunk. *Cosmin — no Costel; hell, I don't know.* Biting deep into his own wrist, he let the blood drip into the boy's mouth.

The boy woke with a choked cough. He tried to sit up. Vlad grabbed him by the hair and held him down to ensure the blood was swallowed.

The commotion woke the brother on the top bunk. "Sergiu, quick give him your blood," Vlad said.

Sergiu shook his head. "I will not be a part of making more of us. You do as you will but this is not for me."

This was the beauty of Sergiu. He did not try to control others. He simply lived his own life the way he knew best.

At the sight of Vlad, the brother on the top bunk sat straight up almost hitting his head on the low ceiling. "Master, what are you doing here?"

His brother gagged and choked. He jumped down from the upper bunk to check on his brother, who had blood dripping out of his mouth. His brother's eyes rolled back in his head. "What happened? Is he dead?"

"That is a good question. What do you think, Serg? Is he dead, or dying? Are we dead?"

"Who can answer such philosophical questions? I truly do not know."

The brother who was awake held his unconscious twin. He looked at the two men as if they were mad. "What did you do to him?"

"The same thing I'm going to do to you." In less than a heartbeat Vlad grabbed the boy by the back of the hair and bit into his other wrist, as his right one was still sore. The twin tried to fight Vlad's ironclad hold to no avail. Blood flowed from Vlad's arm into the boy's mouth. The panic faded from his eyes as they rolled back. The two brothers lay peacefully together on the tiny bed.

They waited for what seemed like an eternity before the two brothers stirred. It would be daylight soon, so it was a relief when they woke. First one and then the other stared at Vlad in bewilderment.

"Welcome to our world." Vlad gave them a mischievous smile.

Sergiu tossed them each a cloak. "You are going to need these when the sun comes up. Now let's go find someone inconspicuous for them to feed on."

"Feed on?" one brother asked.

"I'm so thirsty. I need water," the other brother gasped.

"I'm afraid water will not quench your thirst. Come with us." Vlad leapt out the window followed by Sergiu. The brothers reluctantly followed.

Their first feeding was a debacle. Vlad had to kill two onlookers so there would be no witnesses and they still barely made it out of the city before half the townspeople spotted them.

The brothers were willing to accompany Vlad and Sergiu to the cave — after all, where else would they go? A large stone had been placed in front of the entrance, hiding the cave and the buried treasure within. Cosmin and Costel were relieved to get out of the sun and retire to the comfort of the cave. Sergiu told them what they needed to know about being a vampire. He took them under his tutelage, teaching them and comforting them. This was what he did best, helping and caring for others. It was his life's work and he truly enjoyed it.

Sergiu spent most days in town finishing up Vlad's business. The shop sold first and for the most money. To Vlad's surprise, this came as a great relief. He was finally free and no longer responsible for making sure the shop was run properly. It was not until the shop was no longer his that he fully realized how shackled he had been by it. Yet, there remained an uncertainty about leaving it behind. Managing that shop had been his life for almost one hundred years. *What will I do with myself now? It is past time to move on and find out what else is out there.* The mixture of excitement and trepidation was confusing. At least running the shop had been easy.

Once most of Vlad's other assets — his businesses, homes and farms — sold they would leave Targoviste. It did not come as a surprise that the burnt lot where Vlad's mansion had stood did not sell. The superstitious people of Targoviste wanted nothing to do with that accursed place. So for now it would have to sit.

The twin brothers adjusted to their new life as well as could be expected, thanks largely to Sergiu's support and guidance. Vlad had no patience for coddling them, as Serg did. Although, Vlad had to admit watching them learn to fly was hilariously entertaining.

One night in the cave, Cosmin asked Vlad, "Why did you do this to us?"

Vlad had turned them because of their obedience. Yet, he chose his words more carefully. "My ambitions require me to surround myself by men who will be loyal. If you prove to be worthy then you can become commanders in my army."

Costel's face brightened.

Cosmin was not so easily won. "But we are not warriors. We are smithies in training."

"Aye, you were. But now you are warriors in training. You are no longer common humans, you are vampires."

This worked to win Cosmin over. The two brothers smiled at each other.

The assets that did sell brought in another pile of gold to be buried in the cave. Within one month's time they were finally ready to leave. Vlad could not wait to get out of the cave. For the first time in decades he felt enlivened. The possibilities as a murderous wealthy vampire were endless.

CHAPTER 29 MIDDLE EAST 1354 AD

The first vampires they visited were Sergiu's companions in Trebizond. There they met what Sergiu referred to as a *coven* of vampires. He explained that it was a small coven consisting of only three, a woman and two men. The men were threatened by Vlad from the moment they met him and the woman was intrigued. It was difficult to tell which man was the woman's lover, as they both appeared to be close to her.

Vlad's stay was not a long one. On the third day the men became enraged when they found the woman trying to seduce Vlad. Apparently, they did not want to share her with a third. Vlad had no interest in her, other than a curiosity to know what it would be like to be with a vampire woman. Not having to be overly gentle all the time was an exciting prospect. Vlad was not given the chance to find out.

The men challenged Vlad. Sergiu appeared between Vlad and the angry men. The twins quickly moved to stand on either side of Vlad to show their allegiance. Sergiu managed to talk his friends down and promised that they would be on their way. Though Vlad would have been pleased with a fight, he was also content to get out of there. After only three days with no work to be done he was growing beyond restless. They happily left Trebizond that night.

"That did not go as expected," Sergiu said, as they took flight.

"There can be only one leader, Serg," Vlad said.

"Of course. Then perhaps we avoid established covens for now, as they will already have leaders. What do you propose we do now, *Leader*?" Sergiu said.

"It will be easiest if we do not stay in any one place too long." Not to mention there was a large world out there that Vlad, in all his years, had not explored. "We need to learn to fight. Most of all, I want to find others like Costel and Cosmin. I need warriors if I am to become a ruler."

"It will be best to avoid the powerhouses to the northwest. Namely Lord Chastellain and Lord Ramdasha. We most certainly do not want conflict with them," Sergiu said.

After a couple of hours, they came to a walled city surround by lush green farmlands.

"Let us see what awaits us in Bursa. There is a new ruler here. He calls himself Sultan Orhan. He was born a simple nomad and he, like his father Osman, has become a great ruler. They have a very powerful human army, which allowed them to conquer this region. There should be much to learn from the Osmanlis." Sergiu lectured them in his schoolteacher tone.

They had to wait until dawn for the city gates to open for tradesmen. At this point the city came alive. The hustle and bustle made it apparent that Bursa was very prosperous. Slowly moving amongst the people with their hoods over their heads the four vampires wandered the city streets. They came across a large field where soldiers were sparring. It was not far from the main palace compound and the Mosque of Osman.

"Exactly what we need," Sergiu declared. "These must be the sultan's men."

Cosmin and Costel shrugged to each other, clearly not understanding what Sergiu was talking about.

"And?" Vlad questioned. "What do they have to do with us?"

Sergiu could not believe that his companions did not understand. "These men are your path to the sultan. With your vampire abilities you can quickly move to the top of the sultan's army. You can learn the art of combat from them and they could lead you to the power you are seeking."

"We might as well give it a try." Vlad was skeptical. He did not think they would be welcome, as they were not Muslim. Not to mention they were not as dark-skinned as the locals.

Sergiu boldly approached the men as they carefully thrust toward one another with long thick curved swords, the likes of which Vlad had not seen before. Each was careful to give his opponent plenty of time to block the blow, as they did not truly wish to harm their comrades.

"Salaam Aleichum Sadiqi." *May peace and God be with you my friend,* Sergiu greeted the man who was clearly in charge.

He was an aging warrior who wore a large white turban twice the size of his head. Vlad thought the headpiece was absurd. There were tall billowing feathers secured in the folds. The downy feathers moved gracefully in the breeze and with the man's movements. He sported a large grey mustache that had most likely been as black as the bottom of a well at one time. His greyness surely gave him more status and respect amongst the younger men he commanded.

While the hat was ridiculous, Vlad quite liked the mustache. *In fact, a mustache would make me look older.* Vlad decided that he would have to grow one. He had always remained clean-shaven, a habit formed because Vallachia had always disliked facial hair. But now he needed to look older and a thick dark mustache would help with that.

The commander eyed Sergiu for a moment but as was customary, he had to return the formal greeting. "Aleichum Salaam." *And may peace and God be with you.*

"Tell me, kind sir, what does it take to join the sultan's mighty conquering mercenaries?" Sergiu spoke in perfect Turkish with little to no accent.

"We prefer the term Janissaries." The man eyed Sergiu with suspicion.

"Of course, Janissaries, the elite guard of the almighty Sultan

Orhan — may God always smile upon him. My mistake. Please forgive my ignorance, most merciful Sire."

Sergiu is a master with words — in almost any language. He knows how to lay it on thick, Vlad thought.

It seemed to work because the man issued the slightest hint of a smile as he continued to assess Sergiu. He moved to eye Vlad. Vlad met his gaze with a stern stare. The commander gave a slight nod and moved on to examine Cosmin and Costel — who appeared uncomfortable under the elder's scrutiny.

Finally he declared, "Yes, you appear to be fine, healthy young men. In order to join our powerful army one must prove his worth. Can you fight?"

"We will let our swords do the talking." Vlad's voice was bold. His Turkish was not as good as Sergiu's and his heavy accent dominated his words.

"I sense much arrogance in you, boy. Such an attitude can serve soldiers well. Yet it can also be dangerous. Men come from far and wide to join this great conquering army. Only the best survive and only a select few make it to the top."

"That sounds like a worthy challenge." Vlad issued his wicked smile.

"Your confidence and pride will serve you well, I'm sure of it. My name is Ismail Pasha. I am the seraskier of the Janissaries, as well as the Grand Vizier to the sultan himself." This meant he was the commander of the sultan's army and the sultan's top advisor.

"Well then, we are conversing with the right man," Sergiu said.

"In fact, that is enough talk." Vlad was beyond impatient with all the niceties and sick of the arse-kissing. "Let us show you what we are capable of. Who is your best man?"

Ismail laughed. "I would not recommend taking on my best soldier unless you wish for death."

Vlad's smile broadened.

"I may have been wrong — your confidence may be the death of you," Ismail said.

"Bring your best man forward."

"Very well, perhaps it would be best to put you in your place, boy." With a hand signal from Ismail, a large man approached. He was abnormally tall, at least a head higher than Vlad. He was also much larger, obese as well as muscular. His curved sword was drawn and massive shoulders swayed exaggeratedly as he walked.

"Let's show this boasting young man here what an Osmanli soldier is capable of." Ismail's words got the soldiers attention.

Vlad gracefully drew his long broad sword as the men moved to form a large circle around him and his opponent. Vlad could feel the anticipation of the crowd and relished it. The onlookers' eagerness to see a fight fed Vlad. A rush of energy passed through him.

Vlad let his grand opponent attack first in an attempt to appear timid. He did not strike in the beginning. He only blocked the man's blows with ease, although Vlad had to admit they were quite strong for a human. It was obvious why he was viewed as the best. He was undoubtedly the strongest amongst these men.

Eventually, Vlad picked up the pace as he went on the offense. It did not take long before the man tired from wielding his heavy sword. Some of the Osmanlis shouted supportive cheers to their comrade. That was when Vlad decided to stop toying with him. He gracefully kicked the man's legs out from underneath him. His large form landed hard. Vlad shoved his sword deep into the dirt an inch from his opponent's head. He let the handle sway in the air for a moment — for effect. The large man looked at Vlad with wide dark eyes.

Vlad smiled and gave him a hand to help him to his feet. "I hope there will be no hard feelings, my friend."

The man narrowed his eyes and slapped Vlad's forearm away. He scrambled awkwardly to his feet. He marched off the field in a show of anger, pushing men out of his way and knocking over a sword stand.

CHAPTER 30 NORTHERN ANATOLIA 1354 AD

Ismail applauded. His large brown eyes danced like moonlight off rippling water. "Splendid display, my boy." In that instant Vlad became the old man's primary point of interest and his most favored pupil. "You won because you are fast and strong. Yet, you lack the skill and discipline of a tenured warrior. You hold your weapon all wrong and you need to stand like so." Ismail braced his legs apart with his left foot slightly forward. "Keep your knees loose." He bounced in his stance to show Vlad how mobile he was — ready to take action. Ismail proceeded to show Vlad how to hold the sword more securely and keep his elbow loose as well. "With my training, I will make you into the best warrior to ever walk this earth." His voice boomed with triumph.

Vlad motioned for Cosmin and Costel to pay attention to Ismail Pasha. It was obvious this man knew what he was doing when it came to sword fighting. They could learn much from him. Sergiu cared nothing for fighting and he moved to the shade of a nearby olive tree. Soon he was chatting merrily with some of the soldiers. He never met a stranger.

The lesson continued until midday when the sun grew too intense. The men retired indoors for their studies — which meant a nap for many of them. Cosmin and Costel could not wait to take their hoods off and get away from the bright sun.

"The latest in Arab medicine." Sergiu picked up another book. "The latest in Arab sciences and inventions." He truly did not know where to start.

Vlad was not interested in any of it. He was anxious to get back to training — he wanted to become the best. His brow furrowed as he asked Ismail, "You do not seem concerned that we are not Muslim."

"The Osmanlis judge people on their skills and potential. If a person is of value then we do not care about their religion, or the color of their skin. Look around you; many of the Janissaries are Christian born. The sultan's lead doctor is Jewish and the best doctor to ever roam the earth, I'd imagine. Of course, to gain status and become a commander or even the Grand Vizier one must convert to the religion of the Prophet Mohammed — may God forever protect his eternal soul. While the men may study what they choose, we do emphasize the teachings of the Koran. Of course, we welcome converts but do not require it for lower level infantry."

Sergiu's ears had perked with interest. He joined Vlad and Ismail with an armful of books. "I have heard people in the north speak of you. They say that the wise sultan is infinitely fair. Sometimes the tax to the Osmanlis is less than what they were required to pay under their former Christian rulers. Also the people you conquer tend to be content because they are allowed to keep their religion."

"Yes, the sultan's father, Osman, blessings forever be upon him, believed that it was best to conquer and tax rather than conquer and convert. This way people are much less likely to retaliate. This leads to fewer problems in maintaining the lands we conquer and fewer uprisings. As long as they pay their tribute to the Sultan Orhan, they have our protection and they can live out their lives as they wish — retaining whichever religion they choose."

"That is ingenious." Sergiu looked at Vlad as if to say, *Are you taking note of all this?*

"Aye, the sultan and I were born as nomads and now we command almost all of Anatolia and even up into Europe itself — over half a million people under our command. And we have no intention of stopping."

"Inch' Allah," Sergiu injected.

The Pasha laughed. "Always! Only if God is willing. Always, Inch' Allah!"

Sergiu whispered quietly so only Vlad could hear, "That is a typical overstatement of power. They only control the northern regions of the Anatolian peninsula and they have barely begun to venture into Europe across the Dardanelles."

Vlad chuckled at Sergiu's secret correction of the Pasha's boasting.

When the sun was low in the sky, they headed back outside to train. Late that night after a large meal of roast goat and rice, they sat around a campfire. The man Vlad had bested in the sword fight sat off to himself and glared at Vlad.

Sergiu pointed to the man with his eyes and gave Vlad a shove toward him.

Vlad knew Sergiu wanted him to make peace with the man. "But how," Vlad whispered.

"Go. You will figure it out. I do not want him to cause trouble for us."

Vlad moved to the large man's side and asked if he could take a seat.

The man grunted in response.

Vlad shot Sergiu a irritated glower and Serg nodded for Vlad to continue.

The silence stretched thin between the two men.

"I like the swords you use here," Vlad finally said. It was a stupid thing to say but it was the only thing he could think of. He was not a master of words as Sergiu was.

"They are scimitars," the man scoffed. He quickly brandished his sword from his side.

Vlad reflexively jumped.

The large man chuckled. "You see the broad body and the elegant curve." He ran his hand down the back of his sword as if he was caressing the curves of a beautiful woman.

The men around them watched with interest; some appeared concerned, while others looked hopeful that another entertaining skirmish might break out.

Vlad longed to inspect its craftsmanship. "May I see it?"

The man looked at Vlad as if he were mad, so Vlad continued. "Here." He slowly took his long straight broadsword out of its sheath and offered the handle to the man.

He took it with reluctance and inspected it. The man handed Vlad his scimitar.

"The craftsmanship is quite good," Vlad said. *Not as good as one of my own swords but good.*

"And this is an extraordinary sword."

"I made it myself. It is yours now."

For the second time that day the massive man looked at Vlad with wide eyes.

"An offer of my good will. May it always serve you well, my friend."

The slightest smile crept across the large man's face. "I cannot take this without giving you something in return. You must accept my scimitar."

Vlad studied the lovely sword in his hand. "It would be an honor. My name is Vladislav."

"Vlads ... "

"Vlad is fine."

"They call me Abdullah."

"It is a pleasure to meet you."

"If you think that scimitar is something, you should see my most prized treasure; a gold-handled scimitar inlaid with precious stones. That is simply my common practice sword."

"I see how you are. I give you my very best sword and you give me rubbish in return."

The big man laughed from his belly and Vlad could not help joining him.

This lightened the mood throughout the camp. Soon all were

relaxed and joking with one another as comrades do. Vlad and his men were unofficially part of the Janissaries.

Vlad knew Sergiu would be pleased that his attempt to make peace had worked. Sergiu smiled at Vlad as if he were a proud father. It was a look Vlad had rarely received from his own father. He would have done most anything to earn such favor from Sergiu.

In the days that followed they learned much. It was easy to see the value in training with Ismail Pasha. He had been a skilled fighter and was an excellent trainer. It only took a couple of days before they caught the eye of the sultan himself. He came to examine his new recruits. Ismail informed them that Sultan Orhan had been pleased with what he saw and had invited them to a feast in his palace that night. Sergiu was able to charm the sultan and they endlessly discussed politics. After an hour or so Vlad grew bored and found himself jesting with Abdullah and a few of the other Janissaries.

SERGIU CONTINUED to learn from the sultan — or perhaps it was the other way around — and Vlad and the twins continued their training with Ismail. They accompanied Orhan on several missions that year. Sometimes they set out to maintain Osmanli lands and sometimes they went to conquer new territories. Orhan, like his father before him, would divide any loot acquired during these conquests between his soldiers as a reward for fighting for him. This helped to ensure the Janissaries' loyalty. Vlad desired such loyalty from an army of vampires so he studied Orhan's methods. The man was a down-to-earth leader, as his father had been. He even shod his own horses. Vlad figured this must have originated from their humble background. Orhan was a fair leader and seemed to care about his men and their well-being.

Sergiu and Orhan became inseparable much of the time; a relationship which appeared to concern the pasha. Eventually the sultan would ask for Sergiu's advice as much as he would consult his own pasha.

Rather than spending time with the sultan, Vlad usually preferred the camaraderie of the soldiers. It appeared that without women around, Vlad could get on well with the men. Women and men were kept separate from one another in this society. Women of high status such as Orhan's wives, mother and daughters were kept under lock and key in their own part of the palace and never seen by the Janissaries. They would never venture out to the marketplace or be seen on the streets for any reason. The only women that were seen in town were servants and lower class women who had to sell their goods as a means of survival. Of course, Vlad was not interested in any of those women. His sights were set on the powerful — a woman with a name behind her.

CHAPTER 31 NORTHERN ANATOLIA 1355 AD

Over the next year Vlad and the twins became skilled fighters under the pasha's tutelage. Sergiu preferred to study while they trained. He stayed behind with his books rather than head into battle with the Osmanlis. Most of the lands the sultan conquered were smaller Christian villages and towns. They were not well defended and the fine-tuned Osmanli fighters made quick work of these areas. More often than not it was hardly a fight. The Janissaries did not truly need Vlad and the twins, so Vlad ordered Cosmin and Costel to hang back.

"What would you have us do then, Master?" Cosmin asked.

"Keep your eyes and ears peeled. Our job is to protect the Janissaries. If any of them get into trouble then it is your job to save them."

This was a worthy goal that seemed to pacify them.

Next on Orhan's list of lands to conquer was the Gallipoli peninsula. This was well defended and not the easy raid the other missions had been. The siege at the fortress of Gallipoli lasted for weeks. The men grew weary and bored. They preferred quick and easy loot. Here there was no such compensation for days on end.

This time the vampires played an active role in the battle. They defended the sultan's slaves as they slowly built massive earthworks that would allow the army to ascend the walls of the fortress. Two such earthen ramps were built simultaneously so that the Osmanlis could pour into the city from two different vantage points, thus making it harder for the smaller Gallipoli army to defend the city. Yet with three vampires leading the soldiers over the wall the Gallipoli forces would not be able to stop the intruders anyway.

Vlad fastened several shields together which Abdullah held. From behind this enhanced shield, Vlad would fire continuous arrows at the sentries guarding the wall. Costel would hold a similar large shield while Cosmin fired onto the city wall from the second earthwork. This kept the Gallipolians on their toes and made it difficult for them to fire down upon the sultan's slaves. Vlad saved Abdullah on numerous occasions, knocking away the enemies' arrows time and again, keeping them from finding their mark in Abdullah.

As Cosmin defended the second earthwork, an arrow found its way through his arm. Costel ripped the arrow out and quickly bandaged the wound. After only a couple of hours of rest Cosmin demanded to return to battle. The three vampire soldiers were becoming legends amongst the Janissaries.

It took a couple of weeks before the massive earth ramps reached the top of the outer city walls. This allowed the sultan's men to finally enter the city. Vlad and Abdullah led the way into the city from one ramp, while Cosmin and Costel were in the front line of the other. The Ottomans' superior numbers overwhelmed the Christian soldiers. It was thousands against hundreds.

Sultan Orhan himself wanted to enter the city with his army. And enter he did. Up until this point they had only lost a few men, mostly slaves. Vlad knew there would be more casualties as the remaining Gallipolian forces defended their city. Vlad could not protect all the Janissaries, so he focused on the sultan and Abdullah. He kept them both in his sights at all times.

Ismail was getting too old to be of much use on the battlefield. He hung back, barking commands at the men from the safety of the rear of the army.

The sultan's men flooded the streets like waves of black ants. They would finally get their long-awaited spoils of war and the glory they so desired.

Orhan positioned himself at the top of a small hill in the town square. This was where he planned to deliver his victory speech to the Janissaries. A handful of Gallipolian soldiers crept up behind the sultan. No doubt they understood the limitation of the Osmanlis — which was the sultan himself. All centered around him. If he were to fall in battle, there would be no one who could maintain order and the Janissaries would fall into chaos. They would become nothing more than mercenaries with no leader. If one could get to the sultan he could end the battle, not to mention, win back the city.

With Orhan's attention on the chaos in front of him, not even his personal guards noticed the small group of soldiers about to ambush them. Vlad shot an arrow into the bowman whose arrow had been pointed at the sultan's back. In a flash, Vlad left Abdullah's side and came up behind the enemy from the rear. By the time Orhan heard the commotion behind him, he found the Gallipolians decapitated and Vlad covered from head to toe in blood. Vlad struggled to fight back the long fangs that were threatening to form. He drove a spear into the ground and staked the head of the would-be Gallipolian assassin on it.

"A gift for you, My Sultan." Vlad bowed to Orhan.

Orhan was pleased beyond measure. At the victory celebration in the newly conquered city that very night Vlad, Cosmin and Costel were the honored guests who sat at the sultan's table. He named them the Guardians of the Guard — the Protectors of the Janissaries. There was much cheering and merriment as the sultan had lost only a handful of men and gained much. With the fall of the fortress, the long peninsula of Gallipoli was now under the firm control of the Osmanlis. This gave them a strong foothold in Europe itself and would make future raids into Eastern Europe all the easier.

As their reward, the three vampires were offered first rights to the best of the loot and any captured Gallipolian slaves, who would be Osmanli slaves from this day forth. Vlad did not feel the need for slaves — they would only slow him down. The sultan would have better uses for them. Vlad and the twins settled for a pile of gold coins and a handful of precious stones.

CHAPTER 32 NORTHERN ANATOLIA 1355 AD

Being fully trusted by the sultan and held in the highest regard, it was time for Vlad to find out how high he could rise in this regime.

"If you were to convert to Islam, I would be glad to offer my youngest daughter's hand in marriage," Orhan said to Vlad. "You are the finest young man I have ever met."

"If I were to marry your daughter, I could become the heir to the throne?" Vlad inquired.

The sultan laughed. "No. Of course not, my ambitious young friend. My son Murad will be the next sultan of the Osmanlis. Only a son from the lineage of Osman himself can be sultan. We are not like the Romans. I hear that they have, at times, passed the inheritance of the throne through an emperor's daughter. These are usually for political alliances or in the rare case when there is no male heir. That is why men should have many wives. My son is strong and intelligent. Yes, Murad will make a fine ruler someday."

"Surely you speak the truth, Sire — may his rule be prosperous." Vlad's thoughts raced. He needed to find a princess of the Roman Empire to marry. Then when he usurped the throne it would be seen as legitimate. The Osmanli Empire was set on having a son of Osman as the ruler. Vlad would never be viewed as a legitimate sultan, even if he converted to Islam.

That night Vlad informed Sergiu and the twins that it was time to move on. "We have learned as much as we can here. I want to find soldiers of my own."

"Leaving will make us deserters," Sergiu said. "We will have to sneak away in the night and hide from any Janissaries we may come across, at least until enough time has passed that our desertion is forgotten."

"I want to take Abdullah with us. I think he will be loyal and he is brave and strong."

Sergiu frowned. "Not only are we deserting the sultan, now we are taking one of his best men?"

"We cannot very well stay here forever, pretending to be human," Vlad countered.

"I like it here," Costel complained.

"After the conquest of Gallipoli there is likely to be a period of rest before the sultan makes his next move into Europe. Life here will be a bore until then. We have learned much but our time here is over," Vlad said with finality.

"I would like to see what else awaits us," Cosmin spoke up.

"Thank you, Cosmin. We will leave on the morrow. Serg, you should be content in that I am not going to kill the sultan and his son Murad and take the throne by force."

"That sounds like an excellent idea, Master!" Cosmin lit up. "We will have to feed soon, why not on the sultan and his heir?"

Sergiu exhaled in disgust.

"I like the way you are thinking, Cosmin, but we must be smarter than that. The Janissaries are loyal to a fault. They will follow only a sultan of the House of Osman. Only a son of Osman himself would be seen as a legitimate ruler. Even if I were to marry a daughter of the sultan's, I would never be allowed to rule *as* sultan. Not to mention the entire religious barrier. This would make usurping the throne even more difficult. I don't think we will be converting to Islam anytime soon. We have time. We must be patient and do this right."

"Not to mention the sultan is a good person and a dear friend," Sergiu spat. "They have been nothing but kind to us. They welcomed us with open arms, as if we were one of them."

Sergiu was as close to fuming as Vlad had ever seen him. This meant that he remained calm and collected on the outside but Vlad knew better. It was only the slight redness in his mentor's cheeks that gave proof of his anger.

"Thank you, Sergiu, for being our moral guide. It may serve you well to remember our end goal. It will be easier if you do not become so attached next time," Vlad replied.

"Well, I will continue to do my best to edify the lot of you."

"I hope that is the case, my dear friend." Vlad gave Sergiu a firm pat on the shoulder in an attempt to calm him.

Once the soliders were fast asleep, Vlad and his vampire companions gathered the modest treasure they had gained from their time with the sultan and prepared to take flight. This was more gold than Cosmin and Costel had ever hoped to have during their human lifetime.

Sergiu and the twins headed out of the barracks, while Vlad remained. He shook Abdullah awake.

He had been snoring loudly and woke with a start. "What, what is it!"

"Shh, follow me. There is something I have to show you," Vlad whispered.

"Now?"

"Yes, now, and don't wake the others."

Abdullah reluctantly and noisily followed Vlad out of the barracks. Vlad led him to a quiet part of town.

"What is the meaning of this?" Abdullah's voice was full of irritation.

"You will see soon enough, my friend."

Costel and Cosmin stepped out from behind a vacant building. They secured each of Abdullah's arms and Vlad bit into his own wrist, flinching at the pain that shot up his arm. Abdullah's height required them to force him to his knees so Vlad could pull the hair on the back of his head and force the blood down his throat. This all happened quickly. Abdullah barely had time to get out a word of protest. A couple of heartbeats later he fell face down in the sand. They rolled his large form over onto a piece of leather that had been secured between two sturdy poles. This formed a stretcher which Cosmin and Costel could use to carry the unconscious Abdullah.

"Now, if you are satisfied, let us get out of here before they find we are missing," Sergiu said. Over his shoulder was a bag containing Abdullah's most prized possessions. He had just returned from collecting it from the barracks.

"I will miss the Janissaries and I will miss feeding on Muslim slaves. They are clean, no spirits fouling their blood," Costel said.

They took flight. Cosmin looked back toward Bursa. The others followed his lead, taking in the city one last time.

"Not to fear, my young friend. We will find our own Janissaries. Ones who will follow me... and not grow old and die on us."

Costel smiled.

CHAPTER 33 RHODES 1355 AD

Vlad and his companions flew south. He had hoped to make it to Alexandria before Abdullah woke but shortly after they reached the waters of the Mediterranean, Abdullah stirred.

"Shall we find out if a vampire this new can fly?" Cosmin asked and then proceeded to laugh wholeheartedly with his brother.

"Don't you dare," Sergiu chastised.

"Oh, come now. We are only funnin' you, Serg."

"There." Vlad pointed. "That large island will do. We will need to get Abdullah out of the sun."

"That would be the island of Rhodes," Sergiu announced.

"How does he know so much?" Costel asked.

"If you live to be as old as Sergiu, you too will know a thing or two," Vlad said.

They landed on the beautiful green island. It was a nice change from the dryness of Anatolia. Abdullah's transition went well enough. He was primarily concerned about being stolen away and taken to the land of the infidel. This disturbed him more than being turned into a cannibalistic killer. He took it all rather well, although he did miss his comrades in arms — they were his only family. In fact, they all missed their Osmanli companions.

They, like the great Osman himself, became nomads. They lived remotely in large tents that Vlad paid locals in Rhodes to make. They did not stay in any one place too long. This was not a bad life for vampires, as they did not have to pretend to be human. They could be themselves. As soon as Abdullah was comfortable with flying and could somewhat control himself around humans, Vlad had the tents and their few belongings shipped to Alexandria. They took flight that night.

After a time in Alexandria, they slowly made their way west, traveling south of the Mediterranean Sea. The weather was hot and the sun was unbearable. Days were spent undercover, usually inside the large tents. They trained with every known weapon. Of course, Sergiu preferred his books to training. He read endlessly, studying Arab medicines and sciences. He read histories and philosophies. Sergiu would often tell Vlad, Abdullah and the twins stories of mighty leaders of the past. Such tales were greatly enjoyed by all.

Nights were often spent in local taverns looking for suitable men to add to Vlad's army. He became quite skilled at finding men on the fringe of society, men he knew would become loyal subjects. All Vlad had to do was offer them a small amount of wealth and an even smaller amount of power. This was more than they could have hoped for as humans. Occasionally, one of the new recruits would prove to be too bloodthirsty. If he was unable to stop killing then he was beheaded before he drew attention to Vlad and his men.

Vlad's faith in Cosmin and Costel was not misplaced. They served him well, following every order. They became powerful fighters and helped to train the new vampires. Vlad's growing army of outcasts was working out better than he could have imagined. Since he was always the one to turn them, they would often refer to him as their master. As Vlad had hoped, they were fiercely loyal. He began to refer to these soldiers as his Janissaries — his very own vampire army.

The problem was keeping them busy enough that they did not grow bored. Bored vampire soldiers were very dangerous. Sergiu designed a strict regimen for them, based on the Osmanli archetype. This consisted of alternating between schooling — which many of them disliked — and learning to fight, which most enjoyed immensely. This left them with very little free time, which meant less time to find trouble.

They settled in Fez for the longest period of time. It was the end of the road — quite literally. By the time they were wearing out their welcome in Fez, Vlad's army numbered fifteen; which was not bad for a vampire army. But they had to keep moving in order to not draw too much attention. They made their way east, visiting new towns and cities along the way. It was time for the next phase of Vlad's plan. While he was growing in power, he still needed a name for himself. To become royalty he needed to marry into an imperial family.

By the time they arrived at the new Osmanli capital, in what was now referred to as the Ottoman Empire, Vlad had twenty-seven men under his command and the year was 1415. Sultan Orhan's son Murad had moved the capital during his reign, from Bursa up into Europe. Murad's grandson, Mehmed, now resided in the old city of Adrianople and the name had been changed to Edirne. All of this should have been a clue that much had changed since they left Sultan Orhan all those years ago.

Abdullah was looking forward to returning home. Perhaps Abdullah expected to find the same young Janissaries they had left behind almost sixty years prior. Either way, they were all looking forward to a warm welcome, like the one they had received under the rule of Orhan. Surely this new sultan would see the benefit of Vlad's group of young and superior fighters.

Simply getting an audience with the sultan proved to be difficult. After a couple of days Vlad was ready to move on. He did not see the value in delaying in Edirne but Sergiu was convinced that there was more to learn from the all-powerful Osmanlis, who had continued to rise in strength and numbers, more so than other empires. Their army was the most loyal and the most feared in all the land. It was rumored that the enemy would flee at the sound of the Osmanli war band, resulting in the easy acquisition of the now vast lands of the empire. The leaders of Europe were forever watching to see what the sultan would do next, as he continued to expand Westward.

Finally, Sergiu, Abdullah and Vlad were given permission to meet with the sultan in his palace. He then kept them waiting for almost two hours. Again Vlad wanted to leave but Sergiu persuaded him to stay. Their weapons were confiscated at the front entrance to the palace. They were instructed on how to behave in Sultan Mehmed's presence, which made Vlad want to hurl. This time it was Abdullah who kept Vlad from marching out. With a child's awe, Abdullah wanted to meet the new sultan more than anything.

CHAPTER 34 OTTOMAN EMPIRE 1415 AD

When Mehmed was finally ready to see them, two armed Janissaries led Vlad, Abdullah and Sergiu into a large room where the sultan sat on his throne. On his right was his Grand Vizier and on his left a young man who must have been the sultan's son and heir, Murad II. One of the guards gave a forceful shove to the back of Vlad's head to remind him to keep his head down until the sultan said otherwise. It took every bit of Vlad's self-control not to break the guard's nose. Sergiu and Abdullah prostrated themselves at Mehmed's feet placing their foreheads to the floor as instructed.

Vlad shook his head. *Do it for Abdullah.* He followed their lead more slowly. After what seemed like a long time Sultan Mehmed bade them rise, giving them permission to gaze upon him.

"What is it that you want from me?" Mehmed's impatience was clear.

For Vlad, this confirmed that they should not have come.

"We want nothing, Your Majesty; except to serve you. You see, our great grandfathers served the mighty Sultan Orhan himself, may blessings be upon him," Sergiu said.

"What do you have to offer me?"

"We have twenty-eight well-trained soldiers ready to serve your empire." Sergiu bowed his head to the sultan.

For the first time Mehmed smiled. Then he issued a derisive laugh. "I have no need of simple mercenaries. Their loyalty can never be trusted. I rely entirely on my Janissaries whom we have trained since they were small boys. They are my 'sons,' knowing only my schooling and my laws. They are boundlessly devoted to me. Your band of rabble is of no use to me."

With that, the sultan raised his hand to dismiss them. Vlad could see Abdullah's shoulders sag at Mehmed's insult. This was enough to make Vlad want to sink his teeth into the sultan's neck and drain him of life. Vlad could not wait to get out of there.

Sergiu and Abdullah backed away slowly from the sultan but Vlad spun on his heel and headed for the door. The two Janissaries drew their scimitars and pointed them at Vlad's chest.

"No one turns their back on the sultan," one of the Janissaries declared.

"That's odd, because I believe I just did." Vlad moved around the guards' swords. With the palm of his hand he shoved one of them into the wall. Vlad tried to be gentle but he could hear the sound of bones cracking as the guard's fragile human body gave way to the unyielding stone wall. He shoved his shoulder into the second guard and sent him flying into the adjacent wall. He too was not dead but taken out of the fight.

Vlad turned to Mehmed. "You have made a grave mistake. You do not want me as your enemy."

The three of them disappeared, as the sultan yelled for more guards.

That night they sat around a campfire far outside the city. Abdullah's massive shoulders remained slumped.

"Cheer up, old friend." Vlad spoke in Turkish or Arabic, or some combination thereof. It was almost their own personal language. "We are your comrades in arms. These," Vlad gestured to his men, "are your brethren. Forget about the sultans of old."

Abdullah gave a weak smile. "I don't understand. Sultan Orhan was a great leader. What has happened to my people?"

"That was a long time ago, Abdullah. The modern sultans have become pompous, with an obscene sense of entitlement," Sergiu paused. "Yet our visit was not a complete waste. We did learn that the devsirme, or child soldiers, are indeed how the empire has managed to create the most loyal and possibly the fiercest army to ever roam the earth." Sergiu was forever looking on the bright side.

"Tomorrow we travel to Constantinople," Vlad announced. "I warned the sultan that it would be unwise to cross me. We will offer our valuable services to Mehmed's mortal enemy. Constantinople will be a good place to avoid the sultan's men, who are most likely already looking for us. He will not take our meeting today lightly." *What better place to find a princess to marry than in the capital of the Roman Empire? Hopefully we will be received better by the emperor than the sultan,* Vlad thought.

"Come on, it is time for your Latin lesson," Sergiu said.

This brought about moans from some of the men.

As Vlad's men moved through Edirne on their way south, they came upon a crowd in the street in front of the palace.

"What is going on?" Vlad asked a local on-looker.

"Impalings," a man offered.

"Who?"

"Two of the sultan's top palace guards."

Vlad knew straightaway which guards were to be put to death.

"Why?" Sergiu asked.

"They failed the sultan yesterday. That is the price one must pay for failing the Shadow of God on Earth."

"The Shadow of God, my arse." Vlad let out a grunt of disgust. "You must be jesting." Then he turned to Costel, "Fetch my bow and quiver."

"What are you going to do?" Sergiu's forehead was lined with concern.

"If Mehmed does not want them in his army, then I will try them in mine."

Vlad beckoned for Abdullah to follow. They moved swiftly through the crowd to get closer to the public execution site.

Sergiu went to work preparing the men. "Be ready to move out on my command. We will most likely be pursued by hundreds of the sultan's troops."

Vlad and Abdullah waited with their hoods up, hiding their faces. The condemned palace guards were escorted into the courtyard by four sentries. With his hand, Vlad gestured for Abdullah to take out the two sentries on the right. Vlad shot one arrow followed by the other in a blink of an eye. Abdullah did the same. Each arrow found its mark in its intended guard and the prisoners were left standing alone with cloth bags over their heads.

Leaping with ease onto the low dividing wall to the courtyard, Vlad yelled, "The sultan is nothing but a goddamned nomad."

There was chaos all around. Abdullah threw one of the hooded men over his shoulder and Vlad seized the other. Guards ran toward them from all directions, as they disappeared in a flash.

Vlad and Abdullah paused under cover of a grove of olive trees outside of town. By the time the rest of Vlad's men tracked them down, the two guards lay in the deep transformative sleep with Vlad's blood dripping from their mouths. Their broken bones were already healing.

As the army of vampires entered the ancient city of Constantinople they numbered thirty.

CHAPTER 35 CONSTANTINOPLE 1415 AD

It did not take long for Vlad and his men to find their way into the court of Emperor Manuel II of the Roman Empire. The emperor was impressed with their remarkable fighting ability and readily accepted Vlad's offer to fight with him against the ever-present threat from the Ottomans. Unlike the sultan, Manuel was not picky. Any help he could get was welcome. His continual cries for aid from his fellow Christians in the West, usually fell on deaf ears. Thirty trained fighters were much needed in his small army. Constantinople had once been a mighty empire. In the centuries past, they could easily ward off threats from the Seljuk Turks and the like. However, times had changed; the Ottomans had grown to be far more powerful than the Seljuks had ever been. The ever-shrinking Roman Empire was now surrounded by lands the sultan controlled. Emperor Manuel desperately needed Vlad's help.

Constantinople was an ideal place to usurp the throne, as there had been many to do so in the past. Granted, former usurpers were usually family members of the emperors. They succeeded by taking control of the army. If Vlad were to marry into the family then taking control of the army would be easy. The people would not hesitate to follow a strong leader in these desperate times. Such a change in power would be nothing new to them. This was unlike the Ottomans who had been led solely by the sons of Osman and only a man in his direct line of descendants was viewed as a legitimate ruler.

Vlad's relatively few — yet highly effective — soldiers quickly earned him a place at the emperor's table, along with the emperor's most trusted advisors and the commanders of his army. Over the next year Vlad and Sergiu studied the situation in the palace. Emperor Manuel's most favored child was Isabella. She was his firstborn. It was said that Manuel had fallen in love with Isabella's mother. Yet before their daughter was born he was forced to marry another. Manuel's parents would not allow him to marry his love. As heir to the throne it was his duty to marry for political reasons. So he and Helena wed in order to soothe relations with Helena's royal family in Serbia. These were the facts — what remained was the emotional turmoil this chain of events put in place.

Some viewed Isabella as nothing more than an illegitimate child, though no one would dare say that to the emperor. Yet most viewed her as the grandest of all princesses in the kingdom. This made her Vlad's target.

At the Pascal Feast in the spring of 1416 Vlad and Sergiu sat at the emperor's long table. In the middle of the table sat Emperor Manuel; to his right sat Helena and to his left sat Isabella. Manuel all but ignored Helena and chatted away merrily with his daughter. Vlad ears were focused on their conversation.

"Oh, Father, why must these gatherings be so boring?" Isabella complained.

This was Vlad's cue. He shot Sergiu a devious smile and swiftly left his seat only to appear behind the emperor and his daughter. "Pardon me, Your Majesty. I hate to interrupt you and your lovely daughter but we simply cannot stand for a bored princess. May I offer to lead the young lady in a dance?"

The emperor glanced at his daughter who nodded slightly, accepting the invitation.

"Very well." Manuel frowned. He stood and took Isabella's hand.

Vlad slid her chair back so she could easily stand.

Manuel placed her hand in Vlad's.

Vlad issued a slight bow to the emperor for entrusting his daughter to him. *Let the games begin,* he thought. It had been a while since he had had to charm a woman. Hopefully he was not too rusty.

Isabella and Vlad joined in the circle dance. They held hands and Vlad gave her a warm smile.

Her cheeks flushed and she looked away.

She is perfect — young and naive. This would be as easy as drinking blood, Vlad thought. "Tell me, are you betrothed to someone?"

Isabella looked at him in disbelief. "Of course not. Father would never allow me to dance with you if I were promised to another."

"Yes, of course. I simply wanted to be sure that you are not spoken for."

She smiled and looked away, too shy to hold his stare. "And why is that, kind sir?"

It was a good thing Vlad could hear well for she spoke softly.

When Vlad did not answer, Isabella looked up at him. He gave her a sensual and mischievous grin. He had to steady her by releasing her hand and placing his arm around her waist, as her knees gave way.

This is too easy, he thought. She will be begging her father for permission to marry me. "Where is your mother?"

This brought a scowl to Isabella's small face and her gaze moved to the Empress Helena. "My mother was falsely accused of treason and banished to a faraway convent. I have not seen her since."

"How can you be sure the charges were false?"

Isabella's frown deepened. "Mother loved my father more than anything. She never would have betrayed him and Father knows this. I am sure of it."

Already knowing the answer, Vlad asked, "Who would dare to make false accusations against your mother?"

"It was Helena," Isabella said the name with disdain. "She was always fiercely jealous of my mother and me. Even after Father married Helena, he continued to see my mother. He loves us dearly and spent time with us whenever possible. Such affections he never shows toward Helena. I know that Helena had my mother wrongly accused but I cannot prove it."

"Have you spoken to your father about your suspicions?"

"Yes. He dismisses them. He does not think Helena is capable of such malice. He thinks of their relationship as a business venture. Though it is not that simple for Helena."

"I should think not. They have several children together. For women such affairs are never simple."

Isabella laughed. "That is true." She leaned into Vlad and whispered, "You know, my father still visits my mother from time to time — when he can."

Vlad gave her a warm smile, as if he was entertained by her love story, though be it a sad and twisted one. "Your father does not believe the allegations of treachery against your mother then?"

"I'd like to think not. Sometimes I wish he would revoke the charges so that my mother could return to us."

Vlad studied the ruler and his wife. Helena appeared uninterested in what was going on around her. Yet Vlad knew better; it was a ruse. She was carefully watching *all* that happened in the room. Helena's eyes were sharp and cunning. She was dignified in her aging, as most royalty were. Vlad was more attracted to Helena than to her stepdaughter. Rather than the young and foolish Isabella, Vlad preferred the intelligent and ambitious type. For a brief moment he thought that Helena was the one he should be charming. He could kill Manuel and marry the empress. *No. Helena is smart, she would see through me.* Vlad shook his head. *Stay with the plan. Don't allow yourself to become distracted.* So he turned his smile back to Isabella who blushed and averted her gaze.

CHAPTER 36 CONSTANTINOPLE 1416 AD

One advantage of being a vampire was that one can easily spy on humans. They could move unseen in the shadows and listen to others' conversations from afar. After the feast that night Vlad followed Isabella to her chambers. From a dark corner outside her room he listened to her and her chambermaid.

"Did you see him? He is so handsome." Isabella's voice was wistful.

This resulted in an eye-roll from Vlad.

"Who, my dear?" replied the chambermaid.

"Vlad of course. He asked me to dance. He was a perfect gentleman."

"They always are — at first. Don't you go gettin' too attached to that boy now. You know your father will have you marry a prince when the time is right."

"I will not be forced to marry as my father was!"

"I'm afraid that is the way it works for you lot, you know — you bein' royalty and all."

"No! I will convince my father to let me marry whom I choose."

"Of course, my dear, then he will name you and your husband the heirs to his throne and you will be empress." The chambermaid was being utterly sarcastic.

"That is it! I must convince my father that my future husband and I are best suited to rule this kingdom. Once I am empress I can banish Helena to a convent." This brought about a chorus of girlish laughter from Isabella.

Vlad had heard enough and was annoyed with the young girl so he retreated. However, this is perfect! Isabella has more influence over the emperor than I could ever have. She will be able to convince her father to let her marry me. Then perhaps she can persuade her father to name her as his heir to the throne — this would make my ascension to power even more legitimate. All I would need to do is ask for her hand in marriage when the time is right. Then she will do the work for me.

VLAD DID NOT WANT to seem overly anxious to marry into the royal family, so he waited to approach the emperor about marrying Isabella. It would be best to make it seem as if he were truly falling in love with her. This way when they married it would appear that it was for love — nothing more. He would work to make the public, the emperor and Isabella, believe that he was simply a love-struck young man. He did not want them to suspect his plans to usurp the throne. After all, vampires could afford to be patient.

In the months that followed, Vlad did nothing but exchange the occasional longing glance with Isabella. When Sergiu and Vlad deemed that the time was right, Vlad approached the Emperor about his daughter's hand.

"Oh, no. My baby girl is not ready to marry. She is only a child," Manuel said.

The emperor chuckled and Vlad followed his lead, even though nothing funny had been said.

"I'm afraid that as her father you are unable to see the fine young lady she has grown into," Vlad said. "She is approaching her sixteenth birthday. That is when many a princess is married. If you were to wait much longer, she would be an old maid."

The emperor frowned. "I suppose my little girl is growing up. She will have to marry someday." Manuel sighed, clearly not liking the idea. "You are a fine young man; intelligent, strong and brave. Yet, I am afraid she will have to be betrothed to a prince, not a minor noble such as yourself. She will have to marry for a good reason, you know, for a political reason."

Obviously, the emperor has not spent much time thinking about his daughter's marriage. His ambivalence is exactly what I need. "If I may, Sire. It is obvious that you love your daughter entirely too much to use her as a political pawn. Surely you will not force her to marry someone she does not wish to be with. Give her the chance to be happy in marriage, a chance you did not have." Vlad was not sure if he had overstepped his bounds with this last statement. But the emperor did not appear upset.

Manuel remained thoughtful.

This is my chance, go for the gold. "Of course, Your Majesty, you are correct. She should marry for a reason and what better reason is there than love?"

The emperor's shoulders sagged, as if Vlad had placed a heavy weight upon them. "I do want her happiness."

Vlad smiled. *Soon the throne will be mine.* "Then ask her what she wishes. If she does not want to marry me then I will never speak of this again."

The emperor slowly nodded. "I suppose it is time I deal with this ... matter."

"Thank you, My Lord." With that Vlad swiftly exited the room.

That was it — a bit of convincing was all it took. Isabella was overjoyed by the news of Vlad's proposal and begged her father to allow the marriage. Manuel could not resist his beloved princess's requests. He had never denied her anything, so of course he could not deny her this. The wedding was scheduled for one month after her sixteenth birthdate. This was an arrangement that even Helena was content with. At the engagement celebration Vlad overheard the empress state that it was best for Isabella to marry the likes of *Vlad* — an insignificant soldier boy. This was an ideal arrangement compared to a powerful prince who might have his eyes on the throne. Helena wanted her firstborn son, John VIII, to rise to power, although John was still a small child.

From afar Vlad narrowed his eyes at Helena and took comfort in the thought that soon he would be ruling in her place. He could almost taste it. His dream was close — within reach. *By the years' end I will become the Emperor of the Roman Empire. I will make this kingdom great once again under my rule.*

CHAPTER 37 CONSTANTINOPLE 1416 AD

Now that Vlad and Isabella were betrothed, he was at least allowed to see her, chaperoned of course. This time was spent charming her and fine-tuning their plans. They were both in agreement that she should work to convince her father to name her as his heir. She was only concerned with revenge against her evil stepmother. Vlad doubted she had any interest in running the state. She was highly educated, as all nobility were but she did not think beyond her petty grievances with Helena.

Things were working out impeccably; better than if Vlad had planned all these details himself, such as a favored daughter of marrying age, who held the heart and ear of the emperor.

It was not long after their engagement party when Emperor Manuel announced that his beloved daughter and Vlad would be the ones to carry the crown of Constantinople upon his death. He declared to all in the Great Hall that he had never seen a finer warrior than Vlad and that Vlad would make a strong and worthy emperor someday. Helena quickly rose from her throne after hearing this news. Her cheeks reddened with anger. She glared at her husband for a moment and then stormed out of the Hall in a show of protest.

~

THE DAYS and months crawled by. Vlad could not wait for his wedding day. He had worked hard for this for far too long. He would finally be crowned prince and it could not happen soon enough.

It was the night before the wedding that Vlad received a formal invite to take wine and refreshments in the Great Hall. He arrived to find that the Hall was empty. A servant scurried in with a serving platter. With shaky hands he placed it on the table. The gold tray contained two chalices of wine. Grapes and figs had been elegantly arranged on the platter.

It was not long before Isabella came in with her eunuch escort.

"Is it only us?" she asked as she looked around for others.

"Apparently." Vlad gestured to the two wine cups. "Do you know why we were summoned here?"

"No. I assumed it was something father concocted. I'm not sure why — perhaps to celebrate my last day of childhood." She then turned to her eunuch guard and demanded that he wait just outside the Great Hall. "Leave the doors open if you must. What could happen? We are to wed tomorrow. Then you will *have* to leave us alone." She gave the eunuch a playful shove but the large man remained unmoving.

The eunuch glared at Vlad. Vlad put his hands up as if surrendering. He gave the eunuch a look that said he would behave himself. The large man reluctantly left but Vlad knew he would never venture out of earshot. There was no such thing as privacy within these walls.

"Your last day of childhood, eh? Does that mean you are ready for womanhood?" Vlad gave her a playful smile.

Isabella looked away with blushed cheeks. She picked up one of the goblets and raised it, "To womanhood."

Vlad did the same. Tapping his chalice to hers, they drank. The wine tasted odd. Vlad almost spat it out. He studied the substance for a moment — everything fell into place. The mysterious invite, only two goblets of wine. They were poisoned! He looked at Isabella with wide eyes. Then panic overtook him when he saw that she had drunk most of the cup. He knocked the chalice from her hand and the metal clanked noisily on the marble floor. The small bit of wine that was left in her cup looked like blood on the floor.

"What —" Isabella tried to protest.

"It is poisoned! Someone is trying to kill us."

She smiled. "Don't be silly, My Love. The wine tasted fine to me."

"Of course it did; you are a human. You could not smell or taste it with your dull senses."

"What are you talking about — a human?"

Isabella's concerned escort approached. He must have been alarmed by Vlad's raised voice and the noise of the chalice hitting the floor. "What is going on?"

"Someone has poisoned her ... us." Vlad knew what little he had drunk would not affect him in the slightest. It would take flagons of human poison to kill a vampire and that might not be enough.

Isabella grabbed her stomach and doubled over. Whatever poison was in the wine, it was quick to take effect. She gazed at Vlad, pleading for help and her eyes were full of pain. He caught her before she fell.

"No, no! Go get help! Fetch the royal doctor." Vlad looked to the stunned eunuch. "Now, you fool!"

With that, the eunuch ran.

Isabella reached for Vlad's hand and looked into his eyes. "Helena," she whispered. This was her last word. Vlad could see the life leave her as her heart slowed until it stopped beating altogether.

With her, Vlad's dreams vanished. He slowly lowered her body to the floor, as the rage took over. "Helena," Vlad whispered through gritted teeth.

Vlad had left the hall when Sergiu appeared in front of him. "Teller, wait. What are you going to do?" Sergiu only called Vlad by his human name when he was trying to remind Vlad of where he came from — when he wanted Vlad to remember his compassion.

Vlad sidestepped Sergiu and continued toward the barracks. He would need some of his men to help with this one. "I'm going to kill that aristocratic bitch." Vlad paused to look at Sergiu. "Don't you dare try to stop me."

Sergiu shook his head with disapproval. "Teller, Please... "

"Don't call me that."

CHAPTER 38 CONSTANTINOPLE 1416 AD

When Helena entered her private chambers that night, Vlad was waiting for her. Her dead chambermaid lay at his feet with fresh wounds oozing from her neck. He was half sitting and half leaning on a desktop with his arms crossed.

Helena jumped when she saw him and gasped at the sight of her motionless servant sprawled across the floor. She took a step toward the door. Her mouth opened to yell for her guards.

"You can scream all you want. Only my soldiers will hear you and they will not come to your aid."

Helena's eyes shone with fear. She ran for the door but Vlad appeared in front of her.

"You will not be able to outrun me either."

"What do you want?" Helena's voice shook.

"Your blood."

Her body began to tremble.

"And I want to hear you admit that you killed Isabella."

"What! You have gone mad."

"Ad-mit it." Vlad over-pronounced every syllable.

"I would never do such a thing."

Vlad grabbed her by the throat but did not squeeze. He did not want her dead — yet.

She clawed at his forearm but it was like scaping her nails against frozen marble.

He added the slightest pressure around her throat.

"Fine," she conceded.

Vlad gave Helena a slight shove as he released her. This caused her to fall to the floor.

She sat on her hip and turned to view her maid. "I knew you were an ambitious young man but I did not think you were capable of this. I underestimated you. It appears we are more alike than either of us may have expected."

"To kill your own kin — for what?"

"Isabella was not my kin! She was a bastard child with a commoner for a mother. My husband was blinded by the two of you. He was going to put that bastard and a minor noble on the throne. He is a fool! I could not convince him that it was our son, born in purple, who has the right to the throne. I had to do something. I was born a Serbian princess. My father is Constantine Dragas. Therefore my son is of regal blood and the rightful heir."

"That name means nothing to me." Vlad's voice was full of disdain.

"I watched the two of you. You only wanted the power that marrying her would give you. She was simply too stupid to see that. Do not try to deny it by claiming that you *loved* her. You can't lie to me, boy. You cared nothing for that insignificant little girl." Helen cautiously rose from the floor. Her fear had given way to anger. "Now you are here to avenge her death!"

She glanced around the room for a way out of this impossible situation. Then she changed her approach. She stood to her full height — her dignified empress stance. "I think we can come to some sort of an agreement." Her lips puckered as she reached to undo the silk threads that held her top together.

Vlad smiled. "What are you proposing?"

"You aspire to be the emperor, is that correct?"

Vlad gave a slight nod.

"Well then." She stepped closer and ran her finger playfully down his chest. "Why don't you marry me instead? All you would have to do is kill Manuel."

Helena's scent overwhelmed Vlad. Her large breasts were mostly visible. He smelled a hint of sweet milk, as she was still breastfeeding her youngest child. He grabbed her waist and pressed her body to his. Inhaling deeply at the nape of her neck he fully took in her womanly scent — clean feminine flesh, delicious blood and sweet milk. An inadvertent moan left his lips.

Where the neck met the shoulder was the best part of a female — as far as Vlad was concerned. It had been a long time since he had been with a woman. In fact, he did not remember the last time. A couple of years, maybe five, possibly ten ... he honestly didn't know. Time moved differently for vampires. It seemed to speed along quickly most of the time. Years could seem as if they were merely months.

Are men this easily distracted ... and gullible? Yes. Vlad answered his own question.

He pushed her away and looked into her eyes. "Are you proposing that I get rid of Manuel and then you will marry me and crown me emperor?"

"That is precisely what I am proposing. That way we both get what we want. You will become ruler and I will have a handsome young man in my bed." She tried to further convince him with a seductive smile but Vlad knew she was lying.

Helena was cunning, working the only angle she had in this situation — her sensuality. She is simply trying to save her own skin. As soon as she is free from me, she will run to her husband and he will order that my head be removed for treason.

Helena sensed that Vlad was not convinced so she continued, "Unless, of course, you don't think you can kill the emperor."

"I know I can. That was the plan all along, my dear." Vlad pulled her to him and took another deep breath, inhaling the sweet aroma from her neck. He kissed her naked shoulder. Slowly working his way up her neck ... her cheek, until his lips were on hers.

Helena's chest heaved with excitement.

Vlad ran his hands gently over her breasts. Now it was she who moaned with pleasure. Picking her up he carried her to the bed.

Once he was more than satisfied, they lay next to each other.

"Why are you so cold, my lover?" Helena asked.

"Because I'm a demon. Perhaps even the devil himself."

She narrowed her eyes at him, as if he were mad.

"You are wrong. I'm not like you. I have to kill to survive. I often use it to my advantage. You, however, are human. I expect more from you. Humans should be better than me and my kind. I have no choice but to kill. You had a choice. Killing Isabella was beyond the greatest of sins."

Helena studied him, trying to make sense of the gibberish he was speaking. He took her jaw firmly in his hand and pushed her face to the side. This left her neck fully exposed. His fangs sank into her soft skin with ease. Vlad was her judge and executioner.

THE NEXT MORNING Vlad woke in the soldiers' barracks. His men were moving about getting ready for the day. He sat up slowly and put his head in his hands. His head throbbed. *Dammit, too much blood.* It had been a very long time since he had felt this terrible.

Sergiu handed him his special hot brew. "Rough night, eh?"

Vlad shook his head to try and clear it. "Aye, or a really good one. I'm not entirely sure which." He eagerly took his favorite drink from Sergiu. "Women are trouble. They are seductive and manipulative. If they are ruthless on top of all that, one had best be wary."

Sergiu laughed. "Thankfully not all of them are like Helena. Nevertheless, I find them to be complicated and intimidating. I have told you many times, life is much easier if you leave them alone."

"And I had, for quite some time. Now I am paying the price." Vlad sighed. "We were so close, Serg. I suppose it is time for us to move on."

"I imagine so. I was concerned all along that this scheme was too perfect to last. Everything was falling into place seamlessly. It was bound to come unraveled."

"Master!" Abdullah ran toward them. "We had best be on our way. The emperor is calling for your head. He is accusing you of the murder and rape of his wife and daughter."

"What! That's outrageous. I didn't rape anyone, or kill his daughter for that matter."

"The emperor must protect his wife's image, as she was found naked in her bed this morning. The people cannot be allowed to believe their empress willingly slept with her murderer. Come! Everyone will be looking for you." Sergiu moved quickly around the room placing his precious books in a trunk.

Vlad stood with a frustrated groan and announced, "We move out now, before we have to slaughter all the emperor's men."

Costel let out a disappointed snort. "It would be a fun fight, though."

With a glare from Vlad, Costel shut his mouth and threw some clothes into a large leather bag.

"And we're off," Cosmin said. Under his breath he added, "Because our master has managed to anger the ruler ... yet again."

CHAPTER 39 MIDDLE EAST 1416 AD

Vlad and his army of vampires had to lay low for a time, returning to their nomadic roots. They lived in luxurious tents with every comfort they wanted and then some. They moved about the land, never staying in one place for long.

Ironically, Vlad united the sultan and the emperor in a common cause — hunting him down. Sultan Mehmed had been on the lookout for Vlad ever since his unacceptable display of disrespect. The sultan suspected that Vlad was the one who had foiled his public executions as well. So Mehmed offered to help Emperor Manuel find Vlad. The reward for Vlad's head was one-hundred gold pieces. This was eventually raised to one thousand gold pieces. Vlad's picture hung on every street in every major city in the region. He quite enjoyed being the most wanted man in the world. Yet this meant that he had to become a ghost, which was what he did.

Even in her death Helena got what she wanted. Her son, John VIII, became the next Emperor. As it turned out, her sons would be the last to rule over Eastern Rome. John's younger brother Constantine XI was the last emperor. Constantine had been the suckling babe when his mother died at Vlad's hand. Sergiu claimed that it was appropriate that Constantine XI was the last to rule. The Eastern Roman Empire was founded by Constantine the Great and after one thousand one hundred and twenty-nine years the empire finally fell under the rule of yet another Constantine. Sergiu enjoyed this irony.

Sergiu remembered the time when the Eastern Roman Empire had been magnificent. He was forever telling them stories of Constantinople during its pinnacle. He could name all the emperors by heart. However, his favorite tales were the extraordinary ones of the powerful empresses who ruled the empire, each without a husband at her side; the virtuous Empress Theodora and the cruel Empress Irene, to name a few. Vlad thought Sergiu had an eternal infatuation, or even an insatiable love for the beautiful Theodora, whom Sergiu had actually met. Yes, Sergiu was ancient. Older than dirt itself, or at least this was what they often said in jest.

Sergiu's favorite literature was Princess Anna's copious historical accounts. Being the daughter of Emperor Alexius I, she often wrote about her father's numerous crusades against the infidel — primarily the Seljuk Turks. If only Vlad had a silver stavrata for every time Sergiu would read to them from Anna's many works. The younger men who had not heard the tales a million times over would listen to Sergiu with great interest, while Vlad and Abdullah would entertain themselves by silently mimicking Sergiu as he read. They knew many of the lines by heart and this was an entertaining way to pass the time. Cosmin and Costel would act out the scenes as Sergiu read or told stories. The twins would pretend to be overly dramatic lovers or they would fence with wooden sticks. This would usually end in a rather serious wrestling match in which each brother would try to best the other. The match would often end with a broken bone or two. This was their unsophisticated form of theater. What could Vlad say? They had to do something to pass the endless time on their hands.

As the years continued to tick away, so did the novelty of Vlad's alleged crimes — only half of which he had actually committed. Eventually, he could show his face in public again. By 1453 Vlad was more than ready to get on with his search for a noble wife.

As it would turn out, this was a year that would always be remembered. The formerly impenetrable walls of the Queen of

Cities were finally breached by Sultan Mehmed II's cannons – cannons the likes of which the world had never seen before. It was said that Constantine XI bravely stood his ground, never abandoning the city. He fought the endless flood of Ottoman Janissaries to his very end and the end of an iconic Christian capital.

Sergiu had been relieved when Vlad declared that it was not their fight. Some of Vlad's men desperately wanted to join the battle but it was of no concern to Vlad. He was not overly fond of either side, so leaving the humans to their own troubles was best.

Vlad continued to grow his army. He had taken a number of the emperor's top fighters with him when they left Constantinople. His quest to find a princess of marrying age proved to be more difficult than he had anticipated. The Hungarian princesses had already been wed. Bulgaria's only princess had but recently been born. She had a long line of older brothers to await the throne ahead of her. Not to mention, Vlad was not interested in waiting around for sixteen years for her to grow.

It was not until the year 1455 that Vlad learned of a suitable princess. Posed as a minor nobleman, he made his way into the Moldavian court. The newly crowned prince of the region, Voivode Stefan III, welcomed Vlad to his land. Vlad had grown quite fond of Stefan, which was odd, as he usually did not get on well with men in power. Yet for some unforeseen reason he found Stefan to be affable. He had even begun to consider him a friend. This was also rare, as Vlad had no human friends.

Prince Stefan was the one to inform them that the Voivode of Wallachia, despite having a wife and numerous concubines, had only produced one heir. Her name was Neacsa. This news grabbed Vlad's attention.

"And how old is this princess, Neacsa?" Vlad asked.

"Perhaps going on eighteen. I believe she is to wed an Albanian prince this summer. Her father is my uncle, Voivode Vladislav II of the Draculesti family," Stefan answered.

"Well he has a great name. Then again, half the population in this region goes by some form of Vlad, whether it be Vladislav, Vladnic, Vladismir, not to be confused with Vladimir."

Stefan laughed.

"Draculesti, as in the dragon family," Sergiu interpreted.

"Yes, he calls himself Prince Dracul — the Dragon Prince."

Vlad gave a knowing look to Sergiu, who nodded in complete understanding. They had been together for so long that they often did not need to speak to communicate. They both knew they were headed home, back to Targoviste, as soon as possible.

As they packed for the short trip from Moldova to Wallachia, Sergiu said, "This feels as if it is the right time to finally return."

Vlad smiled. "We have come full circle, my old friend."

"It is ironic. All that traveling and adventure only to end up back where we started so many years ago."

"What has it been? About a hundred years?"

"Give or take."

Much had changed. Vlad's former smithy shop was no longer there. What stood in its place were new buildings. Well, new to them. Most of the humans around here would think of them as old. New, old, it was all relative. A smelly butcher shop now stood where the original tiny smithy building had once been.

Cosmin and Costel were overjoyed at being home. They spent the entire first day touring around their childhood neighborhood. They talked excitedly about each important place from their youth; the field where they used to play, which was now a row of homes. They showed Vlad the place where Cosmin stole his first kiss, where their grandparent's house used to be and the like.

The only buildings that were recognizable were the large stone structures, such as the grand orthodox church and the government compounds. These buildings had been well maintained and expanded as needed over the years. It was indescribably odd to be back. So much had changed, yet the city *felt* the same — it was home.

Vlad's Janissaries numbered just over fifty. This made it the second largest known vampire army in the world, only slightly short of that of the High Court of Elders. Vlad was a force to be reckoned with – largely unstoppable.

Fifty well-armed fighters bombarding the city was a bit more of an entrance than Vlad wanted to make. He took only Sergiu, Abdullah and the twins to meet the Prince of Wallachia. If princess Neacsa was to marry that summer they had to move fast, as spring was on its way. Vlad introduced himself to Voivode Vladislav II that very evening.

With the ever-present threat from the all-powerful Ottomans, leaders in this region welcomed any young soldiers who were ready to fight. It also helped to mention that Prince Stefan of Moldova had sent them to Wallachia to see if they could be of assistance. Vladislav clearly and rightfully trusted his nephew, as Stefan meant him no harm.

The next day Vlad brought more of his men in for a training session. The point of this was to demonstrate some of their abilities to the voivode and his army, which was pathetic. Many of the soldiers were too old and he would have been lucky to have three hundred men in all. Of course, Vladislav was impressed with the newcomers' strength and speed, which they greatly reduced in order to appear as human as possible.

After a long day with the soldiers Prince Dracul invited Vlad and Sergiu to dine with him. The prince was an older man with a grey beard and a kind face. He now wore his simple gold crown, as this was a time for more formal evening attire.

"Your Majesty, if I may? Your army is in need of much work," Vlad ventured.

"Is that so, young man?" His expression made it clear that he thought Vlad was entirely too young to offer any sound advice.

"Please, Sire, do not be fooled by his youthful appearance. He is a very skilled fighter with more experience than you can imagine," Sergiu interjected.

Prince Dracul gestured for Vlad to continue.

"If you would allow me to, Sire, I could make your army great. The first order of business would be to replace about half of them with young, more able-bodied men. Then they need to be trained daily to build muscle and stamina. It appears that they mostly sit about, at this point. My men are some of the best because we train daily with every type of weapon available. Some of your men do not even know how to hold their swords properly. Such techniques I am able to teach them. Allow me to work with your army for one month. I will show you such improvements that you may decide to make me your ... " Vlad almost said son-in-law but caught himself, "your chief commanding officer."

Prince Dracul studied him for a moment. "You are well spoken. I can tell you have had an excellent education."

"Yes, of course. Are not all nobles well educated?" Vlad replied.

"Well *most* nobles anyway. You can lead a man to war but you cannot make him fight." The old voivode laughed, though Vlad did not see the humor.

Prince Dracul cleared his throat before continuing, "You are also well trained in the art of combat. Such a combination can be difficult to find in one man. I do not doubt that you know what you are talking about." Then he frowned. "I have not been able to bring myself to replace some of the older men. They are loyal and they fought beside me at one time. So I keep them on. I do not like the thought of letting them go. How will they support their families without the soldiers pay?"

It would be dreadful to have to get rid of my most favored men. Vlad was grateful that he did not have this problem. As vampires, his men did not grow too old to fight. "Rulers must make difficult decisions. You must think of your people first. If Wallachia were attacked your current army could not defend this land and protect your subjects."

Prince Dracul looked grave as he turned to Sergiu. "You are quite right. Vlad is wise beyond his years."

Sergiu smiled. "You have no idea. You should give him a chance. He will transform your army."

"So be it. After one month's time I will assess the progress of my army."

CHAPTER 40 WALLACHIA 1455 AD

Prince Dracul's commander in chief did not like it that Vlad was given permission to temporarily take command of the Wallachian army — if one could call it an army. The very next day Vlad discharged half the soldiers; if they were too old or too fat, they were told to find other employment. Abdullah began a rigorous training routine with the hundred and fifty or so soldiers who remained. Meanwhile, Vlad set about advertising for new recruits. Only the youngest and strongest would be selected to replace the old and worthless soldiers.

When Abdullah returned from a long distance run with the remaining army, the men were winded and heaving terribly. Some looked as if they might collapse entirely. Yet still others took even longer to return, as they could not keep up. Abdullah, who was breathing normally said, "We have our work cut out for us here, Master."

"Aye, this is worse than I thought," Vlad said.

That night Vlad announced that they were to receive extra portions of meat. Sergiu seemed to think that this would help to build young men's strength. Vlad did not question this as his companion was always right about such matters. Vlad knew nothing of human nutrients and Sergiu had read every medical book he could get his hands on.

The soldiers cheered at this news. Then Vlad announced that their portions of wines, ales and meads would be reduced. This brought about a round of loud protests.

"Who are you to show up here from God knows where with your goddamned Ottoman henchman?" one man hollered. "You can't expect to walk in here and change everything we have done for years. You cannot take away our drink. We will not stand for it."

The men looked to Vlad to see what he would do.

Vlad's eyes narrowed at the insolent man, he placed one hand on the dirk that was always at his side. In less than the blink of an eye, he had thrown the long knife deep into the man's chest. It took all Vlad's effort to control his temper. With clenched fists, he swiftly leapt onto the table in front of him as the protester's body fell to the floor.

"To test me — to see what kind of a leader I am — is one thing. I had expected that; but to insult Abdullah is another matter entirely. Abdullah is my seraskier." Vlad used the Turkish word for commander-in-chief in order to provoke the men. He was taunting them, as he wanted to push them to their limits. This matter had to be settled at once. "Does anyone else here have a problem with Abdullah?"

No one dared to breathe. They stared at Vlad with wide eyes.

"Good. Now if any of you do not like my rules then by all means — go." Vlad swung his arm gesturing toward the door. "I will have only men who are willing to work hard to defend Wallachia in this army. If you prefer the old days where you sat about drinking all day and collected your pay each week for nothing, then you need to leave at once. Those days of leisure are over. I will build a *real* army, one that will actually be capable of defending this great land. I have no room for lazy drunkards amongst my ranks. Does anyone wish to leave?"

A few men stood and headed for the door. "Good. Anyone else? This is your only chance to get out."

Some of the men looked nervous but no one else left.

"Now get some rest. Your training starts at dawn." Under his breath so only vampires could hear, Vlad told Abdullah, "Kill them. Make it look as if it were an accident."

"Gladly, Master." Abdullah gracefully followed the men who had recently left the room. He had taken the man's insult about being an Ottoman henchman to heart and was angered by the others who chose to desert the army.

ANY YOUNG MEN willing to join the Wallachian army had to prove themselves. They had to be able to run long distances without stopping. Those who could not were sent home. Next Vlad designed a series of tests like those his father organized for the annual Ludus tournaments. Only the men who could throw a cannon shot or a spear the farthest were sworn in as new Wallachian soldiers. This created an army that was physically more capable, though they all needed much training in weapons and warfare.

Vlad became absorbed in his new occupation and hardly thought about his original goal.

Sergiu had to remind him. "What about Princess Neacsa? When will you inquire about her?"

Vlad looked up from a training schedule he had been poring over. "Yes, of course. Tomorrow Prince Dracul will see his new army. Once he sees what I have accomplished, then I can turn my attention to his daughter. It is best not to appear overly interested in her anyway."

"Well played. You know — if I did not know better — I would say you are really enjoying yourself. You are a natural at leading armies. It almost appears that you would rather work with the army than pursue the princess."

Sergiu's sarcastic tone was not lost on Vlad. "Yes, well pretending to be a silly love-struck young man again is not an appealing thought. This is easy, simple ... clear. Women are anything but."

This brought about a good laugh from Sergiu. "I have taught you well."

CHAPTER 41 WALLACHIA 1455 AD

The voivode was thrilled with his new army. Over three hundred young and able men stood in perfect unison with their swords resting against their right shoulders. They stared forward unflinching. There were no fat bellies hanging over the belts of uniforms and no more grey hair.

"Their training is going well, Your Majesty," Vlad said. "Their strength and stamina increase every day with my training regimen. They will soon be the most excellent bowmen and swordsmen around. That is, if they remain under my tutelage."

Prince Dracul nodded and moved to walk amongst his men — inspecting them. He stopped to stare at some of the finer-looking men for a bit too long.

Sergiu glanced at Vlad with wide eyes. They were both thinking the same thing; *the prince may have an eye for men.*

"That might explain why he has only produced one heir," Vlad whispered so that only Sergiu would hear.

Sergiu chuckled. "Aye and you had best be warned, as every time he refers to you he calls you Vlad the Handsome."

"Oh no."

Sergiu laughed more loudly this time and had to stop himself when nearby men turned toward him to see what could possibly be funny in this serious situation.

When the voivode returned from his "inspection" of the men, he placed his hand on the old commander in chief's shoulder. "I dread to inform you, old friend, that you are relieved of your duties. Vlad the Handsome will be the head of my army from this day forth."

The old man slumped under this news and exited the training field without a fight or even a word of protest. After all, there was no way he could argue that the army had been better under his command.

Sergiu had not been jesting, as Vlad had hoped; the voivode did indeed call him "the Handsome." Vlad glared at Sergiu who laughed in return. Vlad hoped that that moniker would not take hold.

After much praise from Prince Dracul, Vlad said, "Thank you, Sire. You have chosen the best man for the job. I will not fail you."

"I know you won't."

"The next step in building your army is to increase your numbers. Three hundred humans — I mean men, is not enough. We need more."

"I fully agree. However, there is no money for more troops, as I must pay Sultan Mehmed his annual tribute."

"Why do you pay your enemy?"

"I have no choice, my dear boy. We are but a small country, we will never have the manpower or wealth to be able to take on the infinite resources of the Ottoman Empire."

"*Not* paying the tribute, and using the money to build your army is a good start," Vlad protested. Anger was rising inside at the cowardly ruler who wasted his time trying to make the countries around him happy. Prince Dracul paid the annual tribute to keep peace on his southern border and continually told Hungarian leaders what they wanted to hear. Dracul worked to convince them that he was not on the Ottomans' side. All of this told Vlad that the voivode was a weak ruler who would not stand up for Wallachia.

"You still have much to learn about politics, young man. I have no choice but to pay the sultan," the voivode said.

"With all due respect, Sire, there is always a choice."

"I will not allow the Ottomans to destroy this land over a simple issue of tax. Keeping the Ottomans pacified is the wise thing to do, especially when they ask so little of us. We are allowed to keep our faith and govern ourselves as long as we pay an affordable amount of gold coins each year. He also requires young boys to train for his army. I have plenty of people who offer their sons up to the sultan. Under him they acquire a good education and can rise through the ranks in the sultan's army. A boy who is skilled and proves his worth could become the Grand Vizier. There is much opportunity for these young men in the Ottoman army — opportunities I cannot offer them. Leave the politics to me and you focus on training my men."

"Of course, Your Majesty," Vlad said through gritted teeth. Not only was Vladislav providing the enemy with men for an army but he was also helping to *fund* that army. This was the most idiotic thing Vlad had ever heard.

At a feast that night Prince Dracul announced to everyone that Vlad was his new Commander in Chief, thus making it official.

With a nudge from Sergiu, Vlad reluctantly broached the subject of the princess. "I was told you have a daughter, Neacsa; she never joins us for the evening meals. Why is it that we never see her?"

Prince Dracul sighed. "She is a difficult one. She refuses to leave her bedchambers since I announced that she was to marry the prince of Albania. She takes all her meals in her room. She never wanted to marry. When she was younger I did not mind putting off marriage. She seemed too young anyway. But now I worry that she is too old. What young prince would want to marry an old princess? So I told her that marriage could not be postponed any longer. She has refused to speak to me ever since. I don't really blame her — the Albanian prince is a barmy little fellow. But I have no other options. There have been no other suitors to come forward. I worry for the future of the Wallachian throne."

Vlad could clearly see the story of this man's life. Every day he was faced with nothing but poor options. He believed that all he could ever do was choose the lesser of the evils that lay before him. Vlad actually felt for him. *What a wretched existence.* As a vampire Vlad's life was limitless and yet the prince's was nothing but limited. This was to

Vlad's advantage, as all he had to do was offer him a better option. "Well, why don't you allow her to meet me? Perhaps I could change her mind about marriage."

"You would be willing to marry my daughter?"

Vlad nodded yes, keeping his face serious. He tried to appear as if it was a sacrifice he would be willing to make. He did not want to seem overly zealous.

"Ah, you say that now but wait until you meet her. She is ... challenging to say the least. I don't know what to do with her."

Vlad's eyebrows raised with intrigue.

After a thoughtful pause the voivode added, "Nevertheless, it would not hurt to give it a try. Perhaps she will take a liking to you."

Dracul looked at Vlad with a stare that made Vlad uncomfortable. It was a look that Vlad had received from many women but never a man.

"If anyone can convince her to marry it would be you," Prince Dracul said.

"It is settled then." Vlad excused himself as he stood to leave. The voivode's interest in him was concerning.

CHAPTER 42 WALLACHIA 1455 AD

The very next morning Vlad was summoned to the Great Hall to meet Princess Neacsa. Vlad stood to the right of Prince Dracul when from outside the large doors they heard a woman's voice, "Put me down! I will walk from here."

A rather small young lady came through the door. She kept her head down and walked straight toward her father's modest throne. The throne was a large wooden chair with a tall back that almost reached the ceiling. It had an intricately carved personal roof protruding forward — a roof only for the leader. Vlad quite liked the simple, yet elegant throne.

Neacsa bowed slightly, "Father." She took a seat on his left.

Her head remained down and turned away. This could have been taken as a sign of obedience but Vlad knew better. Her head was turned from them in defiance. He liked her, not because she was overly pretty but because she was spirited; winning her over would not be easy. This would make it fun — a challenge.

"Please, my dear, look at me. I have good news for you." Dracul spoke softly.

"The only good news you could give me is to inform me that I do not have to marry," she quickly replied.

The voivode turned his gaze to Vlad. "You see what I must put up with." She still had not looked at either of them, so her father continued, "My news is even better, as I have found a strong and handsome suitor for you. If you agree, you will not have to marry the Albanian prince. Wouldn't that be nice, dear?"

"You know that I do not wish to marry anyone. Marrying a man who does not even know me and who does not love me is a prison sentence. You might as well throw me in the dungeon now. As my husband tires of me, he will spend more and more time with his endless supply of concubines. I don't want any part of it."

"My darling, we have been through this before; love is something that develops over time. You will grow to love your husband and he you. I grew to love your mother very much, as you well remember. Please, become familiar with Vlad; you might decide you want to marry him. Most women would be elated to have such a fine suitor. I would marry him in a heartbeat ... that is, if I were you."

Neacsa shook her head, remaining unconvinced, so her father continued, "As the Princess of Wallachia it is your duty to provide heirs for the throne. If I had been blessed with any other children, I would not put this burden on you. But you are my only hope for the continuation of the Draculesti family line."

Her stubbornly square shoulders sagged a bit under her father's patient words. Guilt was clearly the best way to get through to her.

Vlad decided that it was time for him to speak, "My Lady Neacsa."

Her body shivered at the sound of his voice.

But he continued, "If it is the idea of concubines that concerns you then I will gladly give up the right to have them."

Neacsa finally raised her head to look at him for the first time. "You would do that —" Her voice had been full of amazement but when she looked into Vlad's eyes she stopped talking. Her lips parted and she slowly stood. Her stare was intense, piercing even. It was as if she could see inside Vlad. She did not see a handsome face, as so many other women had. She could easily see beyond that, as if she could see who he truly was — a killer.

Her skin was pale, her face covered in freckles, with large full lips and even larger teeth. Her eyes were the color of a rich dark honey and full of light — no, a fire. Then fear sneaked into her expression as she continued to study Vlad. She turned her wide eyes to her father, silently pleading with him. When she did not receive a response from him, she glanced around as if she were a wild animal who had been backed into a corner.

"What is it, dear?" Prince Dracul asked with concern.

Neacsa quickly decided on a course of action. She gave a slight bow to Vlad. "Please, sir, would you allow me to speak with my father ... alone?"

"As you wish, My Lady." Vlad bowed deeply before leaving. He shut the Great Hall doors behind him and rested his back against them. He was beyond curious about this mysterious woman and her strange reaction to him. He could easily hear their conversation.

"Father, that is him — the one from my vision. He has haunted me for many years. You must send him away at once! He will be the death of us."

"Please, my dear, not this nonsense again. He is a strapping young man. One of the best warriors I have ever seen. He will make a fine voivode someday. Granted he needs to be trained in proper politics but he will be a great leader and a good husband. Your children will be smart like you and strong like him. They will be able to rule Wallachia for many generations to come."

Not "proper politics" but rather, "passive politics" is what he wants to teach me. Vlad thought. Not a chance in hell. I will not be a weak ruler like this old man.

"Surely you can see it, Father. He is charming you and will use me in order to be crowned prince. Once we are of no further use to him, he will rid himself of us."

"You are correct, in that he is a determined young man who wishes to become a leader of nations. This makes him the right person to take my place but he would not hurt us, my dear."

"How can you possibly be so sure? You barely know him."

"I have known him for much longer than you and yet you are quick to condemn him."

"Did I not foresee mother's death long before she died? I saw it coming and you know this. I can see his future and ours. Why won't you believe me?"

Prince Dracul was silent for a long time. Clearly a part of him believed that there was some truth in his daughter's intuitions. "Is this dream the same as the one about your mother?"

"They are not dreams, Father. They come to me in broad daylight and yes, this vision is the same as the one I used to have about mother — just as vivid. Only there is one difference; this one changes. That mysterious suitor who only moments ago left the Great Hall, kills you in every vision. Yet, in only some of my visions he kills me as well. Other times he lets me live."

This resulted in another long thoughtful silence from the voivode. When he spoke his voice was soft. "Now, let me tell you what I know about this young man. He is what Wallachia needs. He will secure the future of this country. Either way, my wonderful daughter, I see no better option. Let us pray that your visions are misleading this time. Vlad is undoubtedly the best choice for you and for this throne. The little prince of Albania would be a weak ruler. I do not want the Danesti family to take the throne again. Vlad is strong enough to protect you and the throne. I know that he will make Wallachia great. He is more than anyone could hope for in an heir. We must do what is best for our country."

"Even if I managed to have children, there is no guarantee that they would become voivode. The throne you sit upon is not a stable one. Not with the Hungarians and Ottomans always interfering; not to mention the treacherous boyars. Each of these is a threat to your rule. They could have us killed at any time and instate whomever they deem more fit as voivode. There are forces well beyond your control that are always meddling with a secure monarchy in Wallachia."

Neacsa seemed to know a lot about local politics. Vlad felt as if he should be writing this down. *Who in the hell are the boyars?* he thought.

"Yes and Vlad will be capable of dealing with these threats. We cannot give up. If you do not have a child then there will be no one left from the Draculesti family line and the boyars will be forced to instate a member of the Danesti family as the next voivode. We must try to carry on the Dracul family name. Don't you see he is our best chance? God has sent us a gift. Honestly, dear, I can't believe you don't understand this."

"Then you have sentenced us to death."

"My mind is made up. You will marry Vlad this summer."

Vlad heard Neacsa's light footsteps as she made her way toward the Great Hall doors. Under her breath she added quietly so her father would not hear. "You are a fool, Father."

CHAPTER 43 WALLACHIA 1455 AD

Vlad disappeared, speeding past two guards and around the corner. They had given up waiting for the princess, as they were playing chess to pass the time. They barely took note of the breeze that passed over them as Vlad ran by.

Sergiu gave a slight jump as Vlad appeared behind him.

"We have a small problem," Vlad said.

"What is it?"

"Well, perhaps a big problem. It is the princess, she is a ... I have no idea what she is. She appears to have lucid visions of the future. She predicted her mother's death and now she knows that I am here to usurp the throne."

"A witch," Sergiu said under his breath.

Vlad could almost see the thoughts swirling around in that large brain of his. "There is no such thing as a witch, Sergiu. If there were, don't you think we would have seen or at least heard of one in all our years?"

"Seen — no, heard of — yes. One hears tales of witches all the time. Most are children's fairy stories. Nonetheless, the tales are common. We do not see them because they remain hidden, to avoid burning at the stake. They are not entirely unlike us in that manner. Perhaps some of them do not know they are witches. The latter is what I am assuming is the case with your little princess."

"That is absurd. She is not a witch."

"Then how else would you explain it?"

For this Vlad had no answer but he still did not believe in witches. He did not *want* to believe in them. *What would that mean? What other powers could Neacsa possess?* This was disconcerting. "Aside from this minor hitch, it appears that Vladislav is determined to have me marry his daughter, even though she adamantly refuses."

"Well, that is not ideal."

"I would say not. An unhappy bride sounds like a nightmare." Vlad was not sure what he had expected to find in Wallachia but it was not this.

Sergiu remained in deep thought and nodded in agreement.

THE REST of the spring flew by. Vlad and his men continued to work with Prince Dracul's human army. Some days were spent with Vladislav and his chamberlain. They felt that they needed to educate Vlad on how to properly run a kingdom. Most of it was a bad joke. They continually rambled on about how to make everyone happy, Hungary, the Ottomans, the boyars.

"You must play all sides. At the very least pretend to be *everyone's* ally," Prince Dracul would lecture.

Vlad quickly grew tired of this bollock and try to argue with them. They would counter, claiming that Vlad was too young to fully understand and that by the time he took the throne, when he was much older, he would be wiser and better able to understand how best to rule. This was comical as Vlad was old enough be the voivode's great grandfather many times over.

This time spent with Dracul and his top advisor was not a complete waste. Vlad did learn about the important influences that affected this region. He learned how Hungary continually wanted a Catholic ruler here and that they were forever trying to convert the

Orthodox people of Wallachia. They also wanted a ruler who was loyal to them and defiant to the Ottomans.

To Wallachia's detriment, it was located between two superpowers. It was constantly torn in two by Hungary — backed by the wealthy pope in Rome — and the ever-growing Ottoman Empire, which was now controlled by the most ambitious of the sultans ever to rule. Mehmed the Conqueror was quickly earning his moniker. These two powers constantly played tug-of-war with the Wallachian throne. They each wanted a voivode who would be loyal and yet neither wanted to have a direct border with the other. Essentially, Wallachia was all that stood between the East and the West — between Muslims and Catholics — the sultan and the pope.

As if this were not enough there were the boyars and the Transylvanian Saxons. These were two local groups who also had a vested interest in who was on the throne. It was during these lessons when Sergiu and Vlad would pay the most attention. They had much to learn of the way things worked right here at home. The world politics of the Eastern and Western conflicts, such as the endless crusades, were known by all. Or rather, they were known by anyone who was educated. But the smaller happenings within Wallachia were only important to the people of this region.

The boyars were a group of nobles who felt that it was their right and duty to appoint the voivodes of Wallachia. They determined who was in power. They had a long history of overthrowing rulers whenever they saw fit. This could be because they were offered a pretty price from say Hungary or the Saxons, perhaps even the sultan himself. The boyars would also instate new rulers for political reasons; for example, if a ruler was viewed as too weak or too powerful. If a ruler did not step down when the boyars decreed, he was beheaded.

The boyars chose the voivodes from one of two competing royal families, the Danesti and the Draculesti family lines.

On the other hand, the Saxons were wealthy merchants from Transylvania. They relied on selling their goods in Wallachia. They had a vested interest in a voivode who would allow free trade and little to no tax paid to Wallachia. They would intervene as needed to ensure that such a ruler in this region was sympathetic to their need to make cartloads of money off the Wallachian people.

"In order to help ensure the peace and keep my head, I do not collect any tax from the Saxons on goods sold on my land. This has worked out well, as they fully support me. They are one less problem to contend with this way," Vladislav said.

Vlad forced a smile. Neacsa was right — her father was a fool. He needed that tax money to grow his pathetically small army.

"However, I have found a way to deal with the boyars," Prince Dracul continued. "As soon as you marry my daughter, I will name you voivode as well. We will rule in tandem. This way if the boyars decide to kill one of us the other has already been crowned. There will be no need for the boyars to instate a new ruler, as Wallachia will already have one. Think of it as a form of security for my line."

Perhaps he was not a complete fool, as this was an excellent solution to the problem. Not to mention it fit perfectly with Vlad's plan. When Vlad decided to fully take over the throne, he would already have been crowned prince. "That is the best idea I have ever heard, Your Majesty." Vlad's smile was genuine this time. He frowned as his thoughts strayed to Neacsa. *She is another matter entirely. What on earth will I do with her?*

CHAPTER 44 WALLACHIA 1456 AD

Vlad and Neacsa were married in June of 1456. Many of the young noble ladies and even some of the servants were envious of Neacsa's marriage. She did not feel this way. She had remained hidden in her chambers throughout the entire engagement. At the wedding ceremony she kept her head down or looked away from her father and Vlad at all times. Her full lips remained downturned; she never wavered. After the wedding she retreated quickly to her room. She sent a maid to inform Vlad that she had "fallen ill" and could not receive him. This was suitable to Vlad. While he was intrigued by her, he had no interest in sleeping with her. She may very well have been the most curious of all women. Life was easier if he left her alone and so this was what he did.

The day after the wedding, Prince Dracul crowned Vlad the second prince of Wallachia. It was announced that Vlad would rule by his side as an equal from that day forward. The boyars had all eagerly attended the royal wedding and Vlad's coronation. Vlad had made it his business to know who this boyar class was. Many looked displeased and spoke bitterly with one another about Dracul's attempt to maneuver around their power over the throne.

Over the next couple of months Vlad played the role of dual ruler. Prince Dracul insisted that he be called Vlad III. Dracul would muse that it was as if Vlad was his own son, as if Vlad had been named after him.

Vlad never saw his wife. In fact, no one but her chambermaids ever saw her. She continued to take her meals in her room.

Sergiu thought that this was the funniest thing he had ever heard. "Do you know the definition of irony?"

"Of course I know what it means," Vlad replied.

"It means ... you."

"Me? What in the world are you talking about?"

Sergiu laughed. "Irony is the fact that you spent a good portion of your life seducing married women — all the way up to the Empress, no less and now that you are finally wed you do not sleep with your own wife."

"Very amusing, Serg."

Sergiu laughed so hard it brought tears to his eyes. Vlad couldn't help smiling.

It was in September of 1456, when Vlad deemed that the time was right to take the throne for himself. It appeared that people in the castle viewed him as a legitimate ruler. He had complete control of the army. There was nothing standing in his way except for Dracul and possibly Neacsa.

When the night came, Vlad entered Neacsa's chambers through her fourth-story window. He stood silently leaning against an entryway to her large room. He watched her and her two servants as they chatted away merrily about nothing of significance. All three ladies sat on the princess's large bed. Suddenly one of them shivered and slowly turned toward Vlad. It was as if she had sensed his presence. She jumped when she saw him and another of the maids screamed and quickly stood.

"What is the matter?" Vlad asked. "Doesn't a man have the right to visit his wife's chambers?" Vlad stepped forward and one of the maids wrapped her arms protectively around Neacsa.

"Leave us." His voice was dark.

"What are you going to do?" one of the maids asked.

"You are rather brazen ... for a servant. Get out, before I have my guards remove you."

Neacsa wrapped an arm around each of her maids and whispered for them to leave. "I do not want anything to happen to the two of you, so do as he says." She kissed each of their cheeks.

The maids reluctantly left. Neacsa remained seated on her bed. She pulled a plush fur throw up to her neck to hide her body.

"Don't worry. I'm not here for that. If I had wanted that I would have visited here much sooner. Though perhaps you should try it. You might find you like it," Vlad gave her a wicked smile.

"Men are swine. They could never please me as my servants do. Women know what other women want."

"That explains a great deal. What is it they say about the apple not falling far from the tree? You, like your father, fancy the same sex."

Neacsa scowled. "At least do me the honor of sparing me the small talk. Have you decided to kill me?"

"I hope not. You see, I rather like you —"

"You don't even know me," she snapped.

Vlad smiled. *She is indeed feisty*. "I have been around women enough to know that you are different. You are unnaturally insightful and there is a fire inside that burns strong. You will grow to become a very intelligent woman. It would be a shame to waste that. I came here to ask you one question. That is it — only one tiny little question. I want you to answer it carefully and honestly. Do you think you can do that?"

Neacsa looked worried but nodded her agreement.

"Good. All I want to know is, what do *you* want?"

Her large honey-colored eyes widened. "What do *I* want?" she stated each word slowly.

"Yes, if you had the perfect life, what would it look like?" Of all the possible questions, Vlad could tell that this was not what she expected.

"I ... I don't know. No one has ever asked me that before."

"I know. Take your time, it is an important question."

This she did — her brow furrowed as she pondered what the perfect life would be like. Her defensiveness wavered. "The perfect life would be to live alone with my maids, away from all this, perhaps on a farm or in a convent. We would grow our own food and live in complete peace. There would be no men telling us what to do. We would be far away from all the death and war caused by men. No politics, no threats, only ... love and joy."

This was the answer Vlad was looking for. If she had said that she wanted power and wealth or to rule a great nation then she would be dead. Lucky for her she had answered correctly. "I could offer you such a life, one of freedom from human rules and obligations. You would have the ability to survive on your own and not have to depend on anyone. You could do as you please."

"So you have decided not to kill me. What is the price for this 'perfect life?'"

"You see, I knew you were intelligent. Yes, this life I'm offering you does come at a cost. You must leave Wallachia forever. But I will equip you with the strength and power to easily make it on your own."

"May I take my servants?"

"Servants, possessions, some money — though you won't need it. Whatever you want."

"Except for my father. He will not be coming with me, will he?"

"I'm afraid it is too late for your father, my dear." Abdullah was draining the old voivode of life as they spoke.

There was a sadness in her eyes but she did not cry. She had known this day was coming. She had seen it long ago. Her father had been as good as dead since the day he declared that she had to marry Vlad.

"I want it — this life you are offering me." Neacsa's voice was soft and solemn. Like her father she was resigned to her fate.

"Are you certain?"

She nodded.

Vlad appeared next to her bed.

She jumped at his sudden movement.

"All you have to do is drink." He placed one hand on her upper chest and firmly lowered her torso into the pillows. He bit deep into his free wrist and held it over her head.

Neacsa's tiny freckled nose wrinkled. "I have to drink your blood?"

"If you want your perfect life then, yes, you must drink."

Her lips parted and she let Vlad's blood drip into her mouth. Her face scrunched at the horrible taste. She tried to sit and spit it out but he held her down. Soon the fire that was Neacsa was out. Vlad's part was done. He left to see how Abdullah had fared.

Sergiu would be there when Neacsa woke. New vampires were his specialty. He would see to it that she fed from an old slave or the like. Then he would help her with the transition and make the arrangements for her to leave as soon as she was ready.

Sergiu reported that the first couple of days of Neacsa's transition were challenging; the difficulty mostly manifested in the form of her deep hatred of Vlad. She did not attend her father's funeral service. Vlad announced that she had come down with a terrible sickness and could not leave her chambers. Within one month she was ready to head into exile. She had decided to turn her maids in order not to risk killing them. They gladly drank her blood in order to accompany her. Vlad doubted that there had ever been maids more loyal than hers.

Sergiu recounted that at times she appeared thrilled about the prospects of her new life. This was most likely due to Sergiu's silver tongue, convincing her of all the possibilities. He was wonderful about cleaning up Vlad's messes. This was something that Vlad did not take for granted. He knew full well that he would have been utterly lost without Sergiu by his side.

Vlad thought it best for Neacsa to give a speech before she left. This would make things appear normal. The speech was added as part of the negotiations of her leaving. She addressed the boyars and the people of Targoviste with a heartfelt speech about her decision to become a nun and how it would be difficult to leave her people but that God had called her to His service. It went without saying that she must obey God above all else. She stated that while Vlad would miss her he also supported her decision and promised to visit when he could. It was sweet. The people loved it. They cheered for their princess as she and her faithful servants were escorted out of town in a royal carriage.

That was it. Vlad was left with the Wallachian throne to himself. After all those years he had finally achieved his dream. He was now Voivode Vlad III of the Draculesti family. Prince Dracula — of the Dragon.

CHAPTER 45 WALLACHIA 1456 AD

As Vlad had already learned, the Wallachian crown came with many problems, each of which had to be dealt with in turn. The first order of business was the boyar class. Within a month of being the sole ruler it became apparent that the boyars were not convinced that Vlad was a legitimate ruler. They were rightfully suspicious of the relatively sudden death of Prince Dracul. Most of all, they were displeased because Dracul had taken their right to name the next ruler away from them. The boyars wanted to appoint the successor to the throne. Since they had not done so with Vlad, they viewed him as an illegitimate usurper of the throne. There were murmurs of replacing him with Dan, a man born of the noble line of the Danesti family.

"We must deal with these boyars. A group of nobles who feel that it is their right to put whomever they choose on the throne are dangerous," Vlad mused. "They have learned to turn a substantial profit by being ruthless and playing politics. They are nothing more than paid assassins and traitors to the throne."

"They appear to be the most immediate threat to your rule." Sergiu agreed. "I wonder how many rulers of Wallachia they have murdered? The Ottomans can be pacified with their annual tribute of gold coins and boys for the sultan's army. The Saxon merchants in Transylvania will hopefully be pacified with a low sales tax for now. But the boyars — they are a different story."

Vlad nodded. "We will deal with each of these threats in order of importance. The boyars will be easy enough to handle, unlike the Ottomans. We will start by inviting the boyars to a feast at my government compound in Targoviste. Tell the Janissaries that if it does not go well then they will be the ones feasting." Vlad had long since adopted the term Janissaries to refer to his elite corps of soldiers. In his kingdom Janissaries meant Vlad's loyal vampire warriors.

"I will inform them that they must hold off on feeding until this gathering," Abdulla said.

"We will make an example of these nobles. This is what happens if one dares to cross me."

Now that Vlad had become ruler, he was not about to let anything get in the way of his throne. He had worked hard for this for many years. It had been a long time coming, which led Vlad to develop a sense of entitlement. *I deserve this. Wallachia is mine.*

"There are more diplomatic means of solving problems. Must we kill them all?" Sergiu questioned.

"Aye but killing is the surest and easiest means. Especially for vampires, who must kill to survive. This way I eliminate a threat and feed my bloodthirsty men."

Sergiu frowned. "Aye, it must be done."

VLAD PUT on a feast suited for kings. The Great Hall was packed with fifty members of the noble boyars, which included most of their immediate family members. They were all too happy to grow even more fat on Vlad's endless supply of the best wines and meats. He sat at the head of a long table. As always Sergiu sat to the right of Vlad. They ate nothing and drank wine as they listened to the nobles' private conversations. It soon became apparent that a good number of the boyars thought Vlad was a joke of a prince who would not last six months on the throne.

As the evening grew late, Vlad had heard more than enough of their side conversations. This group of men and their families were treacherous. They would sell Vlad out as soon as they saw fit — as soon as they were offered the right price. This would most likely come from Sultan Mehmed, in order to ensure they appoint someone loyal to the sultan. It could also come from the wealthy merchants of Transylvania who did not fancy paying taxes to Wallachia.

Vlad gave Sergiu a knowing nod.

Sergiu graciously excused himself as he went to inform the Janissaries that it was time to feed.

Vlad moved to the side of a beautiful young woman — one of the boyar's daughters. He took the girl's hand and gently raised her from her chair. Her cheeks turned red and she smiled shyly. He led her to the elevated floor at the far end of the Great Hall, which held Vlad's skillfully-carved wooden throne with its own private roof. The room had fallen silent at his strange behavior. Perhaps they expected a marriage proposal — some covert plan to win the boyars over, by marrying one of their beloved daughters.

Vlad took a moment to survey the room and enjoy the complete attention that he had been given. They waited patiently to see what he would do. Grabbing the young girl by the waist he pulled her close and lowered his head to the nape of her neck. He took a deep breath. The sweet smell of young blood flowing just beneath the soft skin made his fangs grow. He had not fed in well over a month and he instantly lost control.

The girl tried to push Vlad away in an attempt to save her modesty. A terrible scream came from her as he bit deep into her neck. Blood streamed from the wound, turning her cleavage crimson. Vlad could hear the crowd as they panicked but there was no stopping him and no escape. They were surrounded by hungry vampires. When the girl's body went limp in his arm he let her fall to the ground. Raising both arms upward, he gave his men the signal to feast. The screams rang in his ears long after every human in the room was dead and his men's lust for blood was satisfied.

"Not entirely discreet, My Lord," Abdullah observed.

"No need for that when there are no survivors." Then to his men Vlad commanded, "Impale the men's bodies. Put them on display in the front courtyard. Everyone must see what the penalty for treason is under my rein."

This the men did without question. As the bodies were dragged from the room Vlad noticed that Sergiu was nowhere in sight. This was not his scene. He knew it was a smart political move, yet his heart was not in it. That was what Vlad admired most about Sergiu — he was practical, smart and yet still caring, even as a vampire.

CHAPTER 46 WALLACHIA 1456 AD

The next order of business was the Germanic Saxons. A letter was sent to the leaders in Sibiu informing them of the tax that must be paid for the goods they sold on Vlad's land. They were invited to his compound in Targoviste in order to discuss this issue. Surely the news of the boyars' ill fate had reached them and they wisely declined the offer to attend a feast in Vlad's Great Hall. Their refusal was also an unofficial rejection of his proposed sales tax.

"I will not be defied and made a fool of by these Saxons. They grow fat off of my people and then refuse to pay even a nominal tax," Vlad said.

"Not to mention they are most likely plotting to replace you with a leader who will be sympathetic to their business needs. They have a reputation for such treachery in the past," Sergiu added.

"We will pay them an unexpected visit." Vlad issued a devious smile.

About one month after the slaughter of the boyar class Vlad and his entourage headed to Sibiu. Sibiu was a strategic place for the Saxon merchants. They could control the trade routes to surrounding areas from there. It was, for all intents and purposes, their headquarters.

In order to keep up their human pretenses Sergiu, Cosmin and Costel rode with Vlad to Sibiu. They pushed the horses hard as they made their way through the Carpathian Alps. Vlad's Janissaries were to meet them there in case negotiations failed. Feeding his hungry men was a constant worry. If he could use their need to feed to take care of his enemies then this was a suitable solution to both problems.

As they rode toward Sibiu it dawned on Vlad that this was as close to Ludus as he had been since the dreadful day Vallachia turned him. Riding a horse was slow and incredibly boring. He tried to focus on the task at hand but his mind would wander home, time and time again. He thought of his family ... but mostly he thought of Vallachia. Soon he would be able to win her back. The thought of her by his side as his wife drove him forward.

The four travelers received a warm welcome. They were seated with the leader at a table of honor in the Great Hall and food and drink were brought in. The wine tasted odd so Vlad did not drink much. The Saxon leader kept encouraging them to drink more.

"Offer us some decent-tasting wine — then perhaps we would drink," Vlad replied.

The man issued a twisted smile. "That is because I have poisoned your goblets with a highly potent mixture. You will all be dead within the hour."

That must have been a cue, for a man entered the room. The man moved to stand by the Saxon leader. The leader continued, "You remember Dan of the Danesti family?"

Vlad's poised smile never left his face. "Aye, I have heard of you."

"Of course you have," Dan replied. "Because, unlike you, I was born of royal blood and that makes me the rightful ruler of Wallachia. You see, after you are dead, my comrades here will declare me as the ruler of Wallachia. Then we will end this nasty squabbling over taxes, as I understand that my dear Saxon friends cannot afford to pay taxes to both Wallachia and Hungary." Dan was clearly pleased with himself.

Vlad nodded to Sergiu, who knew that it was time for their men to lay waste to this modest castle. Sergiu stood to leave.

"And where do you think you are going?" Dan said, as two guards moved toward Sergiu.

"I have drunk too much wine — poisoned wine at that. I must relieve myself. Unless you would rather I do it here." Sergiu gestured to the floor in front of him.

With a wave of Dan's hand Sergiu was escorted out by the guards.

Vlad stood from the long table and moved slowly toward Dan and the Saxon leader. "What you two traitors fail to understand is that we are immune to your pathetic poisons." Vlad forced his fangs to grow. He wanted to see the fear in their eyes when they realized that there was a monster amongst them. He wanted to watch their reaction as they realized that it would be their last moments — not his.

In a flash, he sank his teeth into the neck of the Saxon. When his body became unseeing and unmoving he turned to where Dan had been — but he was gone. Vlad spun around to Cosmin and Costel. "Where did he go?"

"He ran off that way, Master."

"Well, don't just sit there! After him!"

The twins disappeared. Vlad's Janissaries filed into the Great Hall led by Abdullah and Sergiu.

"You have my permission to ransack this town," Vlad announced. "Start with the people in this castle. After you have had your fill impale the bodies outside the front gates. You may take whatever spoils you find as a reward. Do not leave anyone alive who has seen what you truly are."

Vlad's hungry men moved out at once and the screaming began.

"Dan's plan was rather clever. It may have worked had we been human," Sergiu observed.

"Aye and Cosmin and Costel may be too obedient. They must be told what to do at every turn; otherwise they do nothing. They cannot think for themselves."

"I do not doubt this but why bring it up now?"

"They let Dan get away."

"Oh no," Sergiu breathed.

"I sent them after Dan. He will not get far."

When the twins returned their heads hung low. "We lost his scent, My Lord."

Vlad issued a frustrated yell. "He is a mere human, you imbeciles! He could not simply disappear into thin air." Vlad sped out of the door from which Dan had left. He followed his scent, with Sergiu, Cosmin and Costel at his heels. The twins were right. Dan's scent faded away in the middle of the hallway not far from the Great Hall. Vlad looked up and then studied the walls. "There must be a secret passage around here somewhere." Vlad pointed to the wall. "Look here; the mortar between these stones is missing."

"There must be a way to open it." Sergiu began pressing on nearby stones.

Vlad worked his fingers into the gap between the stones. He pulled with all his might but the secret door barely moved. "Help me, you fools," he said over his shoulder to the twins. With their help the door moved more but it was still hung up on something — its hinges, no doubt.

A small stone easily slid into the wall when Sergiu pressed it and the door opened the rest of the way on its own. Dan's scent was stronger in the secret passageway.

"Now follow him." Vlad pointed into the dark musty opening behind the door. "This is your chance to fix your mistake. I want Dan's head on a silver platter. Do you understand?"

"Yes, Master."

"Of course, Master."

The two brothers disappeared into the dark opening. Vlad's breathing was heavy. The anger overwhelmed him. Dan and the Saxons trying to overthrow him — Cosmin and Costel's incompetence — it was almost too much for Vlad.

Sergiu placed a firm hand on Vlad's shoulder. "Everything will be fine. The boys will not let you down again."

Vlad's tense shoulders slowly relaxed under Sergiu reassuring touch and he was able to take a deep cleansing breath and think again. "I plan to take control of Sibiu. Send for my chamberlain in Targoviste. He will be stationed here with twenty, no, better make it thirty human guards to patrol the city. Give him two Janissaries as well, to make sure he stays safe. From here he can better control the trade routes and the taxes. As long as we pay taxes to Hungary for goods sold on their land then they should not worry themselves too much with what we do here. Now we will be able to collect taxes for goods sold in Wallachia."

Sergiu looked impressed. "That is an excellent idea. As long as we are fair with the taxes and King Mathias of Hungary still gets his sums of money from the Saxons he should not blink an eye. He has larger problems that demand his attention. What of the pillaging of Sibiu?"

"My men deserve it. I will allow them the traditional three days of pillage," Vlad said.

Sergiu frowned.

CHAPTER 47 SIBIU 1456 AD

"Where are Cosmin and Costel?" Vlad paced in the Great Hall of the Saxons' small castle. The brothers had been gone for the better part of an entire day. "I should have gone with them. Surely Dan would not be able to harm them." Vlad felt sick at the thought that something terrible might have happened to them. "I should not have been so hard on them."

Vlad looked to Sergiu for reassurance but Sergiu looked worried and simply shrugged. Vlad continued to pace. It seemed like ages passed before the tall doors to the Great Hall flew open and in marched the twins.

"Oh, thank God," Vlad mumbled under his breath.

Cosmin knelt down on one knee and from behind his back he presented a bloody head on a silver platter.

"My dear boys, you succeeded! I never should have doubted you." Vlad laughed and the brothers smiled proudly. "I did not literally mean 'on a silver platter.' It is a figure of speech — but I appreciate the gesture. What took you so long to track down a human?"

"Dan had made his way to Timpa Hill. We slowly followed his scent. It was fortunate that we let him reach his destination because he led us to his family and a number of his followers. We killed every last one of them and burned his fortress. Of course, the bodies are impaled in the courtyard."

"My boys, you did well. Tonight we celebrate!" He turned to Abdullah and handed him the silver platter with its gory contents. "Skewer Dan's head on a spear outside the front gates."

THE FOLLOWING day Abdullah came to Vlad and announced that some of the men had found gifts in the city that they wished to bestow upon their master. Two Janissaries entered with a group of terrified women. Their hands were bound in front of them and the ropes went around each of their waists tying the women together. They were shuffled into the Great Hall in single file. Otherwise they looked unharmed.

One of the soldiers bowed to Vlad and announced, "Master, these are some of the best women in Sibiu. We would like you to have them as a gift. The start of your harem, if you so desire."

Vlad forced a smile. His Janissary meant well. "Thank you for the gesture." Vlad sat down hard on Dan's throne and rubbed his face with both hands.

All rulers in the region had the right to have concubines. Sultans were rumored to maintain hundreds of women in their harems. Vlad chuckled. How do they find the time? I have been completely consumed since I became the Prince of Wallachia. I have not had a second to think about women, save Vallachia. Let alone be with one. Concubines are a large expense — one I do not need. They required at least one servant each to tend to their every need. This would mean a lot of extra food, drink, extravagant clothes, not to mention eunuchs to guard them day and night. Where would I find eunuchs?

Vlad sighed. The idea of maintaining concubines was overwhelming. They would be an added worry and quite costly, neither of which he needed at this time. His Janissary looked concerned that Vlad did not like his offering.

Vlad managed to smile. "Again, thank you for the generous offer. You could very well have kept such beauties for yourself." Vlad stood began to untie the women. "This is no way to treat ladies of the court. They are royalty now."

One of the women actually smiled at Vlad with gratitude when he freed her hands. She was quite tall with long flaxen hair. Her bright blue eyes held his for a moment. *Perhaps having concubines would not be so bad after all.* "You are safe," he whispered to the blonde. Then more loudly he added, "All of you are safe."

Vlad turned to his Janissary. "See to it that they make it to Targoviste. Keep them safe and comfortable at all times. Their every need should be met. It is your duty to make sure these women find their way to my compound. They are not to be harmed in any way."

"Of course, Master." He appeared relieved that Vlad had accepted his princely gifts.

Once the women had filed out of the Great Hall, Vlad let out another sigh. Sitting back on the throne he placed his face in his hands. He could feel Sergiu's stare. Without looking up he said, "What?"

"I'm afraid the pressures of ruling are getting to you, Master."

"No, not you, Serg. You do not call me that. There are seemingly endless political issues to deal with and now this unnecessary distraction. Providing for numerous women is not an appealing thought."

"You are new to this. You will get used to the burdens of being in command. You also may become accustomed to having many women at your disposal. They may be a pleasant and much-needed distraction from all the politics. At least this way you will have women of your own and you can leave other men's wives alone. Not to mention, you do not have to marry any of them. It is rumored that Mehmed has close to six hundred women in his harem."

"Six hundred! How can anyone afford six hundred women? That sounds like a nightmare."

Sergiu laughed. "I'm afraid I have to agree with you, my friend. Having hundreds of mysterious creatures to care for and tend to is not something I would want to try."

"One of them was still a child, not a woman."

"She will grow."

Vlad frowned. "And in the meantime, what does one do with her?"

"Nothing. You will do nothing but wait for her to develop into womanhood."

Vlad nodded. *That poor child should not be a concubine. She should be running free with her friends, climbing trees — falling out of them.* This stream of thought reminded him of the time Vallachia fell and broke her arm as a child. A smile crossed Vlad's face — of course when it happened, he had been panicked but now it was a fond memory. He had struggled to carry her all the way to town. He took her straight to Sofia, who fixed her up in no time. Vallachia had had a wonderfully normal childhood. He felt a twinge of sadness. *Not all girls have it so easy.* He was thinking about his new young concubine.

"If Mehmed, as a mere human, can manage the world's most powerful armies, the largest harem to ever exist, not to mention his unorthodox fancy for young boys, surely you can manage a handful of concubines," Sergiu declared.

"Little boys?" Vlad gave a shiver at the thought, which caused Sergiu to laugh. Vlad was already sick at the thought of little girls, now little boys! "If Mehmed can manage all that then I *will* succeed."

"That is the spirit, my friend!" Sergiu said.

Vlad stood and paced — it helped him focus. "We have dealt with the traitors at home. Now that these threats in the north have been subdued, we will turn our attention to the threats in the south."

Sergiu's eyes widened and his smile faded. "You are certain about this — you will take on the Ottoman Empire?"

"No. I will take on that simple perverted human of a sultan ... Mehmed. This will require more planning and preparation. We will have to be smart." Vlad's mind raced with thoughts of all the work to be done. Walls needed to be rebuilt to withstand the Ottomans' superior cannon fire. In fact, Mehmed had the world's best artillery. His cannons could fire one hundred pounds of steel over one mile. That was how he had managed to conquer Constantinople. Vlad would need to build both of his armies, vampire and human.

That was when it dawned on Vlad. "I will retake Constantinople," he whispered.

Sergiu's eyes grew wider and his frown deepened further.

"I refuse to be another vassal for Mehmed. I will not be a weak ruler like Prince Dracul. He wasted his time trying to pacify both Hungary and the Ottomans. Not only is this an impossible task, it is the sign of a ruler who will not stand up to his enemies. I will not make the same mistake."

"Indeed you have already proven to be quite a different ruler than your predecessor. You are much more of a dragon than he was. The name Dracula suits you," Sergiu said.

THE PILLAGING ENDED and Vlad's chamberlain was secured in the palace in Sibiu. Vlad and his men took flight that night for Targoviste. They had been gone long enough that the lack of a day or two for traveling could be easily explained. There was no need to slowly ride horses back. Vlad was more than ready to return home. While he had been away, he'd felt a constant worry about the state of affairs at home.

About half their trip was over when Vlad spotted the ruins of a castle. He dived down to get a better look. The castle had been located high on a mountainside. There were many steps leading down to the narrow river bottom.

"This was once the castle Poienari," Sergiu declared, as they landed in the ruins.

Only the walls remained, the ceilings had long since fallen in. He surveyed the steep valley. The castle was safely nestled at the end of a box canyon. No human army could reach it from the north. It could only be accessed from the narrow opening facing south. "Sergiu, you are forever telling us the story of Alexander the Great and the uncanny battle of Issus; where the few were able to hold off the many."

Sergiu had been studying the terrain as well and was thinking the same thing. "This appears to be the ideal place to hold off a hundred thousand Ottoman troops."

"Precisely. The first task for my new slaves taken from Sibiu will be to construct a fortress on this spot. It will be difficult for the sultan to get his large artillery up the narrow valley and my Janissaries will be able to keep the Ottomans from reaching this place. They will not be able to surround us with their sheer numbers or get to the women and children hidden away in the new palace. Poienari will be a haven for my court."

"An excellent plan," Sergiu agreed. "It appears that you may have been destined to lead."

"Only because of your teachings, my dear friend."

CHAPTER 48 WALLACHIA 1456 AD

Upon Vlad's return there were more problems which required his immediate attention. He was informed that the people of Wallachia were upset because he had been in office for months now and had done nothing about the crime and indigent populations of the country. With a history of unstable government and the frequent changes in leaders, the country had fallen into a state of perpetual lawlessness. People who were incapable of working were starving in the streets and theft was a common occurrence. Being surrounded by two powerful empires, namely Hungary and the Ottomans, this tiny yet strategic piece of land was in constant turmoil. This game of tug-of-war left the commoners in shambles. They were in a constant state of unrest and uncertainty about the future. This gave way to much crime and suffering. At least this was how it was explained to Vlad.

"I will not spend precious tax money on housing prisoners or welfare to the indigent. This money is needed to reinforce my compounds and build my armies," Vlad declared.

"But, Sire, the people are demanding that, as their new leader, you address these problems," the new chamberlain pleaded.

"Never fear, my chamberlain, the troubles of the people will be dealt with in the quickest and easiest fashion." *Another feast.* "Let them hate me as long as they fear me."

In one month's time, in order to ensure Vlad's men would be hungry again, another feast was held at the government compound. This time it was under the guise of feeding the poor and indigent in Targoviste. Before the feast Vlad went looking for Sergiu; he had gone missing and no one seemed to know his whereabouts. Sergiu had become quiet and distant this past month.

Vlad found Abdullah in the hall. "Have you seen Serg? I have been looking everywhere and I am beginning to worry."

"Yes, I've seen him and I have been looking for you. Sergiu Pasha asked me to give this to you." Abdullah handed Vlad a rolled piece of papyrus.

It read ...

My Dearest Friend Teller,

I am truly sorry but I cannot be a part of your feast tonight. Your actions up until now have been necessary. It is common for leaders to make examples out of their enemies. Even extremely brutal tactics are readily used by many a ruler. Rulers must make difficult decisions for the good of the masses. But what you are doing tonight is not needed. These people are not traitors or a threat to you. They are simply in your way. I fear you may be going too far — perhaps past the point of being able to return. There is good in you. I see it at times. Please do not completely lose yourself in Vlad the Impaler. Remember your humble roots. Deep down, Teller is in there somewhere. Like the Osmanlis, I'm afraid if you continue down this path of cruelty you will lose sight of who you truly are and what you truly want.

Your trusted friend, Serg.

Vlad's first reaction was to argue with Sergiu. He wanted to defend his position that tonight's feast was indeed necessary. Yet there was a part of Vlad that thought Sergiu might be right. Vlad could always count on Sergiu to tell him the truth, whether he wanted to hear it or not.

Abdullah had left Vlad alone in the hallway. He must have read Vlad's reaction to the letter and decided that it was safest for him to retreat. That was wise because Vlad's frustration gave way to rage. He crushed the papyrus and punched the wall with a left and then a right fist. The stone gave way, sending cracks racing up the wall. Two holes remained where Vlad's fists had been. Sliding down the wall, he sat on the cold floor. His bleeding knuckles rested in his lap. He could no longer see what was right. It was as if he had gone blind. "I will try not to lose myself, Serg," he whispered.

NEVERTHELESS, the feast carried on as planned. Vlad fed the poor beggars of Targoviste a royal meal. It was their last supper. This was the least he could do.

After the feast Sergiu did not return. Vlad feared that he might be gone for good. He did not know what he would do without Sergiu. He required Sergiu's wisdom and counsel — his friendship. Sergiu was the Grand Vizier. The fragile hold Vlad had on Wallachia would crumble away without Sergiu's guidance. There were times when panic would overtake Vlad. He could hardly breathe without his companion at his side. It was as if his chest was being pulled apart.

Five days after the feast of the indigent population, Vlad was hard at work reviewing tax papers the chamberlain had given him to sign. Vlad preferred to work at a large desk in his bedchambers. A swoosh of air brushed over him and he looked up to find Sergiu. Vlad wanted to throw his arms around him but refrained. Instead he leaned back in his chair and smiled.

"Truce?" Sergiu asked.

"I count on you to always tell me the truth, Sergiu."

Sergiu gave a weak smile. "I thought that was my job. Some sultans would have killed their Grand Viziers for writing such a letter."

"Yes, well I am not the sultan, now am I?"

"Thankfully, you are not."

CHAPTER 49 WALLACHIA 1456 AD

The criminal population was dealt with the following month — feeding time. Vlad issued a decree to his Janissaries. From that day forward they were to feed on the criminal populations of Wallachia. Any man accused of a crime was fair game. The only requirement was to not let people see that they were vampires. The first order of business was to empty the prisons by drinking from the occupants and then impaling the bodies in the front courtyard — as usual. Vlad sent small groups of Janissaries throughout Wallachia to track down criminals. The message was clear; Vlad would not pay for prisons and lawbreakers would be executed immediately. This sent bands of riffraff fleeing into surrounding countries, closely pursued by Vlad's men.

Six months into his reign, the chamberlain declared, "The people are singing your praises in the streets, Master."

"Is that so?" Vlad asked with genuine surprise.

"Indeed Sire, they say you have brought justice and peace to the land. Crime does not exist anymore and the people feel safe for the first time in many years. They are calling you 'the Law Giver'."

Vlad looked at Sergiu holding his arms outward with the palms up. "Well, what do you have to say about that, old friend?"

"I'll be damned."

"Pleasant unintended consequences, I suppose," Vlad added.

"Having the support of your people cannot hurt, My Lord. There was never any love lost for the boyars, who kept this country in a state of disarray with their whimsical and self-serving coups. And ridding the land of criminals has made you very popular with your subjects."

"We will see if they still support you when they hear the Ottoman War Bands marching this way." Sergiu said this quietly and in Turkish so the chamberlain would not have been able to make sense of it. Loudly he added, "So much for having your people hate you."

"Yes, Sire. It appears that most love you and the rest fear you."

"Perfect." Vlad shot Sergiu a mocking smirk.

Sergiu laughed.

WITH THINGS SECURED on the home front, as secure as possible anyway, Vlad could focus his time and money on preparing for the Ottomans. This became an obsession. All he thought about was drinking Sultan Mehmed's blood and reclaiming Constantinople. By the year's end the renovations to the Poienari Castle were complete. It was the most elegant of palaces, expanded and decorated lavishly. It was truly fit for an emperor. A tall lookout tower had been built which hung over the cliff. Far below was the river Arges. At times, to get away from it all, Vlad would spend hours alone looking out over the majestic mountains from that tower. It was calm and peaceful, unlike ruling Wallachia.

The compounds in Targoviste were more practical. The walls were enlarged around the government buildings in order to withstand the blasts of the powerful Ottoman cannons. This was done by covering the walls with tons of loose rubble. Cannon shot would be absorbed into the rubble, rendering the sultan's cannons useless or at least greatly slowing their destructive power.

Next Vlad turned his sights to Bucharest. This small town was located close to the strategic border crossing at Giurgiu. Giurgiu was situated on the Danube River and was controlled by the Ottomans. This large river was the only thing between Vlad and Mehmed. Vlad started construction of a government compound in Bucharest. This move placed his men closer to the enemy — an early warning system of sorts. They would be sure to see the Ottomans coming.

Most days were spent training new soldiers. The best of these would be turned into Janissaries but most were left as humans.

It was in the midst of this that Vlad received word from the High Court of the Elders.

This was disconcerting on a number of levels. Will they interfere with my plans to reclaim Constantinople? What if Vallachia is with them? What if she is with him? Vlad ground his teeth together at this thought. Interestingly, Vlad had not thought about her as much as he once had. Over this past year something had changed. Perhaps he had simply been too busy. Are my ambitions to overthrow Mehmed replacing my goal of winning her back? No. I must become Emperor of the Roman Empire in order to get her back. Then I will finally be worthy of her. She would not be content as a princess of Wallachia. She deserves to be an empress. Together we can make the Roman Empire magnificent once again. We will reclaim the lands that rightfully belong to us. Vlad pictured the two of them ruling side-by-side from the mighty thrones of the Topkapi Palace.

Sergiu interrupted Vlad's daydream. "How shall we respond to their request to visit?"

"Well, at least I finally have their attention."

"Yes," Sergiu said. "Now that your armies are large and we have come out of hiding, we have gained the interest of our kind. Not to mention, you have now made a name for yourself. They were bound to hear of us. I was curious to see who would learn of us first, the Court or Ramdasha. It appears the Court has better or perhaps more eyes reporting back to them than their enemy Ramdasha."

"Either way, we will not keep them waiting. We have nothing to hide. No humans suspect that we are vampires. Let them come. I will receive them at the Poienari Castle. I want them to see what splendor I have accomplished." Vlad stood to leave for a meeting with Prince Stefan of Moldova. The prince was now a trusted comrade; in fact, he was one of the few humans Vlad fully trusted. They were united in the fight against Mehmed. Since Vlad had married into Stefan's family, Stefan referred to Vlad as his cousin.

"Is that it? Teller, this is what we have been working toward all these years. The Lady Vallachia will most likely be coming to you. This was your goal all along. The end prize."

"I'm not ready. I am not powerful enough for her." Vlad headed for the door.

"Teller, please wait —"

"Stop calling me that!" Vlad was not dim. Sergiu only called him Teller when he wanted to remind Vlad of where he came from, of being human. This was something Vlad had all but forgotten or wanted to forget. As a human, Teller was nobody; now he was royalty, Voivode Vlad III, a ruler of lands.

"I must ask a favor of you ... a small one," Sergiu said.

Vlad stopped.

"Thank you. Answer me one question; are you 'not powerful enough for her' or for *you*?"

Vlad narrowed his eyes. "I don't have time for your riddles Sergiu." *What did he mean by that anyway?*

Sergiu let out a frustrated moan and Vlad was off to meet with his "cousin."

CHAPTER 50 WALLACHIA 1457 AD

After the dreadful meeting with Vallachia and the Court, Vlad sat on the grand terrace overlooking the mountains and the Arges river far below. He had gone numb, his eyes were open but unseeing.

He heard footsteps behind him but still did not move. Perhaps he would never move. He could simply become a statue — forever. Sergiu took a seat beside him. He had wisely given Vlad plenty of time to calm down after Lady Vallachia's visit.

"Well, that was disastrous."

Vlad nodded in agreement.

"Would you mind explaining what happened to you back there?"

"I'm not sure. It was her touch. It made me lose control. When she took my hand I saw ... children, our children. I suppose it was the family we would have had if we had remained mortal. And the sensation ... the shock." He did not have the words.

Sergiu studied Vlad with concern. "That confirms it — you have gone completely mad."

Yet the children had appeared vivid in Vlad's mind, a boy and a girl about eight or nine years of age. They resembled him with olive skin and dark hair but they had Val's large bright blue eyes. *They were chil-*

dren who would never come to be. Vlad shook his head to get rid of the image of the beautiful children — his children. There was a sorrow that threatened to consume him, so he forced his thoughts elsewhere. "Not to mention, I was fuming from the onset." Vlad clenched his jaw and fists. "I would greatly enjoy ripping that oversized guard of hers to shreds."

"And why do you think that is?" Sergiu gave him a knowing look.

"I have no idea. But you seem to have an opinion on the matter."

"Perhaps it is because Riddick reminds you of yourself? And he is close to her."

"Or perhaps you are the one going mad," Vlad spat.

"Very well, fair enough. What are you going to do now?" Sergiu was wisely changing the subject.

"I have ruined my only chance to be with her. She will never forgive me and she has her men. She does not need me." Vlad paused for a moment, not wanting to say this out loud. "The greatest problem is that I'm not worthy of her. You saw her, she is pure and virtuous, nothing like me."

Sergiu eye's brightened with a sudden insight. "That explains your behavior in the Great Hall. You were trying to make her out to be impure, like you, by insulting her —"

Vlad narrowed his eyes at Sergiu.

"Never mind, I should have kept that thought to myself. Please forgive me."

Vlad stood. He'd had enough of Sergiu's philosophical analysis. Rage boiled and churned from within. If it had been anyone else daring to speak to him in such a manner, they would be dead.

"What are you going to do?" Sergiu spoke to Vlad's back.

"Carry on with the only thing that matters — reclaiming the Roman Empire and defeating the Ottomans." Vlad heard Sergiu's disapproving sigh as he exited.

The first order of business was to have a servant send for Ilona. Over this past year she had become Vlad's Kadin — or first lady. She was the concubine who pleased him the most. He had grown to highly covet his concubines. He finally had women who were meant only for him. They were young and unwed when they became his concubines. They were diligently guarded by eunuchs. Vlad did not have to share them with anyone. All twenty of them were solely his.

Ilona, like most of the others, was elated when he called on her. A couple of them did not seem to enjoy his cold touch, so he rarely called on them. Now he needed Ilona. She would be the perfect distraction from his troubles. She resembled Vallachia in some ways. Perhaps this was another reason he favored her most. Ilona was the blue-eyed beauty from Sibiu. She was quite tall and lean, with long wavy blond hair.

VLAD MADE love to Ilona for the entire night. He had dozed off when a soft knock came at his door. He reached for a blanket to cover Ilona's naked body. She was fast asleep.

"What is it?" Vlad said as he stood to dress.

Abdullah entered and looked away modestly when he saw Ilona in bed. "Sorry to bother you, Master but we have a problem; it appears some monks have gone missing. Pasha suspects that Cosmin and Costel may have had something to do with it." Abdullah often referred to Sergiu as Pasha. Many of Vlad's Janissaries also called him by this respectful title. He was a mentor to them all.

Vlad was glad there was work to be done. This way he would not think about the horrible meeting with Vallachia yesterday. "Very well, I will head to the Great Hall at once. Gather the twins and also send for the eunuch to escort Ilona back to the women's quarters when she wakes."

With a nod Abdullah retreated. He was all too happy to leave the indecency of Vlad's bedchamber.

Vlad fastened his long chlamys at his right shoulder with a large jeweled broach fashioned as a dragon's head. He paused to smile at Ilona. His soft conversation with Abdullah had not awoken her. *Poor thing; she will have to sleep most of the day to recover from last night*. Then he was gone.

Once in the Hall he questioned the twins about the missing monks.

They remained silent with their heads down, as if they were two small boys who had been caught stealing watermelons from a neighbor's garden.

"Please, tell me you two did not kill monks." Vlad inquired.

Not looking up, Cosmin answered, "Yes, Master, we did. They came to the front entrance seeking shelter — and to proselytize, no doubt."

"No doubt," Vlad said through gritted teeth. "Need I remind you two of our mission here?" Vlad struggled to keep his voice calm. "We need Hungary on our side. If Hungarian monks turn up missing when they enter our lands, this will not help to win King Mathias's support. We need him as an ally. The Ottomans will soon attack from the south. We only have sixty trained vampires at this time. Even with our abilities and the seven hundred or so human warriors we cannot fight a hundred thousand Ottoman troops while defending our northern borders from Hungary. The downfall of many a great empire has come when they had to fight on different fronts. This divides the troops and leaders, greatly weakening strong armies. Not to mention, it would not hurt to have the Hungarian army join us in the coming fight against the Ottomans. This will not happen if we continue to kill their monks. Do you understand?" Vlad felt as if he were a lecturing schoolteacher.

The twins were silent. Vlad had lost them at some point during his diatribe. Politics was obviously beyond them, so Vlad tried another angle. "Very well. How about this; what happens when we feed off the riffraff?"

"Ah, is this a trick question, Master? Because usually nothing happens."

"Yes! Exactly my point. Nothing happens. Their disappearance often goes unnoticed. Now, what happened when I killed the empress?"

"All hell broke loose and we had to go into hiding for many years,"

Cosmin answered and Costel laughed at the memory of their time in exile.

"Correct again. You must remember that our goal here is to pretend to be human and not draw attention to our true nature. Do not ruin this for me. The point is, no more killing monks. Is that clear?"

"Yes, Master," Cosmin answered.

"Costel?" Vlad searched his face for a confirmation.

"Yes, Master. No more monks." He paused as if not wanting to anger Vlad further, then added quickly. "What about nuns?"

"No! No nuns. That does not bode well either."

"But, Master, they are so delicious. Their blood is pure unlike the drunkards, slaves or whores we must usually feed on."

Cosmin gave his lesser brother a nudge, indicating for him to shut up.

Vlad let out a frustrated groan. "The rule is simple; leave highly revered people alone."

Cosmin knew they had pushed Vlad as far as they could. He bowed. "Yes, Master." He pulled his brother out by the arm.

Once they were gone Vlad complained, "I swear, it is as if we are dealing with children at times. They are obedient to a fault but not the sharpest swords in the armory."

Sergiu and Abdullah chuckled and nodded in agreement.

"So much for my assumption that becoming a vampire increases one's intelligence," Vlad said.

"It appears that becoming a vampire only enhances what one already has," Sergiu said.

"Then apparently the twins did not have much going on upstairs to begin with," Abdullah added.

"And becoming a vampire only increased their lack of smarts," Vlad said.

The three old comrades laughed.

Sergiu redirected them to the matter at hand. "We can send word to King Mathias that we found evidence that the monks were indeed foreign spies posing as holy men."

That was an excellent idea, Vlad thought. "But only if Mathias inquires about his monks. Otherwise we will not open ourselves up for accusation."

Sergiu smiled with pride. "You have come a long way. You also seem to have a knack for politics. As long as you are not plotting to take on the High Court of Elders, I suppose, I should be content — better the Ottomans over the Court."

"The Court of Elders is not my enemy." If for no other reason than Vallachia is one of them, Vlad thought.

"For that I am grateful," Sergiu replied.

CHAPTER 51 COPENHAGEN 1457 AD

Elijah's entourage flew swiftly back to Denmark after the horrible meeting with Prince Vlad of Wallachia. When they landed on Elijah's balcony, Mary gave Vallachia a quick hug and a weak smile that said she was sorry. Mary swiftly retreated, undoubtedly to check on Elizabeth. Elijah ordered the others to go to the Great Hall to update his father on all that had taken place. Elijah glared at Riddick as he left the room.

"Please, Elijah, don't blame Riddick. I commanded them to leave. It was my fault, not his," Vallachia pled.

Elijah put his arms around her. "I'm aware of that, however it is easier to be mad at him rather than you."

"That is not fair. Please don't take it out on Riddick." Val wanted to be sure to keep her promise to Riddick that she would answer to Elijah.

"I specifically ordered him not to leave your side. Yet he did and it got you into trouble," Elijah said.

Val shivered at the memory of her recent encounter with Teller. She buried her head in Elijah's chest and let his arms comfort her. "I don't understand. That was not Teller. He was out of control. At first I thought he was completely void of emotion but in actuality he was entirely controlled *by* his emotions. He had no restraint — no control. He goes wherever his feelings and desires take him." She shook her head as if that would somehow help her to understand. "He has gone mad."

Val thought of Teller's father, Ivan, for the first time in a long time. It is as if becoming a vampire brought out his father's tyrannical characteristics in Teller and amplified them tenfold. Her thoughts turned to Riddick and his lust for power when he was a younger vampire. For many years Riddick let his humanity fade — or perhaps forced it out. He cared only for power and wealth. Perhaps this is what happened to Teller as well.

"I am very sorry, Val." Elijah gazed deep into her eyes. "I truly am."

She could see that he spoke the truth. *I am hurting and it hurts him in return.*

"Your room is occupied with Mary and Elizabeth. Why don't you get some rest?" Elijah gestured to his bed.

It was all she could do to crawl into his bed. She wrapped herself tight in his chlamys and let herself slip into oblivion.

Val woke with a start to the same dream of Teller transforming into a red dragon and devouring her. *It was not entirely a nightmare, it was real,* she thought. Recent events flooded back into consciousness. *The dream makes perfect sense.*

She was surrounded by Elijah's scent, his clothes, his bed, him. It was the smell of comfort, protection and love. She could easily forget her nightmare when Elijah was near. She carefully rolled over. Elijah was still asleep, so she simply watched him. He looked peaceful in his sleep, with no trace of worry or sadness. *Elijah would never hurt me. He has always been there for me. We only want what was best for each other.* Now that she finally knew where Teller was and that it was worse than she could have ever imagined; she allowed herself to think that maybe Elijah was whom she'd been meant to be with all along. *We would be happy together. Maybe now we finally could be.*

Elijah must have felt Val's stare. His eyes opened slightly and he smiled. "Yes?" His voice was full of sleep.

"Nothing, just watching you sleep." Val issued a warm smile.

His eyes widened. "You seem as if you are doing well ... considering."

Val was in high spirits or maybe simply feeling different. She was not entirely sure what came over her. She slid out of his chlamys and threw her leg over him — startling him. Wrapping her fingers in his, she held his arms to the bed. She brushed her lips against his neck before ever so gently kissing it. Her mouth slowly worked its way to his. When his mouth returned her kiss, she thought he had given into her touch. Joy and longing filled her entire body.

Elijah gave her a long hard kiss before he pushed her away with his hands still in hers. "What are you doing?"

"What do you mean?" Val smiled down at him. "You know exactly what I am doing."

In an eye blink, he rolled over on top of her, pinning her to the bed. "Not like this."

"Why not?"

"Because it is not me you want."

There was only sadness in his stormy grey eyes. This shattered what was left of Val's heart. Her joy and longing dissipated, leaving only pain. The pain that she was still hurting Elijah, the pain of seeing Teller as Vlad the Impaler.

Val pushed Elijah off and let out a moan of frustration. She was beginning to see that it was Elijah she wanted. Yet, he was right — as always — not like this. *We should not be together under these circumstances. Not when he is convinced that I would be thinking of another. But I had not been thinking of Teller.*

OVER THE NEXT couple of months Vallachia fell into a dark cloud of sickness. She felt as if she were perpetually falling into nothingness. Locking herself in her chambers, she refused to see anyone. She did not know which was worse: finally finding Teller only to discover that he had become a monster or Elijah's refusal. *Have I lost them both? All those years I kept Elijah at arm's length because of another. The length of an*

arm was the perfect distance, close but not too close. He could almost have me but not truly. Elijah deserves far better than that. She fell into a trap of self-loathing.

Her friends often tried to coax her out of her self-made prison. One such time Mari begged her to open the door. "Please, Val, let us help you."

Val did not respond.

Elijah's voice could be heard, "Val, are you there?"

Silence. The sound of his voice caused Val's eyes to sting as they filled with tears. She stifled a sob in her throat.

"Maybe she has left?" Sonia said.

"Do you want me to kick the door down?" Riddick asked.

"No." Val's voice was barely loud enough for them to hear. "I'm here. I wish to be alone."

"Come," Elijah said. "Let us give her more time."

"She has been alone for far too long already," Mari protested. "She does not need more time, she needs us!" Nevertheless, Val heard Mari's voice fade away as they retreated.

The weeks continued to pass and Val's friends became increasingly worried that she had not fed. Surely they thought she was upset over Teller but in truth Val's thoughts were of Elijah. She had loved him as a friend for a long time. Perhaps more than a friend ... now that she fully admitted that she wanted him. She longed to be with him. *But I can't. I do not deserve him.*

Even worse than this was the darkness that settled deep within Val when she thought of Teller. There was no longing. She did not even know if there was love. I created the most wretched creature to ever exist. How many has he killed? How many has he turned into killers? It is all my fault. I can no longer live with myself. Death cannot come soon enough.

Her friends continued to beg her to at least feed, even if she continued to refuse to see anyone.

After two months of this, Elijah's voice came from outside her door, "Val, if you don't feed, we will bring you someone and you will most likely kill her. You will be too hungry."

"I'm not hungry." This was the same thing as saying that she did not want to live. Val was, of course, starving. Her throat was constantly on fire. She enjoyed it because it kept the emotional pain away. Her body had grown weak and stiff.

All had grown silent outside her door. Val was relieved that they were leaving her alone ... again.

Her balcony doors flew open. The tall elegantly carved doors hit the adjacent wall and shattered. Splintered wood scattered across the floor. Val was too weak to move. Riddick stepped into the room carrying a human figure in his arms. Elijah was directly behind him.

"The girl is alive," Elijah explained. "She has been given a heavy dose of herbs to render her unconscious."

The sweet scent of the human hit Val with the force of a thirty-foot wave. She instantly lost control. In a fraction of a second the monster was in control. She didn't remember standing and moving to the girl. All she was aware of was the sweet blood as it ran down her sore throat —soothing the pain. She felt strength flow back into her body.

"Val, stop. You are going to kill her," Elijah said.

His voice sounded distant and muffled. The monster did not care. It had to have more.

With his arm around her waist, Elijah pulled while Riddick pushed her off the woman with his hand on Val's chest. It took both their efforts but she released the poor girl.

Vallachia took a couple of deep breaths and let her eyeteeth recede. She had to shake her head to fully get the monster out. "Oh God, did I kill her?" She put her ear on the woman's chest. There remained the faintest heartbeat.

"Take her to the infirmary to ensure that she will make it," Elijah said.

Riddick left with the unconscious woman still in his arms.

Mari appeared at Val's side and threw her arms around Val.

Val hugged her in return and laid her head on Mari's shoulder. Val felt as if she were a child who had been lost and finally found her mother.

"No more of this, you hear?" Mari whispered.

Val nodded. She forced herself to face Elijah, his eyes were iron grey and full of pain. He thinks I am this upset over Teller. Teller can go to hell. Elijah does not know how I truly feel. How can I fix this? Should I even try to win him back, when I am not worthy of him?

Sonia ran into Val's chambers, followed by Mary and Elizabeth.

Elijah gave Val one last icy glance before leaving.

Val went to the washbasin and splashed her face with the cool water. The water in the basin turned bright red. She looked at herself in the mirror for quite some time. Her gaze moved to her friends' reflections. "Look at us. Look at what we have become. We are all killers. Demons killing demons or demons killing humans. None of it matters."

Val's girlfriends exchanged worried looks with one another at her cryptic words. Teller was right — she had turned him into a killer. Then he had killed her father, which was justice, she supposed. How many deaths was she responsible for because she had created him, including that of her own beloved father? At that moment she vowed to never turn anyone again.

CHAPTER 52 WALLACHIA 1458 AD

Over the next year, most of Vlad's construction projects were completed. Government buildings in Targoviste and Bucharest were reinforced to withstand a long siege from the Ottomans. Wells were dug in the atriums and the cellars were stock-piled with grains, dried meats and wine. This was for the people of Wallachia, to keep them alive and safe when the time of war fell upon them. The castle at Poienari was also well supplied with provisions and made ready to protect Vlad's people while his soldiers fought the endless horde of Ottoman warriors in the valley below. He would often spend nights making weapons for his troops. He was almost ready.

Only two years into his reign Vlad decided it was time to stop paying the annual tribute to the sultan. In order to buy more time, Vlad sent a letter to Mehmed requesting a three-month leeway on this year's payment. This the sultan granted, for an extra fee, of course. Next Vlad requested that the sultan come to Wallachia to collect his money as opposed to it being delivered to their border town of Giurgiu, as was customary. It came as no surprise that Mehmed refused to come in person but he did state that he would send men to

Targoviste to collect the tax. This was an indication that the sultan was willing to compromise as long as he received his annual tribute.

Vlad instated a law that made it illegal for Wallachians to offer their boys to the sultan to be educated and trained as Janissaries. When he made this decree to the people, he delivered an overly zealous speech — which Sergiu had written — about no longer providing soldiers to the infidel. Vlad spoke passionately about standing up to God's enemies and that it was a Christian's divine duty to fight for their own true religion — not Islam. It was a bunch of bollock, none of which Vlad actually believed, but the people rallied behind him. Soon every Bishop and Deacon around was preaching Vlad's — or Sergiu's — propaganda. The people were ready for another crusade against the nonbelievers.

After this speech, many men came forward volunteering for the army. They were untrained and Vlad was not sure how much use they would be. It took a lot of time and effort to train the ever-growing human army that Vlad already commanded. There was not enough time to properly train all these men who were offering to fight for God.

Not to mention, Vlad planned to rely mostly on his Janissaries. They would be all he truly needed to defeat the sultan. The humans were largely for show — to make it more plausible that Vlad's small yet elite army could defeat the mighty Ottomans.

Nevertheless, the morale of the people was excellent and this would help when one hundred thousand troops marched their way.

The night before Sultan Mehmed's men were to collect the nonexistent gold coins, Vlad decided to summon Jusztina to his bedchamber. She was one of the concubines whom he rarely called upon. She did not seem to enjoy his affections so he largely left her alone. But this night was an exception, after all Jusztina was quite attractive. When she entered his bedchambers, she kept her head down. Her face was rounder than he had remembered. This was not unusual. A concubine's life was one of leisure with servants to wait on their every need. Many of them grew plump.

Vlad noticed her hands were shaking and he could hear her heart racing.

"What is the matter? You need not fear me."

She remained silent with her head down.

Vlad rose from his bed and moved toward her. She flinched away. "Come now. Am I that terrible?" He spoke softly.

Jusztina shook her head no. "It is ... just that I had hoped you would not call on me for a while longer."

"And why is that?" He put his hands on her upper arms and her body went rigid at his touch. "Tell me, what is wrong." He still spoke softly, trying to calm her.

A tear ran down her cheek as she moved her hand down the front of her silk brocade pulling it tight to reveal her now-large round belly. She was with child.

Vlad's vision blurred as anger overtook him. He instinctively backed away. "Who did this?" His voice was louder but still calm.

She shook her head no and cried into her hands.

"Who is the father?" His rage was taking over. As he stepped toward her she shrank away, protectively clutching her stomach and the baby inside.

"Please, don't hurt us!" she yelled. She sat on the floor with her arms wrapped around her legs. "I had hoped that some of the other concubines would be large with child by now, so that you would not find out. But they are all talking. We wonder why none have become pregnant. As much as you fancy Ilona she should be with her second child by now, yet her belly remains flat. It is becoming apparent that you are not capable of fathering a child." She knew that talking was the only thing keeping her and her unborn child alive.

"Who is saying this about me?" Vlad asked through a clenched jaw.

"Our servants have heard rumors that many people suspect that you are ... unable to have children or that you are ... fond of men. Which we concubines know is not true. So the former seems most plausible to us."

Vlad had been mad before but now he was fuming. As he stepped toward her Sergiu appeared between them. Vlad's bare chest slammed into the palm of Sergiu's hand as he stopped his advance on Jusztina.

"What is going on?" Sergiu demanded.

Vlad growled at Sergiu and paced. "Show him!"

Jusztina slowly used her shaking hand to pull her gown tight against her round belly.

"Oh no," Sergiu whispered.

"I've been betrayed by her, by my guard, by the father of the child and God knows who else," Vlad spat.

Jusztina wrapped her arms around Sergiu's leg. "Please don't let him kill us!"

"Be easy, Teller." Sergiu spoke too softly for Jusztina to hear. "Let's be rational about this. Perhaps we should at least hear her story?"

As Vlad moved about the room like a caged lion, Sergiu was careful to stay squarely between Vlad and the girl.

"I will not take this lightly! This is treason!"

Sergiu gestured for Vlad to calm down with his palms facing outward and slowly moving his arms up and down. Sergiu knelt down on one knee so he could face Jusztina. "My dear, this is serious. Many a woman has lost her head for such betrayal. I will try to convince Vlad to let you live but first you must tell us how this happened." Sergiu spoke soothingly as if he were a loving parent.

Jusztina nodded. Tears ran down her face. She began slowly. "I was betrothed to another, well secretly anyway. My love and I made plans to marry as soon as he could afford it. Then your men ransacked my city and I was forced into slavery."

Vlad stepped toward her and Sergiu quickly stood and stopped his advance. "You are not a slave! You are a concubine," Vlad yelled.

She kept her head lowered. "They are one and the same."

Vlad let out a frustrated yell and returned to his pacing. "They are not slaves! I provide every comfort in the world for them!" The finest of silks, servants who do everything for them, tutors to educate them, if they so choose. Anything they ask for they receive. This does not make sense — most of my women appeared to be content with the life of leisure I provide. Why isn't Jusztina?

"Please, dear, do not antagonize him. Continue to tell us what happened." Sergiu's peaceful and rational presence was the only thing keeping this situation under control. It lessened her fear and deterred Vlad from acting impulsively. Sergiu walked a fine line and he knew it.

"My ... love followed me here from Sibiu. He works in the castle. A man who often guards us was also taken prisoner in Sibiu. He was chosen to become a eunuch. This guard knew both the father of my child and me when we lived freely ... in Sibiu. The three of us had grown up together. This was not how we thought our lives would turn out. It was this guard who allowed me to make occasional visits ... " She was careful not to name the father or the eunuch who had betrayed Vlad. "We made plans to run away after he was able to save enough money."

"What is his name?" Vlad demanded.

Jusztina shook her head. "I can't. You will only have him killed as well."

Once again, Sergiu stopped Vlad's advance. "Who knows about this?"

"Only the three of us, the guard and the father. As well as my handmaiden."

"You have not told any of the other women?" Sergiu asked.

"No, of course not. They are a jealous lot. Many would be glad to rat me out. I have been able to hide my growing belly under my clothes — until now. They think I am growing fat."

Sergiu nodded, apparently believing her story. He placed both hands on Vlad's shoulders and backed him a safe distance away from Jusztina. He spoke quickly, quietly and mostly in Turkish. "This is perfect. All we have to do is make sure no one else finds out. Banish the eunuch, the maid and the father."

"Or kill them," Vlad said through a clenched jaw.

"No, banish them and claim the baby as your own. You need an heir to the throne if you are going to be able to keep this human façade up for much longer. Plus this will stop the rumors that are quickly spreading that you are not able to have children. This is an excellent solution — for everyone." Sergiu appeared to be proud of himself.

Vlad was skeptical; killing them still sounded like the best option.

"Her story is not unlike the story of your youth. You had once secretly planned to marry as soon as you were more stable. What if the Lady Vallachia had been captured and forced into a harem?"

"She *was* taken from me!"

"Fair enough. I ask only that you put yourself in Jusztina's place. It should not be too difficult, since this is much like your past."

Vlad studied Jusztina's lovely tear-stained face. She glanced between Vlad and Sergiu with wide brown eyes — wondering what they were saying — wondering what her fate would be. She reminded Vlad of Mari, in some ways. He took a deep breath.

Sergiu heard Vlad's heart slow. "Good. Let me speak with her. Please — stay back." He knelt down beside Jusztina again. "We have a proposition for you, my dear. If you tell us the names of everyone who knows about your infidelity then no harm will come to them or you. The only thing you must do in return is to let it be known that the baby is Vlad's. As long as you keep this nasty business a secret, all will be well."

"What will happen to the father and the guard ... and my maid?"

"They will be banished, yet unharmed. You have my word."

"I don't have a choice, do I?"

"I am afraid not, my dear."

Jusztina slowly got to her feet with Sergiu's help. She looked Vlad directly in the eyes for the first time throughout this entire ordeal. "Do I have your word, none of us will be harmed?"

With his arms crossed firmly in front of his bare chest, Vlad nodded his agreement.

CHAPTER 53 WALLACHIA 1458 AD

The following morning, after Vlad had fully calmed down, he decided that this was a grand opportunity. He was fond of the idea that people would think that the child was his. He and Sergiu sat in their favorite place, the tower at the Poienari castle.

"How is it that you always know when to intervene?" Vlad asked.

"I have told you before. It is my job to keep an eye on you and that fierce temper of yours. I do not want you to do something out of anger that you will regret for the rest of your life."

"Thankfully you have always been there for me. You are my voice of reason when all reason leaves me."

It was back to work. Vlad had the sultan's emissaries to drain of blood and impale on the front lawn — all in a day's work. This would be the start of war with the Ottomans. By putting off payment as long as possible, Vlad had managed to postpone his true intentions until the fall. After today it would become clear to Mehmed that Vlad would no longer be his vassal. However, the sultan's army was known to be fair-weather fighters. They would most likely not attack until spring at this point. It was entirely too difficult to feed a large army on the move in the winter. Not to mention, the sultan's men grew more impatient and irritable when they were cold and hungry. They would not come in full force until winter had passed. This would give Vlad even more time to prepare.

After the sultan's men were suspended in the air in front of the compound in Targoviste, Vlad sent Abdullah to take as many of the Janissaries as he thought he needed to Giurgiu. They were to take control of the strategic border crossing from the Ottomans. Abdullah was to leave a handful of vampires there to keep watch over the Ottoman lands to the south.

~

A COUPLE of nights later Vlad summoned Ilona to his bed. One might think he would have learned that women are trouble — he had not. As soon as he bid Ilona to enter, she ran to him and buried her head in his chest.

"What is the matter?"

Vlad's chest grew wet with Ilona's tears. *Something must be terribly wrong. Did someone die?* "What it is?" he asked again.

"It is not fair," she managed.

"What is not fair?"

"Jusztina, she is to bear your child, when it is I who wants your children more than anything!"

"Ah, I see. Well, God works in mysterious ways." It seemed like the correct thing to say. Although Vlad knew God had nothing to do with Jusztina's pregnancy or with why Ilona was not with child.

"I'm scared, Vlad. What if it is me? What if I can't have children? You will lose interest in me entirely. You will find another Kadin and perhaps even marry her." The tears fell faster and harder. Ilona buried her face in her hands and sobbed.

Vlad took a blanket and wrapped it around her to protect her from his coldness. He sat with her on the bed and held her tight.

"You have no need to worry about that. I will not lose interest in you. You are faithful and that is worth all the children in the world."

These words slowed her tears.

Women are overly emotional about such affairs, he thought with no small degree of irritation.

"If I were to have your son, then perhaps you would make me your wife. Now you will marry Jusztina, especially if the baby is a boy."

Oh no, not the marriage talk again. Ilona wanted very much to become Vlad's new wife. "I promise you that I will not marry Jusztina." Marrying an unfaithful woman who most likely despised him sounded like hell on earth.

Vlad held Ilona close and ran his fingers through her thick blond hair until she fell asleep out of emotional exhaustion. He, of course, was wide wake. His thoughts strayed to the fact that he should allow Ilona to marry another, so that she could have the children she desired. She was a lovely woman and still young enough, barely twenty. Surely a widower in town would gladly marry her. Since she was a concubine and therefore no longer a virgin, her choices would be limited. But still Vlad could find her a man who would provide for her. He grew tired of thinking about women and all the problems that came with them. Being careful not to disturb Ilona, he slipped away and headed for the armory. Pounding on metal always helped to clear his head.

While he made a handful of scimitars it became clear that he would not let Ilona go. She was his. Unlike Vallachia, he did not have to compete with the Prince of Vampires to win her affections. With or without a eunuch guard, Ilona was devoted to him and he could not stand the thought of her married to another.

Ilona was still wrapped tight in the blanket on his bed when he returned. He gently lay beside her. When he woke she was staring at him. A smile crept across her face.

"I'm glad to see you are feeling better," he said.

"It is because it has come to me."

Vlad shook his head in confusion.

"I know what we must do. We must pray! If we repent for our sins, then perhaps God will be merciful and give us a child."

Vlad rolled away from her. He had not prayed since he was a human and even then it was because Vallachia seemed to think that it would help ... somehow. Even as children she would guide him in how to "properly pray." What a terrible joke — it had all been for naught.

Besides, what could young, innocent Ilona possibly have to repent for? Perhaps she had impure thoughts about a boy next door when she was fifteen. That would require extra days of fasting at Pascha. Vlad could almost hear a bishop telling her this. What a load of shit. No amount of praying would ever give him the ability to have children. Though for the first time, he wished he could, only to make Ilona happy. He would do most anything to please her.

"Please, Vlad! This is why we have not conceived. We must have done something to anger God."

Vlad rolled over to stare at her with his devilish smile. "I am afraid, my dear, that my sins are too great to ever be forgiven."

"No. That is not true! God forgives *all* sins."

In that instant, Ilona reminded him of Vallachia more than ever — her beautiful innocence and her religious rhetoric. Vlad had had enough. He rose to his feet. "God does not exist!"

A tear ran down her cheek. "How could you say such a thing?"

"If there was a God, He would never allow creatures such as us — me to exist."

Ilona held her hands to her face to hide the tears. Her shoulders jerked with each sob.

Thankfully Abdullah barged in unannounced, interrupting this conversation that was only growing worse by the moment.

"I'm terribly sorry, Master but it is the sultan's men — they are marching toward Giurgiu." He spoke low and in Turkish so Ilona would not have understood even if she could have heard him.

"How many?"

"Only a couple hundred. It does not appear to be a full-scale attack. Mehmed is most likely concerned with reclaiming the strategic border crossing before winter is fully upon us."

"Inform my Janissaries that we will take flight for Giurgiu at once — it is feeding time."

With a smile and a nod Abdullah was off.

Vlad moved to the chest that held his armor. He fastened a shiny dragon-embellished breastplate to his chest

"You are going to war?" Ilona whispered.

He kissed her forehead. "I won't be long. Don't worry about me." As he left, her sobs turned to grief-stricken wails. He disliked leaving her in such a state.

CHAPTER 54 WALLACHIA 1458 AD

As the sultan's men approached, Vlad stood at the top of the Giurgiu tower with Abdullah on his right and Cosmin and Costel on his left. The already-cool fall breeze blew across them. Costel's fangs protruded from his lips.

The sun was setting when the sultan's army finally drew near. This was ideal, as not having the sun in their eyes would make the vampires more comfortable. When the enemy reached the border crossing, Vlad and his small band of men were waiting at the southern entrance. There were over sixty in Vlad's vampire army. Some held torches and some held crimson flags inlaid with the white Draculesti family dragon. The previous Ottoman guards, who had manned the tower before Vlad took control, had been impaled along the main road as a greeting for the approaching army.

As soon as the enemy was within human earshot Vlad stepped forward and yelled in a powerful voice, "Why does this army march on my border crossing?"

The man who stepped forward as the leader wore a large black mustache, much like Vlad's. He moved gracefully — too gracefully. Vlad gave Abdullah a knowing look.

"They call me Mustapha," the Ottoman leader declared. "I am the sultan's new seraskier. We are here to see to it that this fort remains under the sultan's command, blessings be upon him. It is a relief to see that you are here in the flesh, Vlad the Impaler. That way when I kill you, your people will easily be subdued under a new voivode. One who will, of course, serve the mighty sultan. This will also save us a full-fledged war in the spring. Think of all the lives I will save by killing you tonight?"

"Only a coward of a ruler does not personally lead his men into battle. Why is your *precious* sultan not here? Is he hiding behind his harem, or perhaps the little boys he truly favors?" That was enough talk. With a hand signal from Vlad his archers rained arrows down upon the enemy.

Many of them were able to take cover under their shields. They had expected this predictable first line of attack.

Vlad advanced and his men followed. His sights were set on Mustapha. Without a doubt he was the biggest threat. Only the best became seraskiers of the sultan's army and he was young and new. Vlad had a growing suspicion he was not human. It was easy to find Mustapha amongst the colliding armies, because Mustapha was also seeking Vlad. Their swords rang out as they met with great force. No human could have stopped such a blow. Mustapha's and Vlad's eyes met briefly in a moment of recognition — neither of them was human. Worry flashed across Mustapha's face.

Vlad issued his wicked smile. "Finally, a real fight."

Vlad's attack was fierce. It took Mustapha a moment to gain his footing but eventually he was able to do more than simply block Vlad's mighty swings. Mustapha was not bad but Vlad was better. Their swords collided numerous times until Vlad found his opportunity. He thrust his sword deep into Mustapha's side. It was the perfect swing, landing between the front and back plates of his armor. Vlad kicked his opponent's sword out of his hands as Mustapha fell to his knees. Vlad removed his sword from Mustapha's side with a kick to the chest and a twist of the wrist. This was so the sword would do more damage on the way out. Mustapha landed hard on the ground with a moan. He grabbed his side. Vlad moved in to sever his head, as two men attacked Vlad from either side. They were human and Vlad easily thwarted their advances.

When Vlad turned back to find Mustapha, he was gone. Vlad searched the multitudes of dying humans as his men easily walked through them. The men in the back had retreated with vampires quickly hunting them down. Yet, there was no sign of Mustapha. Vlad scanned the sky and in the far distance a large bat-like figure could be seen fleeing. He had an uneasy feeling he needed to stop Mustapha now or he would be trouble in the spring. Vlad leapt to take flight when a sword cut deep across the back of his lower leg. He landed on the ground with a thud and ran his sword into the chest of the remaining brave soldier who had managed to slash his leg. Vlad had to fight off more men before he could turn his attention back to Mustapha, who was now out of sight. Not even Vlad's vampire eyes could spot him.

By the time Vlad's men slayed or bled-out the remaining soldiers, Mustapha was most likely halfway back to Mehmed. Vlad would not be able to catch him before he reached Istanbul. Hopefully the sultan would have Mustapha's head for his great loss that night. Very few disappointed the sultan and lived to tell about it. Yet Vlad was concerned. He had a terrible feeling that Mustapha would survive and be back in full force at winter's end.

"He was one of us, wasn't he?" Abdullah asked, as they both stared to the south where Mustapha had disappeared.

"Aye," Vlad said.

"Should we go after him?"

"It is too late, he will be back to Constant — I mean, Istanbul in no time. It would not be wise to attack him on his own land. Besides, haven't you had enough blood for one night?" With a smile Vlad smacked Abdullah on the shoulder.

There were no humans left. More bodies were impaled along the road. But there were too many. The rest of the bodies were put in a large pile to be burned. Vlad did not want them rotting on the main road. They were also careful not to leave any signs that vampires had been responsible for this massacre. Bodies with bite marks on the neck were burned. The putrid smell was hard to ignore as they took flight for Targoviste. Abdullah, as well as a handful of the other Janissaries, stayed behind in order to ensure all remained secure at the border crossing.

UPON VLAD'S return he and Sergiu decided that Mustapha must have been either a lone vampire who was able to easily prove himself to the sultan, or a Janissary who had been turned into a vampire. Either way he was most likely pretending to be human. They speculated that the sultan did not know of Mustapha's true nature.

"I wish we had a spy in Mehmed's court," Sergiu pondered when Vlad returned with the news of the battle. Sergiu usually remained behind to keep an eye on things while Vlad was away. Sergiu was granted full governing powers in Vlad's absence.

"Now that we know the sultan has at least one vampire fighting for him, we must be extra vigilant." Vlad paced. It helped him to think. "It is imperative that my people are able to quickly fortify themselves in the government compounds in Targoviste and Bucharest. We must have more sentries on watch at all times to ensure that the people can get to safety in time. These extra precautions must be made in case the Ottomans were to get through our front lines or in case they were able to catch us unaware."

Vlad had not been concerned about a surprise attack before; the Ottomans always announced their arrival with loud war bands. But a vampire enemy who could stealthily fly through the night could easily catch them off guard.

"Yet, it is not overly concerning if the sultan has only one vampire amongst his ranks," Vlad added.

"If they are smart and they most likely are, the sultan would send this one 'extraordinary' soldier to kill you in the night. They know that without you the threat in Wallachia would most likely dissipate. You should be better guarded," Sergiu said.

Vlad had never needed personal bodyguards before. The idea

seemed ridiculous. "Who could possibly protect me better than myself?"

"You must sleep at some point."

Vlad pondered this for a moment. "Very well. Perhaps sentries should be placed outside my chambers while I rest."

After leaving his meeting with Sergiu, Vlad bathed away the evidence of the battle. He was in a hurry to find Ilona. He rarely entered the women's chambers, as it was designated a safe haven for the women of the household. No men were allowed, including Vlad. Of course, eunuchs were the exception but they were arguably no longer men. As the voivode of the houschold Vlad could break the rules as he saw fit — or at least bend them on occasion.

Ilona sat outside in the secluded atrium for the women. No doubt she was enjoying the last of the temperate fall days before winter drove her inside for months on end. A maid tended to her hair. Vlad watched them silently for quite some time. Ilona was solemn. Her eyes were open but unseeing.

It was taking entirely too long to braid her hair. "That is quite enough. You look lovely, my dear." Her hair did not need to be braided anyway, as it was Vlad's intent to mess it up.

The maid started and Ilona's face brightened into a wide smile. She held up the front of her silk brocade so she could run to him. Her hair fell around her face as the maid's hard work came unraveled. The maid let out a frustrated moan, as she would have to start all over.

Ilona threw her arms around Vlad's neck. "You are alive!"

Vlad was glad his long chlamys covered the fresh scar that had formed across his calf.

"I told you not to worry."

"You are back so soon. Oh, thank God! I was worried sick."

"We made quick work of the sultan's men. They will not be back for some time, I imagine." It was good to see her smile. "Gule Gule." Vlad whispered.

Ilona cocked her head to the side and furrowed her brow.

"It is a Turkish saying, which directly translates to something like, go smiling ... with goodbyes."

It was a bad translation but she understood. "Never leave on bad terms."

Vlad smiled and kissed her gently. "We have some unfinished business. Will you visit my chambers?"

She smiled playfully and took his hand to lead him out.

The maid was relieved that the two lovers were leaving. They were making her uncomfortable. She did not like his presence in the women's quarters, though she would never tell Vlad so. This place was the only sanctuary women could have from men. Vlad was an intruder.

Ilona gave Vlad a concerned glance as they approached his chambers. "What are they doing here?" she asked.

Sergiu had already stationed two Janissaries at the door.

"We are simply taking extra precautions. The sultan will not take last night's defeat lightly," Vlad said.

Ilona frowned. Once inside, Vlad swept her off her feet, cradling her in his arms.

"But they will hear us," she whispered.

They were vampires so she had no idea how well they would hear everything that went on in this room. Vlad's smile was full of mischief. "Then we will make their shift more entertaining for them." He easily tossed her onto the large plush bed.

Ilona laughed with delight, temporarily forgetting about her worries of the sultan and an impending war.

CHAPTER 55 HOLY ROMAN EMPIRE 1458 AD

Ramdasha sped through the streets with only his two most trusted advisors and a small satchel that held his most prized possessions. Ramdasha had become an expert in hiding and in running. He continuously drifted between remote areas and bustling cities, mostly in Southern Europe. This region was safest for him, as he had the most allies in the south. When he was not on the move he was preparing to move. The Court's scouts were never far behind. The most he had been able to stay in one place, since his attack on Prince Elijah and that whore of his, was about one year. Granted, after a decade or so he could return to previous places of residence; or rather, previous places of hiding.

An inconspicuous row of adjoining peasant homes provided good cover. In one of these homes, near the center, were two of Ramdasha's guards pretending to live there. They dressed as commoners, leisurely drinking and playing games. A rug covered a thick wooden door in the dirt floor. This door led to a narrow passageway. A smooth earthen floor spiraled gradually downward. At the end of the passage were the living quarters for Ramdasha and his most trusted men.

His men had dug these tunnels and shored up the walls with

wooden beams. They had built the long row of tiny homes as well, starting with the one over the top of the entrance. These homes were meant to house humans. It was more difficult to catch the scent of vampires when masked by the strong smell of humans. Thus, this arrangement provided an extra layer of protection against discovery by Lord Chastellain's men.

Ramdasha felt more secure when he was underground. He was always on edge when they lived in one of his above ground homes.

For the lord of a growing vampire army he lived modestly. He had left many luxuries behind. This was a sacrifice he was willing to make in order to defy the Court. He lived as if he were a peasant himself. Of course, this was for the benefit of his kind. Someday the world would belong to vampires. Then he would have it all. But until then, he lived underground — only a shadow in the night — unseen by most and concealed from the Court.

Ramdasha and his closest comrades always had a strategy for a quick retreat. It was vital that Ramdasha had a flawless plan for his next move. When the Court's men grew too near, he and his cohorts would disappear and regroup quickly without being discovered.

This time the Court had almost found him. They had been close — too close. Usually Ramdasha's sentries would spot the Court's men well in advance, giving Ramdasha plenty of time to flee. But this time one of the scouts managed to find the entrance of the small house that led to Ramdasha's current underground hideout.

The scout had gotten by Ramdasha's sentry quite by accident. From atop a nearby rooftop, the sentry's attention had been drawn away by two drunken humans fighting in the street — something about a woman was all the sentry could gather.

The Court's scout past by unnoticed on the street below. The scout caught the scent of vampires outside the nondescript home. As soon as Ramdasha's guards inside the home spotted the Chastellain "C" on the scout's breastplate they drew their swords and the scout was killed. The guards alerted Ramdasha and they barely made it out a secret exit before the scout's companions flooded into the underground tunnels.

Ramdasha and his men separated, as always, to make it harder for the enemy to know which vampire scent to follow. Ramdasha knew he needed to get to water quickly so that he could no longer be tracked. When the smell of the Mediterranean filled Ramdasha's nose, relief flooded through him — another narrow escape. It was a rush that he rather enjoyed. At least these moments of excitement broke up the monotony of hiding. They also gave him confidence and made him feel powerful. No one had been able to elude Lord Chastellain for as long as he had.

ONCE SAFELY IN their new hideout, Ramdasha and his men regrouped. They settled into a modest home in an isolated region of the French Alps. No humans and hopefully no vampires would find them for quite some time. In fact, they would have only one sentry keep watch until spring. For now the vast amounts of snow would keep most anyone away.

"That was close, My Lord. Thankfully, no one saw you," Sebastian said. Sebastian had taken Riddick's place and was Ramdasha's best warrior and most trusted servant.

"Must we keep running, My Lord? Why can't we stay and fight the Court's scouts?" one of Ramdasha's men complained.

"You know why," Ramdasha snapped. "The scouts never travel alone — not after we killed many of them in the beginning. The Court sends them out in small battalions and I only allow the five of you at my side at all times. I don't fully trust anyone else. Not after Riddick's betrayal ... over a stupid woman."

"Surely if we were to call all our allies together we could stand up to the Court. Mendoza and Belleaire have succeeded in growing their forces, as well as your sympathizers in the East. We are many," Sebastian said.

"Even with all my sympathizers, we do not outnumber Lord Chastellain's armies," Ramdasha said. "He controls all of the North. I can't seem to win any of them over. Which is surprising, to say the least, because this world is all wrong and it is the Court's fault — no, I don't like to give it an abstract name — this is all Lord Chastellain's doing. Why can't any of his allies see him for what he truly is? He and he alone is to blame for this backward world vampires are forced to endure. In his barbaric mind he believes that the weak should rule this earth. Well let me tell you, in my experience it is always the strong who survive. In the human world, the sick of body and mind do not live long prosperous lives. The healthiest and strongest of humans are the ones who survive and then go on to thrive. Why should it be any different for vampires? We are far superior to humans, yet we have to remain underground, hidden away, like bats in a cave, never seen by the light. We are the strongest, oldest, most intelligent creatures on earth and yet we are not allowed to flourish. We, the superior beings, must remain out of sight. I will not rest until we are free! It is the vampire's right to rule this world."

It was a tirade that Sebastian had heard many times, yet he never tired of it. "Of course, My Lord, with you as our supreme leader."

"It is taking us far too long to rebuild." Ramdasha tapped his fingernails impatiently on the wooden armrest. "We lost many in the vampire plagues. Creating a more disciplined army is much more difficult than simply turning large numbers of humans into vampires and setting them loose in the streets. Although that was an exciting time." Ramdasha smiled at the fond memory. "It is difficult to see why Chastellain has numerous supporters. How can so many of our kind not see that he works to keep us suppressed? It is as if we are nothing but animals. We are less than humans in his eyes. He allows pathetic humans to prosper while his own people languish. That is why we must resist him at any cost." Ramdasha's eyes burned with anger. This topic would forever impel him.

"Any rational vampires in the North must be too afraid of Chastellain to cross him," Sebastian offered. "Or they love the prince and that tramp of his."

"No!" Ramdasha glared at Sebastian. "No one loves them and I've warned you, do not mention her in front of me. I refuse to acknowledge her existence. She is dead to me and she would be dead if I had not been betrayed." Vallachia was forever the one who had escaped him. She had cost him dearly. For Ramdasha this was still a fresh wound. In his mind it was as if her treachery happened only yesterday.

"But, My Lord, I hear that in the North they call her the Great Snow Queen and they all but worship —"

"Enough! I said, do not discuss her in my presence. Is that clear?"

"Yes, of course, My Lord. Those miserable human-loving vampires must be stopped. Humans are nothing more than food — like sheep." Sebastian wisely changed the subject.

"No, humans are lower than sheep. At least sheep provide wool, as well as food," one of Ramdasha's men said.

"That is correct. Humans are not even as useful as sheep," Sebastian said.

This brought about a round of laughter.

"Humans should be rounded up and controlled by their masters — us," Ramdasha said.

"Out with the old and in with the new!" This was their mantra and it brought about a round of toasting.

This helped to lighten the mood and calm Ramdasha. He studied his men with approval. "There is one hope. Our informants have come across a new coven of vampires in the East. Well, perhaps an army is a better description. They are large in number and well trained in the art of combat. They do not appear to be in league with the Court. As far as my emissary can tell, they are ruled by one. He goes by the name Prince Vladislav Dracula."

Sebastian lit up. "Then we must go to him at once. Surely he can be persuaded to join our worthy cause."

"Let us hope so. With his numbers we could easily defeat Chastellain. We would finally be ready to attack and we could come out of hiding forever," Ramdasha declared.

Sebastian jumped to his feet. "Then what are we waiting for?"

"Patience, my dear comrade. We must be smart at all times. Acting in haste is what gets people killed. Prince Dracula may be dangerous, should he choose not to side with us. I have already sent word to our allies in Bulgaria. We are to meet in two days' time. They will accompany us. I need more guards to protect me — in case this Dracula is hostile."

CHAPTER 56 WALLACHIA 1458 AD

Ramdasha and his entourage made their way to the Poienari Castle — Vlad's display of wealth and power. The splendor of the castle alone worked to convince Ramdasha that Vlad was exactly the man he needed as an ally.

Vlad looked forward to the meeting as well; even though Sergiu did not like the idea. Sergiu wanted nothing to do with Ramdasha. Yet, Vlad was curious about this elusive vampire.

Ramdasha smiled when Vlad entered the room. Vlad returned the gesture with his confident and sarcastic smirk.

"So you are the great vampire prince my informant told me about?" Ramdasha spoke first.

"Aye and you are ... ?"

"Lord Ramdasha."

"Ah yes. I have heard very little of you. In fact, I have heard nothing of you since your time during the great plagues of Europe. What was that? A hundred years ago. I thought you had given up or perhaps you were dead."

"Not in the least. My resolve to defeat the High Court of Elders is stronger than ever. That brings us to why I am here. When you join my mighty forces, we will be unstoppable —"

"And why should I join you?"

"The Court despises its own kind. Of course, it is up to us to stop them. Surely you do not like having to pretend to be a human at all times. Imagine if you could be yourself! Our people want to come out of hiding. Our kind needs your help. I am here to offer you the privilege to fight with me to free vampires from Lord Chastellain."

"If you are so determined in your cause then why are you only now coming to me? The Court found me over a year ago."

Ramdasha narrowed his eyes. "Chastellain is a very powerful man, he has many eyes and ears. Yet I too am powerful and together your forces and mine would be capable of defeating the malevolent ruler."

"Believe me, Chastellain is no friend of mine —

"Wonderful! We will finally answer his call to war. We will begin preparations straightaway. How many men do you command —

"Not so fast. I have my own plans and I am not about to be distracted in order to help you — a complete stranger."

"I assure you, it is not for me. It is for the good of all vampires."

"You honestly believe your own rhetoric, don't you? Vampires need humans to survive." Vlad thought of Ilona. There were humans he cared about as well. "This is entirely about you. You want nothing more than to rule the vampire world."

Blood rushed into Ramdasha's cheeks. This was not going as well as he had hoped but he was not willing to give up. "Do not believe the lies you may have heard about me. I am a kind and generous soul. I only want to help my people."

"You said, 'your people.' You wish only for power. I will not help you overthrow the Court for your own personal gain. I serve no one. I will tell you exactly what I told the Court. I am in this for myself. I have my own aspirations. My business is my own and I will leave you to yours. That is the only agreement I will make with you, is that clear?"

Ramdasha's glower deepened. "They have already gotten to you." It dawned on him that this might be a trap. Through clenched teeth he added, "Then we had best be on our way."

"That would be wise," Vlad threatened.

~

NOT ALL WAS LOST for Ramdasha. While he had developed a dislike for the arrogant Prince of Wallachia, he managed to find a treasure on this trip to the East. Something even more valuable than Vlad's vampire army. He found himself a soothsayer.

On his way back to France, he caught the scent of vampires. This led him to a small cabin in the woods of Thessaly. Ramdasha had never been in love before but when a young female vampire stepped out of the cabin, he knew he had to have her. Her skin was pale — unlike his — and she had enticing full lips.

Ramdasha bowed. "My Lady, I am Lord Ramdasha and these are my men."

His men glanced at one another in confusion. They did not know what had gotten into their leader. He never showed this kind of respect to anyone, let alone a woman.

The woman smiled, revealing her dimpled cheek and Ramdasha thought his knees might buckle. She had intense honey-colored eyes; he could not look away. "What may I call you?"

"My given name was stolen from me. I now go by Elda."

"Elda ... that is beautiful." Ramdasha felt awkward when she stared at him. He was a fish who had been firmly hooked by a fisherman's line. He was powerless. "Do you mind if my men and I rest here? We are returning home from a diplomatic errand."

Again his men looked at one another with uncertainty. They had only just begun their journey home and were far from needing to rest.

"What errand?" the mysterious woman asked.

She is shrewd. Ramdasha saw that she could not be fooled. "We paid Prince Dracula of Wallachia a visit."

Her jaw tightened at the name Dracula. "And did your visit go well?"

"I should say not! He is an arrogant arse. Pardon my language, My Lady, but he is not capable of seeing beyond his own mundane desires."

Elda revealed her dimpled smile. "Well then, you should stay and we should see what else we have in common." She knew that this strange vampire might be trouble but she could not help herself. She too had never been in love — with a man. Much to her surprise, she found him irresistible. The dark-skinned stranger was simply glorious.

CHAPTER 57 WALLACHIA 1458 AD

Late one morning in the dead of winter, a servant knocked rapidly at Vlad's chamber doors. Vlad had been poring over some parchments at his desk.

The servant bowed briefly. "Master, it is the Lady Jusztina. She has gone into labor."

"And does everything appear to be well?"

"Yes, Master."

"Excellent. Inform me when the baby arrives."

It was not until early the following morning when the servant returned. "I am pleased to announce that the Lady Jusztina has given birth to a healthy baby boy."

"That is wonderful news."

"What will you name your firstborn son?"

"Vladislav Dracula IV."

"Of course, Master. Excellent choice."

Vlad dismissed the servant with his hand.

The servant bowed and turned to leave. He stopped at the door. "But, Master, don't you wish to see your firstborn?"

"Oh ... "*Not really,* Vlad thought. "Yes, of course. Yet, there is much work to be done at this time. I will allow the mother and baby some time to recover and ... " *I don't know what they do?* ... "bond," Vlad guessed.

No doubt Jusztina would still be afraid of him. Vlad had not seen her since that dreadful night he found out she was pregnant. He did not want to worry her now with his ... overbearing presence. She needed to focus on the new baby.

"As you wish, Master."

A COUPLE of weeks later Sergiu said, "You know, people will speculate about why you are not interested in your firstborn child. You should at least see him."

Vlad appeared in the doorway of Jusztina's relatively small chambers. He had given her her own quarters. She no longer lived with the other women. He watched as she patted the back of her fussy newborn. When the baby's cries ceased, she lowered him into the bassinet. She covered him as she sang a lullaby. Vlad decided that she would be a fine mother to the heir of the Wallachian throne.

"How is he faring?" Vlad asked.

Jusztina jumped and he chuckled. He didn't understand why startling people had always amused him so. Yet it never seemed to grow old.

She protectively moved to stand between Vlad and the baby.

"Please do not be afraid. I am no longer angry; in fact, I'm rather pleased with our arrangement. I will not harm either of you, you have my word." Vlad tried to further reassure her with a warm smile.

While she did not return the smile, her shoulders relaxed.

"May I see him?"

Jusztina nodded in agreement and moved to the side of the bassinet.

Vlad stood over the sleeping baby. "He is ... incredibly tiny. How will he ever grow enough to become a warrior?"

"You don't have much experience with babies do you?" she asked.

"No, none." It had been a very long time ago when his little brothers had been born. He could not believe that they were ever this small.

"Little Vlad is a perfectly normal baby and he will grow to be big and strong. Under your tutelage he will become a great defender of Wallachia." She gave her newborn a warm smile. "Do you want to hold him?"

"No! Certainly not. Surely I would break him."

Jusztina chuckled even though Vlad was not joking. He was confident that he would somehow accidentally hurt the baby if he even so much as touched the fragile creature.

He placed his hand gently on her shoulder. "I'm grateful that the two of you are well."

Vlad was almost out the door when she stopped him. "Vlad."

He paused.

"Thank you."

"Don't thank me, thank Sergiu."

VLAD INCREASED Wallachia's defenses all the more, as they had learned that their enemy was even stronger than they had originally thought. Vlad had prepared for an attack from the world's largest human army but now they had to take precautions for a vampire attack as well. Not to mention the battle at Giurgiu had been a clear display of Wallachia's strength. The sultan would know that Vlad's army would not be easily defeated. The Ottomans would need to regroup and prepare to fight an army that was stronger than they had anticipated. Plus the sultan had lost hundreds of his best men at Giurgiu. This left Wallachia with some time before the sultan would make his next move.

Vlad did not want to attack the Ottomans. He preferred that his enemy come to him, as his men knew their own land best and they would be more prepared if the sultan had to bring the fight to Wallachia. Vlad wanted every advantage and he took great precaution. He would do this with as few of his own casualties as possible.

The Wallachian court was doubly on guard for an attack throughout the entire spring but none came. Vlad worried that Mehmed was building his own vampire army.

"Perhaps his defeat at Giurgiu made it clear that he cannot beat us," Abdullah pondered.

"This is Mehmed the Conqueror we are talking about. He will never settle for a loss. He is carefully planning something," Vlad said.

Sergiu arranged for two of their trusted Turkish Janissaries to discreetly make their way to Istanbul to see what they could learn. Interestingly, the first to volunteer for the mission were the two palace guards Vlad had saved from Sultan Mehmed I's execution. These soldiers had no devotion to the sultan, they were perfect for the job.

THE YEARS CONTINUED to fly by with no attack from Mehmed, yet Vlad did not let his guard down.

As little Vlad grew he became the object of much of Vlad's attention. The precious little boy brought him much joy. The boy's favorite pastime was when Vlad would throw him up high. The child would squeal with delight as he gently landed in his father's arms.

The first time Jusztina witnessed her baby flying through the air she screamed. She snatched him from Vlad's arms. "You will surely drop him."

"I would never do such a thing."

Little Vlad reached his pudgy arms out for his "father" to take him again. Vlad reached for him.

But Justina turned away. "It is his nap time and you are getting him too excited."

Vlad did not argue, as women knew best about such matters.

Vlad waved goodbye to the little boy as he cried for his father.

As for Jusztina, Vlad left her alone, never calling her to his bed. Her heart belonged to someone else and she appeared to prefer this arrangement.

As the boy grew, Vlad carved him a small wooden sword. It was not the best of carvings, as Vlad was not skilled in working with wood. Nevertheless, the boy cherished it. He would "sword fight" with his father until his little arm grew too tired to hold the sword.

Overall, Vlad was content. The problem was Ilona. With every year that passed, she remained childless and she grew more depressed. She also became fiercely jealous of Vlad's "son" and all the time and affection Vlad lavished on him.

Vlad decided to consult Sergiu about what to do with Ilona.

"On matters of politics, even war, I can be of service; but when it comes to women, you may need to find yourself another Grand Vizier," Sergiu mused.

"Come now, Serg. I am beginning to think that women are not as complicated as you say. They only want to be cared for and to have children."

Sergiu laughed. He was clearly not convinced.

"I could marry her to a widower who could care for her and give her the children she desires." The thought of Ilona with another caused a rage to stir inside but Vlad was concerned for her wellbeing. He was trying hard to put his needs aside and think of hers.

Sergiu laughed again. "Have I not taught you anything after all these years? Ilona does not simply want anyone's child — she wants *your* child. If you were to release her from her duties as a concubine she would most likely be heartbroken at your rejection."

Vlad had not thought of this. "It seems you may know more about a woman's heart than you think."

That settled it. Vlad would keep Ilona for himself and do his best to make her happy. He immediately sent for a servant to head to the market to buy a new silk gown and a gold necklace. *Surely that will please her.*

CHAPTER 58 WALLACHIA 1462 AD

From what Vlad's spies could gather, Mustapha had managed to recruit no more than five vampires to serve the sultan. That made six with Mustapha in the lead. It was also apparent that Mehmed did not know of their true nature — they were simply the best of his warriors. Mustapha knew that Vlad was a vampire but he did not know that Vlad's elite men were vampires as well. Mustapha was under the impression that Vlad and perhaps only one or two of his closest men were creatures of the night. Mustapha believed that he had found enough vampires to conquer Wallachia.

When a hundred thousand troops crossed into Wallachia, the populations of Targoviste and Bucharest were barricaded safely within Vlad's compounds. He sent his concubines and their entourage to the palace of Poienari and left two Janissaries there to guard them. Two of his top men were all he felt he could spare. Vlad's soldiers were needed on the battlefield. Sergiu was to remain at Poienari as well.

The summer of 1462 was an unusually hot one. The unyielding sun beat down upon the two armies as they collided near Targoviste. Most of the day was spent fighting. Vlad and his Janissaries killed hundreds of the sultan's men but there were thousands to replace the dead. Not to mention, the handful of vampires in the sultan's front line kept Vlad's best men occupied. Abdullah, Costel, Cosmin and Vlad focused their attention on the enemy's vampire soldiers. Vlad's time was spent fighting Mustapha, who had greatly improved over the years. Vlad was unable to kill him during the initial assault. It was going to take longer than Vlad thought to defeat these numbers. The hampering effects of the relentless sun on his Janissaries did not help matters.

The Ottomans aimed their artillery at the government compound in Targoviste. They wanted their spoils of war — women and loot. Their cannons fired endlessly on the rubble walls. Vlad did not know how much longer the walls would hold out.

"Fall back!" he yelled to his men. They had to lead the army away from Vlad's people. "Retreat to the valley opening at Poienari!"

The sultan would assume he had Vlad on the run. As Vlad had hoped, the Ottomans pursued the Wallachian army, thus leaving the compound and its contents locked safely within.

When Vlad reached the valley opening he yelled, "Hold your ground!"

As planned, his soldiers prepared a front line of defense across the narrow valley opening. Vlad had lost two Janissaries to cannon fire, as well as a handful of human warriors. This was more than he had ever lost before. They may have slaughtered five hundred or more Ottomans, and Abdullah had killed one of the sultan's vampire soldiers. Yet the enemies numbers were so large that it did not seem to make a difference in the endless supply of men who kept pouring down upon them.

By the time the Ottomans arrived at Poienari, it was growing late. Thankfully, Vlad and his troops were safe from cannon fire, as the enemy could not get their large artillery through the mountainous pass.

The sultan's men did not attack. They busied themselves with setting up a well-guarded camp for the night. They would attack at dawn.

"He thinks we are trapped in this box canyon," Abdullah said. "He will let his troops rest until morning. Then he thinks he will be able to finish us with ease."

"Good. Little does he know that this is right where I want him. We will be able to limit the number of men we have to fight at one time in this narrow valley. We will kill every last one of them, if we must. Then I will be able to march into Constantinople and easily reclaim it."

Abdullah and the twins smiled as if they could taste the victory.

They had begun to let their guard down and Vlad's human troops were exhausted. "We camp here tonight. Janissaries, you keep watch. The rest of you get some rest. We have a big day ahead of us tomorrow," Vlad announced.

Sergiu appeared in front of Vlad.

"What are you doing here?" Vlad did not want Sergiu in harm's way. He was not a fighter.

"It is Ilona. She has gone missing. Her guard has looked everywhere in the castle but he can't find her. He found this on your bed."

Vlad snatched the papyrus from Sergiu's hand.

I AM sorry that I must leave you, my love. Life is meaningless since I am not capable of bearing your children. I will not be a slave to the Ottomans. It is time for me to leave this life.

Ever yours,

Ilona

VLAD'S TEETH CLENCHED. He let out a growl and headed toward the castle in a flash, pausing only long enough to leave Abdullah in command. As soon as they could, Sergiu and Vlad took flight for the hilltop palace. In Ilona's chambers her sweet scent was not fresh but still lingered. The chamberlain and Ilona's eunuch looked distraught. They joined Vlad as he followed her scent. It led them to the tower overlooking the river bottom. Filled with dread at what he would find, Vlad ran to the overhang — perhaps he could save her. Her broken body lay on the river rocks far below. Her white silk brocade moved gracefully as the shallow water flowed around her lifeless body.

"Vallachia!" Vlad yelled.

Without a single thought for pretending to be human, he leapt from the tower. In no time he held Ilona's limp body. "No, no, no, Val. I'm so sorry."

Vlad heard the faint sound of Sergiu landing behind him.

After a long moment, Sergiu spoke softly, as if he were afraid of Vlad's reaction. "You do realize that she is not the Lady Vallachia?"

"What are you talking about? Of course I know that!"

"You called Ilona Vallachia ... twice."

"I did not ... Did I?"

Sergiu gave a solemn nod.

Vlad studied Ilona's face. Now that it was motionless, the resemblance to Vallachia was almost gone. Vlad shook his head to clear it. "I destroyed her. I should have let her go a long time ago. She is dead because the one thing she wanted more than anything was the one thing I could not give her."

"It is time you end this charade. You should go to the one you truly love. She may still wait for you in the North. That is the only way you will find happiness."

Vlad was hollow. Ilona had filled a void and now that she was gone it was as if half of him was missing. What replaced the emptiness was anger. It consumed him — making him whole again. He gently laid Ilona's body on the riverbank. A furious yell escaped from him as he stood, taking flight for the Ottoman Camp. Vlad imagined the disapproving look on Sergiu's face. Though Vlad did not turn to see it for himself, he knew it was there. *Yes, let us end this charade.*

With his human pretenses gone, Vlad landed at Abdullah's side at the head of the army. "We end this now."

Abdullah nodded.

Vlad addressed his men. "Janissaries, it is time to finish this!" He spread his wings to their full extent and took flight for the enemy's camp, with his men close behind.

With no irritating sun in their eyes, Vlad's army of vampires laid waste to the sultan's men. Vlad searched everywhere for Mustapha but he was nowhere to be found. Soon the overextended Ottomans retreated in terror, even as their leaders yelled at them to continue fighting. After all, they were only humans. They had been fighting all day and their human bodies were beyond needing to rest.

As for Vlad and his men, well, the night belonged to them. Now filled with rage, Vlad slaughtered more men than could be counted. This seemed to drive his soldiers as well. They rallied around him and fought better than they had earlier that day.

Cosmin and Costel killed two more of the sultan's vampires, yet that still left three and they were nowhere to be found. Vlad's men, as well as the few human soldiers who could still stand, pursued Mehmed and his men as they retreated. Vlad followed them as far as Targoviste but once it was clear that they would do no more harm to his people, he ordered them to push the enemy far back into their own land and then return to protect the border.

Vlad had a terrible feeling that he must return to Poienari at once. Perhaps his concubines were in trouble. *Jusztina, little Vlad!* He heard the screaming before he reached the castle. His wings could not carry him fast enough. Racing to the women's chambers he found the two Janissary guards fighting off Mustapha's men. Mustapha himself had recently broken through the large doors to the women's quarters.

Mustapha's upper body was well protected with armor so Vlad threw a dirk into the back of Mustapha's upper leg. As he fell Vlad sped toward him and sent him flying across the room with a hard kick to the back. This caused more screams from the already terrified women as they moved away from the two blood-stained men.

"Get out!" Vlad yelled.

This they gladly did.

Mustapha lay on the floor against the adjacent wall. He slowly pulled the knife out of the back of his leg and moaned in pain. He smiled. "I wondered when you would show up. Since you prefer impaling so much, we left a gift for you on your front lawn."

Sergiu! No! Vlad thought. Mustapha threw Vlad's knife and Vlad quickly dodged it.

In no time Vlad was on him. With his knee pressed hard against Mustapha's chest, Vlad used all his might to twist Mustapha's head from his body. Vlad quickly returned to the men who had been fighting in the hall. One of Vlad's guards lay dead and Mustapha's two men were about to kill the last of his Janissary guards. Vlad threw another of the dirks from his belt into the throat of one of them. This distracted the other of his vampire enemies and he moved in quickly to cut off his head with his sword.

"Will you make it?" Vlad asked his wounded soldier.

He nodded.

"Where is Sergiu?"

The guard shook his head no, as he clutched his bleeding side and squeezed his eyes shut in pain.

"Wrap that up tight to slow the bleeding." Vlad would have done it himself but he was frantic to find Sergiu.

Mustapha's last vampire soldier pulled the knife out of his throat, choking on his own blood. Vlad finished him with his long sword and the slightest flick of the wrist.

"Serg!" Vlad called as he ran toward the front entrance. "Pasha!"

There was no answer. As promised, on the front lawn there was Sergiu's head impaled on a spear. Vlad's entire world came out from under him. He fell to his knees. Ilona was right, this life was not worth living. If he could have died right then and there he would have. He prayed for the first time since becoming a monster. He prayed for God to end his life. But God refused to listen. Vlad did not blame Him, as he did not deserve the mercy that death would bring.

CHAPTER 59 WALLACHIA 1462 AD

It was unclear to Vlad how much time had passed before he was capable of moving. He had to take Sergiu's head down. Sergiu required a proper burial. Numbly, Vlad dug two graves, one for Sergiu and one for Ilona. They would be buried next to each other in front of the castle Poienari. Vlad almost had the graves complete when a vampire landed in front him. Vlad did not look up; he knew it was Cosmin by his scent.

Cosmin surveyed the two large holes. "Abdullah sent us to check on you. He did not feel he could leave the troops unattended. What are you —"

Costel's cries rang out. "Pasha! No! Pasha!"

Cosmin ran to his brother's side and knelt down beside Sergiu's body and detached head, which Vlad had laid on the ground by the fresh graves. Their wails of grief were too much. Vlad left to retrieve Ilona from the riverbank and laid her in her final resting place.

Vlad's only surviving castle guard joined them. He was mostly healed.

"Are the women safe?" Vlad's voice was flat.

"Yes, Master."

"Go to Abdullah. Tell him to bring my Janissaries. Leave only a few to stand guard. Inform him that it is time to mourn for our pasha." Vlad wanted to get this over with as quickly as possible. He did not know how much longer he could stand this grief without falling apart entirely. Informing his men of the loss had to be done and he wanted it over. Sergiu meant so much to all of them. He had been like a kind and loving father to them all.

Vlad thought Abdullah was going to come unhinged when he saw Sergiu's body. He lifted Sergiu into his arms as he knelt on the blood-stained ground. Vlad had never seen so much as a drop of moisture in Abdullah's eyes but tears ran down his cheeks and fell on Sergiu's headless form. Vlad could take no more. He could not bear his own grief, let alone theirs. Leaving them to finish burying the dead, Vlad took flight without knowing where he would go — it did not matter — nothing mattered.

VLAD ENDED up at Sergiu's cave. There he would sleep for as long as possible. He prayed he would never wake.

Yet, he did. He started out of the cave entrance hoping beyond all hope to find Sergiu there — making his special brew. But Vlad was alone. Slowly he moved to sit outside the cave. He gazed at the mountaintops without seeing them. This was where he would stay forever, unmoving. If only there was a way to gain a moment's relief from the pain. He would have done anything to escape his own thoughts but he was trapped. There was no reprieve in sight. Perhaps once he petrified he would not feel any more. Surely this would end the unbearable torture. He didn't know how many days he sat perfectly still before he heard distant voices.

Vlad was barely conscious of Cosmin. "The cave is around here somewhere, I know it."

"This way. I have his scent," Abdullah said.

They landed in front of Vlad. He did not move or even blink.

"Master!" Costel moved toward Vlad.

But Abdullah stopped him. "Please, Master, we are all mourning the loss of our beloved pasha but you are the leader of Wallachia and our people need you now more than ever."

Vlad stared into space. His voice was hoarse when he finally spoke. "I will not move from this spot."

"How long do you plan to stay here?" Costel asked.

"Forever."

Cosmin put his head down in sorrow.

Abdullah stepped closer. "We beg of you, Master, our pasha is gone, we cannot lose you as well."

These words breathed some life back into Vlad. It slowly pulled him out of the deep chasm he had fallen into in an unsuccessful attempt to escape the pain. Vlad had not thought of anyone but Sergiu and his own suffering. Yet there were others who needed him. There were others he cared about.

I must be strong ... for them — but how? Vlad thought. He put his head down and shook it. His neck felt like grinding stones when it moved. He had been still too long; perhaps he had already begun to petrify. "I cannot do this. I can't do any of it without him. Nothing matters anymore."

"I know," Abdullah said as he sat beside Vlad and placed his arm over Vlad's shoulder. "But we must try to carry on — for Sergiu. He would not want you to waste away forever."

Vlad looked at Abdullah for the first time since he had arrived. "That sounds like something Sergiu would say."

"He taught us well. His wisdom lives on through us."

The slightest smile crossed Vlad's face. "And here I thought he was gone. But you sound just like him. Will I never be free of his annoying edification?"

Abdullah chuckled — his eyes full of moisture.

Vlad had to gather his wits. He had to go on — somehow.

Cosmin took Vlad's hand and pulled him to his feet.

Vlad felt as if his body was breaking out of a stone mold.

"It is time to go home, Master," Costel said.

Vlad found a river to bathe in. He was still covered in dried blood from the battle.

Soon they landed outside of Targoviste.

"Your people will be glad to see you," Abdullah said.

"Don't they know that I am not human?" Vlad asked.

"There are many rumors flying about but most humans cannot be sure of what they saw the night we ran the Ottomans from our lands. Most humans were hidden away and saw nothing. They do not care *how* you did it. They only know that you managed to defeat the world's largest army with few casualties. You are a war hero of the greatest measure," Abdullah said.

None of this was making Vlad feel any better, because none of it mattered.

CHAPTER 60 WALLACHIA 1462 AD

People gathered as they spotted Vlad. They mumbled things such as, "There he is, Prince Vlad." "He has returned!" "God bless you, Voivode!" Soon it seemed that everyone in town lined the streets and cheered. Vlad nodded as he passed but could not manage a smile.

"It is ironic; being their hero was never my intention." Vlad spoke quietly and in Turkish.

"Yet you took extra precautions to protect them and you ran the enemy off of their land. You have made Wallachia a better place," Abdullah said.

Once in the Great Hall, Vlad sent a servant to retrieve Jusztina and little Vlad. He had to see for himself that they were alive and well.

Vlad's human chamberlain scurried in. "How wonderful that you have returned, Master. It is beyond all hope to see you alive — after your terrible fall off the Poienari tower ..." He waited for an explanation as to how Vlad could possibly be standing in front of him.

Vlad offered none.

Under Vlad's hard stare the tiny fellow continued. "Yes, well — to business then. If I may advise, Your Majesty, now would be the time to march on Istanbul. The sultan's forces are greatly damaged and the

Mother of Cities is at its most vulnerable. With you leading our superior army I do not see how you could fail."

"We will not march on Istanbul. That is no longer of importance."

"But, Master, that was your plan — your desire all along. We must reclaim our land from the infidel. If anyone can accomplish this it is you."

Has this chamberlain truly believed my rhetoric? Do my people honestly believe that we are fighting — no killing — for God? What God would actually want war? Vlad thought. He decided that the chamberlain was unable to see this for what it had been — simply Vlad's own lust for power. All this death has occurred because I alone wanted more. Perhaps Voivode Dracul was right all along. Making peace with one's neighbors is much more difficult than making war. If one wants a fight, they will surely find it — but peace. How does one obtain that? Impossible.

"It no longer matters." Vlad finally said. In fact, it never mattered. How many times did Sergiu try to tell me this? I retake Istanbul and call myself Emperor. Then what? I still would not be satisfied. What would it take — to conquer the world? I could. But then what? Would I be happy then? No. Why didn't I listen to Sergiu? It took his death for me to finally see. I must put a stop to this madness.

The last words Sergiu spoke to Vlad rang through his mind. "It is time you end this charade. You should go to the one you truly love. She may still wait for you in the North. That is the only way you will find happiness."

Until that moment Vlad had no idea what he would do next. He had not even given the future a second thought. This was because he had only hoped for no future at all — just death. But now he knew what he had to do. "No more blood," he said to the chamberlain who was patiently waiting for his response. *Blood,* Vlad grabbed his throat as he became acutely aware that he was starving. "How long was I away?" he asked Abdullah in Turkish.

"Almost six weeks, Master."

It was as if it had taken Vlad's body this long to fully wake from his long stillness. In one swift motion he stood from his throne, stepped close to the human chamberlain and sank his teeth into his neck. After draining him of life, Vlad held the man's body up with one hand under his upper arm. He handed the body to Cosmin. "Get him out of here before Jusztina and the baby see him." In reality, little Vlad was no longer a baby, he was going on five years old.

The twins quickly dragged the body out of the room.

Abdullah handed Vlad a cloth to wipe away the blood.

Vlad looked at the rag, which was stained dark red. "Yet we never truly get away from the blood, now do we?" He shook his head in despair. *The little man had been an excellent chamberlain. At least I did not hurt little Vlad.*

Loud human footsteps approached. Vlad handed the bloody cloth back to Abdullah who quickly hid it behind his back.

Little Vlad pulled his hand from his mother's when he saw Vlad and ran toward the only father he knew. "Baba, baba," he yelled.

Vlad picked him up and held him tight. His tiny arms around Vlad's neck felt like Heaven. Vlad never wanted to let him go.

"I knew you would come back. I told Mama not to worry."

Vlad nodded a greeting to Jusztina. "You were worried about *me*?"

"Yes, well — Wallachia would fall apart without you. I'm glad you returned."

Vlad threw his son high up in the air and the boy laughed at the thrill.

"You must have grown an entire length since I last saw you. Perhaps you are ready to take over as voivode?" Vlad proclaimed.

"Yes, I'm ready! Can I, Mama?" His voice was soft and sweet.

Jusztina shook her head in disapproval. "You should not encourage him so."

At first, Vlad had thought that little Vlad's presence would allow him to remain in power for a couple of generations by disappearing for a time from the public's eye while placing his "son" as figurehead. Vlad would continue to run the kingdom from behind the scenes. Then eventually he could come back as Vlad V and so on. It would have been tricky but it might have worked. However, Vlad had a new plan but first he had to make a trip north.

"I have to go away on business but I will return as soon as I can," Vlad said.

The boy wrapped his arms around his father's neck. "Don't leave us again."

"I will not be gone for long."

"Take me with you," the boy pleaded.

"I'm afraid I can't, son."

"Why not?"

Vlad tapped his finger lightly on the child's tiny chest. "Because you have to stay here and look after things in my absence. You are the man of the house while I am away. Besides who else will keep your mother out of trouble?"

"Oh, wonderful. Now he will be an insufferable boss while you are away." Jusztina appeared truly concerned.

A servant burst through the Great Hall doors. "Master, Master! It is your chamberlain. He was murdered in the street. His body was found in front of the compound."

CHAPTER 61 WALLACHIA 1462 AD

Vlad looked to Abdullah in disbelief.

"Oh no," Jusztina said. She sensed that it was time for her and her son to leave. She snatched little Vlad from his father. "Vlad, I am sorry for your losses."

Vlad put his arm around her shoulder. "And I'm glad the two of you are safe." He kissed her forehead and kissed the little boy's cheek.

Little Vlad teared up as his mother took him away.

"Don't cry, my little prince. You must be strong. I will see you soon, I promise." Once they were gone, Vlad turned to Abdullah. "Those two imbeciles left the chamberlain to be found twenty lengths from here! What if little Vlad had found him? They cannot be entrusted with the simplest of tasks. One would think that the disposal of a body would be easy for vampires." Vlad sighed. "I am going to have to strangle them."

Abdullah chuckled and shook his head. "Unbelievable."

After briefly pretending to be surprised and concerned at the chamberlain's "mysterious death," Vlad headed to the women's quarters. There was one last order of business to attend to before he headed to Copenhagen. Many of his concubines were gathered in their common room. The mood in the room changed dramatically when Vlad entered. They had previously been at their leisure but grew tense and silent at his appearance.

"Master, you have returned!"

"We were worried."

Vlad studied them for a moment. Honestly ... he could not remember some of their names. Soon it appeared that all eighteen of them and a handful of maids had come from their side rooms to see why he was in *their* quarters.

"We are sorry about Ilona. She was a dear friend. I told her that she should have faith in you. I knew that you would defeat the infidels."

The concubine's words seemed sincere. She must have been a true friend of Ilona's. Vlad nodded to acknowledge her kind words. "I have come here to inform you all that I am relieving you of your service to me." He studied their reaction.

Some gasped and one girl cried into her hands. Yet a couple of others seemed to brighten at the news.

"What will become of us?"

"No one wants to wed older women who have been concubines. They want to marry young virgins. We will be thrown into another harem or we will have to fend for ourselves," another concubine added.

"No. I would never do that to any of you. I will arrange for you to travel to Moldova. You will be safe there. Voivode Stefan will see to it that you are found suitable husbands. You will not become Stefan's concubines and you will each be given the chance to have a proper family and children of your own."

A couple of women smiled at one another with hope and excitement.

The woman who had been crying said, "Why? Don't you want us anymore? Are we no longer good enough for you?"

One whispered to another, "It is because he wishes to replace us with younger girls."

This was not meant for Vlad's ears.

"You are all lovely women. I will not be replacing any of you. The truth is I do not want to hurt any of you like I did Ilona. You deserve better. You are young enough to have many children of your own and to have a husband who loves you. Not to mention I don't want my enemies coming after you again." This was true but his unspoken list went on; such as the fact that he was planning to leave the throne, he did not age while they did and the most important — it would not impress Vallachia if he had a harem waiting for him back home. "You must be set free." Vlad was finally taking Sergiu's advice, *It was time to end this charade.* "Pack your belongings. Carriages will be here in the morning to carry you to Moldova. Your maids, eunuchs and a handful of my best warriors will see to it that you remain safe and comfortable. I wish you all the very best."

Many of the women blinked at him with a stunned expression.

Vlad paused outside the room to listen as the women burst into an entire range of emotions once they thought he was gone. Some cried as they most likely had hoped to become Vlad's next Kadin or — even better — his wife. Others were elated, perhaps because they would have the chance to have children and a normal life.

Vlad shook his head. Women are indeed complicated creatures.

The final order of business was to name Abdullah as Vlad's new Grand Vizier. He was given complete rein while Vlad was away. Some of the Wallachian court muttered their disapproval to one another. They thought Abdullah was too young or too Turkish. Not that any would dare say this to Vlad. This was side talk only vampire ears could hear. It was apparent that some had hoped to be granted Sergiu's job but there was no one Vlad trusted more than Abdullah.

The following morning, before Vlad headed north, Abdullah was beside himself. "You are going to face the largest known vampire army on your own?"

"I will not be alone. I'm taking the imbeciles," Vlad said.

"That does not make me feel any better. I should be by your side."

"You are the only one old enough and intelligent enough to maintain control while I am away. The Janissaries know and respect you. There is no longer anyone else who can take my place. Would you rather I leave the twins in charge?"

Abdullah laughed. "That would be a disaster."

"Precisely. I am not going there to start a war. I'm going there to offer my allegiance and get her back."

"Yes, *her*. That sounds like war to me."

"I need you here. You are all I have left."

Abdullah nodded. His down-turned mouth mimicked his large black mustache.

They both felt the full impact of Sergiu's absence.

CHAPTER 62 COPENHAGEN 1462 AD

Things slowly returned to normal for Vallachia after finding Teller and the subsequent sickness that overtook her. However, her relationship with Elijah had never been more strained. He kept his distance and she no longer knew how to approach him. She feared that he would reject her again. Not to mention, it was difficult to shake the thought that he deserved better. Elijah deserved someone who loved only him — someone who had never loved anyone else.

"Perhaps we should join Teller in his quest to reclaim Constantinople," Vallachia said.

Samuel and Mari looked at each other in a way that said, "Here we go again."

Elijah appeared out of nowhere. Val smiled at him but he scarcely looked her way.

"You know that it is against the Court's laws to interfere with human affairs. What does it matter if the Romans or the Ottomans control any given city or region at any one time? Someday the Ottomans will fall and a new kingdom will rise. We cannot afford to become distracted from our main goal. We must remain focused on protecting humans from our kind at *all* times. If we were to send an army or even some of our best fighters to help Wallachia then this would leave us vulnerable to an attack."

"But surely we could afford to —" Val started.

"I know that you are fond of the empire under which you were raised but in such cases the Court must lead by example. We simply do not intervene with human trifles and conflicts," Elijah said.

"But surely some human struggles are worth fighting for?" Val would not give up so easily.

Elijah glared at her, making it clear that the debate was over. He turned to Samuel and asked if he wanted to join the men for an afternoon foxhunt.

As the two men headed out Mari said, "This is unbelievable! They are running off for a leisurely hunt while our people suffer under Ottoman rule."

"Actually, conditions are not that terrible under the sultan's reign."

"In that case, why are we having this conversation?" Mari said.

Val decided it was time to consult with Mari about her feelings for Elijah and their relationship, or lack of a relationship. She could not stand his coldness any longer. When Val told Mari that Elijah deserved a woman who had never loved another, Mari's jaw fell open in exasperation. "Such a woman does not exist, Vallachia. After all, I fancied boys in the village before I met Samuel."

Val shot her a disapproving look. "I had more than a childish *fancy* for Teller."

"I should say so; I do not remember those boy's names and you waited for Teller for — what has it been — two hundred years?"

Val nodded. "And now I have lost Elijah. I am such a fool!"

"You and Elijah are perfect for each other. You love each other."

"We do?"

"Yes, everyone knows this except the two of you."

"I'm not sure about that."

"Maybe you are a fool."

Val gave Mari a playful shove. "He appears to have given up on me — he barely speaks to me. Who could blame him for moving on? How do I get him back?" Vallachia knew nothing of romance or how to have an intimate relationship. She had spent her long existence avoiding such matters. "Where do I start?"

"You are thinking entirely too much. This is not a stranger we are talking about — this is Elijah. Simply go to him. Tell him what you told me. He will be yours in an instant."

"You make it sound simple."

"It *is* simple! He loves you."

Mari gave Val confidence and hope, two things she currently lacked. "I pray you are right," Val said. Another rejection from Elijah would probably destroy her. Val gave Mari a hug. "Thank you. I should have talked to you a long time ago."

"Yes, you should have. That is what friends are for."

In a flash Val ran to her balcony and took flight. There was one more thing she had to do. She had to formally let Teller go. She landed on the riverbank not far from the castle.

It had been over five years since Vallachia had found Teller. It was time she moved on — in fact it was long overdue. He knew full well where she was and he did not care, perhaps he never had. Teller was dead and the evil Prince Vlad was all who remained — a cruel and heartless monster.

Besides, I love Elijah. I want to be with him. He is good to his very core. Maybe it is as easy as Mari said over two hundred years ago, all I need to do is choose him. That is it — I choose Elijah! He is much more than I deserve, more than I could ever hope for in a companion.

With this decision relief washed over her. *It is unfortunate that I did not choose Elijah a long time ago. Elijah is worth the risk. I must try to get him back. No more waiting for someone who will not come.* She felt as if a chain that had been tightly wound her chest had suddenly given way and she could finally breathe. Waiting for Teller had been suffocating — holding her back. Now she could live!

On the other hand, there was a part of Val that felt guilty for giving up on Teller. If she truly loved him then she should never abandon him. She should go to him and try to help — try to find him buried deep inside Vlad.

She had already tried that and failed miserably. *Besides, if he truly loved me he would have found me a long time ago.* She could argue with herself forever. In fact, she had been having this same conversation with herself for far too long. *It has to end!*

Vallachia reached for a star-shaped white flower with six pointed petals, growing on the riverbank where she sat. Mari loved flowers. She had once informed Val that this particular flower was the Danish Orchid. A tear rolled down her cheek. She threw the flower into the river and watched it float away. As it vanished out of sight she whispered, "Goodbye, Teller." That was it. The decision was made. Vallachia would move on.

Back at the Chastellains' castle Val had to find out if Elijah would have her. She dressed in a long white silk tunic. Since she had spent her life avoiding intimacy, she was nervous. Not to mention he had already turned her down once.

I am a fighter, not a lover. Yet, how hard can it be? Here goes nothing. What a stupid saying that is. It should be, here goes everything. Taking a deep breath, she walked across to Elijah's room and entered quietly without knocking. He was fast asleep. She lay down beside him.

CHAPTER 63 COPENHAGEN
1462 AD

Elijah stirred. "Val? What are you doing?" His voice was full of sleep.

Vallachia did not answer. She put an arm across his chest and kissed his cheek.

"Why are you wearing —"

Val pressed her lips to his. He was reluctant, so she kissed him harder.

He placed his hands on her shoulders to push her away.

"Please don't." Val threw herself on top of him. She continued to kiss his neck and lips.

Elijah's body remained unresponsive and tense. Her heart raced as panic consumed her. She could not handle another rejection from him. She prayed that he would give in and that he still wanted her — that he still loved her.

It seemed like ages before his shoulders relaxed. With a resigned sigh, he let himself lose control. She could feel him letting go of his reason, as strong as it was. In a flash he rolled her over and his lips were on hers. Each kiss more eager than the last. Her lips parted and his tongue brushed across her lower lip. He moved to kiss her neck.

Relief flowed through Val. I did it! He is mine. An overwhelming sense of freedom came with this realization. I should have done this years ago — as in a couple hundred years ago. No more resisting. No more waiting.

Elijah ran his hand up her leg pushing her tunic up to her thighs. His touch was gentle. She pulled his tunic over his head and ran her hands over the smooth muscles in his chest. He was simply beautiful. When she felt like she would explode from his hungry touch, he paused.

Please, don't stop! Val thought.

Elijah studied her. "Are you sure you want this?"

"Yes."

"And it is me you want?"

"Yes," Val breathed.

Elijah looked into her eyes for a moment longer. Deciding she was sincere, he pressed his lips to hers, cradling her back with his hands. She arched her hips toward his and he was inside her.

Val let out a painful moan.

He pulled away.

"Don't," Val placed her hand on his lower back to stay him. "I will be fine."

Elijah lost control, allowing a long-awaited pleasure to consume him. She was overjoyed in his satisfaction.

Afterwards they lay wrapped around each other, content and still.

"There were times when I thought this day might never come," he said.

"I'm sorry I waited so long," she whispered.

Elijah kissed her forehead. He pulled away enough to gaze at her. "What changed?"

His eyes were a bright blue, the grey sadness was gone. "Since you rejected me, I thought I had lost you. That is why I grew sick. I do not deserve you." She hesitated. "And I finally let go of ... the past." She could not bring herself to say Teller's name, not while in Elijah's bed.

Elijah nodded in understanding. "Why didn't you tell me?"

"I should have but I thought you deserved better."

"I did not reject you. It was simply that that was not the right time because you were upset over Teller. I did not mean to hurt you."

"While I was sick it dawned on me that you were the one I wanted. Though I have loved you for a long time. I can't be without you." Val's eyes filled with tears.

Elijah gently brushed his lips across hers.

Val rested her head on his chest.

He held her tight. "Does this mean you will marry me?"

"Yes." Tears of joy fell onto his chest. *I will marry!* She still did not think she deserved this wonderful man. *It is a blessing that he was patient with me for so long — too long.*

They stayed like that for hours as if they had become a great spina; two separate entities, yet when intertwined they became an unbreakable column.

CHAPTER 64 COPENHAGEN
1462 AD

At first light Elijah rose and dressed. "I must tell the Elders the good news and I do not want to give you time to change your mind."

"I'm not going to change my mind," Val said. "That is why I took so long in deciding. I'm sure that you are who I want."

With his fingers in her hair, he pulled her in for a deep kiss. Then he was gone.

Vallachia was not fully dressed when Mari and Sonia barged into Elijah's chambers unannounced.

"Is it true? Are you finally to wed?" Mari's large brown eyes danced with excitement.

Vallachia covered her bare chest with her tunic. "Don't you knock? And how did you hear already?"

Sonia squealed. "It is true!"

"We saw Elijah as he entered the Great Hall," Mari said. "I told you that all you had to do was go to him. Finally you two will be married! By the looks of things, it is not a moment too soon. He must make a virtuous woman out of you."

Mari and Sonia laughed and Val tried to glare at them but could not.

The ladies moved across the hall to Val's room.

Sonia braided Val's hair and Mari set out a fancy gown. Val had to get ready for the big announcement. It took almost an hour before she finally looked like a proper lady of the Court. Dressing as a woman was uncomfortable and time-consuming. Val already longed for her breeches.

When the three companions entered the Great Hall the room fell silent. The place was crowded, it appeared that everyone had turned out. Val did not like all the eyes on her so she focused on finding Elijah. The usual storm in his eyes had calmed. He was truly happy. This filled Val with confidence; she had made the right decision. She would give anything to see him like this. Her only regret was that she had not done this sooner. She had wasted so much time on a childish dream that would not come true.

Val took her new place to the right of Elijah amongst the thrones for the Court of Elders. Lord Chastellain rose to address the crowd.

There was one more regret; the pleasure this would bring Lord Chastellain. Val imagined him telling his son that he had been right; that all the horrible things he had done to Val were justified. Chastellain's plan was finally working out the way he had intended and Val would be his son's prize bride. It took them two hundred years but they finally won her over.

How has this happened? Val mused. *I once vowed that I would never serve the lord or marry his son.* She could see her father's warm expression as he said, "Never say never, my spring flower." After all, never was a very long time for a vampire. She pushed these thoughts away. *This is not about the lord — it is about Elijah. He is all that matters.*

"Ladies and Gentlemen of the Court!" Chastellain declared. "It is my pleasure to announce a long-awaited marriage. My son and Lady Vallachia are to wed. The ceremonies will take place as soon as they can be prepared."

The Great Hall came alive with applause and chatter. Val noticed some of the ladies looked disappointed, as their young lord was spoken for. She smiled at Elijah and he took her hand. When the noise died down a loud exaggerated clap from the back remained. The audience slowly made way for the clapping figure. Elijah was on his feet before Val recognized who it was.

"What are you doing here?" Elijah's voice boomed. He took a step forward with his hand on his sword.

Val could not believe what she was seeing. Her heart pounded against her ribs.

"Well, My Lord. I came here for two reasons," Teller said, as he approached the long row of thrones.

Teller was flanked by Cosmin and Costel, who wore defiant expressions. They were ready to fight the entire room of vampires if their leader deemed it so.

"It appears that I am too late for one of those reasons." Teller gazed at Val for a moment too long.

Teller's eyes sparked like emeralds, not the dark cruel eyes of Prince Vlad. Yet his expression remained emotionless. He was not the monster whom Val had seen the last time they'd met; yet he remained ... hardened or maybe saddened. He was clean-shaven. The thick dark mustache that had hung fashionably around his mouth was gone. This made him appear younger. He looked exactly like Teller from her childhood, kind and protective. Only his sad eyes gave away his true age. Val could see the knowledge they held.

Elijah took another step forward. Others, including Samuel and his own father came to his side. Even John moved from his place behind the lord's throne to stand by Elijah. Riddick appeared at Val's side.

Val wrapped her arm around her stomach. She felt as if she was going to throw up. Her mind raced with confusion.

Teller put his hands up in a non-threatening gesture. "Do not fear, I came here in peace. The other reason I am here," he gave Val one last glance, "is because I want to offer my allegiance to the High Court of Elders. My armies in the South are many and well trained. We will fight with you against Ramdasha and his allies." Teller ended with a bow to Lord Chastellain.

The lord's face lightened. He placed his arm across Elijah's chest to stay him. The lord stepped forward and clasped Teller's forearm as a gesture that sealed their new alliance. "This is a wise decision, Prince Dracula." He turned to the audience. "Let it be known that from this day forth the great armies of Wallachia under the rule of Prince Dracula are allies of the Court!" He held Teller's arm up in the air to further symbolize their new partnership. More cheers and applause came from the audience.

Lord Chastellain put his arm around Teller's shoulders and walked him closer to the Elders' thrones.

Teller gazed at Elijah with a blank expression. "Sorry to steal your big moment."

Lord Chastellain swiftly stepped between them as Elijah drew his sword. Val was grateful for the lord; he was the only thing standing between these two. The only two men she had ever loved. She was grounded to her chair — unable to blink, let alone stand.

"You must stay for the festivities tonight," the lord said to Teller.

Elijah's spoke through gritted teeth. "Father, please!"

Father and son glared at each other for a moment. Elijah spun, grabbed Val's hand and they were outside the Great Hall in a blink.

Val was immensely grateful to be out of there. She hunched over, still holding her stomach. She could hardly breathe. *Why now? Now that I finally let Teller go! How could he?* Her thoughts raced. Elijah led her to his room. They stood on his balcony looking over the city in the distance. The sun was only a minor irritation, as long as Val looked away from its bright rays. The two lovers said nothing for a long time, both lost in their own thoughts.

Elijah broke the silence. "It appears that I am destined to never have you for myself."

"No! You *do* have me. Nothing will change my mind." She put her arms around him and pressed her body to his. "I love you. I choose you." She kissed him.

"You say that now but I know the power he has over you. He will be at our engagement party tonight."

"Then we will not be there." The storm was back in Elijah's eyes. "Let's go to your cave. No one will be able to find us." She ran her hand through his thick dark hair. Wrapping a long leg around him, she pressed her lips to his.

Before she knew it, they were on his bed. His mouth moved up her neck to her lips. He slid his hand under her brocade when a knock came at the door. They stood in an instant and Val smoothed her silk gown.

"What is it?" Elijah said with more than a hint of irritation.

Their closest friends poured into the room. First Mari and Samuel followed by Sonia and Aaron.

"We came to see how you were faring?" Mari's voice was full of concern. She was the only one — besides Elijah — who knew the whole story and the magnitude of Teller's appearance in the Great Hall. Mari knew full-well how Val felt about him.

Val refrained from saying what she was thinking; *We were faring very well until you barged in.* After all they were genuinely concerned.

Mari placed her arms around Val.

Val had to swallow the knot that formed in her throat.

"Come," Mari said, "you need some time with the ladies."

Something told Val that she did not need any "time with the ladies". She wrapped her arms around Elijah in a brief hug and whispered in his ear, "I will see you tonight. Before the engagement party we will leave."

Elijah nodded. His expression was grave.

Val was dragged away by Mari and Sonia, leaving the men to themselves. Val did not want to go. Elijah looked equally reluctant. The women retired to Val's room across the hall. *At least they did not take me far,* Val thought.

CHAPTER 65 COPENHAGEN 1462 AD

"What are you going to do?" Mari whispered.

"Do about what?" Val's voice was distant and cold. She knew exactly what Mari meant.

Mari gave Val a disapproving glare.

"Very well, I will do nothing. There is nothing *to* be done. My decision is made, that is final," Val said.

Mari shook her head. "What timing Teller has. I can't believe it. After all those years you waited for him and now he shows up a day too late. He most likely only pledged his armies to the Elders to gain your approval. To show you he has changed."

"He has changed." Val's voice cracked. "He is no longer the evil Prince Vlad, he's Teller — our childhood friend."

Sonia seemed to gain a full understanding of the problem. She looked at Val with wide eyes. "You would not leave Elijah for that foreign prince, would you? It would destroy Elijah, probably forever." Sonia was fiercely loyal to the Chastellains.

"No. Of course not. I told you, my mind is made up. That is that. Let us discuss it no more." Val's voice was flat.

"Poor Teller!" Mari knew the human Teller. She knew his good side. Her allegiance was divided between Elijah and Teller.

Mari's ambivalence made Val's confusion worse. The thought of hurting Teller sent a pain through Val's chest. She tried to rub the ache away. "Look, I can only have one of them and I choose Elijah. Besides Mari, you once said that you and me married to Samuel and Elijah was the perfect arrangement. What happened to the dearest of friends being married to two dear friends?"

"That was when I thought Teller would never come for you. For all I knew he was dead, like everyone else from our childhood. Besides this is not about Samuel and me, it is about what is best for you," Mari said.

"Could we please talk about something else!" Val said through gritted teeth.

"Right, this is not helping," Sonia said. She went to Val's wine rack and chose an old dusty bottle of the best. "Let's play your favorite game."

"First I must send for Mary and Elizabeth. I would like them to be here for the wedding preparations. I also want to send a formal wedding invite to Lord Alexandru." The more people who knew of the engagement the more real it would feel. It made it more probable that their wedding would take place. The more people who expected a royal wedding the harder it would be to back out.

"Wonderful idea!" Sonia said.

Mari's frown deepened. "Please listen to me! As your life-long friend I know you better than anyone. I must ask you to do one thing for me, then I promise I will leave it alone — forever."

Val gave her a wary look and said nothing.

"Please take some time to think about which man is the best choice ... for you. I know you care about Elijah. He is wonderful. But Teller ... he is your true love."

Val grabbed her stomach and ran to the privy to throw up for the first time since she had had food poisoning when she was a human. Her head spun. All she felt was anger toward Teller. *How could he possibly show up now? Even two days ago, things may have turned out differently. Now it is too late.*

Sonia ran to Val's side and rubbed her back. "Will you let it go? You are not helping." Sonia glared at Mari.

"You see? I knew it was not that simple for her," Mari said.

Sonia said what Val would have if she had been able to speak, "Shut up!"

"Very well. My point is made." Mari slid down the wall and sat helplessly on the floor ... in silence.

Val drew her legs to her chest and wrapped her arms around them. Sonia unbraided Val's hair and ran her fingers through it. They stayed like that for quite some time, silent statues. Finally, Val took Sonia's tiny hand. "Please send for Mary and Elizabeth and take a wedding invitation to Alexandru while you are at it."

Sonia smiled with relief. "Of course." She swiftly jumped to her feet.

Mari and Val exchanged a knowing look. Mari nodded.

Val knew the nod was not an agreement with her choice but an acceptance of it. Mari understood.

Val took flight as soon as she could. When she was far out over the water she sped up into the clouds. Wrapping her wings around her body like a cocoon, she dived downward spinning through the air. She barely made a splash as she disappeared into the water, where she transformed from an oversized bat to an oversized fish. She would hide from the world in Elijah's cave and wait for him. This would also ensure that she would not see Teller. One shocking touch from him and she was afraid her resolve would crumble.

It seemed like an eternity before Elijah's head broke the surface of the water in his cave. He sighed with relief when he saw Val. He appeared in front of her in a flash. "You're here?" he whispered.

"There is nowhere else I want to be."

His wet lips were on hers. Her clothes were soaked as he pressed his body to hers. There was a desperation in his touch. Their wet clothes came off. Soon Val was lost in his caress. She could feel his need to claim her. She gladly let him. She was his. It was over quickly.

"Sorry," he whispered. Elijah moved to lay beside her on the blanket. Val put her hand over his racing heart. It was enough to simply feel his excitement. She wrapped a leg and arm around him and placed her head in her favorite place — his chest. For hundreds of years she had found comfort when she buried her head in his chest.

Time was lost, as they lay together.

"Let me make it up to you," Elijah whispered. "I can show you how good this can be."

He did.

This must be what Heaven is like, Val thought. For hours she was consumed by him. All else was forgotten, even Teller. Now it was her heart that raced.

"I can't believe I have been missing out on this all these years." Val had the urge to try to make up for a lifetime — or several lifetimes — of chastity and never leave this cave.

"The sun should be on the rise," Elijah said. "We had better get back and answer to Father. He will be wondering where we were last night."

Val did not want to go anywhere. Elijah had to peel himself out of her arms.

"I suppose it is time to face everyone," Val said. "We cannot hide forever." She was not looking forward to her friends' disapproval, as she had not attended her own engagement party.

In no time, the two vampires landed on Elijah's balcony. They knew when they entered his chambers that they were not alone. The scent of another vampire was strong. They knew who it was before they saw him. Elijah and Val exchanged a knowing look.

"Here we go," Elijah's voice was barely audible.

Lord Chastellain sat in a chair in a dark corner. "It is considerate of you to make an appearance. I sent Riddick to search for you," Lord Chastellain slowly stood. "Imagine my embarrassment — holding an engagement party for absent lovers."

Vallachia lowered her head. She felt as if they were adolescents who had been caught doing something wrong. Elijah was almost a thousand years old and Val was no spring chicken. Yet, in this world, time stood still. They looked as if they were eighteen and the lord *was*

Elijah's father, after all. Such roles were never lost, especially when one didn't age. Val was abashed.

"At least you are together. I did not know what had happened. Is this wedding to take place or not?" the lord demanded.

It was Val who spoke, "Yes, My Lord. I have already sent for my friends in London and an invitation has been delivered to Lord Alexandru telling him the wedding date is in one month's time."

Elijah took Val's hand. His eye's shone blue. They stared at each other for a moment. Val could feel Chastellain's hard stare.

"Very well. One month, that is not much time. We must send the invitations to the rest of our allies today. There is much work to be done. It will take all my best people to ensure that the wedding can take place in one month."

Vallachia could almost see the lord's mind turning with all that needed to be done. He was ready for the challenge. This was his best side.

When the lord reached the door he paused. "You are both aware that we need Prince Dracula as an ally if we are going to stand against the South and their growing forces." He directed his all-too-common serious stare toward Elijah. "You, my son, will have to learn to control your temper." He turned his intense gaze to Vallachia. "And you will have to learn to be faithful." He looked between the two lovers for understanding.

Again, it was Val who pacified him. "Of course, My Lord."

The lord stared at her for a moment until he decided she was indeed sincere.

Elijah watched the door long after his father was gone. He gave Vallachia a questioning look.

"He is right, Elijah. We need Teller on our side. That means we both have to control ourselves if we are to be together and be his ally. A fight is coming and we need his army. This is bigger than you or me. We must find a way to move forward with Teller in our lives at times."

Elijah crossed his arms. "You never cease to amaze me. Still, you agree with Father?"

"Stranger things have happened, I suppose."

"And to think, all these years I only needed you to help appease my father."

"Well, that only works when I agree with him and that is not usually the case."

"One month, are you sure?"

"We have waited long enough. It is as if we had the longest engagement in the history of this world. I am ready to be married. No more waiting."

Elijah pulled Val to him. His lips found hers. This time it was Elijah who had trouble letting go.

"I need to change," Val whispered. He reluctantly let her slip out of his arms.

CHAPTER 66 COPENHAGEN 1462 AD

As soon as Vallachia stepped into her chambers she regretted it. The scent of a different vampire greeted her. It was a scent she would never forget. The door slammed shut behind her. She turned to find herself only inches from Teller. Panic caused her heart to quicken. With every step she backed away, Teller moved forward. Val put her hand up to stop him — it trembled. "Don't. Don't come any closer."

"I'm not going to hurt you," Teller whispered.

"I am aware of that."

"Then what are you afraid of?"

"What are you doing here?" Val tried to avoid his question.

"You are afraid I will be able to change your mind. You're afraid of how you feel about me."

Perceptive observation. Val clenched her jaw. "No, of course not," but this did not come out as convincing as she had hoped. "Shouldn't you be gone by now?"

"Not without you. Hopefully I have made it clear that I came here for you."

"You are too late." Being reminded of how he never came for her caused her cheeks to redden with anger.

"I know, Mari told me — I am a couple of days too late."

"No, you are two hundred years too late." Her emotions seemed to change with each new heartbeat. She forced the tears back and tried to ignore the knot that threatened to choke her. "Why did you not come for me before — all those years I waited for you?" She didn't know how she managed to get these words out but a tear betrayed her as it rolled down her cheek. What she saw in his face made her feel even worse. His eyes were dark green, as she remembered them and full of sorrow and ... love.

"I was lost. You saw me. I had become a monster. When I killed your father, I knew you would never forgive me. I spun out of control with the new power you gave me. When I first heard word of you, it was only to learn that you were here, with Elijah. This crushed me, which made it all the more easy to continue to spiral out of control." He stepped forward to wipe the tear from her face.

Val slapped his hand away. It would not be wise to touch him. She remembered, all too well, how it felt when their skin came in contact. It would be difficult to remain in control. She backed away and this time he let her.

"If it is royalty you want, then I will make you my empress."

Vallachia welcomed the flash of anger that this foolish comment invoked. "You see, you do not know me in the least. If it were not for the threat from Ramdasha, I would have nothing to do with the Court. There was a time, most of my life actually, when all I wanted was the poor smithy's son."

A flicker of pain shone in Teller's eyes. He lowered his head. "I'm beginning to understand. There was a dear friend who tried to tell me this but I did not listen." His voice was that of utter dismay.

Val had to know. "Why come for me now?"

"It was seeing you again, years ago — to learn you were not married and ... the way it felt when we touched. Yet, I could not compete with the Prince of Vampires. I wanted to become a powerful ruler in order to be worthy of you. Now it is clear that that was not needed to gain your favor. I finally listened to some sound advice that led me here."

Val could not stand to see the pain that consumed Teller's face.

He reached for her but she pulled away.

"Please don't do this. Don't marry Elijah. Give me a chance to ... win you back. Wallachia is your home, come back with me."

"It is not my home anymore."

"If you were to rule by my side, we could restore the Roman Empire — our empire. You could become the Empress of the East."

Rather than a queen in the West. The queen of vampires. For the blink of an eye Val could see it — Teller by her side as they ruled the great empire of the East. That is his dream — one I do not share — or do I? A queen or an empress? A choice between the West and the East. She shook her head. "You need to leave."

"Please." He stepped toward her.

"Leave!" Val yelled so that Elijah would easily hear it across the hall. She glanced toward the door. Then back to Teller. His emerald eyes were full of agony that cut her. It felt as if a knife scraped across her heart.

Teller disappeared as her door flew open.

Val fell to her knees and Elijah was at her side. "What is the matter?"

With her hand over her heart, she tried to rub away the pain. She wiped the tears away with the other hand. *Pull yourself together,* she thought, *for Elijah's sake.* She stood. "All is well." She tried to reassure him with a smile.

"He was here wasn't he?" Anger raged in Elijah's eyes. He glanced toward the balcony where Teller had recently disappeared. Elijah moved to follow him.

Val grabbed his arm. "No, Elijah, don't. Let him go. I did my part, now you need to do yours. We promised your father."

"He has the audacity to come into your chambers, in my home!" Elijah's eyes burned with fury.

Val wrapped her arms around his neck and held him tight. "He is gone. It is over."

Elijah took a deep breath. "I hope you're right." He wrapped his arms around her.

This helped to calm her. The pain eased as it was replaced with Elijah's love. She could feel Elijah's body relax as well. *As long as I am with him, I will be fine — we will be fine.*

CHAPTER 67 HOLY ROMAN EMPIRE 1462 AD

On the other side of Europe, Ramdasha and his new bride, Elda, plotted.

"The Court will not find us before we are ready, as I can see them coming long before they can find us," Elda said. "You no longer need sentries. I can keep us hidden. Our armies will not meet until we say so. That much I can assure you, my love."

"How can you be so sure of this, darling? Your sight can be limited at times. You have said so yourself," Ramdasha said.

"My sight is clear on this. Sometimes images of the future are blurry and other times they are vivid. This one is vivid. Even as a human I could foresee important events in my life. It appears that as a vampire my visions are even more precise."

Upon his return from yet another disastrous encounter with Vallachia, Teller instructed the twins to head back to Targoviste. "Make sure Abdullah is faring well."

"It is not Abdullah Pasha who I am worried about, Master." Cosmin wore a deep frown.

"I will be fine. Allow me some time to myself."

The faithful brothers reluctantly headed for Targoviste without their leader.

Teller needed Sergiu. Landing by the two mounded graves outside the Poienari castle, he knelt by Sergiu's final resting place. "I have lost her, Serg. I waited too long. If only I had listened to you. Then none of this would have happened; you would still be here and she would not be marrying another."

Eventually, Teller fell asleep using Sergiu's grave as a backrest. That was how Abdullah found him. He kicked Teller's leg to wake him. Teller moaned and rolled over to try to force himself back to sleep; yet he knew it would not work. Unfortunately, he was awake.

"I take it that it did not go well in Denmark?" Abdullah spoke to Teller's back.

"One might say that," Teller mumbled. Teller knew Abdullah would not leave him alone so he begrudgingly sat up.

Abdullah plopped his mass down beside Teller. They gazed at the valley below.

"I have lost everything, Abdullah."

"Oh, come now, you still have us. For many years your men were all you needed. We will continue to be all you need."

"Wonderful, I am stuck with you lot." Teller gave Abdullah a nudge with his shoulder.

"I am afraid so, Master. Your men need you. You are our Maker. And Wallachia needs you as well. You have freed your country from the boyars and now the Ottomans. They need your guidance more than ever."

"I can't." Teller lowered his head and shook it. "You know I cannot rule a country without Sergiu."

"Yes you can and you must — we must. You are not alone."

That was how Teller had felt — alone. Yet, Abdullah was right, he did have faithful companions and people who counted on him. "Come. There is work to be done." He stood. "And my name is Teller."

"Teller?"

"That was my given name and I wish to leave Vlad behind."

"You want me to call you ... Teller?"

Teller nodded.

Abdullah frowned. "Very well."

Giving up Vlad was a task he did not know how to accomplish. But he must try to find himself. He longed to start a new life. Taking his true name back seemed like the place to start.

THE MEMBERS of Teller's court in Targoviste were relieved to see their fearless prince return. They worried that the fragile hold they had on Wallachia would easily slip away without Vlad.

"It is time for me to abdicate the throne," Teller announced. "My son is to be crowned the ruler of Wallachia."

"But, Master, he is only five years old," the new chamberlain said. He appeared all too happy to step up as chamberlain. Which he might not have been so eager to do, had he known how his predecessor had died.

"I will not leave him to rule on his own — not yet. He is to be well educated and trained in the art of combat, while we run the country until he is ready to take an active role in the matters of state. I shall rule from behind the throne. I will be here to guide and protect my country. But Vlad IV will be the crowned prince." Teller planned to remove himself from the public's eye. It would not be long before his agelessness became a topic of much discussion. Originally, he had planned to wait a couple of decades or so and then come back as Vlad V but now everything had changed. He would not be coming back. He would see to it that Little Vlad would rule Wallachia until his death.

Teller could see that his chamberlain was concerned, so he continued, "Many a ruler has crowned their predecessors while they were young. Mehmed the Conqueror was made the ruler of the Ottoman Empire when he was twelve. It is rumored that he was given decision-making powers, as well. My son will not have such power until I deem that he is ready." He had explained himself enough. Teller's mind was made up and it was time to move on to other matters. "Did the concubines find their way safely to Moldova?"

"Yes, Master. Safe and sound," the chamberlain said.

"Good. Were you able to find him — the man I asked you to retrieve from his exile in Moldova?"

"Yes, Master. He is here."

"He is alone — he has no family?"

"He never married."

"Excellent. Have him brought to me, then fetch Jusztina and my son." It was time for the boy to meet his true father. Of course, the chamberlain would not do this himself he would send servants to fetch them. This was how nobility worked, send someone to send someone else and eventually the job would get done — usually.

When Jusztina and her son entered the Great Hall, Vlad took the excited boy in his arms. "I have a surprise for you," Teller announced to Jusztina. "It is time you married."

She put her head down in sorrow. "You will have me marry you then, My Lord?"

"No. Not to me, to him." Teller gestured to a large tapestry and the man he had instructed to wait there stepped out from behind it. "If it pleases you," Teller added.

Jusztina's mouth fell open. "You are here and you are alive!" She looked to Teller as if for permission.

"Go," Teller said.

Jusztina ran to her love and threw her arms around his neck. "I never thought I would see you again."

The man wrapped his arms around her waist. "I knew we would be together someday, somehow."

Teller could hear their private whispers as clear as day.

"Who is that man?" little Vlad asked.

"You are a very lucky boy. Do you know why?"

"Because I am a prince," he sang in his sweet childish voice.

Teller laughed. "Yes and because you have two fathers. Not every boy is so lucky." The boy was glorious in his innocence. Teller wished that he could remain this way forever. He did not want the beautiful child to experience the many horrors of the world.

The boy frowned. "That man is my father?"

"Aye."

He buried his tiny head in Teller's large shoulder and hugged him tightly. "No. You are my baba."

"Yes. That is true as well. I love you and guide you and I provide for you; that makes me your father. You will now have us both by your side. We will be here to make sure you are ready to rule Wallachia on your own someday." Teller raised the boy's head with his thumb and finger on his chin, so he could see his son's eyes. "Perhaps you will have baby brothers and sisters."

The boy's face lit up. "I have always wanted a baby sister."

"You see? Things will be even better now."

Jusztina was all smiles and her eyes were full of tears threatening to spill down her face. She clung to her man as if he might disappear forever if she let go.

"He is so big. What a beautiful boy," little Vlad's father said.

Teller set the boy down. "Come meet your other father."

The boy shook his head no and hid behind Teller's leg holding on tight.

"We will give him some time. He will come around as he gets to know you," Teller said.

Little Vlad held his arms up for Teller to hold him. Teller threw him high in the air and his father gasped in terror. Little Vlad laughed with delight as he landed safely in Teller's arms — as always.

"You two are free to marry, if you wish. Within the month I will crown Vlad Dracula IV as Voivode. At which point I will rule from behind the throne. We," Teller gestured to the three adults, "as well as my court, will see to it that the kingdom runs smoothly until little Vlad is ready to take over." To the small boy Teller added, "This is an enormous responsibility and you have much to learn if you are to become a great ruler."

"Yes, baba. I will be a great ruler, like you."

"No, you will be better than me." Teller wanted him to be like Sergiu — merciful and kind, firm only when it was needed.

Jusztina threw her arms around her son and Teller. "Thank you," she whispered as tears of joy fell on Teller's shoulder.

CHAPTER 68 COPENHAGEN 1462 AD

Lord Chastellain's castle was abuzz. The excitement was palpable — nothing but high spirits to be found. No one spoke about politics or impending war. All of that was forgotten as everyone turned their attention to the upcoming royal wedding. Allies and friends from afar arrived and the castle was once again crowded.

Every corner of the castle was cleaned; chandeliers were washed, thousands of pieces of the Court's finest cutlery was scrubbed and the silver was polished. Not a single cobweb could be found. The Great Hall was transformed with modern — and very expensive — décor.

Elijah dragged Val out of his bed to show her the Great Hall. When he uncovered her eyes she could hardly recognize where she was — even though she had been there a million times. Bright new paintings and tapestries stood out the most, as they were in stark contrast to the old dingy ones they had replaced. Intricate statues — some marble, some bronze — stood in corners or acted as sentinels on either side of doorways. New, even larger thrones sat at the far end of the Great Hall.

"It is beautiful," Val said, "but I don't need any of this."

"I know, yet we must humor father," Elijah said. "This is his display of wealth. It is for him more than for us."

She put her arms around him. A bright light danced in his light blue eyes. She had never seen him so carefree. He spun her around and they danced to imaginary music.

~

THE NIGHT before the wedding their friends pulled Elijah and Val apart.

"There will be plenty of time for that later," Samuel said.

The men carried Elijah out of the room — literally. They held him over their heads as they disappeared from sight.

Val could not help but laugh. "What is going on?"

"The men thought they should be with Elijah on the last night before he is married. Therefore, we are here to entertain you in his absence," Elizabeth explained.

This makes sense, Val thought. I should be with my girlfriends on the night before my wedding.

"It is good to see you happy!" Sonia said. "In fact, I have never seen you like this."

It was nice to be in such high spirits. Val had not felt like this since becoming a vampire. The last time she had felt this alive was when she and Teller had made plans to marry. This thought, however, caused her to frown.

"Well," Mari said, "what shall we do on your last night of being unattached?"

"I am spoken for," Val corrected. "Though at times I did not think I would ever marry. I cannot believe this is actually happening."

"Aye, we can't believe it either," Elizabeth said.

"It is going to be odd — you being yoked and all. I do not like it," Mary said. "I don't understand why anyone would want to commit herself to a man. I mean, to give up all the precious freedom we have as vampires. Now you will only be able to do what your husband bids of you." Mary's face twisted, as if the thought tasted bad.

"You know Elijah is not like that."

"That is what they all say. The point is that you had better enjoy tonight," Mary said.

"I know, let's take to the sky," Val said. It seemed that they only flew when traveling on Court business. It would be nice to stretch her wings and float in the clouds simply for fun, with no specific destination in mind.

"Great! You lead the way," Sonia said.

In a flash, Val stood on the balcony rail. She looked back at her girlfriends briefly then did a backflip, spinning completely around. She let herself fall a couple stories before spreading her wings — taking flight only moments before hitting the ground. It was not long before the vampires landed on a snowy mountaintop in Norway overlooking the jagged coastline of the endless fjords. Glacier water formed pale green pools far below. Beyond the mountains nothing but ocean could be seen. Moonlight reflected on the water like diamonds.

"This place is wonderful." Mari was breathless.

"You truly should get out of the castle more often," Val teased. Val had traveled through Norway on several occasions but Mari still preferred to stay behind most of the time.

Mari grabbed a handful of snow and tossed it in Val's face. As Val brushed the snow away a snowball hit the back of her neck. She turned to find Mary and Elizabeth pointing at each other in blame.

"What is this — pick on the bride?" Val said. "Well, if that is how it is ... " She kicked snow onto Mari and quickly threw two snowballs at Mary and Elizabeth. Soon all five ladies were covered in snow and laughing.

Mary stood with the toes of her boots over the ledge of the cliff. To her right a small stream spilled over the edge. She pointed to a handful of lights in the distance. "Let's have a drink." Mary gave them a mischievous smile before she stepped off the ledge.

"This could be trouble," Val said.

Sonia frowned and nodded her agreement.

Yet they followed. They let themselves free-fall for a time. The five friends raced the water as it made its way to the fjord many lengths below. The sound of sails catching the wind could be heard as their wings unfolded. They glided toward the lights of the isolated fishing village.

Inside the small tavern were a half-dozen men sitting about. Most of them had grey hair and lined faces. Their mouths hung open as they stared at the group of strange young women who entered. Mary, Elizabeth and Val were dressed in breeches, of course. Mari and Sonia were dressed as if they were royalty. Either way, women in this village did not wear such clothes.

"What are young ladies such as yourselves doing in these parts?" the innkeeper asked.

"We are celebrating the fact that this lady is getting married tomorrow." Mary slapped Val's shoulder — hard.

It actually stung.

The innkeeper studied Vallachia. "Well, the groom is a lucky man."

"No," Val corrected. "I'm the lucky one." Val gave the man a broad smile and a wink.

It appeared that the poor fellow's knees might give way.

"Let's liven this place up, shall we." Mari turned to the men whose mouths remained agape. "Do any of you fine gentlemen play an instrument?"

One man reached for a small lute and began to strum a melody. The singing began slowly but soon most of the men were singing and tapping their feet to the beat.

"Lovely," Mari said.

Mary ordered ale for herself and a couple flagons of wine for the others. They danced traditional circle dances and tried to learn some of the local songs. Val grabbed one of the old men and literally pulled him up to join the dance. He seemed delighted.

When the men were too tired to stand and the ladies had drunk most of the wine supply, Mari said, "We had better be getting back. We still have to get Val ready for her big day."

Mary scoffed at the many comments about how young ladies should not be out by themselves at this late hour.

The men did not want to see the lovely maidens go. Val gave the innkeeper a handful of gold coins, which more than covered the cost of their drinks.

"That is very generous. Thank you, My Lady ... and Congratulations!" he hollered as they disappeared into the cold night.

CHAPTER 69 COPENHAGEN
1462 AD

After long baths and much primping the ladies of the Court were ready.

"I refuse to put that thing on my head," Val said.

"Come now, it is all the fashion in Western Europe," Mari protested.

"That thing will make me look like a billygoat with those pointed horns coming out of my head."

"It will not make you look like a goat. The veil covers the headpiece so it will not resemble horns." Mari was always well aware of the latest fashions.

"No thank you," Val said. "I prefer Sonia's handiwork with hair. It is *my* wedding and I want my hair tastefully woven. No headdresses for me."

"I find it unbelievable that you are dressing as if you are an old crone from the East."

"I am an old crone from Eastern Europe."

"Fine, if you prefer to look completely out of fashion on the most important day of your life then ... I cannot stop you."

"Val will not be out of fashion. She will look ... classic."

"Thank you, Sonia," Val said.

Mari crossed her arms and rolled her eyes.

Sonia worked magic with Val's hair and carefully placed white flowers in the braids.

"It is perfect! A timeless simple elegance," Elizabeth said.

"It suits you. I knew you would like the flowers." Sonia was proud of her handiwork.

Mari frowned with disapproval from beneath her goat-horned headdress.

Val's gown resembled the brocades of old but it was more revealing on top and a tight belt was fastened under the breasts. Thus her breasts were more defined and visible than she was used to but Mari would not budge on this — Val simply had to wear *this* gown. It was quite lovely with its silky white color and bright red trim, so Val decided that she would have to tolerate the revealing top.

As they approached the Great Hall Val's stomach fluttered. She was not sure why? *Is it because Teller might be here?* He had been invited, along with all the Court's allies.

Of course the ceremony was too much. In addition to the makeover, the Great Hall had been decorated with large bouquets. Val did what she had done before at the engagement announcement; when all eyes were on her, she focused on the prize — Elijah. This way she would not be distracted by who was in the crowd, meaning Teller.

Mari was the maid of honor and Samuel the man of honor, of course — there were no others better suited for these roles. Sonia, Mary, Elizabeth, Aaron and Riddick were honorary members of the ceremony as well. Lord Chastellain walked Val down the aisle and performed the ceremony. Elijah and Val knelt on pillows facing each other.

It seemed as if time sped up. Before Val knew it, they were pronounced man and wife. To end the formal ceremony, the lord indicated that they should rise. He stepped between the newlyweds and took Val's hand raising it high above their heads. "I give you Lady Chastellain."

The crowd went mad.

The lord placed Elijah's hand in Val's and Elijah pulled her to him. Elijah's lips pressed against hers in a passionate kiss.

The crowd cheered even louder.

To start the festivities, the father customarily had the first dance so the lord presented his arm to Val and the crowd made a large circle around the two as they moved gracefully around the dance floor.

"You seem pleased with this decision," Lord Chastellain said.

"I am, My Lord."

"Today I became your father. You don't have to call me 'lord' anymore."

Vallachia's eyes widened. "Are you saying that you want me to call you 'Father?'" He does not resemble my real father in the least. Is it disrespectful to my father to call someone else by that title?

"You have been like a daughter to me for a long time. Now you are officially my daughter, so you should call me Father."

"I will ... try." Val had unfinished business with him. It felt as if this was the perfect opportunity, especially now that he was her father-in-law. "May we speak freely?"

"Of course."

Val leaned in close and spoke softly. "Are you sorry for the things you did to me in the beginning?"

"No." The lord's tone was flat.

She pursed her lips and nodded. That was it — that was all she would ever get from him. At least he was honest. She was disappointed but not surprised. He was who he was, good, bad and everything in between.

He watched her carefully. "Surely you see it; you were meant to be with us. I simply did what I had to do."

Everything fell into place, like the final stone being set in an impenetrable wall. The past couple hundred years had been a long-drawn-out political maneuver all preordained by Lord Chastellain. He needed Vallachia in order to remain in power. It was as if he knew she would balance his ruthless rule with mercy and compassion — making him and the Court unstoppable.

Yet, how does one forgive someone who is not sorry? Val thought. There would always be a rift between them. She would never get an apology. She still hated him at times and the rest of their relationship was solely business. *Now he wants to be my "father."* An angry heat rose from her stomach.

Thankfully Elijah came to take his father's place and they danced for another song in the middle of the crowd before others joined them on the dance floor.

"Did Father upset you?" Elijah asked.

"Is it that obvious?"

"I'm afraid so."

"He is simply ... " Val sighed, "your father. I am grateful that you are not like him." Elijah had a way of making everything seem right. Past troubles faded away when she was in his arms. She lay her head on his shoulder. "We did it," she whispered.

"There is no turning back."

"I don't want to turn back."

"Good," he whispered.

"What about you? You broke a lot of hearts by getting married. Your mistresses will miss your company."

"I only had them because I could not have you."

Elijah spun Val around and dipped her down until her head almost touched the floor. When he pulled her up, his lips were on hers. They kissed for what seemed like ages.

"That is quite enough. Save it for later."

Val glanced over Elijah's shoulder to find Riddick.

"May I?"

CHAPTER 70 COPENHAGEN
1462 AD

Elijah gladly gave Vallachia's hand to Riddick. As they moved around the dance floor, Elijah pulled Mary out of her seat. They had convinced her to wear a dress, only for the wedding of course. She looked lovely — even with her short hair. Yet she was visibly uncomfortable.

Riddick and Val chuckled as they watched Elijah trying to teach Mary to dance. Mary moved awkwardly and Elijah glided gracefully around her.

"It is good to see you like this. It makes me realize how sad you were before," Riddick said.

Was that true? Had I been sad for over two hundred years? More often than not, I suppose. That is a depressing thought. That will have to change.

"You should have done this a long time ago," Riddick continued.

"That is surely the truth!"

"Plus then I could have moved on a long time ago as well." Riddick's dark eyes shone with warmth.

Val laughed. "I wish you the best of luck with that."

"I don't know what you did to me. At one time I would have been unbearably jealous to have to attend your wedding. Now I only feel content because you are happy."

"That is what it means to truly care about someone. I hope you find love and happiness as well."

"I am happy."

Riddick had changed. Of course, in many ways he was still Riddick, for which Val was grateful. The change was most noticeable after they helped him learn to feed without killing. Once vampires were able to stop killing, their humanity could return. Having to kill made them hard and, over time, more cruel but they could heal from that once they stopped killing.

"Time's up, old friend." Elijah spun Val out of Riddick's arms and back into his — where she belonged.

Val focused on Elijah and tried not to worry about the crowd or who was in it — possibly Teller.

"I wish my father and brother could be here," Val said.

"They are watching over you, I'm sure of it," Elijah said.

"As is your mother."

"I was so young when she died. She is barely a memory."

Val frowned. If she were his mother watching over him from heaven it would break her heart to learn that he only vaguely remembered her. He no longer misses her ... How sad. Of course, I do not remember my mother either. Will I stop missing my father and brother someday? I don't know if I want that. Time heals all, I suppose.

"He is not here," Elijah whispered.

Val knew exactly who he meant.

"Good. So when can we get out of here?"

Elijah laughed. "Patience, my love and soon — I hope."

A tap came at her shoulder. Val's stomach dropped, as she thought it might be Teller despite what Elijah had just told her. She turned to find John — Lord Chastellain's faithful minion.

"I am terribly sorry to bother you, My Lady but there is a man at the front entrance who says he has a message for you. He is rather persistent and says he will not leave until he personally delivers the message to you."

Val gave Elijah a questioning glance.

Elijah shrugged. Worry creased his forehead. "Go ahead. I trust you," he whispered. He thought it must be Teller as well.

"Thank you for trusting me. I think you should come." She grabbed Elijah's hand and they headed for the main entrance.

Riddick, Samuel and Mary spotted them leaving and followed. They had been together on so many missions over the years that it was as if they moved as one. They were in tune with one another — protectively watching.

The man at the door was the largest man Val had ever seen, larger than Riddick or Teller. He had dark skin and even darker black hair. His black mustache hung over his mouth like a thick bucket handle and stopped just below his chin. It reminded Val of the one Teller had once worn.

The man bowed. "My name is Abdullah. I am the commander in chief of the Wallachian army. It is a pleasure to finally meet you." His voice was low and deep. He spoke with a heavy accent.

Val returned the bow. "Likewise."

"I bring you a wedding gift ... from my Master." The man gestured to a large wooden crate. "He sends his apologies for not being able to attend the royal wedding himself. He sent me to give you this as well." Abdullah reached under his silk chlamys.

Riddick drew his sword.

Abdullah presented a rolled parchment, which he handed to Vallachia. With one last bow he disappeared.

Val and Elijah glanced at each other with curiosity. He was as confused as she.

Human men unloaded the massive crate in the courtyard. It was at least three stories high. The crate was carried on a large cart. It took eight horses to pull the weight of whatever was in the crate. The crate was rolled into place on logs as the men unloaded it with pulleys and ropes.

Val opened the letter ...

. . .

My Dearest Vallachia,

I could not bring myself to attend your wedding. Surely you know why. Please accept this as a gift to remind you how I feel about you. I am terribly sorry that things ended up this way.

Tel.

Vallachia watched as the men broke open the wooden crate to reveal a statue of an angel. The angel's face resembled Val's. She did not try to stop the tears. She crumpled the note and threw it as she disappeared into the castle. At first, she did not know where to go. She found herself in Elijah's bed. That was where she wanted to be. Against her will, the tears fell.

Elijah entered. He held the wrinkled note from Teller.

Val wiped the tears away the best she could. She watched Elijah move to the fireplace and set the note ablaze. She hugged her knees and they watched the parchment turn to smoke. *If only it were that easy to burn away the past — instantly be able to move on — never look back, never wonder, What if ... ?*

Val swallowed hard, forcing the tears away. She had to stop them ... for Elijah. *I must find a way to forget about Teller. But how?* Val slowly moved to stand by Elijah but no words would come.

"He managed to do it," Elijah said. "Without even being here, he ruined our wedding night."

"No," it was barely a whisper. Val put her arms around Elijah's neck. "I won't let Teller ruin this for us. *We* can't let him ruin what we have."

Elijah did not return her embrace. It was as if she hugged an obelisk. *No!* she thought. *Teller will not take Elijah from me.*

"I should let you go." Elijah's voice was flat. No pain, no sadness.

Val had never seen him like this. Her heart raced. "You promised me a couple of hours ago that you would never let me go. 'Till death do us part ... '"

Elijah looked into his wife's eyes for a long moment and found what he was looking for. Her crystal-blue eyes told him how much she needed him. It was enough to break through his numbness. He pressed his lips to hers and wrapped his arms around her waist. *She is mine.*

Val was filled with relief. "I can't lose you," she breathed.

He picked her up and carried her to bed.

CHAPTER 71 COPENHAGEN 1462 AD

The sun was on the rise when Vallachia finally drifted off to sleep. She had not slept the past two nights. Her girlfriends had kept her up the night before the wedding and Elijah had kept her occupied last night. But there was no time to rest, as a loud knock came at the door. Val could hear their friends outside. She let out an irritated sigh. With one eye open she looked at Elijah. He too had been dozing.

"What on earth could they possibly want?" Val asked. "They can't leave us alone for one day?"

"Today is your big day."

"No, yesterday was *the* big day."

Elijah chuckled at the confusion on her face. "Do not tell me that you have forgotten what happens the day after a royal wedding?"

"What?" Val was too tired to fully take in what he was saying. She did not truly care.

"Today, Father will pronounce you Queen."

Val moaned and buried herself in the bedding. *That is something that happened to other people, not to me*. "I honestly would rather sleep."

"Oh, come now, don't be that way. We have to get up. Our friends grow impatient."

Elijah's door swung open.

"For Christ's sake, let her up," Samuel said.

Elijah laughed.

Mari found Val's head under the blankets. "We have to get you ready ... and it looks as if we have a lot of work to do." She pulled Val up by the arm and was careful to keep her naked body wrapped in the bedsheet.

As Val was dragged across the hall to her room, she gave Elijah an irritated glance. His pale blue eyes danced as he gave her a reassuring smile. He rested with his arms behind his head. He was barely covered by a blanket, leaving his bare chest visible. She wanted nothing more than to return to bed.

"Come on." Mari gave Val a firm tug. "We are going to be late."

"Look at your hair!" Mari said. "We may never get it untangled."

Val had to laugh. Mari's irritation was adorable.

"It is not funny! Look at this mess!"

All the ladies laughed, furthering Mari's irritation. Though she had nothing to worry about; after a long bath and a good oiling, they had Val looking like a proper lady of the Court once again.

It was Val's turn to be irritated, as her movement was limited by the long sleeves of a golden brocade and it was too tight around her bust. "I cannot wait to get back into my breeches."

Mari frowned at her in disapproval. "Women would kill to have such a gown as this."

"You look as uncomfortable as I was yesterday wearing that thing you forced me into. I swear I don't know how you women wear that bollock," Mary said.

Only one more day. Val told herself.

The first thing Val noticed when she entered the Great Hall was Elijah. He was dressed in royal splendor. Placed atop his head was a jeweled golden crown. His shoulders were draped in a red silk chlamys with black fur trim. Lord Chastellain was dressed much the same. On a pedestal in the center of the thrones was a slightly smaller but no less bejeweled crown resting on a purple pillow.

Val's stomach fluttered. *Is this truly happening? I am not a queen. I'm a poor village girl.* She was instructed to kneel in front of Lord Chastellain. He gave a speech about using the power of the Court to bestow the crown to Lady Vallachia.

All she could think about was how this was not right. *I am no ruler; I don't want to be a queen.* The pressure of this new role was already threatening to crush her. She felt as if she could not breathe. Being a queen would entail much more than being an emissary to the Court. It was an inescapable commitment to the followers of the Court. A queen could not turn her back on her duties. Val could not focus on much of what the lord said. It was all she could do to keep her breathing steady.

Lord Chastellain took the crown from the pillow and placed it on Vallachia's head. It was heavier than she expected and uncomfortable. She resisted the urge to take it off.

The lord took her hand and raised her to her feet. She faced the crowd of vampires. John draped a red robe over her shoulders — it had the same thick black trim as Elijah's. John placed a jeweled scepter in her hand.

"I give you the first Queen of the High Court of Elders — Queen Chastellain," The lord announced.

The crowd cheered before taking a knee.

No, no! I don't want this — people bowing to me, Val thought. Handing the scepter back to John, she moved down the steps to the people directly in front of her. She pulled them up to a standing position. "Please, everyone stand."

This they did.

"I am grateful that you would make me your queen. However, I am still simply Vallachia and I will continue to serve the Court as I always have. It is I who serves you."

This brought about loud cheers and someone yelled, "All hail Queen Vallachia." Soon everyone was chanting, "All hail Queen Vallachia."

Val shook her head. That was not what she was trying to achieve. She was trying to tell them that she did not want this and that they should treat her the same as before. She looked to Elijah for help but he only smiled with pride. He stepped forward taking her hand and raising it high. This brought about more cheers.

How has life become so complicated? I was supposed to marry a simple man, in a simple village and have a simple family; then die of old age. None of that has come to be. How did I get here? I do not know how to be a queen. What does that mean? How will this change my life?

The crowd came forward picking Elijah and Val up. They passed the newlyweds over their heads. It was a strange sensation, to be held up by many hands, moving across the top of the crowd. Val held onto Elijah's hand and they let the energy of their people carry them.

Elijah joined Val that night on his balcony after they managed to escape the second day of celebrations. She rested her elbows on the thick stone railing. "I don't want to be queen."

"I know and that is why you should be queen. The fact that you don't want it will be what makes you one of the best queens to ever rule." Elijah put his arm around her.

"So you think I will be a good queen?"

He nodded yes.

"It is a lot to think about being a wife; and only one day later I have to wrap my head around being the first queen to ever rule the vampire world. I don't know what that entails."

"You are not alone and you are a natural leader. You will do fine."

"You make this all sound ... *commonplace,*" she said.

"It is normal. Granted it is not the life we would have chosen but it is *our* life. Ergo ... *normal* — for us anyway."

"The sooner I get used to it the better, I suppose?" She leaned into him wrapping her arms around his waist.

"You were astounding today. Our people love you."

"No, you are the incredible one. Anyone else would have given up on me a long time ago. I love you."

Elijah's arms tightened around her. "If it were easy it would not be worth it. I knew you were worth waiting for."

Val was not sure about that. She hoped to be everything he deserved. "We have to get rid of that idiotic statue."

"Oh, don't worry. We will." With that he left her side and appeared on his bed. He looked at her in a way that made her weak in the knees. With his hand he gestured for her to come to him. In an instant she was on top of him, her lips all over him. She ripped his tunic off so she could run her hands over his smooth chest — her favorite part of his body. He was simply perfect.

"Thank God you are mine," she whispered as he kissed her neck.

CHAPTER 72 COPENHAGEN 1462 AD

Elijah wanted to destroy the statue Teller had given to Vallachia. In fact, Elijah wanted to demolish it with his own hands.

Val convinced Elijah and the Lord to donate it to the city of Copenhagen. It was finally agreed that the statue should be placed in the city square. A water fountain was built as its base. It was adorned with a plaque which read, *Donated by Lady Chastellain to the city of Copenhagen, 1462 A.D.* That was the year Vallachia married one love and lost the other. It was a year of equal parts joy and heartbreak.

The day after the coronation, Lord Chastellain summoned Val to the Great Hall. The vast marbled floor was virtually empty. This was an odd contrast to the previous days of celebration. The decorations and flowers were gone. All that remained in the central area were the Elders' thrones. The servants must have worked endlessly to accommodate them and their aristocratic desires.

The lord sat on his throne. His fingertips were pressed together as they rested against his chin. Val glanced around; there was no one else in sight. No guards, not even John — who was always at the lord's side. *This is odd.* Val narrowed her eyes. *What does he want with me?*

The lord did not acknowledge her approach. He remained deep in thought until she stood directly in front of him. His expression softened when he looked at her.

Val exhaled. She hadn't realized she had been holding her breath. She bowed. "You summoned me ... Father." She had to force herself to call him father.

"I have a wedding gift for you," he said.

This was not what she expected. "That is far from necessary. You did too much already. The wedding festivities were entirely over the top."

"I know but this is a gift you will actually be fond of." He revealed something that had been hidden in his robes. He slowly unwrapped the object from a purple silk scarf.

Val's mouth fell open. She greedily reached for the object. She wanted it — if only to touch it, even once would be enough.

The lord held her father's hand-carved patriarchal cross. "I want you to have this."

"You ... " the knot in her throat kept her from saying any more.

"Yes. I kept it all these years." The lord had to complete her sentence as she eagerly took the cross. "I oiled it regularly and it hung over my bed for the longest time. Eventually it was put into storage and I recently came across it. Well, that is a bit misleading. I tore our storage rooms apart until I found it."

Val chuckled at the thought of the lord rummaging through hundreds upon hundreds of years of possessions. "Thank you," she whispered. She held the cross to her chest. She'd often regretted leaving behind the cross her father had made her. She had been angry with God for forsaking her, so she gladly left it behind in Ludus all those years ago. She had only taken a handful of essentials when she left home for good.

As time passed, Val had wished it had not been lost to her. It was a piece of her father. He carved them to protect the people of the village. Of course, Chastellain was the one they had needed protection from. Plus they did not appear to shield people from evil — Teller had been right after all. All this had upset her back then. Yet, now the cross was physical proof of her father's existence. It was all that remained. It represented his gift for working with wood and his deep devotion to God. He had cared immensely for others and had done everything he could to try to keep the people around him safe.

"That is one thing I regret." The lord interrupted Val's thoughts.

She forced her eyes from the beautiful cross so that she could give the lord a questioning look. *He does have regrets after all, or at least one. What does this man feel guilty about?*

"What I did to your father."

What does he mean by this? Something told her that she was missing something — some important piece of information. "Do you mean killing my father, because that was not entirely your fault?"

The lord shook away his inner thoughts — thoughts of long ago. He forced himself back into the present. His face was lined with sadness. Val had never seen him like this. He was often concerned, angry or frustrated but never ... sad.

"Yes, well your father's death was never my intention."

"I know. Nor was it mine." Nor had it been Teller's intention. Val fully understood this now. At first, she had blamed Lord Chastellain for her father's untimely death. It was easier to blame him rather than accept the role she played in the tragedy — or Teller's role for that matter.

"Your father was a great man. Your mother could always see that."

"You knew my mother?"

The lord swiftly stood. "No. Of course not. I'm merely assuming that that was why she loved him so."

Val watched him leave. There is more to be said but he is suddenly done talking; perhaps because he has said too much already. The way the lord spoke about my mother sounded as if he had known she cared deeply for Father. How could he have been so sure of this? Why won't he tell me more? Her eyes narrowed with suspicion as she watched his dark green chlamys move like the branches of a weeping willow in the wind.

~

THE COURT'S relationship with Prince Vlad started when they coaxed Elijah and Val out of their room for a meeting of the Elders. For months Elijah and Val rarely left his chambers. The new lovers had a lot of catching up to do. Only when it was deemed urgent would they bother to join the Court and even then it was with great reluctance.

At one such meeting Lord Chastellain ordered Riddick to take some of their men to Wallachia to work with Prince Dracula and his army. Riddick was to make sure they were well trained and work with them on any weakness they may have. They were to create a strategic plan for coordinating Vlad's role so that they would be ready at a moment's notice, should Ramdasha attack.

"No," Riddick said.

The room fell silent. Vallachia's eyes widened and there were more than a few open-mouthed gapes. This was the first time Riddick had ever questioned — let alone refused — a direct order.

Val thought daggers might quite possibly come from Lord Chastellain's eyes. His face turned crimson.

"With all due respect, My Lord," Riddick said, "I do not think I am the man for the job."

"And why is that?" Lord Chastellain spoke through gritted teeth.

"Personally, I cannot stand the man. He is arrogant and rude. I can hardly resist the urge to slam my fist into that pretty face of his. Honestly, I would go to war against him before I would work *with* him."

Elijah smiled and Val's chuckle was cut short when the lord turned his glare her way. Riddick was completely unaware that he too was arrogant and rude. He was not fond of Teller because he resembled Teller. They were too alike to ever be able to tolerate one another, let alone get along as comrades.

Lord Chastellain rubbed his forehead with his thumb and index finger. "Very well, Samuel will go." The lord's tone made it clear that this was final.

Samuel's shoulders slumped. "Wonderful."

"That is an excellent idea My Lor-Father," Val said. "Mari should go as well. She grew up with Tel-Prince Vlad." All these titles and names were confusing, especially when all she wanted was to be alone with Elijah. "Mari may be of great help. It might make him more ... stable and open to working with us." Val honestly believed this and she hoped that Mari could help Teller. There was nothing like a friendly face from home to remind someone who he was and where he had come from.

"It is decided then." The lord seemed pleased that Val had agreed with him.

However, Samuel looked even more disappointed. "Excellent," he sighed.

Poor Samuel, Val thought. We need Teller as an ally but no one wants to work with him.

Elijah stood. "If that is all, Father, are we free to go?"

The lord nodded and Val quickly rose — eager to leave.

"You two are pathetic," Riddick smirked.

Samuel laughed. "Oh, come now, Riddick, you are simply envious."

"Who wouldn't be? You two should take a honeymoon."

"Have you gone mad, talking of moons and honey?" Elijah said.

"No, honeymoon, one word," Riddick corrected.

"It is nothing but a ridiculous notion. Something Riddick made up," Val said.

"It is not ridiculous! Newlyweds want to be alone, so they should take a holiday — to get away. Not to mention, they would not bother the people around them."

"Yes, like you are bothering us," Samuel added.

Elijah's eyes brightened. "That is a grand idea, Val. We should go to our estate in Ludus. We have not been there in ages."

"You see? Honeymoons will become popular, just you wait and see." Riddick was quite proud of himself.

The lord gestured for Elijah and Val to leave with a wave of his hand. His face was twisted with irritation. They were disrupting his important meeting with their gibberish. Val took Elijah's hand and they were gone.

CHAPTER 73 HOLY ROMAN EMPIRE 1462 AD

Over the next handful of years Teller slowly gave up his reign over Wallachia. Under the pretense of being a human ruler this was inevitable, as it would soon become apparent that he was not aging. His time was divided between Targoviste, Venice and Copenhagen. He was continually checking on affairs at home to make sure things were going well for the people of Wallachia and his son.

He continued to maintain his large vampire army. He moved into the Court's majestic castle in Venice. He was appointed a lord for the Court of Elders. He oversaw the Court's affairs from Venice to Istanbul. Lord Chastellain thought it wise to bequeath Teller with the title and power his large army deserved. The lord would do most anything to keep Teller as an ally. It was ironic how things had changed; when Teller was nothing but the son of a smithy in a small village he meant nothing to the lord; in fact, he had tried to rid himself of Teller. Now that Teller had made a name for himself, he was in the lord's favor.

Teller's position was of great importance, as it was the front line. Venice marked the farthest southern outpost controlled by the Court. Once again Teller found himself between two powerful forces, Lord Chastellain in the North and Lord Ramdasha in the South. This was exactly where he wanted to be, as there was never a dull moment.

This move to Venice also placed Teller less than one hour away from Vallachia. He could easily attend all important Court meetings.

After leaving one such meeting, he caught up with Vallachia. She looked around only to find that they were alone. *Oh no,* she thought. Her strategy for being around Teller was to avoid being alone with him.

"We can't very well become friends again with you ignoring me," Teller said.

Val said nothing and kept walking. Having her childhood friend back did sound nice but Val knew it would not work. After all, they had been engaged — though be it briefly. If they touched, it would be all too easy to lose control. She had to keep him at arm's length — no beyond that, even farther away.

"You know why I attend all these meetings in Denmark?"

"I can imagine the reason."

"I have to be able to see you ... if I am to win you back."

Val shook her head. "You see? This is why we cannot be friends. We moved beyond that a long time ago and there is no going back."

Teller grabbed her arm to stop her. She quickly jerked it away as the strange shock of his touch ran through her.

"You cannot win me back. I am married and I am happy, so please let me be. You need to move on as well."

"There is no moving on, Val. I know how it feels when we touch. I have never felt that way with anyone else and I never will. You don't feel it with Elijah, because you were meant to be with me."

Val narrowed her eyes. "How could you possibly know that? Maybe I do feel the same way with Elijah."

Pain flashed across Teller's dark eyes. Val felt awful for saying it. Teller is right — that strange sensation between us is unique. It will always be there, tempting us, pulling us together.

Teller stepped toward her but Val disappeared. She ran as fast as she could and locked herself in her chambers. She paced as she gathered her thoughts. *I will have to put up a wall to keep him out, an invisible shield for my mind and heart.*

Teller left Val alone. He knew how stubborn she could be when her mind was made up. He also knew that time was on his side. *After all, we have plenty of that in this never-ending life.*

Vallachia was aware of this and it worried her. How long would she be able to keep her wall up? It took every drop of her strength to refuse him.

After an intense combat training, Val and her friends decided to meet in Elijah's chambers for games and drinks.

"Why don't you join us?" Mari asked.

"I would love to." Teller took Mari's arm in his.

Mari is all but pushing Teller on us. Val thought. Surely, she would not do this to Elijah and me? Would she?

Samuel and Riddick exchanged a concerned look. Riddick was not growing any fonder of Teller and the feeling was mutual.

Val could not imagine those two ever getting over their similarities. She smiled at Elijah and he put his arm around her as they headed to his quarters.

Abdullah and the twins joined in the festivities. They rarely left Teller's side. Val was glad that Teller had such faithful companions. They would follow him anywhere and he would do anything for them in return. The addition of Teller and his friends to their circle did change the dynamics. Samuel, Elijah and especially Riddick did not like these newcomers. These handsome men were a threat. Riddick, Samuel and Elijah had enjoyed having their ladies to themselves. Aaron was the exception. He welcomed the new additions with his usual carefree manner.

As time passed, Teller slowly won Val's friends over — except for Riddick. It took a couple of years but even Elijah accepted him. Eventually, Val lowered her guard as well. The wall crumbled a bit, at least when she was in the safety of others. She treated Teller like she did all her friends. The rare times Teller would catch her alone, she was good about retreating behind her double-layer brick wall. It was nice to have him in her life. At least when he visited Denmark she knew where he was and that he was safe and even content.

CHAPTER 74 COPENHAGEN 1475 AD

It was a clear night and thousands of stars shone brightly. Vallachia was reading on her balcony when something jabbed her in the ribs. She let out a scream and leapt to her feet only to find Teller laughing heartily. He looked and sounded almost exactly the same as he had the day she realized she had fallen in love with him. His emerald eyes sparkled. This was too much, so she focused on her irritation.

"You made me lose my place," she snapped.

"Vampires are not easy to scare, yet I managed to make you jump ten feet." He laughed again. "I can't believe I can still scare you. It is nice to know some things never change."

Val could not help smiling. "Well, I was enthralled in my book. I was reading one of my favorite volumes of Princess Anna's works. She wrote mostly of her father's reign. That was almost four hundred years ago. It was even before our time," Val mused.

"Indeed, it sounds like a page-turner. The description alone bores me."

"This is about a very important time in Roman history. Princess Anna lived during the height of our empire."

Teller proceeded to quote Anna's work, word for word, "Such were the words of the Golden Bull. Men may perhaps marvel that my father, the Emperor, should have shown so much honor to his mother and handed over everything to her, whilst he himself, so to speak, took his hands off the reins of government whilst she metaphorically drove the chariot of state; he only ran alongside and merely shared with her the title of ruler."

Val spoke the last words along with him. "You *do* know her work. You were fooling me — again."

"I know every word by heart. And now her empire is dead, our empire, lost forever." There was a bitterness in his voice. "I should have intervened and stopped Mehmed from taking the city. At that time I was unhappy with the leaders of Constantinople."

"Constantinople lives in books such as these."

"That is not good enough."

"I know." It was barely good enough for Vallachia. Part of her held onto that secret dream — Teller and her as Emperor and Empress of Constantinople — restoring the Roman Empire. She shook her head, *another lifetime perhaps.*

Teller sat down in Elijah's chair next to her. He leaned back and looked up at the stars. "I want to thank you."

Val furrowed her brow. "For what?" *Why on earth would he thank me?*

"My life has gotten better since you found me. You saved me."

"No, I did not. I gave up on you." Admitting this caused pain to form in her chest. She tried to rub it away. I should not have abandoned him when he needed me the most — either time — after he killed my father or after we found him in Wallachia.

"Since Mary and Samuel taught me how to feed without killing, I feel as if I am becoming more like myself."

"Then they are the ones you should thank. Not me. I have a theory about that. When we do not have to kill anymore we can regain our humanity. I have seen it happen many times. Riddick is a good example. I'm glad you have found yourself."

"Your friends are splendid. I'm glad you are surrounded by people who care about you."

Val smiled. "My friends are wonderful. We have always been there for each other."

Teller frowned. "I'm sorry that I was not there for you all those years."

"No, I am sorry I deserted you. I regret it every day," Val said.

Teller smiled. A glimmer of hope shone in his eyes. Val was speaking openly with him. She had let her wall down. He reached for her hand but she moved away.

"Don't push your luck," she said.

"It feels so good. How do you resist?"

"I have to."

"I know. You are stronger than I." He looked up at the stars. "This life is really amazing, is it not?"

Val followed his gaze. "Yes, it is. You know ... it is good to have you in our lives."

Teller's smile was radiant. Val was glad she was sitting down because her knees felt weak.

"I ... should go ... find Elijah." He was the only thing that could clear her head and keep her out of trouble. She worried her legs might falter but she made herself stand.

Teller's knowing smile said, "You will be mine — someday."

He truly is arrogant. Where is my wall? Val glared at him. "You will do well to be careful. You know what the penalty for adultery is in a royal court."

Teller nodded to indicate he knew full well the consequences. "That is why I will have to convince you to run away with me. But for now I will settle for being friends."

Val shook her head with disapproval and left to find her husband.

Queens in the West as well as empresses in the East would be put to death if they were caught being unfaithful. Of course, this was unfair as a king often had a long line of mistresses.

While the world of vampires was more relaxed in their social norms, they were still a product of their culture. Vampires were more lenient, as there were no offspring. A vampire man did not have to worry about whether or not he was the father of his wife's children.

Val did not want to find out what her father-in-law would do if she were unfaithful. She assumed that he would not be merciful. The lord had already tried to kill Teller and that was long before she was married to the lord's son. More importantly, Val would not hurt Elijah. She was determined to be the faithful wife he deserved. Of course, she also had no intention of leaving her friends in order to run away with Teller. Her companions were her only family — her life.

CHAPTER 75 COPENHAGEN 1500 AD

Elijah handed Vallachia a small leather-bound book. His expression was stern and the storm raged in his eyes.

"What is this?" Val asked, even though she was certain she did not want to know the answer.

He nodded toward the book, so she took it and read the title, The Story of a Bloodthirsty Madman Called Dracula of Wallachia.

"This is circulating all over Europe, thanks to the printing press. You should read it. Teller may not be who you think he is."

Val's stomach turned before she even began reading. She did not move so much as a hair until she had finished the tales of Teller's past. It was not long before she slammed the book shut. She rubbed her stomach as its contents threatened to come up. *This can't be true. I must find out!* She stood with determination and leapt off her balcony taking flight for Venice. In her state of dismay, she did not stop to tell anyone where she was going. Elijah would not want her to travel alone, for her own protection. She did not care. She had to speak with Teller immediately and by herself.

Within the hour she landed at the entrance to his palace in Venice. The guards swiftly stepped aside and opened the tall doors for her.

They knew full well who she was. She stormed past them without so much as a word.

"What is this!" Vallachia demanded as she barged into Teller's chambers unannounced.

Teller had been sitting at his desk poring over some parchments. She threw the small book on top of the papers.

He laughed. "I have read it. It is entertaining and comical."

"Comical! There is nothing funny about this horrid book."

"It is comical that someone had the imagination to create such outrageous stories."

Vallachia's eyes had been full of anger but that gave way as a tear rolled down her cheek. Her anger he could handle but the pain in her bright blue eyes was unbearable. "Val. Please do not believe this rubbish. It is full of lies, well mostly. It was made up by a poet with an overactive and rather sick imagination."

"Why would someone write such horrible things about you?"

"It started when the cowardly King Mathias of Hungary had this published and began circulating the stories in order to make me look bad. You see, when I took on the Ottoman Empire with only my small army, praise was sung for me from the Knights of Rhodes to the Pope in Rome and beyond. The useless King of Hungary was all too happy to take large sums of money from the pope to fund another crusade, one that would never come. You see, Mathias needed the money to buy his crown — quite literally the crown of St. Stephen — and therefore be seen as a legitimate ruler. With the pope singing my praise this put great pressure on Mathias. He had to do something, so he had me labeled as a traitor and slandered my name with this bollock. All this did not matter in the end as I had already stepped down from the Wallachian throne."

Val's eyes searched Teller's. She was desperate to see the truth. She folded her arms across her chest.

"Val, you must believe me. I have done horrible things, you know this. I would never lie to you. But the senseless acts in this book are ridiculous. One cannot believe everything they read."

"True enough. Which parts did happen?"

Teller picked up the small book and flipped through the pages. "Well, the bit about the beggars. Only my men fed from them, I did not burn them alive."

Her eyes were filling with moisture.

"Look, this is not important. Please know that this is a load of shit and that I am no longer Vlad. I'm Teller ... again. I implore you to understand that."

He moved around the desk and tried to take her hands. She pulled away. Every time she did that, pain formed in his chest. If only she would let me touch her, I could win her back. Of course, she knows this, which is why she tries so hard to stay away.

"And the concubine, cutting the baby from her womb?" Val's voice was barely audible.

"No! I would never ... *Well, I might have, if Sergiu had not stopped me.* He sat down on the desk and put his head in his hands. It was an attempt to cover the pain, the guilt and the confusion that overwhelmed him. *Would I truly have killed Jusztina and her unborn baby — my precious little boy? Undoubtedly, I would have.*

"I don't know what is wrong with me," Teller whispered. "I have an anger inside that takes control. Maybe it is simply the way I am. I'm like my father and there is nothing I can do to stop it. Only Sergiu Pasha could reason with me when I lost my senses. My father could inflict damage when he was enraged but when the fury takes me, people end up dead. You are right. I have done unforgivable things. Maybe not those terrible things." He pointed to the book. "But terrible things nonetheless."

It took a long moment for him to find the courage to look at Val. He expected her to be utterly disgusted — judging his past sins.

Her eyes were no longer angry or full of pain. Only compassion and love could be found as she silently watched him. This made Teller feel all the worse. He would never deserve someone so perfect. *How can she forgive me so quickly?*

Val wanted to put her arms around him but refrained. Instead she placed a hand on his shoulder and gently rubbed, as Sergiu used to do. This, along with her powerful touch was more than Teller could handle. He put his arm around her waist and pulled her to him. He buried his head in her soft stomach and let the tears fall. He had never fully mourned for Sergiu, for all the dead at his hand, for ... everything. It felt miraculous, as if a heavy burden was slowly vanishing.

Val rubbed her fingers through his hair. Teller was relieved and grateful that she finally let him hold her. In that moment he needed her more than anything in the world. Life appeared clearer. Hundreds of concubines could never have taken Vallachia's place — she was the one he needed. This was the start of letting go of the past and fully healing.

As his tears slowed, a vision of two children appeared in his mind's eye. There stood a boy and a girl. They had olive skin and Teller's dark hair. Yet they had crystal-blue eyes and a strong jaw like their would-be mother's — Vallachia's. Children that were meant to be born but would never come to be. These wonderfully beautiful souls had nothing else to do, except haunt their father.

For what seemed like a long time Teller enjoyed Val's loving touch and the sight of their children. When she pulled away, she sat next to him on the desk. He picked up the idiotic book. "They did get one thing right — the bloodthirsty bit."

Val chuckled and snatched the book from him. She threw it across the room. It landed in the fireplace. Moving swiftly she followed it and lit the book on fire. She returned to his side and they watched the book burn.

Val took Teller's hand and turned it over to examine his wrist. She ran her finger across the numerous white marks that remained. Both of his wrists were nothing but scars. Her soft touch over the pale skin sent an extra shock through him.

"How many of us have you created?" she asked.

"There is no way to be certain, upwards of a hundred, I suppose. Not all the men I turned worked out in my army. We killed the ones who could not control their thirst and yet others chose not to follow me."

"The past is done. We must look only to the future." She smiled and her sky-blue eyes sparkled.

He wanted to put his arm around her again but feared she would reject him.

"I suppose I am paying the ultimate price. I lost the two most important people in the world, you and my pasha."

"Pasha? You are referring to Sergiu and you mean he was like a father to you?"

"Pasha is a title of respect like a ... " he searched for the Greek or even Latin words but all that came to mind was, "Grand Vizier."

Val shook her head still not understanding.

He had to hunt harder for a translation. "A Vizier is a ... most trusted advisor. He was the wisest amongst us."

She nodded. "Tell me about him. What was he like?"

"You would have loved him ...

CHAPTER 76 HOLY ROMAN EMPIRE 1551 AD

"It is time," Elda said. "I have seen it. Their leader is sure to fall if we attack now."

"You are certain of this, my darling? Chastellain's reign will finally end?" Ramdasha replied.

"Since becoming a vampire my visions are much more powerful. Still at times, they are vague and they can change. Yet at other times, they are clear as a virgin mountain lake. And this is one of the most vivid visions I have experienced. We are finally strong enough. If we attack now, their forces will be diminished and their leader will die in battle."

Elda was in her woolgathering trance, the one where she was seeing things that others could not. Ramdasha fully trusted her. He had witnessed the power of her sight first hand. With her powers she had managed to keep them hidden from the Court all this time.

"Surely this will allow me to take over," Ramdasha said.

With a triumphant nod and a vengeful glimmer in her honey-colored eyes, Elda issued her lovely dimpled smile to her beloved husband.

~

THE HIGH COURT OF ELDERS was beginning to think that Ramdasha would never have the courage to meet them in an all-out battle. That was, until Ramdasha sent three emissaries to deliver a letter to Lord Chastellain. The messengers handed the sealed scroll to a palace guard at the front gates and quickly fled. The Lord summoned Elijah, Vallachia, Riddick and Samuel to the Great Hall. John was already there, of course, waiting to fulfill any order the lord may have. Chastellain broke the dark green wax seal, which had been pressed with the symbol of a tarantula. He read the message aloud. ...

IT IS time we settled our differences once and for all. In order to determine who is best suited to rule the world of vampires, I challenge the Court to meet me in combat. There is a large meadow to the northeast of Mount Blanc, which is isolated and should suffice for a battlefield. Dusk on January 15th 1551 will be the date.

Lord Ramdasha, the rightful king of vampires

LORD CHASTELLAIN'S face had gone red by the time he finished. Val looked to Elijah who returned her concerned gaze. She moved in close and laid her head on her husband's shoulder.

There would be a war — a war that would best any human war — and they would have to be on the front line. This was what they had trained for. Now that war was certain to come, it seemed frightful. It would not be like training.

"No! We *will* meet him in battle but ... on our terms," the lord declared.

Val had seen him angry many times but he was beyond that. He crushed the parchment. Val wondered if it would disintegrate under the immense pressure. It was a good thing for Ramdasha that he was not present. Lord Chastellain could have killed Ramdasha with his enraged stare.

"How will we get a message to him with our terms for battle?" Val ventured. Let the power struggle begin. Chastellain and Ramdasha will argue

over when and where the battle should take place — if we can manage to get a message to him.

A wide-eyed panic flashed across the lord's face as he realized replying to the message would be tricky. They did not know where Ramdasha was. That had been the problem all along. "Riddick, take the closest guards and track the messengers down. Bring them to me alive!"

Riddick disappeared in a blur before Chastellain had finished.

Samuel was brave enough to fill the silence that followed Riddick's departure. "Ramdasha has the nerve to make war sound as if it is *his* idea. We have been calling for him to face us head on for centuries. We even left some of his men alive so they could deliver the message."

"The fifteenth day of January is almost upon us — it is less than two days away. We need more time to prepare," Elijah said.

"That is, no doubt, why he set the date so near. The less prepared we are, the better for him. We must have more time to gather some of our remote allies," Val added.

"We will not play his game!" the lord said. "We will go to war on our terms. If he wants a fight two nights from now then he will have to come to us. We are prepared for that. Our armies would annihilate them on our own lands."

"That is why he has not attacked this castle and I would wager that he would not be that stupid. He is, unfortunately, cunning," Samuel said.

"At least he has finally answered our calls to war. We cannot miss this opportunity to end this. If we have no other choice then we must fight him on his terms," John said.

Vallachia was fond of the idea of getting it over with, rather than dragging it out. They had been waiting a long time for this. It was overdue. On the other hand, the enemy would be more prepared and she did not fancy the idea of them having that advantage. There was most likely a good reason why Ramdasha had chosen that meadow. "Surely he has a plan that will give him the upper hand."

"Yes, he obviously feels prepared to fight us. Something has changed for him to come forward now. He would not challenge us to war unless he was certain he could defeat us," Chastellain said. His anger had subsided and there was work to be done. This was what he did best — think.

"We must respect the fact that he is prepared to fight us. He must have something we do not know about — a new weapon perhaps, more warriors than us, any number of possibilities," Samuel said.

"With Teller's army, surely he could not outnumber us," Elijah said.

"It looks as if we are about to find out," Val said. She moved to the window wondering how it was going for Riddick. Perhaps she had hoped to see him return. *I should have gone with him,* she thought. Most likely the emissaries had fled straight into the Oresund so that it would be difficult to track them in the water.

"Where is Riddick?" The lord paced in front of his throne.

"Let's go after him," Val took Elijah's hand and headed for the door.

But there was no need to leave as Riddick appeared in the doorway. In either hand Riddick held two unfamiliar men. Behind him one of the guards held a third prisoner — a woman. Others in the castle, mostly guards, had gathered around Riddick. This was out of curiosity rather than to help him. Riddick did not need their help.

"Riddick, my dear boy, what on earth would we do without you?" The lord beamed.

Thank God the messengers were not smart enough to head straight for water. Did they not know that vampires could track anything on land as well as in the sky? Riddick was better than most in this area. He could track a spider, let alone three reeking vampires.

The lord was in his element and ready to play with his prey. He smiled with malice, as he studied the three vampires kneeling before him. One man rubbed his arm where Riddick's grip had been. The lord wandered away, peering out the window. He was a cat looking uninterested as the wounded mouse tried to scurry away. When the mouse was almost out of reach, the lord would pounce, sinking his teeth and claws into the poor helpless creature. The mouse never truly stood a chance.

"Well, well. What have we here? It appears Ramdasha has decided to act like a real man. Perhaps he does have a cock after all."

One of the prisoners glanced at Vallachia with wide eyes. It appeared that he thought such vulgarity should not be spoken in front of a lady. Val thought his concern for the innocence of her ears was endearing. Of course, she had lived long enough to hear far worse.

Val gave Elijah a questioning looked. He shrugged in response. Apparently he did not know what had gotten into his usually pedantic father either.

"Does Ramdasha actually believe that he stands a chance against me? He is finally ready to answer *my* calls to war?" the lord said.

The prisoners remained silent. It was the woman who found her courage. "Yes, I believe that is his intention, my... "

"My what?" Chastellain demanded.

"My Lord." It clearly pained her to call him by this respectful title.

"That's better. What traps has he set for us on the fifteenth of this month?"

"No traps, My Lord. He wants an evenhanded battle. No skullduggery, I promise," the woman answered and the men were happy to let her do so.

"Please, My Lord, are you going to kill us?" one of the men blurted. The suspense was torture, he simply must know his fate.

"Of course not. If you think that I would kill you, then you have been misled. You see, contrary to what you may have heard about me, I am a benevolent and fair ruler."

Vallachia refrained from rolling her eyes, as this statement was debatable. *The lord is in rare form.*

"To demonstrate how benevolent I truly am, I will ease your mind by telling you exactly what will happen. I will send one of you with a message for the cowardly Ramdasha. The other two will remain here and I will not harm a hair on your mangy heads. You have my word."

"What message?" the woman asked.

Val had to admire her — she was brave.

"Do not worry about that, my dear. You will not be the one sending it," the lord said.

Val knew he would not send her — she was entirely too brazen. Chastellain eyed both the men for a long moment but Val already knew which one the lord would pick to send the message. He would send the weakest one — the man who had not said a word — the one with the slumped shoulders and who stared only at the floor.

Val was right.

"Send these two to the dungeon and, as I promised, do not harm them," Chastellain ordered.

In no time only the weak one remained. "Please, My Lord, I don't know where Ramdasha is. He is already on the move."

"Liar! You were running right back to him when we caught you. For the first time in centuries I don't give a shit where that bastard is." The lord softened his tone and smiled. "To further demonstrate how gracious a leader I am, I will not have you followed. As long as you deliver my message to your spineless master, your companions will go unharmed. I will even set them free to fight against us in battle. You see not only am I merciful, I am also brave. All I want is an honest fight. My armies, against Ramdasha's in a battle to decide who should rule. If I can be defeated in a fair fight then I will gladly hand over my throne. Tell Ramdasha that the battle must occur in two weeks' time and on neutral grounds. We will send a parchment with you. It will contain our terms for war."

The man's head had remained lowered throughout the lord's speech.

"Do you understand?" Elijah demanded.

Vallachia recoiled at the darkness in Elijah's voice.

"Yes ... I ... I think so, Your Majesty." The prisoner was shackled and surrounded by guards as the parchment with the new terms of war was prepared and sealed with gold wax and the Chastellain coat of arms.

CHAPTER 77 COPENHAGEN
1551 AD

Samuel was the Court's weapons expert. Ever since they were trapped in Ramdasha's old cavern he had studied from humans or anyone he could find who knew about explosives and guns. He experimented on his own as well. He trained the Court to fire guns. Val was not fond of the awkward contraptions. They were unbearably loud and had to be reloaded after each shot.

Nevertheless, the Court's soldiers learned to reload quickly and to shoot accurately. Yet in battle, guns would only be useful in the beginning, as their enemy would not be stopped by the bullets — only slowed temporarily, if one was lucky. When they went to reload, their opponent would be on top of them.

Thus, the focus was on sword fighting and archery. The Court's soldiers were trained in all areas of combat but they had an entire battalion dedicated to archery. They consisted of the Court's most accurate shooters. Vampire combat was much more difficult than human combat because, like bullets, arrows would not kill vampires either; only slow them down. Yet, they had to utilize all possible weaponry.

Many of Val's friends developed a propensity for their favorite weapons. Elijah was an expert with the whip or rather whips. Not just any whips — Samuel lined them with the sharpest of razors. Elijah kept two such whips fastened to his belt whenever he left the castle. With these he could easily sever the head of a vampire from a distance. This was one sure way to kill his opponent.

As it would turn out, Mari had an aptitude for archery. She was the head of the Court's archers. Samuel, of course, was the best with guns — he kept two in holsters on his belt at most times. He also invented explosives that were small enough to hold in the hand. They ignited on impact. He called them grenades. It would blow one's opponent back and possibly take them out of the fight; yet again this would not kill a vampire. They would heal from the blast, as Val and her companions had after the explosion in Ramdasha's old cavern.

Riddick was the best with his double axes. He used one in each hand — they had one incredibly sharp edge and metal spikes on the back. Teller preferred the crossbow. He kept this with his arrows strapped to his back. For hand-to-hand combat, Teller fought with a scimitar in one hand and a wicked spiked club in the other.

Val was most lethal with two double-edged long swords and numerous knives, which lined her belt. Learning to use a weapon in either hand allowed them to defend themselves better and increased the chances of being able to issue a lethal blow.

Most of them would be carrying bow and arrows on their backs as well as their preferred weapons. Men and women alike would wear metal breast and back plates with the Chastellain Coat of Arms on the chest. Their tunics and breeches were made of a flexible black material, which allowed them to move as quickly and freely as possible. The finishing touch to their battle garb was thick black leather boots.

Two days before the battle it was no surprise to find Elijah in the horse stables. He was feeding Hollis apples — well Hollis's great, great, great, great ... grandson. Elijah had bred Hollis's line well and his offspring were the largest and strongest breed — the mighty Clydesdale. The Scottish claimed to have been the first to breed the Clydesdales but they bought their original stud from Elijah. Elijah's horses had a reputation for being the best and were often sought after by humans far and wide. Little did they know that the line for these magnificent horses came from an orphaned foal who was almost a warm winter meal for wolves.

Val joined Elijah and Hollis, Jr. She ran her hand down Hollis's neck. This fine specimen was over nineteen hands high. He was at least twice as muscular as the average horse and his hooves were three times the size. People paid a high price for Hollis to breed their mares.

"Will you ride him into battle?" Val asked.

"No. I will not risk him."

"Yet, you will risk me?"

"No. If I had it my way you would not be fighting. But I know you — all too well. You will fight no matter what I want."

"Well, all that time spent training would have been for nothing if I did not fight. We cannot let all my hard work go to waste." Val gave Elijah a warm smile. Of course, she would not let their people fight for her. She had to be in the front line by Elijah's side — leading their people. This was what just rulers did. And this fight was worth dying for.

She ran her hand playfully down his chest and wrapped her arms around his waist. "Let's spend the day in our cave — the two of us. Then tomorrow, the eve of battle, we will spend with our family."

Elijah's arms held her close. "That sounds perfect. Tonight we will have to feed."

THE EVE of battle seemed as if it would never end. Like the stories of hell, it was prolonged torment. They had been busy preparing for battle since the date had been set. They'd had little time to think about much else. Up until that point they had spent much time perfecting their strategy. Then came the day before the battle; at this point everything was planned and ready and reviewed a million times over. There was nothing to do but wait. They were supposed to rest because at dusk they would take flight for the battlefield. But how could anyone possibly sleep at a time like this?

All the people Val cared about would head into battle the next day.

They would be in mortal danger and she knew that the chances of everyone surviving were slim. She prayed that most would and that they would finally end this war over vampire domination. The entire human race was at stake. The Court must fight to the end. No matter what that end might be. If Ramdasha won, the world would change forever. They simply could not allow that to happen.

They started out in the Great Hall. Elijah, Samuel and the lord reviewed parts of the plan one last time but it had all been finalized so eventually everyone fell silent. Val laid her head on Elijah's shoulder and Mari's arms were around Samuel's waist. They had nothing left to say but it was as if they did not want to leave one another's company. It was not likely that they would ever be together again — not all of them.

"Everyone should try to get some rest," Lord Chastellain said.

Val's closest friends found themselves in Elijah's chambers. Val curled up at the head of their large bed and rested against the massive pillows. Mari joined her. Samuel and Elijah followed. Val laid her head on Elijah's chest for some much-needed comfort. Sonia sat in a tiny ball on Aaron's lap. Elizabeth's head was on Mary's shoulder. Teller and Abdullah gazed out the window but did not take in the view. Riddick stayed on the other side of the room from Teller. The twins sat on the floor each using the other as a backrest with their elbows resting on their knees. They looked as if they were perfectly paired bookends. Wine was opened and passed around but no one felt like playing games.

They sat in silence, no longer taking one another for granted. The only thing that mattered was that they were together. There was no predicting what tomorrow had in store for them. As immortals in a time of relative peace, they'd had little apprehension about the future. The future was a given, they always had tomorrow. That was no longer the case on the eve of battle; it would be a battle with others who were just as fast and strong.

Now that their seemingly everlasting life was in jeopardy, Val imagined that it felt worse than it did for humans. Humans could die at virtually any moment from any number of causes. They were less likely to place confidence in their future. That was not the case for them. It was painfully clear how much they had complete faith in their futures, which could end tomorrow.

"It will be an immense relief to get this over with. Imminent war has been our life for far too long. Soon we will no longer have to worry about a pending battle." Elijah broke what had been hours of silence.

"Let us hope we are able to end this once and for all," Samuel said.

Val nodded. She had only one burning question, "What do you think happens to us when we die?"

The heavy silence that fell on the room was suffocating. No one spoke because no one knew the answer. They'd had this conversation many times with no resolution. Val regretted bringing it up now. It was not helpful for creatures who may not have a soul to ponder such things before heading into battle. If only they knew where vampires came from, maybe they could answer Val's question. It was on most everyone's mind but only Val had the courage, or the stupidity, to voice it.

Where did they come from and where do they go? If things went poorly then they'd find out tomorrow. These were unanswerable questions and yet the most important at a time like this.

"I want everyone here to know how much I love you." Val tried to lighten the mood, which was an impossible task.

Mari's eyes filled with moisture.

This made their comrades even more uncomfortable, so they slowly retired to their own quarters.

Val gave everyone a tight hug before they left. The shocking sensation that Teller gave her when they hugged was unbearable. His touch made it even more difficult to hold back the tears. Val did not want to let him go. For a brief moment she wished they had run away, leaving this war far behind. She felt terrible for having this thought.

"We will all be fine," Teller whispered.

Only Mari and Samuel remained. Mari and Val curled up together at the head of the bed. Samuel lay beside Mari, putting his arm around the two women. Elijah did the same. Yet no one slept. They remained silent statues for another hour until the sun was low in the west.

To make sure they had plenty of strength for the fight, Elijah and Val had fed the night before. The rest of their time was spent in their cave, lost in each other. She was grateful for that time alone and this time with her dearest companions. If this was the end, then there was so much she still needed to do, things she wanted to say. But it was too late. All that remained was stillness.

CHAPTER 78 COPENHAGEN 1551 AD

The four closest of friends headed to the courtyard at dusk. Lord Chastellain was already there, organizing the armies for departure. Lord Alexandru, with Hector on his right and Mary on his left, would lead a separate army numbering about sixty. They were to break off from the main army. Teller's men — who numbered about seventy — were to do the same. They would wait until the main army had fully engaged with Ramdasha's forces. Then they would attack from either side, Alexandru from the west and Teller from the east. They hoped to surprise and overwhelm Ramdasha's forces with this tactic.

Mari was to lead the battalion of twenty archers to the nearby hill. This would give them the best vantage point to attack and help the soldiers on the ground. Lord Chastellain was to remain in the rear of the main army, which was comprised of one hundred and fifty soldiers. Elijah, Riddick, Samuel and Vallachia would lead the primary army.

Lord Chastellain wanted to be by Elijah's side but they convinced him that the Court needed to separate their first in command — himself — from the second in command — Elijah. They could not risk losing both King and Prince early on in the battle. Since Elijah was the better fighter it made sense for him to lead the army.

Riddick and John tried to convince Elijah and Val — the second and third in command — that they too needed to split up. But neither would budge on this. Riddick would not leave Val's side and Lord Chastellain would not have put his son in the front line without Riddick anyway. In the end, it all worked out. This strategy was the most logical, as it put their best fighters first.

It worried Val that she would not be able to watch after her other friends. Being separated from them would be hard. However, Elijah, Riddick and Val would be Ramdasha's primary targets, as he had a very old vendetta against them. Perhaps being away from the front would help to keep Val's friends safe — she hoped.

The most worrisome thing was that they had no idea what tricks Ramdasha had in store for them. No doubt he had surprises of his own. He now felt ready to take on the High Court of Elders, who had reigned supreme for over a millennia, so they needed to respect this fact. He must have some secret weapon or scheme. He would not have agreed to meet the Court in combat unless he was certain he stood a good chance of winning. Hopefully the Court's strategy would be enough to defeat him.

Before they took flight, Val found Teller and threw her arms around him one last time. She had to feel his special touch, in case there would never be another chance. "Take care of yourself," she whispered as she enjoyed the shocking sensation that ran through her. He kissed her forehead, which made her knees give.

"I will find you as soon as I can," he whispered.

Val found her other friends and gave each an embrace.

"I will see you for the victory celebration." Mary tried to smile.

Val wished that she shared Mary's confidence. Returning to Elijah's side Val took his hand, as Lord Chastellain gave the command for them to take flight. Over three hundred vampires rising into the air was quite a thing to witness. They blackened the sky and the noise was deafening. The wind created by their wings swirled dirt in all directions.

Vallachia wondered what humans would make of this sight. No humans lived near and none would be this far out of town at dusk. Had they been, they might have assumed it was the end of the world. If the Court failed, it *would* be the end of the world.

Val gave one last nod to Teller and another to Mary before they broke off from the flock with their respective armies. As they neared the battlefield Val grabbed Mari's hand and gave her a knowing nod that it was time for her and her archers to branch off. They were to slip around the back of the highest hill. This would give her archers the best vantage point to rain down their arrows on Ramdasha's army. Then she too was gone. Val's heartbeat quickened. *What if Mari is ambushed?* Val had to take several deep breaths to calm herself. *She will be fine.*

They landed on the outskirts of the battlefield. Their trusty scouts approached.

"All is quiet and clear, My Lord," a scout informed Elijah. "No sign of Ramdasha and the field is safe. No explosives have been set."

"That is good news," Elijah said. His head turned toward the south.

Val could smell it as well — vampires and lots of them. They watched Ramdasha's army as it landed and march in unison onto the field.

"Here we go." Elijah took Val's hand and with the other motioned for their men to move forward. They needed to remain out of range of their enemies arrows. Elijah held up his fist. As if they were one massive creature the Court's soldiers halted.

The Court's crimson flags with the gold Chastellain coat of arms rippled in the breeze. They were answered by Ramdasha's forest green flags, inlayed with a black tarantula. All else was motionless — the world stopped.

"How many do you think they have?" Val whispered.

"It looks like no more than two hundred." This confirmed Val's guess as well. That was more than they had behind them. She was grateful they had more vampires on the way.

"He does have the numbers," Val said.

Elijah put his hand across her chest to stay her, as he stepped forward. It was all she could do not to move with him. She wanted to be by his side no matter what. Ramdasha stepped from behind his front line, revealing himself for the first time. He had a well-armed woman to his right and a large man to his left — undoubtedly Riddick's replacement. The fact that the woman stood to his right — giving her more status — indicated that she must be Ramdasha's wife. They had heard rumors that he had married.

Val searched the front line and spotted Rosalia. Her gaze was intent on Vallachia. No doubt she was anxious to get on with the fight. She was more than ready for a long-awaited revenge. Val knew she would not have gotten over the Chastellains killing her love.

Elijah's voice rang out in the silent night. "While we are glad you are finally willing to face the High Court of Elders like a man, I must warn you that this is your last chance to surrender. You can still avoid a war."

Ramdasha's laughter echoed around them. "Today the rule of the High Court of Elders will end."

This response was not a surprise. Both Elijah and Ramdasha gave a hand signal for their forces to engage. Ramdasha's front line quickly raised a wall of shields. The Court threw grenades into the shields, which blew them apart. Arrows rained down on Ramdasha's men. Val was relieved to see this, as it meant that Mari had made it safely to the top of the hill.

CHAPTER 79 THE ALPS 1551 AD

A second round of Samuel's explosives were thrown into the front line. Elijah seized this opportunity and ran forward with his army behind him. The second blast stopped most of the enemy's front line.

Ramdasha had quickly retreated when the shields went up. *Coward,* Val thought. She leapt into the middle of Ramdasha's army and finished off the wounded, while fighting others back. With a sword in each hand, Val managed to keep her attackers at bay.

A wide circle formed around Elijah, as his lethal whips took off the head of anyone who got too close. In the east, a blood red flag with the head of a dragon flew high in the sky as Teller's army collided with Ramdasha's forces. Val glanced briefly to the west as Alexandru's army attacked from that direction. This was excellent timing as Ramdasha's forces had pushed the Court's front line back. This turned the tide of the battle as the enemy had to fight against three different fronts.

A loud explosion came from the rear of the Court's army. Val's first thought was of Lord Chastellain. Elijah and Val glanced back to find that across the rear of their army there was nothing but black smoke and debris. Elijah turned and blocked an attacker by twisting one whip around the man's sword. He severed his neck with the other whip. Val took flight. She had to find Lord Chastellain. But a sword cut through her wing shearing it from her body. As she fell to the ground she cut the leg of her attacker with one sword and when he fell to his knees she cut his head from his body with the other sword. She hit the ground sending a fresh shock of pain through her back. A scream escaped her lips.

"Vallachia!" Elijah yelled. In an instant he stood over her, keeping the attackers at bay with his whips.

Val managed to get to her feet. "I'm fine," she said, as she swung her swords around readying them. Elijah nodded and moved to attack and to get her out of the way of his whips.

Val quickly scanned her surroundings. Teller had fallen to his knees. She ran for him. It looked as if he was in pain, yet she could not see any wounds. He quickly stood and shook his shoulders as if to shrug off the pain. Teller gave Val a brief nod before turning to attack. Once Val was sure Teller was well, she charged after her enemy.

Riddick, Samuel, Abdullah, Teller, Elijah and Val formed a circle covering each other's backs. "We have to find Ramdasha. It is the only way to end this," Elijah yelled over sounds of metal colliding. This was intermixed with the occasional grunt, moan or wail of pain or grief.

Ramdasha's men were numerous and well trained. It was difficult to tell which side was stronger. *This could go on forever or until everyone is dead,* Val thought.

Several knives flew in Val's direction. She knocked one away with her sword. One knife glanced off her arm. The cut was deep but she had to ignore it. She fought the desire to see if the lord was well. *Elijah is right; we must focus on killing Ramdasha. It is the only way to end this.*

"There," Teller yelled. They followed his gaze. He had spotted Ramdasha.

Out of the corner of her eye, Val saw an arrow heading straight toward Teller. She threw her sword up knocking it aside before it hit his leg — her sword narrowly missed him. He gave her a quick nod of thanks.

"Stay in this circle and move as quickly as possible toward Ramdasha," Elijah ordered.

They fought their way toward him. He had surrounded himself with his best fighters. His wife — if that was indeed who she was — was nowhere to be seen. As they approached Ramdasha, two of his men charged and Elijah swung his whips wrapping one around each neck and with a flick of his wrists their heads fell to the ground.

"Surely you are man enough to take me on, Ramdasha?" Elijah taunted.

No, Val thought.

Ramdasha glared in response.

"Only the weakest of rulers hides behind his men," Elijah continued. "Have you not seen enough bloodshed for one day? Let us end this now and the winner will rule the vampire world."

If Ramdasha wished to save face in front of his men there was no way he could refuse. "Very well but it must be a sword fight. You must get rid of those whips."

Elijah let his whips slide out of his hands. They coiled on the ground as he crossed his arms drawing two swords from their sheaths at his hips. He spun the swords around, pointing them at Ramdasha. This happened so quickly that the human eye would not have been able to make out what had happened. The swords would have looked as if they appeared in Elijah's hands.

Elijah expression said, *Come on.*

No, Val thought. For some unknown reason she looked to Teller.

He gave her a reassuring nod.

Val hoped he was right — that Elijah would win. He had wagered everything on his ability to beat one man.

Ramdasha stepped out from behind his men with his sword drawn. Val was relieved to see he only had one. This would give Elijah an advantage. Elijah attacked fast and hard. Ramdasha was able to avoid or block his blows.

One of Ramdasha's men moved to attack Elijah from behind. Riddick threw a knife into the man's throat and sped toward the would-be attacker. As Riddick removed the knife from the man's throat, he severed his head. Holding the head up by the hair, Riddick pointed at the enemy in warning. "Back off cowards. This is their fight!"

The fighting around them slowed as it became apparent that the two leaders were fighting for the title of victor. Elijah was more skilled. He cut Ramdasha's arm. He hit his breastplate several times but Ramdasha kept his neck well protected.

Val screamed as pain shot up her leg.

This distracted Elijah. Ramdasha swung hard, aiming for Elijah's exposed neck. Elijah threw himself back, the sword leaving a gash across his neck.

Val had been focused on Elijah and had not noticed a group of Ramdasha's men sneaking up from behind. Val slowly pulled the knife out of her upper leg. She barely had time to block Rosalia's blow.

Rosalia and her comrades forced the Court leaders to resume fighting and they could no longer protect Elijah from Ramdasha's men. Val blocked swing after swing. They were not the blows of a mindless soldier. They were determined and full of hatred. Val could see that Rosalia was a tormented soul, her eyes were wild. *If only I could help her.*

"Rose, stop!" Val blocked another blow.

"Only friends call me that. You are *not* my friend."

"Rosalia, please! I did not want them to kill Orrick."

"Save it, Queen Chastellain. For all I know it was you who killed him."

"I didn't but he did try to kill me." Val tried to reason.

"Shut up, *Queen!"* She said the word queen as if it were a curse word. "I have been waiting for this moment for a long time. Let us see how the North does without their precious Queen."

Val shook her head in sorrow and whispered, "I'm sorry." Val knelt down on one knee, trying to ignore the searing pain in the back of her leg. She drove her sword up under Rosalia chin. As Rosalia fell Val removed her sword and stood in one movement. Val swung with her other arm which held the knife she had removed from her leg. Rosalia's head rolled away from her body, bringing an end to her physical and emotional pain all at once. Val reunited Rosalia with her beloved. It was the least Val could do.

Val searched for Elijah and the others. A knife glanced off her breastplate as she ran toward Elijah. Ramdasha's sword slammed into Elijah's breastplate and threw him back. His feet came off the ground from the force of the blow. Elijah reflexively brought both swords forward removing Ramdasha's head from his body. Elijah landed hard on the ground.

A man attacked Elijah but Val was there to stop the sword from going through Elijah's neck. Val flicked the sword from the man's hand and placed her blood-soaked weapon to his neck.

"It is over." Her voice was dark. It frightened her.

The man put his hands up in surrender.

Elijah leapt to his feet and grabbed Ramdasha's detached head by the hair. Holding the head up high, he echoed Val's words with a roar, "It is over!"

CHAPTER 80 THE ALPS 1551 AD

Time stood still as Vallachia surveyed the battlefield. Slowly they regrouped and the fighting halted. Without their leader, Ramdasha's men lost heart.

What now? Val thought. They had planned, trained and prepared endlessly for battle but what happened afterwards? She had no idea what to do, so she tore off the bottom part of her breeches from her injured leg and tied it around her bleeding wound.

Val was grateful when Elijah took control. He was a true leader and forced himself back into action.

"Capture every last one of them. If any try to run, kill them!" Elijah commanded.

Some of Ramdasha's men did run and they were beheaded. The rest were shackled with heavy iron restraints and made to kneel. Elijah gave a knowing nod to Riddick, then to Val he indicated with his head that she should leave.

Val gladly limped away. The pain in her back and leg was tolerable because of the relief that filled her. A huge burden was no longer — Ramdasha was dead. They had won. After hundreds of years it was finally over. That was all that mattered. She did not stop to think about what Elijah and the others were about to do. All she cared about was finding the ones who matter to her. She was half in a daze as she searched.

Val found Mari first. Mari ran to her and they embraced. They nodded to each other, as an indication that each was alive — not well — but alive. Mari headed for Samuel, who was a mess, and went to work tending to a deep cut on his arm.

In the distance, Val overheard Elijah, "No one wages war against the High Court of Elders and lives to tell about it. You all know full well the penalty for challenging us. You are to be executed."

Val did not watch, as she knew Elijah meant they were to die straightaway. Val had seen enough death for one day ... no, for a lifetime ... no, for many lifetimes. She was grateful that he was willing and able to finish the job. She didn't think she could have. The Court could not let them go. They would regroup and another leader would rise. Elijah was finishing this now so they would not have to fight again; at least not anytime soon. The human race would be safe for many years to come.

The Court did not have enough dungeon space to lock them all up. Plus feeding them would be a problem. They were not willing to do that to humans. *They are better off dead.* At least this was what she told herself. Of course, in her heart she knew not all of them were bad. Some of them only followed Ramdasha because they knew no better and believed his rhetoric against the Court or they were scared to cross him. Locking them up would allow them — well Val mostly — time to determine who should live. She could save some of them that way. There could be others like Sonia and Aaron — good vampires who lived under Ramdasha's rule. She had saved many of them over the years. She shook her head, *No; it is too late. Let this end now.* She was tired and the pain from her injuries was growing more intense. This made her content with the safest and easiest path.

Val limped up to Mary. Mary was trying to splint Elizabeth's leg. Lord Alexandru and Hector were holding Elizabeth down as she screamed. Her leg had been almost completely severed. Val did not think she could possibly feel worse but the helpless feeling that overwhelmed her at the sight of Elizabeth was indeed worse.

"If we can hold the leg in place it will heal on its own. I'm sure of it. It has to." Mary cried. "She needs something to ease the pain, so that we can hold her still and properly stabilize her leg."

Val ordered a woman standing nearby to find one of the doctors.

The woman ran off straightaway.

"Vallachia!"

Val turned to find Sonia racing toward her. Aaron was at her heels. They were blood-spattered and bruised but well enough. Relief flooded through Val as she moved to embrace them. *My friends are alive,* she thought. *We made it!*

The look on Sonia's face said otherwise.

Val's heart skipped as it leapt into her throat. "Where is he?"

"You must come ... now," Aaron said.

In a flash they were gone. When they reached the back of the Court's army, blood ran down the back of Val's leg. Her running had reopened the knife wound but she did not care. ...

Laying before her was the charred form of Lord Chastellain. His head lay not far from his body. "No, no, no!" She fell to her knees and let the tears flow. She thought they might never stop as the reality of this dreadful day overwhelmed her like a waterfall beating relentlessly down on her. There was no way to escape the endless bombardment. She was drowning. *War is truly the most dreadful thing on earth.*

It was not long before she heard Elijah. "Father! No!" He dropped to his father's side across from Val. Elijah put his head in his hands. Then he let out another furious scream. His suffering sent a fresh round of grief over Val. It was now a sharp physical pain through her heart. She didn't know how long they stayed there like that but it seemed forever.

Once again time stood still, as the survivors took time to mourn their losses.

~

"YOUR WING," Elijah whispered.

Val had forgotten about it. She did not care. A numbness had fully consumed her.

"What about her wing?" Mari asked.

"It was severed from her body," Teller answered.

"What are you saying? That she will never fly again?" Mari said this as if it was the worst thing in the world, as if Val might as well be dead.

Never fly again. Never fly again. Never fly again ... The words echoed in Val's head. Death would be better than all this.

Mari unfastened Val's armor and gasped at the sight of all the blood. She lifted the back of Val's tunic. "It is difficult to tell through all the blood but there appears to be a long cut down your back where the wing used to connect."

Val pulled her shirt down and looked at Elijah. "I will be fine." Then she looked to Mari. "I'm fine." Only this was not convincing.

Val shook her head. "There is much work to be done." It was her turn to take over. She had to stay busy or go mad. "We do not have time to worry about petty things like a missing wing. Tents need to be set up in the adjacent clearing. We can rest for a couple of hours. Then Ramdasha's men must be gathered and the bodies burned. Our soldiers need to be prepared for burial. We will move forward and honor our fallen."

With this, the men went to work. Riddick led the way, he appeared content to have work to do.

Elijah moved to Val's side and put his arms around her. She ventured a glance at his storm-filled eyes and looked away. He had not looked this troubled since before she'd agreed to marry him. They had been happy for a long time. She could not stand to look into the endless greyness of his eyes, so she buried her head in his chest.

Over Elijah's shoulder she found Teller staring at them. He too looked grave and battle worn. They all were. He nodded and turned away. She supposed he was making sure she was in good hands. The tears returned; the torment was unbearable. While she was relieved that her friends had survived, this made her feel overwhelming guilt for all those who had died, including her father — her lord.

Val had thought Lord Chastellain was the safest of any of them; since he was in the back. Surely nothing could ever have been powerful enough to kill him. He had seemed like the strongest entity on earth. She'd been sure he would live forever. She wished she had given him a hug as she had done for the others she cared about. If only she had said goodbye. There were many things that needed to be said. Now it was too late.

"You need medical attention," Elijah said.

Val ran her finger along the cut across his neck. Thankfully it was not deep. "First, I must check on Elizabeth." Val limped over to where she had left Mary and Elizabeth.

Elizabeth was fast asleep.

"The doctor was able to get her to take enough pain-relieving herbs to knock her out — or perhaps she passed out because of the pain." Mary rose from Elizabeth's side. "We set the bone and the doctor is stitching her up. She thinks the leg will heal."

Val wrapped her arms around Mary and shared in her relief.

Elijah took Val's hand. "Let me bandage your wounds. You need to rest."

That sounded like the best idea in the world. Val's entire body ached. Val could slip into oblivion and not think or feel. That was exactly what she did. They claimed the first tent to be erected. Val was asleep before Elijah was done tending to her injuries.

CHAPTER 81 THE ALPS 1551 AD

Wallachia was awakened by an intense itch running down her back. Her attention turned to the throbbing sensation in the back of her leg. Many other less-annoying sensations plagued her body. She moaned and tried to scratch her back but could not reach it. Elijah must have already woken because he appeared next to her cot.

"What is the matter?"

"It is my back — it itches terribly!"

Elijah rubbed it gently. This made it worse. She moaned again, "No, scratch it."

This he did with reluctance, as he did not want to hurt her.

"I wonder ... " he said. "Does it feel like it is healing?"

Val rolled over to face him. "Aye, that is precisely what it feels like." She thought back to past wounds and how they had itched as the flesh rapidly healed.

Elijah helped her to her feet. "See what happens when you try to fly."

"I don't know if that is a good idea," Val said.

He reassured her with a smile, so she tried.

Two wings spread out behind her as she transformed. The new

wing was different — it was softer and weaker. The old wing was a deep black that glistened with an iridescent purple when the light touched it. The new wing was not as dark or as shiny.

Val looked at Elijah in wide-eyed amazement. His eyes danced. She wrapped the new wing around her so she could inspect it.

Elijah ran a finger along the wing. "It is wonderful."

It was delicate — like caressing a lamb's ear. Val did not think it was ready for flight but she had a feeling it would be soon.

He picked her up, as she transformed back to normal.

She pressed her lips to his. "We will fly together again!"

"Forever!" His arms held her tight. "I wonder if we lost a leg or an arm, would they grow back?"

Val pondered this. "I'm not sure. Wings are magical, the way they appear and disappear. Either way, I'm not about to cut my arm off to find out."

"Perhaps a finger then?" Elijah said.

Val chuckled. "Not today."

"Come, we have to tell the others. They are very worried about you."

As they emerged from the tent, Val assessed the scene with fresh eyes. A plume of thick black smoke rose into the air where Ramdasha and his men were burning in the center of the blood-soaked battlefield. The smell was nauseating. Others dug graves for their fallen comrades. The atmosphere was solemn.

The leader inside Val took over. These people — her people — needed their queen. She swiftly leapt onto a supply cart. "My dear people," she yelled to get everyone's attention. "You all sacrificed so much on this day." Soon all eyes were on her. "We have all suffered great loses. Everyone fought bravely. For that, you are owed more than can ever be repaid. Those who died today did not die in vain. We will be able to move forward in peace. This was the war to end all wars. Humans and vampires alike are safe. We will heal and thrive once again." With that she spread her wings to their full extent.

This prompted loud cheers and applause. Val studied the crowd. Her gaze met Mari's whose eyes were full of tears.

The chanting began, "Long live our queen!"

Val raised her arms to silence the crowd. "We owe much to our brave king. He ended the horror of this day with the skilled swing of his sword." With this she held her hand out to Elijah. He gracefully leapt to her side and raised both their hands in victory.

This provoked more cheers and applause. The crowd chanted, "Long live our king!"

Elijah and Val smiled at each other, yet the truth could be seen in his eyes. The storm raged — on the inside he was falling apart. She knew exactly what he was thinking. His father was supposed to be the king — not him. It was his father's title and the fact that Elijah was king meant only one thing — his father was dead. The reality of it fully set in.

Nevertheless, he swung Vallachia up into his arms and kissed her. The crowd loved this the most — the cheers were deafening. It was as if they needed to see affection after so much death. It was a form of healing. There was also comfort in seeing that their leaders were united and well. If leaders were secure then the people felt secure, even in such an uneasy time.

Elijah knew he had to put on a good face, for the people, no matter how he felt. He was truly selfless. Val was more in love with him than ever.

CHAPTER 82 THE ALPS 1551 AD

Now that they had cleaned up, rested and healed — physically anyway, the Court began to investigate what happened during the battle. Samuel, who looked much better, had investigated the explosion that had taken out the rear of their main army, which included Lord Chastellain. John was completely distraught over his master's death. He too had been thrown back by the blast and badly burned. This was the last thing he remembered before his world went black. He reported to Elijah and Val that before the explosion he had noticed some of Ramdasha's men sneaking along behind their army. They must have been running oil-soaked rope and setting up the barrels of explosives behind the army.

"I had no idea what they were doing. Our attention was on you, My Lord," John explained. "I was about to point out the men behind us when we were blown away. The lord must have been rendered unconscious allowing someone to behead him. It was most likely one of the men who had set the charge." John lowered his head. "I am terribly sorry, My Lord, I was too late."

Elijah narrowed his eyes in suspicion.

What is that about? Val wondered.

"How is it that you still have your head?" Elijah inquired.

"Truly, I do not know, My Lord. They must have only gone after your father. Or perhaps they did not have time to behead others who had been knocked out by the blast, as our remaining army attacked."

Riddick appeared. There were dark circles under his eyes. "My Lord, we have disposed of all Ramdasha's men. We accounted for the top in command, including Lord Mendoza and Lord Belleaire. Only the lady who appeared at Ramdasha's side before the battle is missing. She was nowhere to be found. She must have fled during the fight."

Elijah and Val exchanged a worried look.

"We did find the body of his commander in chief," Riddick finished.

"Who do you think she is?" Val asked.

"I know her." Teller's voice came from behind them as he approached. "Her name is Neacsa. She was once a princess of Wallachia and ... my wife. I suppose she is still my wife, since we are both alive and we were never officially divorced."

"Your wife!" Val spat. The worst of feelings consumed her. One she had not felt for many lifetimes. In fact, she had not felt this way since she was a young girl who had recently fallen in love for the first time. Unlike when she was a naive young girl, this time she easily recognized the ugly feeling — it was jealousy — an emotion which apparently only Teller could cause her to feel. "You said you killed your wife."

"No. You inferred that and I did not bother to correct you. What I said was, 'she became *indisposed*', meaning I turned her."

"You made her one of us!" Val yelled, as the jealousy raged. It was all too much, the battle, her father-in-law's death, now *this*. Any ability to control her emotions was gone.

Teller smiled with amusement, fully enjoy her reaction. "Yes, well, I would have killed her. Perhaps I should have."

"Why didn't you?" Val demanded. "Now she is our enemy and she is out there ... somewhere!"

"Val, calm yourself," Elijah said. In order to change the subject Elijah put his hand on Riddick's shoulder. "Thank you for the update. Now get some rest. You have more than earned it, my dear friend."

Riddick's body relaxed under Elijah's touch as he finally realized how weary he truly was. He nodded and headed straight for the tents without the slightest protest.

Elijah led Teller away from Val with his arm over his shoulder and continued to ask him about Neacsa. This was good because Val might have tried to strangle Teller. She stormed off in the opposite direction. Before she was out of earshot, she overheard Teller explaining that he had not seen Neacsa since he took control of Wallachia in 1456.

"There is something else you should know about her," Teller said. "She very well may be a witch — if you believe in that sort of thing. At the very least she had an uncanny means of seeing the future. I have no idea what that means now that she is a vampire. Val is right; I should have killed her when I had the chance."

THE LORD'S body was returned to Denmark. He would be buried in the great catacombs under the Chastellains' castle. The fallen soldiers were buried near the battlefield. Family and friends said passing words for them. Finally, they were ready to head home. Val could not wait to leave this cursed place. Her new wing had fully grown in. She had never been more grateful for the ability to take flight.

Upon their return there was little time to rest, as there were several days of ceremonies to get through. First was Lord Chastellain's funeral. As with royal weddings, the day after a royal funeral was Coronation Day. This time it was Elijah's. Then there was to be a victory celebration on the third day. This was good because it gave Elijah and Vallachia little time to sit about and think, yet they did not feel like celebrating. They had lost eighty-seven of their fighters, including their father and they had slaughtered over two hundred of their enemy's men. The vampire population had been greatly reduced. This would once again put the world back in balance. The human population could flourish. Val had to remind herself of the real reason they had fought so hard and sacrificed so much.

"I would be honored if you, my dear wife, would speak at my father's service," Elijah said.

"Are you sure? My relationship with your father was ... complicated, to say the least," Val said.

"Yes. You are precisely the right person. I don't want his flaws to be overlooked. I want someone who really knew him to speak the truth about him, good *and* bad. Anyone else would talk about him as if he was a saint and he was not."

Val nodded but she was not certain it was a good idea. How would our people receive a less than perfect remembrance of their former leader?

WHEN THE TIME CAME, this was what Vallachia said ...

MOST OF YOU know that Lord Chastellain and I had our differences over the years. He was a man that I hated and loved in equal measure. The lord was not always easy to get along with. He could be both fierce and gentle. However, this duality was what made him a great leader. He could show compassion when needed and he would not hesitate to cut his enemy down. He was always willing to do whatever was necessary to lead and defend his people. He remained focused and dedicated to our worthy cause until the end. He sacrificed his life for us and for humans. I know that he would not have had it any other way. Dying in battle was the most honorable death for him. He gladly sacrificed his life to keep vampires and humans alike living in harmony, so that both races can thrive. We will do our best to follow in his footsteps and continue his legacy...

VALLACHIA MADE the mistake of glancing at Elijah. Tears filled his eyes and the knot in her throat became too tight for her to speak. Lord Alexandru stepped up and Val was grateful to be able to take her seat between Elijah and Mari. Mari placed her arm around Val. Alexandru went on to deliver a wonderful speech.

CHAPTER 83 COPENHAGEN 1551 AD

Elijah's Coronation Day was more festive. Val was the one who crowned him king, which was a great privilege; yet looking out over the crowd of vampires she still wondered how on earth she had gotten there. This life was entirely surreal.

Somehow, they made it through all this to the victory celebration. The queen and the newly crowned king led the way onto the dance floor.

"What do you make of Ramdasha's wife's disappearance?" Val asked Elijah as they glided around. They had not had much time to talk or even think about such things over the last couple of days.

"It is concerning indeed. The thought of a vengeful wife out there somewhere planning to rebuild an army is quite worrisome. The Court will need to make finding her a priority."

Val nodded in agreement. She knew he was right — as always. She had hoped this would be over forever. But now there was another threat. Peace does not last forever. "One comforting thought is that it will take a long time for an army to rebuild. For now we will have peace," Val said.

Elijah smiled. "Yes, for now we will enjoy a long period of peace, however long it may last." Elijah frowned. "It appears that Ramdasha knew Father was in the rear of our army. Father was specifically targeted. Ramdasha most likely thought that if Father was killed then our forces would fall apart. This has been the downfall of many great armies. If their leader is defeated, the soldiers lose their fortitude and can then be conquered, as Ramdasha's were."

"Thankfully, that is not the case with our warriors. They follow you as much as they followed Father. It was a wise move to separate our top in command," Val said.

"I suppose. However, I may have been able to save Father if I had been near."

"Then you too would be dead and all would have been lost."

Elijah nodded. "Yet, how did Ramdasha know to set his trap in the rear of our army, where Father would be?"

"Maybe he did not know the lord would be there. Perhaps it was simply the most convenient place to set the explosives without being seen."

"Perhaps." Elijah did not look convinced. "Or there is a spy amongst us."

"Only those closest to us knew our specific plans before battle," Val said. "The infantry were only told what to do and where to go before we took flight for the battlefield. One of them could not have possibly warned Ramdasha of our plans in time. Yet, he had known to attack the rear of our forces well in advance of the battle. I fully trust those closest to us. Who would betray us?"

Elijah nodded and looked thoughtful. "Who indeed?"

Her thoughts regarding who would possibly betray them were interrupted when she spotted Teller. He asked Elijah for permission to dance. Elijah willingly gave him Val's hand. Elijah was secure in their relationship, as he should be. She would not do anything to harm him.

Yet when the now familiar sensation went through her body as Teller took her hand and put his arm around her waist, she could feel herself falter. She could not stop the irritated moan that came out, "Ah, what is that? It is so ... frustrating."

Teller laughed. "It is not frustrating, it is wonderful. Simply enjoy it."

"You know I can't allow myself to do that," Val spoke through gritted teeth. The feeling was sensational.

"Someday you will." He smiled his confident and — yes — arrogant smile.

She could see why Riddick would dislike him. He was infuriating.

"Imagine what it would be like to make love," Teller whispered in her ear.

"Honestly! You are relentless." She tried to push him away but he tightened his arm around her waist so she could not put any distance between them.

"You have no idea."

She scowled at him.

"I'm only joking."

"You are not." However, it was too late as the thought was in her head. He was incredibly stubborn and so was she. This was going to be a test to see which one was *more* stubborn. She shook her head at him and tried to change the subject. "What was that during the battle, when you fell to your knees?"

"I don't know." His brow furrowed. "I was running toward you when the man cut your wing off and I fell to my knees as a searing pain ran down my back. I thought that a sword had slashed me as well but it had not. The pain subsided rather quickly."

This confirmed Val's suspicions, he had felt her pain as she had once felt his, so many years ago. "That happened to me before as well."

"What happened?"

"When Lord Chastellain broke your neck, I felt a sharp pain run through my own neck and back. It was intense but relatively brief," Val said.

"You mean we can feel each other's pain? That is madness."

"How else would you explain it?" Val wrapped her fingers in his to emphasize the point about their odd — whatever it was. She let herself enjoy the sensation.

"It all must mean something. It has to mean that we were meant for each other. We are ... connected." Teller frowned. "Why can't you see that it is me you should be with? How much proof do you need?"

"Maybe we were meant to be together at one time but that can't happen now."

"I don't see why not, unless you do not love me?"

"You know I love you. I always have and I always will." This was going too far. She could see that Teller wanted to kiss her, so she changed the subject. "How are you recovering?"

This did the trick, and pain moved into Teller's eyes. "Considering that I lost many men, I suppose we are faring well. I am grateful that Abdullah and the twins were not harmed. All the bloodshed took me back to my time in Wallachia. That was not something I wanted to relive."

Guilt balled up in Val's stomach. He needs me and I cannot be there to comfort him, to help him through these tough times.

"And how are you faring?" he asked.

"Moving forward, I suppose. I would be lost without my friends. We will get through this."

Teller nodded. "Elijah is a good man. He is a worthy king. I was impressed with the way he took on Ramdasha."

Val looked for Elijah and smiled when she found him. "Yes, he is wonderful, brave and selfless."

"Don't sell yourself short, you are a remarkable leader as well. You are able to be rational without losing sight of what matters. You two resemble a benevolent king and queen who are only found in children's fairy stories."

"Why then are you always trying to come between us?"

"You know that I cannot help the way I feel about you. I have no control when it comes to you. I could not stay away if I tried. So I keep coming back to torture myself by having to watch you happily married."

Pain moved into Val's chest. It would be awful to have to watch Teller blissfully in love with someone else. Her eyes threatened to tear up so she pulled away. Everything about him was overwhelming — his touch, his emerald eyes, his words. She would have to put her brick wall back up.

EPILOGUE

Every couple of years Vallachia would return to Ludus to see how her lineage was faring. One such time she came upon two lovers sitting on a blanket in the forest. She jumped into a nearby tree to get a better view and remain unseen. The boy was blond with blue eyes. She knew he had to be related to her ... somehow. Val could almost see her brother in him. The girl had long dark hair, olive skin and green eyes. She greatly resembled Teller's family line. She had to be his distant kin.

Val felt the branch move slightly. She knew who it was and did not turn to him. "What are you doing here?" she whispered.

"What do you think? I'm looking for you. Elijah said you wanted to be alone. I assumed that this is where you would come," Teller said.

"Why are you looking for me?" Val's thoughts turned to Elijah. "Is something wrong?"

"Everything is fine. Ramdasha is dead — remember?" Teller watched the couple for a moment. "You know, in a way, it is as if we live on. As humans I mean — through them."

Val nodded, knowing exactly what he meant. She had watched history repeat itself many times over. For the past four hundred years their two family lines often came together. "They *are* us, in a different lifetime. They get to live the life we were supposed to have."

The trembling boy mustered up enough courage to kiss the girl.

Teller stepped toward Val wrapping his arm around her waist. He reluctantly put his lips to hers as if he was sure she would stop him.

Val let the shock run through her body as their lips touched. *Only for a moment,* she told herself. Perhaps it was a moment too long. When she came to her senses, she placed her hand on his cheek and put her thumb between their lips. "Stop," she whispered.

He placed his forehead against hers. "I hate it that I lost you. We were meant to be together," he looked at the couple, "like them."

"I know but that was another life — one that would long since be over. We have to let it go."

"I followed *you* here — remember?"

His point was made; clearly Val had not let go.

"Touché but I am not yours." She laid her head on his shoulder.

In his arms she could pretend, even if only for a moment, that they were truly home. That they had never left and were still human. They were not monsters — killers even. She could see the life they should have had together. There would have been ten children. He would have taught the boys to compete in the town tournament and to be smithies like him. Her daughters would have been good cooks under her tutelage. Then they would have grown old and their children and grandchildren would have taken care of them. They would not have seen the world — the good or the bad — the war, the death. They would have been poor ... and together ... and happy.

The End of Book Two

Help others find this book by leaving a review on Amazon.
Sign up to Lynne's email list at www.lynnehill.com to get a free eBook. Plus, never miss a new release.

OF GODS AND GODDESSES

BOOK 3 IN THE LORDS AND COMMONERS SERIES

Does the world wake from the stagnant times of Medieval Europe only to fall into darkness...forever?

Vallachia knows a lot...

Well she should — she ancient.

However, even her vast knowledge is not enough.

Much to her surprise she still has a lot to learn.

The enemy will not play to her strengths this time.

They will prey on her weaknesses.

This battle will not be won with a war...

It will be won by conquering one's own mind.

The key is to uncover the mysterious origin of the vampire race.

which could save them all...

Start your next adventure today!

What Critics are saying ...

"This book [Of Gods and Goddesses] is a great conclusion to the series! A definite page turner. This book covers loyalty, bravery, sacrifice, betrayal and truth. I found myself emotionally impacted by the plot twists and found myself racing through the book praying for my favorite characters to make it out alive. This series is NOT your average vampire story, it is so much more. I highly recommend it!"

—Jennifer

ALSO BY LYNNE HILL

The Lords and Commoners Series

Of Lords and Commoners Book 1

Of Princes and Dragons Book 2

Of Gods and Goddesses Book 3

A Gods and Goddesses Novelette

A Woman's World Series

A Woman's World Book 1

Lost Powers Book 2

A Collision of Worlds Book 3

LIST OF CHARACTERS

The High Court of Elders

Lord Chastellain

John (right hand man)

Prince Elijah (the lord's son); Patricia (Elijah's lover)

Vallachia (Val, lead emissary)

Riddick (commander in chief); Leopoldo and Natalia (from Riddick's past)

Samuel (Elijah's closest friend)

Mari (Val's closest friend)

Sonia

Aaron

English branch of the Court

Lord Alexandru

Hector (right hand man)

Mary (commander in chief)

Elizabeth

Teller's Clan

Sergiu (trusted advisor)

Abdullah (commander in chief)

Cosmin and Costel (twins)

Ivan (father)
Petru (innkeeper)
1st Family Teller Meets
Darius (smithy/father)
Martina (oldest daughter)
Sabina (youngest daughter)
Ramdasha's Clan
Sebastian (Riddick's replacement)
Elda (wife, FKA Neacsa Dracula)
Lord Mendoza of Portugal
Lord Belleaire of France
Rosalia (her love, Orrick, beheaded by Elijah)
Real Historical Figures
1. Sultans of the Ottoman/Osmanli Empire
Orhan I (son of Osman, ruled from 1324-1360)
Ismail (head of the army, fictitious)
Mehmed I (ruled from 1413-1421)
Mehmed II, the Conqueror (ruled from 1451-1481)
Mustapha (head of the army, fictitious)
2. The Last Rulers of the Byzantine Empire
Emperor Manuel II (ruled from 1391-1425)
Isabella (firstborn, illegitimate daughter)
Empress Helena (wife)
Emperor John VIII (son, ruled from 1425-1448)
Emperor Constantine XI (son, ruled from 1448-1453)
3.Wallachian Nobles
Vladislav II Dracul of the Draculesti family
Neacsa (adapted to fit the story)
Dan III of the Danesti family
Ilona (Vlad III's 2nd wife)
Jusztina (Vlad III's 3rd wife)
Prince Stefan III of Moldova (Vlad III's cousin)

VOCABULARY LIST

- Dracul = Dragon
- Dracula = of the Dragon
- Voivode = prince
- Janissary = soldier
- Seraskier = commander in chief/head of the army
- Grand Vizier = top advisor (usually to the Sultan)
- Pasha = a respectful title for a high ranking official
- Kadin = most favored concubine/1st lady
- Eunuch = castrated male
- Devsirme = children trained to become Janissaries
- Dirk = short sword/long knife
- Scimitar = curved Arabian sword

ACKNOWLEDGMENTS

This book would still be lacking much if it were not for all the wonderful support around me. Thanks to my mothers. Yes, mothers. I am blessed to have four of them, a birth mother, a godmother, a stepmother and a mother-in-law. They are great preliminary readers and encouragers.

Many thanks to my fellow writers and editors, who have helped me to improve and have provided much needed support and guidance. Thanks to Marcia; good editors are hard to find. A special thanks goes to David VanDyke for sharing his knowledge and experience. His candid wisdom about the industry is much appreciated! The thing I admire most about fellow writers is their willingness to help new writers. Thank you all!

Thanks to the historians/authors whose works helped to guide much of the history in this book; Lars Brownworth, Anthony A. Goodman, Sir Jens and Tracy Barrett. You are all wonderful! Many thanks!

ABOUT THE AUTHOR

Lynne Hill is the author of the *Lords and Commoners* series and the *Woman's World* series. She made the short list for the Chanticleer Book Awards and was awarded a 5 Star Reader's Favorite Award. She was born in Colorado and raised in a small town of eight hundred people. Lynne holds a Doctorate of Psychology in criminology and justice studies. She is an advocate for Restorative Justice, a theme that is incorporated into her novels. Her extensive travels overseas and her work as an American Peace Corps Volunteer in Jordan helped to inspire her writing.

Find out more at www.lynnehill.com and sign up to her email list to get a free eBook. Plus, never miss a new release.

www.ingramcontent.com/pod-product-compliance
Lightning Source LLC
Chambersburg PA
CBHW030627310726
48979CB00003B/919
9781736724965